CW00545383

HAUNT OF THE WENDIGO

CHAPTER ARCHIVES #1

DEVIN HANSON

Haunt of the Wendigo
Chapter Archives #1
Copyright © 2020 Devin Hanson
Published by Hudson Indie Ink
www.hudsonindieink.com

This book is licensed for your personal enjoyment only.
This book may not be re-sold or given away to other people. If you would like
to share this book with another person, please purchase an additional copy for
each recipient. If you're reading this book and did not purchase it, or it wasn't
purchased for your use only, then please return to your favourite book retailer
and purchase your own copy. Thank you for respecting the hard work of this
author.
All rights reserved.
This is a work of fiction. Names, characters, places, brands, media, and
incidents are either the product of the authors imagination or are used
fictitiously. The author acknowledges the trademark status and trademark
owners of various products referred to in this work of fiction, which have been
used without permission. The publication/use of these trademarks is not
authorised, associated with, or sponsored by the trademark owners.

Haunt of the Wendigo/Devin Hanson - 1st ed
ISBN-13 - 978-1-913904-45-6

INTRODUCTION

The Chapter Archives series is a parallel story plot to the Halfblood Legacy, following Ryan Halsin. It can be read as a standalone series, or preferably combined into one series in the Halfblood universe. The suggested reading sequence is:

The Halfblood's Hoard
Shadow of the Ghoul
Wylde Fire
Haunt of the Wendigo
Lilin's Wrath

CHAPTER ONE

I pushed open the swinging door to the pub and stepped in, out of the hammering rain. Water streamed from my jacket and puddled at my feet. I shook the worst of the water from myself and scanned the pub, looking over the patrons. I spotted the man I was looking for in the back and headed that way, still dripping.

Summer in Maine was not what I had expected. Ten minutes ago, it was sunny and nearly warm enough to make me regret wearing the jacket. Then in the space of a few minutes, clouds came scudding in from the east and the deluge began. Just my luck I had decided to walk to the pub from my hotel room.

I reached the table I was aiming for and shucked the canvas jacket off my shoulders. I threw it over the back of a spindly chair, sat myself down, and rubbed a hand through my close-cropped hair sending rainwater sprinkling down onto the table. The man I was sitting across from put down his fork and gave me a level look.

"Is that necessary, Ryan?"

I leaned forward and put my elbows on the table. "I don't

know, John. You tell me." I held John's gaze and reached over to steal one of his fries.

John sighed. He was an older man who had kept himself in shape for the majority of his life, but a desk job for the last handful of years had let him grow a bit of a gut. "I know you're upset."

"Nah. It's not like that. I'm not upset about wasting the last six months doing absolutely fuck-all. I do, however, have other things that I want to do, and none of them are in Portland, Maine."

"Your sister."

I grimaced. Memory of meeting her as an adult for the first time came back with perfect clarity. She had been in bikini underwear and a cutoff shirt that barely covered her ribs, a wet dream walking. Only the knowledge of how dangerous she could be had kept my head straight around her. "Yeah. She needs me. To help keep her perspective, if nothing else."

"You're not falling for her, I hope."

"Absolutely not. She terrifies me, if I'm being honest."

"She should. I still don't understand why the Chapter has let her live."

"Fortunately, you're not on the council, and that decision is not yours to make. Can we focus, please? Alexandra is not why I'm here."

John bought time for himself with a bite from his burger, then cleared his mouth with a swig from his soft drink. "If you're looking for permission to go back to the west coast, the answer is no."

"Oh, come on. Why not? Six months, John. I've spent half a year looking in every corner of this city. If there's something hunting people here, I haven't been able to find it. Or even evidence of something existing. I hate to say it, but Portland doesn't have a monster problem."

"You might be right."

"Then why can't I go?" Frustration and unfocused anger made my voice tight, and I gripped the edge of the table, trying to calm myself.

"Can I get you anything, dear?"

I looked up and forced a smile for the slender serving girl. She had her hair up in a high ponytail and wore an apron with the pub's logo on it. "I'm not staying long. Just having a word with my friend here."

"You came all this way, Ryan, and it's still raining out. You might as well eat." John pushed his plastic cup over to the edge of the table. "I'd like a refill, please. Diet coke."

"Certainly." The girl picked up the cup and looked at me expectantly.

"Oh, for... fine. What's good?"

"Burger's decent," John said around another bite.

"We have a chowder specialty. Fresh clams, harvested this morning," the girl said helpfully.

Every dive in Maine seemed to have a chowder specialty. It was either that or lobster. "Do you have anything without so many carbs? Steak and salad would be right for me. Medium rare."

"We can do that, sir. Anything to drink?"

"Water, no, wait. Coffee, black is fine."

"Okay, it'll be a few minutes. I'll be right back with your drink."

I watched her go, then turned back to John. "You haven't answered my question." The interruption had given me a chance to get my anger under control, but I still wanted answers.

"It's why I asked you here, Ryan. There's been people going missing."

"Not in Portland, there's not. I would have heard about it."

"No, not Portland. Further north, in the country. In a town called Kingfield."

"Haven't heard of it."

"I'd be surprised if you had. It's small. A resort town, if you can call it that. It caters to the skiing season on Sugarloaf Mountain."

That didn't sound promising. After Los Angeles, even Portland was small. "Let me guess. One street, probably called Main Street?"

"Kingfield has a Main Street, yes, but it's not *that* small. I believe it has several streets. Thank you, dear."

The serving girl set a mug in front of me and poured it full from a hot carafe. "Your steak will be a few more minutes. Can I get you anything else while you wait?"

"No thank you," I shook my head and waited for her to walk out of earshot. "How many people have gone missing?"

"You know how it is. It's a country town. They aren't too open to outsiders, and that includes reporting unusual deaths. That we've heard anything at all suggests there's a bigger issue there."

"Well, that's something at least. Any chance it's the same thing we've been hunting?"

"So far away? I don't know, Ryan, it's a hundred miles from here. Could be, I suppose, but it begs the question why it would travel so far when there's plenty of viable victims closer."

"Wonderful." A hot plate with a steak on it appeared over my shoulder and set down in front of me. It looked like a New York strip, grilled over a wood fire. The part of the plate that wasn't occupied by the steak was piled high with a chopped salad. My mouth started watering immediately. "Oh, this looks good. Thank you."

"You're welcome," the girl smiled brightly at me. "Refill on your coffee?"

"Please. Thanks." I started eating and found I was hungrier than I had thought. The steak was seasoned well and medium rare, the salad was... a salad. The hot food and coffee had chased off the lingering chill from getting rained on, and my mood started to improve.

"I've got a contact for you that knows you're coming. A Forest Ranger by the name of Hall."

"In the know?" I asked around a mouthful.

"We've worked with Hall before."

"That's something, at least."

"I've also set you up with a room at the local bed and breakfast. There's a hotel, but the B and B has more comfortable accommodations. Or so I've heard. And it's a little more isolated."

I grunted. "Where will I find this Hall?"

"At the police station, probably. It's the sticks out there, so the Rangers help with the police work when needed. By all accounts, Hall is well-liked by the locals. Could help you get past their reticence, if they see you working together."

"I don't really do partners," I frowned. "It's dangerous enough without having to worry about protecting someone else."

"You're a flatlander," John shrugged. "Without some local assistance, all you'll get is a cold shoulder out there."

"Fine." I didn't like it, but John was right. "What kind of backup is there available?"

John popped the last of his fries in his mouth and rolled a shoulder. "Not much. Other than Hall, you won't find many friendly faces."

"The local church?" I didn't have to ask if there was a church or not. Any place in America where more than two streets came together, someone inevitably threw up a church.

"First Baptist and a United Methodist. You won't find help from them."

"Well, shit, John. Sounds like you picked the absolute worst place for me."

"I didn't pick it. Blame whatever is out there killing people. You think I want you in Maine? You're a pain in my ass, Ryan."

I grinned. "Aw, don't be like that. You'll hurt my feelings."

He snorted. "When can you leave?"

"I've got nothing holding me here. I find this thing, whatever it is, and then I can go back to California?"

"You'll go where the Chapter needs you. Right now, that's in Maine. After you get back, who knows? As much as I don't like the idea of a Nephilim operating out in the open, your sister has things locked down in Los Angeles. I don't see the need to send you out there, too. But maybe the council will send you, just to get you of my hair."

"One can hope." I drained the last of my coffee and stood up. "Thanks for the meal."

"Hey, I didn't..." John trailed off and shook his head. "Whatever. It's a two-hour drive. You better get started."

I pulled my jacket off the back of my chair. A glance out the window told me the rain had stopped again. "I'll see you around, John."

With a wave, I headed out of the pub and into the patchy sunlight. The humidity wrapped around me like a soggy blanket. The car I was leasing was a couple blocks away. I ducked my head down and started walking. The sooner I got to Kingfield and found whatever was killing people, the sooner I could get out of Maine.

J ohn Baptiste's two-hour estimate for the drive turned out to be dead on. Highway 27 was a two-lane asphalt crack in the endless sea of forest. After I left Farmington behind, there was little that interrupted the trees. Every few miles, enterprising souls had carved out little pockets of cleared land, but the trees pressed close around the boundaries of their land with palpable eagerness to reclaim what was taken from them.

There was an undeniable beauty to the land. I've been all over the world, and there are few places as vibrantly green as the Maine back country. The county road was well-maintained and the clapboard houses were quaint.

I stopped to get gas in New Vineyard at a little two-pump station, one for diesel and one for gas. The pumps were antiques from the '40s, long before credit cards. The register had a little cardboard sign taped to it with fading duct tape, cautioning that the credit card reader was out of service. Judging by the age of the tape on the sign, the last time this place took plastic was during the Reagan administration.

Glad I had thought ahead to take out cash, I paid the sleepy attendant and returned to my car. I could hear the pump down under my feet groaning and chortling to itself as I filled my tank. It took twice as long as it would have at a modern station in Portland, and I found myself musing over how antiquated everything was.

At least I didn't have to crank a pump by hand to pull gas up out of the reservoir.

Back on the road, the land started climbing and the mixed deciduous trees along the side of the road began changing over to fir and pine trees, mixed with the occasional birch. It came as a shock when the land on either side of the road turned abruptly into open fields growing soybeans and corn.

I started passing buildings, the clapboard siding freshly painted, the tin roofs in good repair. There was an aura of wealth that had been lacking in New Vineyard, no doubt the result of the seasonal tourism. I started paying attention to my GPS, and soon turned off the highway to the bed and breakfast John had arranged for me.

The gravel road rattled the shocks on my little economy sedan as I pulled into the parking lot. I climbed out of the car with a sigh, and took a moment to stretch my back and look around. It was cool enough to make me reach back inside for my jacket.

The main building was a sprawling, two-story structure that looked like four or five houses merged together into one continuous building. The inevitable clapboard was in good repair, the grey shingle roof only patched in a few places. In the back, there was a separate barn. The Hilton it was not, but I reserved my judgement for when I had a chance to see the inside.

I got my duffel bag from the trunk, made sure the car was locked, then headed for the entrance. The reception area was done up in rustic style, with a dozen framed photographs of various weddings hung on the walls. Apparently, the bed and breakfast doubled as a wedding reception for hire.

There wasn't anyone behind the desk. I stepped up and hit the little bell on the counter. From the back, a woman called out, "Be right with you!" A moment later, a cherubic lady in her sixties bustled out of the back and gave me a cheery smile.

"Hi, I'm Ryan Halsin. I should have a reservation with you."

"Ryan! It's good to meet you. I'm Sylvia Toole. Yes, your assistant reserved our honeymoon suite for you. She paid for a week, but said you might stay longer?"

I shrugged. "My business in Kingfield might take a while."

"Oh, what business is that? Sorry, we don't get many visitors during the summer months. Not like during the winter. We're usually all booked up once the snow gets deep enough for skiing on the mountain. You're our only guest right now, though." She took a breath, then seemed to realize she had been rattling on and gave me an embarrassed smile.

I smiled back. "It's nothing that exciting. I'm a naturalist doing a survey of the local wildlife."

It was a cover I'd used before, and she ate it up, nodding and smiling. "How lovely. I'll show you to your room, then? If you've got other luggage, I can help you with them."

"Just the one, thank you."

"Okay, follow me, then!"

The honeymoon suite was two rooms in the back of the sprawling building, on the second floor. The furnishings were modern enough. A king-sized bed with a hand-crafted shaker-style headboard and matching side tables. There was a fireplace across from the bed, and an afghan rug on the floor in muted greens and blues. The second room had an overstuffed leather couch, a desk, and a sixty-inch TV.

"We've got satellite TV, along with a library of DVDs that you can check out from the front desk. There's wi-fi, but it's slow, sorry. We normally offer a free continental breakfast, but since you're the only guest, I'll just have it brought to your room in the morning. What time do you get up?"

"I'm an early riser," I said absently. I set my duffel on the bed and went to stick my head into the bathroom. It was as modern as the rest of the place, a good twenty years out of date, and styled to be rustic.

"Will you be wanting a wake-up call?"

"No, that won't be necessary."

"Okay. How are the rooms? Can I get you anything?"

"The rooms look great." I nodded at a telephone sitting on the side table. "If I need anything else, I'll just call the front desk."

"Perfect. If you decide to extend your stay, just let me know."

"Thank you, Sylvia. Is there a place around here I could get dinner?"

"There are plenty of places on Main Street, not a few minutes away."

I thanked her again and she left me alone. I took a minute to hang my shirts and throw my socks in a drawer. I used to scoff at unpacking a travel bag. What was the point when you only had two pairs of pants and a handful of shirts? Then, as I got older, I found there was something comforting in not having to dig past dirty boxers to find the clean stuff. It was a semblance of civilization that I slowly began to insist on.

Then, with my room starting to feel a little more like a temporary home, I headed back outside again. It was getting on in the afternoon, almost five, and the air was starting to feel nippy. There were light clouds in the sky, but nothing that looked like rain, and I decided to walk to the town to get food and meet Hall.

It was about a quarter of a mile away. I walked along the grassy verge and enjoyed the clean air and lack of traffic. The houses started growing closer together, then the verge turned into a seamed sidewalk. The road hooked around, following the bend in a river that ran alongside it, and just like that, I was in town.

If I had been driving, I would have passed right through the town before I realized I was in it. There was half a block of businesses, a hotel, a gas station with modern pumps, and that was it. The next block was back to residential. I knew from looking at Google maps that there was a grocery on the other side of the river, along with a general store and a few other businesses.

Sylvia's 'plenty of places' was a choice between a tiny diner and a sandwich bar across the street that shared floorspace with the gas station. I figured it would be harder to mess up a sandwich than a cooked meal, and headed that way.

Five minutes later, I was outside again, chewing on a passable turkey sub and trying to decide what to do next. I hadn't seen a police station on the way in, or in my exploration so far. I got my phone out and did a quick search. The result gave a spot a hundred feet away, so I walked in that direction.

A bridge spanned the Carrabassett river next to the sandwich shop, and I walked out onto it, following the GPS. The running water under my feet was peaceful, and I leaned against the railing, eating my sandwich and watching a pair of ducks chase each other around.

I felt completely out of place in this tiny little country town. The whole of Kingfield had a population around five hundred people. A town like this wasn't even a blip on the radar. Still, something was killing people here, and a place this small would feel the murders deeper than a larger town would.

"Hey, stranger, see anything interesting?"

I straightened up from my slouch against the rail and turned with a polite smile on my face. A young woman had walked up to me while I had been deep in thought, and was leaning against the railing ten feet from me. She was wearing utilitarian clothing, but I could see she was fit under her open jacket. Dark brown hair was pulled back in a ponytail running through the back of a baseball cap. She was a few inches short of six foot, tall for a woman. She had darker skin, with a slight exotic tilt to her eyes.

"Not really," I said. "Just wondering why the police station is in the middle of the river."

She laughed. "You looking for the police?"

"Not exactly. A Forest Ranger, actually. By the name of Hall."

"Well, you're in luck."

I raised an eyebrow at her. "I am?"

"I'm Hall."

I felt a grin grow on my face. "Is that right?" This pretty girl was my Chapter contact? Somehow, I couldn't bring myself to believe it.

"You must be Ryan, then. John Baptiste said you were tall, but you really are a big bastard, aren't you?" She stuck her hand out to shake.

I shut my mouth and shook her hand. She had a strong grip and I could feel callouses on her fingers. My estimation of her climbed up a notch. "Sorry. You're not what I expected. Ryan Halsin."

"Harper Hall. Why would the police station be in the river?"

It was my turn to laugh. "Just trying to follow my GPS. Guess it's not high on the list of priorities for the local department to update Google maps."

"I doubt Sergeant Bunnings even knows what Google maps is. There isn't a lot of crime out here in Kingfield. Most days, the sergeant is out fishing."

"Most days?" Something in the way she had phrased it made me follow up.

She shrugged and her green eyes shuttled sideways out to the river. I read the hesitation on her face. "He's been drunk for the last week straight."

"Not a great response to a crisis," I said carefully.

"Willard is like eighty. The most stress he's had to deal with for the last forty years has been the occasional angry drunk. We don't *have* crime out here, Mr. Halsin."

"Ryan is fine. Maybe you better start from the beginning. Tell me what's happened, from as early as you can."

CHAPTER TWO

"The first anyone knew something was wrong was when old Mrs. Wilson went missing."

We had gone to my rooms at the bed and breakfast. According to Harper, there wasn't really anywhere in Kingfield that would give us any privacy, short of going for a walk in the woods. It was going to be getting dark soon, so we took her old beater truck to where I was staying.

"When was that?"

"Early April. We still had snow on the ground, and Mrs. Wilson had an old diesel truck that had a hard time starting when it was cold out. Pam from the grocery store mentioned to Willard that Mrs. Wilson hadn't been in for a few weeks."

"Did he find a body?"

Harper shook her head. "Nothing. She was just gone. Truck was still there, meal left out uneaten on the table. It was like she just got up and walked off into the woods. We organized a search party and combed the woods around her place for a few days."

"And nothing, huh?"

She shivered a little. "I keep expecting someone to stumble

over her body in the woods. It's bound to happen eventually, and it isn't going to be pretty."

I was sitting in the desk chair and Harper was sprawled out on the couch, her long legs tucked up beneath her. We had the TV on, playing some made-for-TV soap. It was turned down low enough so we could talk, but loud enough to blur our conversation in case Sylvia was prone to listening at doors.

"So, Mrs. Wilson was the first. Who was next?"

"Around ten days later, someone called in a car abandoned on the side of the road. We ran the plates and found it belonged to an older man who lived by himself outside Madison. He has a cousin that lives in Kingfield. Had a cousin," she corrected herself. "After Mr. Langston went missing, his cousin went fishing a few days later and never came home again. We found his boat at the bottom of Embden pond."

I frowned. "How come nobody reported the missing people?"

"What was there to report? An old lady who probably had dementia wandered out of her house with snow on the ground and froze to death under a bush somewhere? A fisherman capsized his boat and drowned? We don't have the equipment to dredge a lake the size of Embden."

"What about the guy from Madison?"

"Willard passed it on to Madison's police department. After everything else that happened, I haven't thought to follow up."

"Damn." I eyed Harper and picked up the weariness in the way she slumped back against the couch. She'd seen person after person go missing for almost two months. I was surprised she wasn't in a panic. No wonder the sergeant was day drinking. "And the pattern of missing people continued?"

"What pattern?" A flash of anger tightened her green eyes. "There's no rhyme or reason to the disappearances! Sometimes a few weeks goes by before someone else goes missing. Then two or three in a matter of days. Nothing is ever stolen. There's no vandalism or motive, no bodies, nothing!"

I made a calming gesture with my hands, worried that Harper's raised voice would carry outside the walls of my rooms. "Okay. I get it. I just wish that I had learned of this sooner."

"Yeah? How come? Are you some super-sleuth? A modern-day Sherlock Holmes come to teach us backwoods yokels how to solve a missing person case?" She had straightened up and swung her feet to the floor, and was leaning forward aggressively like she wanted to leap across the space between us and let her frustrations out on me with her fists.

"No. I work for the Chapter."

She snorted her derision and slumped back against the couch cushions. "Wonderful. And what is the Chapter, anyway?" She eyed me with disdain. "I'm not an idiot, Ryan. I know there is more in the world than humans. Is that what this is? A djinn of some sort going on a rampage?"

"Unlikely," I said mildly. "The Fourth Chapter is more concerned with hunting down monsters."

"Monsters." Harper spread her arms out across the back of the couch and smirked at me. "Like bigfoot?"

"Why would we hunt bigfoot? He's never hurt anyone."

She gave a mocking laugh. "Okay, mister big shot monster hunter. What's the last thing you've saved the world from?"

"An army of the walking dead in Los Angeles." They were being controlled by a djinn called a ghoul, and I hadn't killed the ghoul myself, but that was detail that Harper didn't need.

Harper watched my face for a moment, waiting for me to crack a smile and laugh it off. When I stayed serious, she frowned. "I'm guessing they weren't from the TV show."

It was reflexive sarcasm, understandable under the

circumstances, and I didn't rise to the bait. "Not these ones, no."

"Shit." She looked over at the TV for a minute. I watched her patiently, letting her work through the situation herself. Then she sighed and looked back at me. "I guess it's a good thing I reached out to John, then."

"If you don't mind me asking, what is your relationship with the Chapter? How did you know to call us?"

"When I was young, I got lost in the woods. I was led off the trail by a will o' the wisp. A hinn found me, and she had to turn into an elk to carry me back home before I froze to death. I met John Baptiste and he explained the djinn and the rest of the hidden world. We've kept in contact since then."

I nodded. It was common practice to recruit people who had been exposed to the supernatural. It was useful to have contacts everywhere, particularly in places on the edges of civilization where the weird shit happened more frequently.

"Do you have any idea what is making people disappear this time?" she asked. "Not another wisp, I hope."

"Honestly, I have no idea. Tomorrow, I'd like to visit some of the places where people went missing. Maybe I can find something that had been overlooked."

"It's as good a place to start as any," she shrugged. "Which one do you want to visit first?"

"I'd like to see Mrs. Wilson's home."

"Really? Not something more recent? It's been nearly three months since she went missing. Any clues you're looking for are going to be long gone."

"Maybe, maybe not. I won't know until I look. And the first scene might contain some evidence that the others do not."

"Well, you're the expert." Harper got up and stretched, reaching for the ceiling. I got an eyeful of her toned abs as her shirt lifted up, and jerked my eyes up to her face before she settled back down. "I'm beat. I've been getting up before dawn for weeks. Should I come pick you up tomorrow?"

"That works for me." I followed her out to the bedroom. "One thing, before you leave."

"Mm?"

"If you can be armed, you might want to start carrying."

She frowned, one hand on the doorknob. "Why?"

"Once we start hunting, the monster, whatever it is, will notice. And it will object. Better to be prepared."

"We've been trying to find it for months! If it was going to attack openly, it would have by now."

I shook my head. "This is different. It's not worried about the police."

Harper blew out a breath and her frown deepened. I could see her trying to decide if she should be offended or not. "And what about you? Are you armed?"

In response, I lifted the side of my shirt up and showed her the holstered handgun there.

"It'll look weird if I'm seen around town carrying," she said after a moment. "But I can put a rifle in my truck."

"Not good enough."

"Sorry?"

"How long would it take you to run to your truck and get your rifle out and ready to fire?"

"Depends on how far away I am," she said.

"This isn't a joke, Harper. I don't know what this thing we're hunting is, but if it's aggressive our survival could depend on bare seconds of response time. Get a gun. Wear it."

She eyed me for a beat and said stiffly. "See you in the morning, Ryan." Then she pulled open the door and left.

I sighed and sat on the bed. "Nice going, Ryan. Way to make friends with the locals."

Sunrise was going to come quickly. I shook off the worry

about Harper and went to take a shower. Then I set my alarm and went to bed. The mattress was softer than was I was used to, the pillows too fluffy. I stared up at the ceiling, wondering what it was that we were hunting. Unbidden, images of Harper's tight abs kept intruding into my thoughts.

Sleep was a long time coming.

I woke before my alarm. Grey, pre-dawn light was filtering in past the curtains. I stayed in bed and watched the time on my phone tick over to six o'clock, then muted the alarm when it went off. With a sigh, I rolled out of bed and got dressed.

My handgun was on the bedside table where I had left it, and after a pause for consideration, I dug my shoulder holster out of my duffel. Carrying a gun under your shirt hem might work in the city, but it would take precious extra seconds to draw if I actually had to shoot something. I'd just have to keep my jacket on and hope the day didn't get too hot.

I opened my door and stepped out, and almost tripped over the covered plate lying next to the door. I had forgotten about breakfast. I wasn't hungry, but checked under the cover just to see what was on offer. A pair of blueberry muffins, still steaming from the oven, their tops crispy with crumble. A banana, some strawberries and a few slices of cantaloupe.

Well, maybe I could eat after all. I grabbed the muffins and the banana and headed outside. As early as I was, Harper was already there waiting for me, the windows of her truck fogging in the chilly morning air. I climbed in and handed her one of the muffins.

"Morning. Sorry about last night." There was a large-bore lever-action rifle sitting on the gun rack behind her head and a worn revolver butt was visible sticking out of her hip holster.

Harper took the muffin with studious disinterest. "Don't think this buys you any points," she warned me. She bit into it and her simmering anger melted away. "Oh my god," she groaned.

I grinned and bit into my own muffin. Sweet, tart blueberries. Delectably soft, almost cake-like muffin with just the right amount of cinnamon in the crumble. It was hot and moist, and sent a fresh plume of steam into the air.

"Oh, that *is* good. Well, if you don't want yours, I'll have it back."

"Not a chance, Halsin. So, Mrs. Wilson's place?"

"That's the plan."

Harper nodded and crammed the rest of the muffin into her mouth before putting the truck in gear and rolling out of the parking lot. The suspension on her truck handled the rough ground a lot better than my car had.

"That yours?" she nodded out the window at my car.

"It's a rental," I shrugged.

She smirked. "Somehow I doubted you were the type to drive a Civic."

"Part of the perks of working for the Chapter," I said sourly. "The bean counters pick your rentals for you. You know how much it costs to lease a truck in Portland?"

"Aw, I'm sure you're man enough that you don't have to compensate. I won't judge you either way."

"You already did," I grumbled. "You want some banana?"

"Sure."

I snapped the banana in half and handed her the piece with the stem on it. "Tell me about Mrs. Wilson."

"What is there to say?"

"I don't know, describe her for me."

Harper got us out onto Main Street, and in less than five minutes we were off the paved roads and bouncing down a gravel track. Beyond the ditches on the sides of the track, it was solid, unbreakable forest. She peeled her banana while navigating the turns with a deftness that told me eating on the road was a common practice for her.

"She was pleasant enough, I suppose. She could be crotchety if the mood was on her, but what old person isn't?"

"That's fair. Was she well-liked in the community?"

"She kept to herself for the most part. When there was a picnic or a barbecue in town, she would come in. I think she had a running spat with Mr. Cheney, but if you've lived for seventy or eighty years, you're bound to have a history."

"Not to be an ass or anything, but it seems to me you're being a little defensive of her."

"Am I? I guess a bit. I don't like speaking ill of the dead."

"I understand that. All I'm interested in is why she was targeted. I have no horse in this race."

She nodded. "I know. I'll try to be objective. So, I suppose Mrs. Wilson was like most of the people around here. Pleasant and kind, until you crossed her. Or she thought you were crossing her."

I didn't say it, but to me that sounded like Mrs. Wilson was a bit of a bitch. "Okay. A known loner makes a convenient target. That could be something."

Harper laughed without humor. "Ryan, that describes ninety percent of the population around here. You don't live this far away from everything unless you want to be alone."

"Right. Damn." I looked out at the impenetrable forest going by and tried to fight the feeling of despair. The monster could be watching us go by not twenty feet away and we wouldn't find it in a thousand years. It was entirely likely we would never find whatever it was. The population in Kingfield would dwindle away until the survivors fled, too terrified to remain.

"What are you thinking about?" Harper asked.

I looked over at her and gave her a wan smile. "Just thinking ahead. Finding this thing and getting rid of it won't be easy, I'm afraid."

"Are you certain it's a monster?" she asked carefully.

"What do you mean?"

"I mean, people die out here all the time. We've got a large population of seniors, and the nearest hospital is forty-five minutes away. If someone has a heart attack or a stroke, they often don't make it. It could be that Mrs. Wilson felt her time was coming and didn't want to be a burden on anyone."

"And what about Langston and his cousin? And the others? Surely not everyone who disappeared was a geriatric."

"Well, no. But those could be unrelated incidents."

I sighed. "It could be. The only way we'll find out is by looking, though."

"I know. I just... I want to be sure you're not seeing monsters when all there is are humans."

"Believe me. Nobody would be happier to find out this was all just a serial killer than me."

Harper slowed and pulled off the gravel track onto a two-rut dirt path. Saplings grew between the ruts and slapped against the undercarriage as we drove over them. I braced myself against the dash as our wheels seemed to find every dent and divot in the path. Tree branches scraped against the sides of the truck on both sides.

"Not exactly keeping up the with Joneses, was she?" I asked. I had to speak carefully to avoid having my teeth knocked together.

"There isn't a whole lot of material rivalry out here," Harper shook her head. "Most people are just happy if they have the extra cash to repaint their houses every few years."

"Still," I protested, "it doesn't take money to go out with a pair of loppers and keep your road open."

"She was like eighty, Ryan."

Before I could respond, we came to the end of the path and the oppressively close forest opened up into a clearing. Maybe 'clearing' was too generous. The forest had reclaimed most of the land and young trees were growing right next to the house. An ancient diesel pickup was parked in front of the sagging front deck, its hood partially propped up by a pine that had grown up through the engine compartment and was fighting to find sunlight.

Harper slowed to a stop and we stared at the house through the windshield, neither of us speaking. The house hadn't been in good repair to begin with, but two months of it being unoccupied during peak growing season had all but buried the house in new greenery.

Blackberry brambles snaked up the side of the house and had pulled the shutters from the windows. The paint had already been peeling, and the vines were doing their best to strip it all down to bare wood. The siding was cracked and warped where moisture had rotted the boards, the roof was sagging and missing shingles near the peak.

"Jesus," I muttered.

My exclamation seemed to energize Harper and she swung her door open and dropped to the ground outside. Before I could remind her, she reached back in and snagged the rifle from the gun rack. I nodded approvingly and exited the truck.

I caught up to Harper before she reached the porch and touched her shoulder. "Maybe let me go first," I said softly.

She looked at me and opened her mouth, then shut it with a nod. "Okay."

I drew my handgun from its shoulder holster, checked the mag and breach, then flicked the safety off. "You know how to use that thing?"

"I've been hunting since I was old enough to hold a rifle," she sniffed. "I'm probably a better shot than you are."

"Right. Cover me."

I walked carefully up the sagging porch steps, handgun held out in front of me, my trigger finger resting alongside the guard. The wood creaked under my weight alarmingly, but held. At the front door, I leaned over to peek inside. The gloom in the front room was broken by a few errant streaks of sunlight. I waited for a few seconds, but nothing moved.

Gingerly, I dropped a hand to the doorknob and pushed it inward. The door creaked as it swung open. The top hinge was starting to become unseated from the jam and the leading corner of the door scraped over the floor, following the arc of wear markings.

I stepped inside and let my senses soak in the silence of the house. Other than Harper shifting her weight from foot to foot in the doorway, the house was empty. I relaxed a little and lowered my gun to the floor.

"It's okay. House is empty."

Harper stepped inside and slung her rifle over her shoulder by its strap. "You seem pretty certain of that."

"Not a big house," I pointed out.

It wasn't much more than a cabin. If it had been in a city, I would have classified it as a loft apartment. There was one big room, with a partial dividing wall in the middle. On the left was a kitchen and dinette. An old wood-burning stove was against the dividing wall, and doubled as the heat source. The walls of the kitchen were lined with shelves, half-filled with canned food in mason jars. On the right was a four-poster bed hung with tatty curtains. A handmade wooden ladder was propped up against the wall on that side, giving access to the cramped loft space.

Other than the necessary tools and equipment to sustain life outside of the comforts of the city, there weren't any luxuries or extras. The inside of the house was neat and organized. I had been expecting the classic loner cabin, stacks of newspapers, dishes piled in the sink, roaches scurrying away from underfoot. My expectations couldn't have been further from the reality.

It didn't look like the house of someone who had given up on life.

"What are we looking for?" Harper asked.

"I don't know." I flicked the safety on my handgun and put it away. I stepped into the kitchen and looked closer at the jars on the wall. Venison, unless I missed my guess, along with a few rows of fish and assorted vegetables. Dried beans and rice were in sealed glass containers over the stove. Enough food for months.

There was no running water, no electricity. An antique propane lantern sat on the dinette table. A door at the back of the kitchen gave me a view down a short path to a well-built outhouse. A hand-cranked well pump was by the back door, its handle polished from decades of use. The house had been constructed shortly after the turn of the century and never connected to the grid. Mrs. Wilson and her husband had lived frugally and simply.

I could read the slow deterioration of the house in the small patches to the tools and furniture. After Mr. Wilson had passed, the widow had done her best to keep things going. There was a quiet desperation visible, now that I looked closer. The rising costs of food and goods, the dwindling savings, and the inexorable knowledge that her own time wasn't far away, had driven her to keep what she had working as long as possible. Twine that bound a broken chair leg back together again. Chipped china plates set neatly in their cubby on the wall. Hand-carved wooden cooking utensils. An old tin teapot on the stove, dents carefully hammered out again.

"Shit," I muttered.

"What is it?"

"Mrs. Wilson didn't kill herself."

"She didn't?"

"No. She wasn't ready to die. Look. Her bed is made. Dishes are washed and put away. She's a hunter, there's an ammo box by the door, but I don't see a gun. Did the sergeant take it away?"

Harper shook her head, her ponytail swaying. "No, it wasn't here, or in her truck. We figured she had taken it with her."

"Not something you do when you're ready to die," I pointed out.

"Was she attacked?"

"If she was, it wasn't in here. I don't see any signs of a struggle." I looked out the window at the rampant growth that had taken over the clearing. Any tracks that had been out there were long gone. Short of finding the old woman's body, there wasn't anything here that would offer more clues. I sighed and shook my head. "I don't think we're going to find anything else useful here."

"Are you sure?"

"No. But that's how this works. I take in details until things start to make sense. Until that happens, all we can do is keep looking."

She pursed her lips, then shrugged. "Okay. What's—"

The radio on her belt squelched, cutting her off. She snatched it and held it to her ear, listening intently. From where I was standing, I couldn't make out what was being said. She grimaced and met my eyes. "Roger that. I'll be there as soon as I can."

"Trouble?" I asked.

Harper shrugged. "After a fashion. We found a missing person."

CHAPTER THREE

Sugarloaf Mountain was one of the biggest tourist attractions in Maine. Harper told me about its history as we drove. A third of a million people went down its slopes every year and brought a massive economic boost. One could argue that without Sugarloaf drawing tourists, the eastern half of Maine would be entirely empty of human habitation.

Out of three hundred thousand people, there were inevitably a few people who were more adventurous than they were intelligent. As I was beginning to understand, the woods of Maine were no joke. A few hundred people got lost every year, even with GPS, and search parties were a weekly occurrence.

Last February, a group of cross-country skiers set out despite warnings of an incoming storm. A blizzard dumped five feet of snow that afternoon. By the time the storm passed and the search parties were allowed to go out, there was no sign of the group.

"It happens every once in a while," Harper shrugged. "We can't always protect people from their own stupidity. Someone finally stumbled over the skiers. I've been expecting this call for weeks."

"How many people in the group?"

"Six. Three boys and three girls."

I winced. That was a lot of people to have die all at once. "Damn."

"The families hired searchers and they've been combing the mountain since before the snow melted. Looks like they finally found them."

"The families will be there?"

Harper shook her head. "No, we keep them out until we can get the bodies properly interred. Nobody wants to see their loved ones chewed on by the carrion eaters. No matter how much they might insist otherwise."

"That's something, at least. Why did they call you?"

"I've asked to be notified of any missing people. The Rangers will have things covered. It's routine. They only let me know as a courtesy."

"Huh. They going to have a problem with me tagging along?"

"I'll make up an excuse," she assured me.

I nodded and looked out the window. We were starting to climb up the foothills and the view was starting to have something other than endless trees. Sugarloaf rose ahead of us, massive and out of place among the rolling hills.

It didn't take long before we were pulling into a parking lot outside a sprawling resort complex. After the isolation and dated technology of Kingfield and the surrounding areas, it was a little shocking to step out of the truck into a truly modern resort. I felt a little like a man who had been stranded at sea finally drifting to land and finding himself at a Caribbean five-star hotel.

A man in an olive-green Ranger uniform waved at Harper when she got out of the truck and jogged over to us.

"Hey, Harper. That was fast. Who is your friend?"

"I was already in the area," she said. "Ryan, this is Miles Ashford. Miles, Ryan Halsin."

I shook his hand. "How do you do?"

"Fine, thanks. Are you a civilian?"

"Ex-army," I shrugged. "A mutilated body or two isn't going to turn my stomach."

"Uh-huh. Harper, why is he here?"

"He's a... private investigator. He's helping with a missing person case. He was with me when the call came in. I couldn't just leave him on the side of the road."

Miles grunted and eyed me for a moment before waving a hand. "Whatever. He can come if he wants, but I can't have civilians wandering around the scene, investigator or otherwise."

"Thanks, Miles," Harper gave him a broad smile. "I'll keep him on a short leash."

"Fine. Come on, we've got a bit of a drive ahead of us."

We followed Miles around to the back side of the hotel where he had a six-wheeled all-terrain vehicle parked. There was a bench seat in front, but the rear seats had been removed to give the vehicle a longer bed. It was empty except for a cardboard box of rolled up body bags.

Harper grudgingly sat in the middle of the seat. With Miles at the wheel and me on the passenger side, we were pretty cramped. Harper was pressed against me from shoulder to knee. Other than her holstered revolver jabbing into my hip, I found the experience rather pleasant. The top of her head was right under my nose and I could smell the faint residue of the tea tree conditioner she had used. The engine roared to life and we pulled out of the parking lot, heading straight for a dirt track that cut into the trees.

I had a brief regret for the rifle we had left in Harper's truck, but Miles was conspicuously armed with a blunt-nosed revolver in a vest holster and had a rifle of his own in a locked case alongside the bed of the vehicle. He caught me looking at the iron he was wearing and flashed me a tight smile.

"It might not look like it, but we're out in the wilds here, Mr. Halsin. We have wolves and cougars and bears, and any of them might want to challenge a couple humans over a free carrion meal."

"Not criticizing. I've just never seen a revolver that large unless it was a fetish."

"You don't stop a bear with a .22," Miles laughed. "You've seen the rifle Harper carries with her."

".444 Marlin," Harper said. "Bear rounds. Overkill for wolves."

"Not that you need to shoot a wolf," Miles clarified. "They're smart enough to recognize a rifle and piss off without you having to fire a shot."

"Most of the time," Harper corrected.

"Mostly," Miles agreed.

"Where are we headed?" I asked, mostly to turn the conversation away from guns before someone asked me what I carried.

"Around to the south-east side of Sugarloaf," Miles said.

"Do we know what happened to them yet?" Harper asked.

"We can guess. They were all college kids with a reputation for being thrill-seekers."

Harper sighed. "Wait, don't tell me. The slopes weren't exciting enough."

"There are a couple trails that are skiable down the eastern slope, if you're good," Miles nodded. "I wouldn't try them on cross-country skis, but then again, I wouldn't go out with a storm warning on the radio."

Miles, it seemed, didn't have an issue trash-talking the dead.

"So, they skied down the trails, then what?" I asked.

"It's hard to say for sure," Miles shrugged. "They made it about halfway down. It could be they went further and got caught by the storm on the way back. Current theory is they decided to head uphill when the storm hit. It's as good an idea as any. If they kept going uphill, eventually they'd hit the slopes, and it'd be an easy ride down to the resort from there."

"But they didn't make it," Harper concluded. "Did you find all six?"

Miles glanced at her then shook his head. "Two. Pam Tauter and who we think is Shane Ashen."

"What happened to the other four?" I asked.

The two Rangers shared a look, then Harper said, "If the wolves found them, we might find scraps of their clothing later." The tone of her voice suggested that was highly unlikely.

"Oh."

"We'll keep searching, of course," Miles said. There was an undercurrent of resignation in his voice that added a silent, *as long as the families keep paying us to* look.

"Of course."

We rode in silence for a while. The jostling of the vehicle over the rough ground forced us to go at barely over a crawl. I shifted my hips around, trying to find a position where Harper's gun wasn't digging into me, but it was a lost cause. I considered asking her if she wanted to sit in my lap, but couldn't see that going anywhere but wrong.

Fortunately, my suffering didn't last much longer. We came around a ridge in the mountain and I caught a flash of red through the trees.

"There!" I pointed.

Miles nodded. "Yep. You've got sharp eyes, Mr. Halsin."

We drew up alongside another all-terrain vehicle and Miles waved to the Ranger already at the scene. "I've brought Harper, and a friend of hers." He threw the parking brake and climbed out.

The other Ranger snuffed his cigarette out on the sole of his boot and came up to my door. "Who are you?" he demanded. He was an older gentleman, with a bushy white mustache and a shotgun slung over one shoulder.

"Ryan Halsin, a private investigator," I said. "Don't worry, I'll stay out of your way."

He grunted. "Sure you will." He thumped a hand on the roof. "Scene's over there, behind that rock. Don't wander too far. If we have to organize a search party for you, we'll charge you every red cent it costs us."

"Considering why we're here, I think I've learned an object lesson," I said wryly.

"Good man. Come on, Miles. We've wasted enough time already. I want to get this done before we start losing light."

"Be right there," Miles said. He leaned into the vehicle. "You gonna help, Harper?"

"Soon as this big lump gets out of the way," she said, and gave me a push in the shoulder.

"Yeah, yeah." I got out of the vehicle and stood back as the Rangers went to work.

I had promised not to interfere with the scene, but that didn't mean I couldn't get a look from a distance. Once the Rangers were busy, I hiked uphill and circled around so I could see down into the little depression where the bodies were.

There was a little bit of underbrush, but the soil in this area was thin and didn't support dense vegetative growth like it did around Kingfield. There were a lot of scraps of pink nylon scattered around, with clumps of insulation stuck to the underbrush. It took me a minute to spot the bodies, and it wasn't until Miles squatted down that my eyes picked out the long shapes of the bones.

Of Pam Tauter, there wasn't much left besides the bones. Animals had picked most of the flesh clean, leaving the matted scalp hair and the gristly bits untouched. Even from where I was, I could tell that Pam had suffered a break in one leg.

I looked uphill, and could make out the path the kids had followed while skiing downhill. There was an opening in the trees that ran down the slope. I wasn't a big skier, but to my untrained eye, it looked far steeper than what I would be comfortable with.

There was a spur of granite that stuck out of the slope a little uphill from where I was. I tried to imagine how it would look in the winter when it was covered in snow. Coming downhill, trying to control your speed, the spur would look like a fun jump.

I climbed uphill toward the spur and stood on the lip looking down. From twenty or thirty feet higher up the slope, it looked manageable, but from the edge, it was a twenty-foot drop straight down. If you had any speed, it would be thirty or forty feet down before you finally hit the ground. Even for a skilled skier, that was dangerous.

As Pam had found out.

I crouched down, reconstructing how it probably had all gone down. Maybe one of the boys had gone first and had made the jump. He likely had called out, warning that it was a further drop than it looked. Pam, coming second, had already been committed. She would have put on the brakes, tried to avoid the spur, and taken it at an off angle.

Then, everyone crowding around, debating what to do. The storm was coming. If they had all been hale, it would have been easy enough to turn around and beat the storm back to the resort. But with one of their number injured, it was suddenly a much more dire situation.

I thought about what it had been like for me at their age. If the men had been raised with any sort of morals, they would have refused to leave a wounded woman behind. The women would have refused to separate, partially afraid of braving the storm on their own, partially out of solidarity for their injured friend.

So, all six, stranded in the woods. They were adventurous kids, they would have likely been familiar with broken bones and the proper first aid. They would have splinted her leg with ski poles and tried to make a stretcher out of their skis. But climbing uphill through uncompacted snow was back-breaking labor. The men would have taken turns stomping down a path and dragging Pam uphill bit by bit.

They would not have gotten very far. Even without the storm coming, they would have realized fairly quickly that they weren't going to make it back uphill to the slopes. They would have tried to make a shelter.

I turned about, scanning the forest, looking for clusters of dead branches. The men would have spread out, breaking off long branches and cutting down saplings with their knives. I didn't see any evidence of that, though.

I frowned, my narrative broken by the lack of evidence. The base of the granite spur would have made a good place to build a shelter. A couple dozen good branches would make enough room for all of them to huddle together for warmth. With luck, the storm wouldn't completely smother them. It would be a long, miserable night, but they would have survived it.

They must have found a better solution. I looked closer at the surrounding trees, searching for the blonde hints of recently broken pine. I found it eventually, but the breaks were a lot smaller than I had been expecting. Pine fronds had been snapped off where the branches were only half an inch thick, but they had broken a lot of them. Bedding, then, rather than shelter supports.

Had they found some other form of shelter? The broken fronds were more frequent in an area to my right where another granite outcrop stuck up from the ground. In fact, it seemed like every branch within reach of the ground had been stripped of its smaller growth.

I climbed down off the spur and headed in that direction. As I came around to where the branches had been stripped, I saw a tree had fallen. The branches had been crushed up against the face of the granite outcrop. At first, I thought it would make an ideal shelter, even better than against the spur, but then as I got closer, I saw there wasn't much space between the trunk and the ground.

I walked along the length of the tree anyway, looking for any sign that the kids had used it as a shelter. I didn't find any scraps of cloth or chewed bones. I made another pass, just to be sure, but there was nothing. This wasn't where they had made their shelter. I was about to give up and search for another explanation when a cold draft gusted against me.

Goosebumps climbed up my neck and I shivered. I backed up a step, my hands spread wide, searching for the draft again. I found it once more and I leaned toward the fallen tree, trying to see past the clustered brown pine needles.

There was something behind the tree, but I couldn't make out what it was. I kicked at the branches, breaking them off so I could get a better look. It didn't take long before I saw where the draft was coming from.

A cave opening was hidden in the outcrop. It wasn't wide, maybe three feet across at the widest part, and maybe four feet tall. The tree trunk had fallen against the side of the outcrop, blocking off most of the cave opening. There was about a foot of opening above the trunk, but it was only a few inches wide at that point.

From within the cave, a steady stream of cold air flowed

past my face, carrying with it the faint but unmistakable scent of rot.

"Harper!" I shouted. "Harper! You need to come look at this!"

A minute later, Harper came jogging through the trees. Her worried look relaxed when she saw me. "What is it? What did you find?"

"I hope you have a chainsaw in one of those vehicles," I said. "I think I found the other missing skiers."

The sun had dropped below the peak of Sugarloaf Mountain by the time Miles made it back with a chainsaw. The older Ranger, who had grudgingly introduced himself as Slate, made no effort to exclude me as Miles bent his back to the saw.

I cleared out of the way, along with Harper and Slate, in case the tree became unstable and decided it wanted to roll down the hill. The saw Miles had managed to find had a dull chain on it, and the going was slow.

"What I don't understand," Slate grumbled, "is why they left the girl out in the snow? Assuming your hypothesis is correct, they would have put the girl into the cave first."

"We don't know how deep the cave goes," Harper rationalized. "Maybe they were afraid of a bear."

"With an opening that large? Nah, not unless there's another entrance somewhere."

"There's a draft," I pointed out. "Could be there is."

"Or maybe there's something else going on here," Slate said darkly. "But let's not borrow trouble. If the stink is coming from our missing kids, there's a reward in it for you, Halsin."

I grimaced. I didn't want anything to do with that kind of

blood money. "Split it among the searchers. I'm sure they would have found the cave eventually. All I did was follow the last little bit of trail."

"Broken branches," Slate shook his head. "You're being modest, man. That was some shrewd thinking."

"And good eyesight," Harper added.

The snarl of the chainsaw dropped down to an idle, saving me from having to respond. "Last few inches!" Miles called out. "She's about ready to fall open."

"About damn time," Slate growled.

The chainsaw roared back to life again. I could hear the pitch of the saw change as the last of the wood gave way. The chainsaw cut off and we saw Miles scurry to take cover behind a thick pine. "Here she comes!" he cried.

There was a chorus of snapping pops and the segment of trunk that Miles had cut loose broke free. It started rolling downhill, but the stump of a branch kept fouling in the ground and after a few rotations it tipped over and slid to a halt. The rest of the tree settled a few inches, but didn't move any further.

"Damn bad luck," Slate said. "Kids did everything right, and then a tree falls over their cave. Like some kind of cruel joke. Well, come on then. Let's see what's inside."

Slate led the way, a big revolver in one hand and a high-powered flashlight in the other. The other two Rangers had flashlights and their own weapons out. Amid all the firepower, I didn't bother drawing my handgun and had to satisfy myself with my cell phone light.

The entrance to the cave was tight, but it opened up quickly, with the craggy roof of the cave high enough over my head that I could stand up straight. There was a big nest of piled pine fronds close to the entrance. I had expected to find the bodies of the other four lying among the browning pine needles, but other than some discarded clothing, there was nothing.

"Cave keeps going," Miles said. "We should look further back. It's clear the kids were here."

Slate scowled back at the entrance. "Fine, but I'm calling it in. I don't want a repeat of what happened to them. Half an hour, tops, then you come on back out. Stay in the open areas of the cave. Don't go through any passage you can't walk in easily. If you can't see clearly where you're putting your feet, don't step there."

I nodded, taking the advice to heart. Spelunking in an unknown cave was dangerous enough when you had all the proper equipment. If it wasn't for the nonchalance on Harper's face, I would have gone to wait outside with Slate.

"All right. Harper, I'm sticking with you," I said.

"Suit yourself," she shrugged.

Slate ducked back outside again. I held my phone up to watch him go, then went to examine the opening of the cave closer. There were scratch marks in the granite around the opening. Our footprints had smudged the dirt there, but I could see where the sand and small rocks had been scraped away down to the bare granite. The granite at the bottom was stained with red where they had scraped their fingers raw trying to make the opening just a little bit bigger.

Seeing their desperate attempt to escape brought home to me just how awful those last days must have been. They had water in the form of snow, but without food, their lives were on a timer ticking inexorably down. The cold hadn't helped matters, as it would have made their bodies work harder to stay warm.

A healthy human with access to water could survive for a month without food. How long had they made it before starvation had cut away the last of their will to live? Two weeks? Three?

"Hey, are you coming?" Harper called.

I gave myself a shake and turned away from the opening. "Yep."

"You okay?" she asked.

"Just an over-abundance of empathy."

She nodded with a small, sad smile. "No shame in it if you want to wait outside."

"You kidding? Come all this way just to hang out with Slate?" I caught up to her and jostled her with an elbow. "Not a chance."

"I'm going this way," Miles said, and pointed toward the back where a bend in the cave led deeper.

"Then we'll go over here," Harper said, and waved toward a narrow opening. "Call if you find anything, and stay safe."

"Yeah, yeah."

I watched Miles go, then turned to follow Harper. My phone light didn't reach very far, and I kept it aimed at our feet. We weren't here hunting for our monster, but I couldn't help but feel tension ratcheting tighter in my shoulders.

"I've got a bad feeling about this," I muttered.

Harper spared me a look. "Anything I should know?"

"No. But if you were starving to death, wouldn't you stay where someone could find you easily? Something happened in this cave."

"Maybe there's another exit," Harper shrugged.

I didn't argue it, but I had my doubts. You don't scratch your fingers bloody when there's a better option available. The little cave we were following got a bit cramped and I had to turn sideways to follow Harper's lithe form, but it opened up again after a few steps.

There were two lobes to the cave here. Sunlight streamed in through a crack in the granite overhead, not more than an inch or two across. The ground beneath was marshy and algae grew in a thick mat on the floor. In the other lobe, clothing was piled haphazardly.

Harper muttered an exclamation under her breath and went to the clothes and started digging through them, cataloging what she had found out loud. My attention was drawn to the puddled water and what I saw sticking out of the mud there.

I crouched down and brushed the clinging algae away from the length of the femur. It had been cracked open and gnawed on. I snapped a picture with my phone, then skimmed away the algae from the surface of the puddle.

"Harper."

I heard her footsteps behind me, then her intake of breath. The pool of water was deeper than it had seemed, and it was full of bones.

CHAPTER FOUR

"That was kind of you to give the reward to the searchers."

I grunted something noncommittal and stared at the trees going by outside the window.

"Seriously," Harper continued, "eight thousand dollars is not a small amount of money."

"They need it more than I do."

"I had no idea hunting monsters paid so well. If I could afford to shrug off eight grand, I'd definitely move out of Maine. I love the land here, but not that much."

"My family has been in the business for centuries. And the Chapter compensates its people well, otherwise we'd be off doing something safe with our lives instead."

"Family business, huh? The Halsin clan has been around a while, has it?"

"Not really, that's an Americanization of our name. You've probably heard of our European family name."

"Oh yeah?"

"Van Helsing."

She snorted her amusement, then did a double take when I didn't join her. "No. Really?"

"Erik Van Helsing was one of the founding members of the Chapter in the sixteenth century."

"Holy shit."

"The records are a little fuzzy, but there's ample evidence that the Van Helsings had been fighting monsters for centuries before that."

"Well, I'll be damned. So, what are you? Last of the line? Fated to save the world?"

I laughed and shook my head. "No, nothing exciting like that. There are dozens of Halsins in America, and more family overseas. Not all of us go into the monster hunting business."

"You must have some interesting family stories to tell."

"You could say that."

We were silent for a few minutes. I could tell Harper wanted to ask me for a story or two, but I wasn't in the mood.

"So, are we going to talk about it?" I asked.

"About what?"

"There were only three skeletons in that pool."

"What are you, a savant at identifying bodies too? How could you tell that?"

"I counted the skulls," I said.

"You mean you counted the skull fragments? There was a lot of mud there. The animal could have buried pieces. Or maybe there were only three in the cave to begin with. The last one could have tried hiking back to the slopes alone and died in the storm." Harper sighed. "Even if you're right, what is the point of making the distinction? If the last kid was alive, he would have found his way back to civilization by now. This way, the families get closure."

"You're right. It's not worth worrying about." I rubbed at the back of my neck and stretched it until it popped. "Besides, we've spent enough time on it. We wasted almost the entire day."

"Not exactly wasted," Harper protested. "I think those kids would agree that finding their resting places was worthwhile."

"Harper, they're already dead. They don't give two fucks whether their bones are rotting in a puddle or buried in state. I'm more concerned with finding out what is making living people disappear. Those we can still save. That's why I'm out here."

She didn't respond, just focused on the road, her eyes hurt.

I sighed and relented. "Still. I suppose it was a good thing that they were found. All five or six or however many. And it did rule out that the kids weren't disappeared by our monster. If nothing else, we've narrowed our window somewhat."

"Well, *I* think it was worth doing."

"All right, fine. It was worth doing. But since we wa... spent most of our day at Sugarloaf, we should plan out tomorrow so we can get right to work."

"Okay. I agree."

"I'd like to look into the most recent person to go missing. Seeing where Mrs. Wilson had gone missing was helpful, but any clues that had been there were long gone."

"Okay. I can arrange that. What kind of clues are you looking for?"

"Honestly, I have no idea. I still don't know what kind of monster it could be."

"I have a question about that, actually. How will you know what it is?"

I pursed my lips. "That's a good question, actually. What is your understanding of the fae?"

"The fae? Like faeries?"

"Not exactly. Okay, so, the fae is like another dimension

45

that is parallel to ours, the mortal. It holds all the creatures and monsters and things that are in legends."

"Like werewolves?"

"Yes, like werewolves."

"And vampires?"

"No. Those are in the real world, unfortunately."

Her eyes widened, and I hurried on before she could derail my explanation with more questions.

"We have legends and stories of monsters because they actually existed. In modern times, monsters are all but gone because the connection between the fae and the mortal is disrupted by iron. There are a few that find their way through every now and then, but nowhere near as many as in the old days before iron was everywhere in the world."

"You mean like Grimm's fairy tales?"

"Sure. The Germans have their monsters. But so do the Japanese, the Indians, the Middle Eastern peoples, the Native Americans in both North and South America. The US is a mixing-ground of cultures, which makes things more challenging. The fae tend to exist where people believe in them. So, our first order of business is figuring out what the monster is. From there, we figure out how to kill it."

"And it's always a monster that we know about?"

I shrugged. "The fae used to define their existence by their interactions with mortals. And we mortals do love to tell our stories. I've run into obscure monsters and wrongly guessed monsters, but never unheard-of monsters."

"I... see."

I smiled to myself. Harper wasn't the first person to have a hard time believing. Most people who didn't grow up fighting monsters had the same reaction. At least she was taking me seriously.

"Once we know what monster it is, then we start researching. There are some nuggets of truth to be found in popular fairy tales or folk legends. But they're rarely perfectly accurate."

"And then we kill it?"

"There are two types of fae, broadly speaking. Those you can communicate and have meaningful dialog with, and those that try to eat your face. If it's one of the first category, we might try and find out what it wants and get it to return to the fae on its own. If it's the second category, well, the fae hate iron and steel."

"We shoot it?"

"Right in one."

"But if it's from the fae, won't it just come right back again?"

"Probably not. The circumstances have to be just right for them to cross over in the first place. Once we kill it, it won't return."

"Probably?"

"Hey, nobody said monster hunting was easy."

We drove into Kingfield, and a minute later had crossed the town and pulled into the parking lot of my bed and breakfast. We came to a stop next to my rental car and I gave Harper a tired smile.

"Well. That was a full day. I'll see you tomorrow morning, same time?"

"It's a date." I was already turning away and I looked back at her with an eyebrow lifted. She ducked her head and cleared her throat. "I mean, I'll see you then."

"Don't forget to arrange that meeting to look into the missing person," I said. "Goodnight, Harper."

"You too, Ryan."

I got out and waved as she drove off. For a minute, I looked after her, watching her tail lights recede into the distance until the trees blotted them from view.

"Real smooth, Ryan," I muttered.

I rubbed at my eyes and yawned. We had been in that cave putting bone fragments into body bags for the whole afternoon and into the evening. Other than a short break for food around sundown, we hadn't stopped working for nearly four hours. I walked into the reception area and waved at Sylvia behind the desk. "Good evening," I called.

"Oh, Mr. Halsin?"

"Hm?" I stopped and squashed the sudden feeling of irritation. I just wanted to go to bed. "What can I do for you?"

"You have a message from a Mr. Baptiste." She came out from around the counter and handed me an envelope. "I wrote it down so I didn't forget."

"Oh. Thank you, Sylvia."

"No problem. How did you enjoy your breakfast?"

"It was delicious, thank you."

She nodded and gave me a sly smile. "You spent the day with Harper Hall?"

I nodded. "She's helping me with my work."

"What do you think of her?"

"I don't know. She's nice enough."

Sylvia sniffed. "She's just as much of a flatlander as you are."

If I hadn't been so exhausted, I would have picked up on the undertone of Sylvia's questioning earlier. I kept my mouth shut until the urge to respond to the snide comment went away. "She seems to know the area well. I thought she grew up around here."

"Oh, she did. But you know how it is. Her family moved here from Portland. You can tell she doesn't belong just by looking at her."

It had been a while since I had encountered any blatant racism, and hearing it from the cherubic lady gave me an unpleasant jolt. "What do you mean?"

Maybe she missed the undercurrent of anger in my voice because she waved a hand cheerfully. "Oh, you know. Just look at her. Dark skin and dark hair. She has native blood in her."

"I hadn't noticed," I said coldly.

"A nice man like you should find a good woman to settle down with," she bubbled on heedlessly.

"That's good advice, thanks. I've had a long day. I think I'm going to go turn in."

"Oh, certainly. Gave a good night, Mr. Halsin!"

I forced a smile and headed off to my room. What the hell was Sylvia's problem with Harper? Harper was intelligent, beautiful, and strong both in mind and body. She clearly had the respect of her fellow Rangers.

There was no understanding it. I took a quick shower and toweled off, still feeling angry. I put on a fresh pair of boxers and climbed into bed. The sheets were cold, and it took me a few minutes to get comfortable. In the end, I chalked the racism up to the insular nature of these tiny backwoods communities. When everyone you know is a blonde or a redhead, it's easy to paint someone with Harper's complexion as 'other'.

That didn't make it any less reprehensible, though. I finally fell asleep, still playing back the conversation with Sylvia and imagining scenarios where I gave the older lady a piece of my mind.

I woke sometime later. It was still dark outside, and I listened for a moment, trying to figure out what had woken me. The night was quiet. A glance at the retro alarm clock on the side table told me it was just after four in the morning.

After a minute, I closed my eyes and started going back to sleep. There was a thump of a door shutting in the distance that popped my eyes open again. For a moment I focused, listening intently, then I heard soft footsteps coming down the hallway toward my room.

I slipped out of bed, grabbed my handgun from the side table, and padded softly to the door. The footsteps stopped outside my room, then there was a rap of knuckles on the door. I reached out and snatched the door open, then swung out to cover the hallway, gun raised at shoulder height.

Harper gave a surprised gasp and her eyes flew to the gun in my hand. "Ryan, I—"

"Shit." I lowered the gun after checking behind her to see if there was anyone else in the hallway. "What the fuck are you doing here, Harper?"

Now that there wasn't a gun in her face, her eyes dropped from mine and she looked down at me. Her throat bobbed as she swallowed. "Sorry, I... you said to let you know if... I mean, there's another person missing."

"Oh." I realized I was standing in just a pair of boxers. "Why didn't you call ahead? I would have met you outside." I stepped back and swung the door open wider. "Well, you're here now. Come on in. It won't take me long to get dressed."

"Um, I thought I'd just stay out here in the hallway."

"Don't be stupid. You've already seen me in my boxers. I'm not shy."

"Clearly," she muttered. After a moment's hesitation, she stepped into the room and went to go stare out the window.

I dressed quickly and started interrogating Harper as I threw my clothes on. "Who went missing?"

"After I dropped you off last night, I checked in on the family that had one of their sons go missing. They agreed to answer any questions you have in the morning. Then, ten minutes ago, I got a call from the daughter that the other son had gone missing."

"In the middle of the night?"

"Tammy, that's the daughter, said she got up to go to the bathroom, and checked in on her brother. His bed was empty, so she called me right away."

I stamped into my boots and knelt down to tighten the laces. "How old?"

"Tammy is sixteen. Henry, the youngest who just went missing is twelve. The rest of the family is Liam at nineteen and Owen at twenty-two. Owen went missing the day before you arrived."

"Kind of old to be living at their parents' house, aren't they?"

"It's not uncommon around here. There's not much regular work to be had, so most children work in the family business."

I shrugged into my shoulder holster and put my handgun away. "All right. I'm ready to go."

Harper turned around and looked relieved that I was clothed once more. "I told Tammy we'd be over as soon as possible and to wake her parents. They should be expecting us."

"Let's not keep them waiting, then."

T he Davis family had a homestead off the 142 going west from Kingfield. It was a relief to see open fields growing high with hay grass instead of the solid walls of trees. Round bales of hay were stacked along the side of the property, with a hand-painted plywood sign offering the bales for sale.

The homestead itself was a sprawling clapboard building. Over the years, it had been continuously added onto as the needs of the family living within had grown. At a guess, it was around eight or nine bedrooms now.

Lights were on in the house. As we pulled into the

driveway, the front door opened and a young girl in pajamas and slippers came running out to greet us. Harper killed the engine and climbed out.

"Hey, Tammy. I came as fast as I could."

The girl's happiness to see Harper was tempered with a frown as she saw me get out of the truck. "Who is that, Harper?"

"Hi, I'm Ryan Halsin. I'm helping Harper investigate the missing people."

"Are you a detective?"

I smiled and nodded. "A private one, yes. You must be Tammy."

She gave me an uncertain smile back. "Are you going to help find my brothers?"

"That's why I'm here," I said reassuringly.

"Are your parents awake, Tammy?" Harper asked.

She nodded. "They are getting dressed."

"While we wait for them, do you mind if I ask you some questions?" I asked.

Tammy looked at Harper and got an encouraging nod. "Okay."

"Does Henry like to go on early-morning walks?"

"He hates getting up early. Even when we have hay days, he's the last one to get up."

"I see. Has he been having nightmares? Acting strange recently?"

"Um… I don't think so. We've all been worried about the people going missing. Mama doesn't let us spend the night with friends, even though school is out for the summer. Henry likes to go fishing, but Mama's making him stay home, so he's been upset about that."

"All right. How have you been? Are you dealing with everything okay?"

"I guess. I'm scared. What's happening? Where are people going?"

"We're trying to figure that out, sweetie," Harper said, forcing cheer into her voice.

"One last question," I said. "Does Henry have anywhere he would go to hide if he was scared?"

"There's an overturned tree down past the field where we would play. It's a good hiding spot."

"Maybe you could show us once the sun comes up," I said.

"You think he's hiding there? Why would he leave the house to hide out in the woods?"

"I don't know, Tammy. I'm just making sure we haven't left any stones unturned."

She nodded, but before she could respond, the door banged open and a heavyset redheaded woman stormed out onto the porch. "Tammy, get back inside!"

Tammy flinched and ran for the house. I glanced at Harper and saw her expression had frozen into a polite smile.

"Hello, Mrs. Davis," Harper called. "We came as fast as we could."

"Waste of time," Mrs. Davis said sourly. "Henry will be home before you know it. He's probably just out looking for Owen."

I glanced to Harper to take her cues. That wasn't the response I expected from a mother who just found out her youngest son was found missing from his bed.

"Maybe, maybe not," Harper said peaceably. "But on the off-chance he really is missing, I was hoping you'd allow my partner and I to look at Henry's room. And Owen's, while we're here."

"Your partner?" The woman's brow furrowed and she glared at me. The barely concealed hostility in her posture relaxed as she looked me over. "I didn't think Rangers had partners."

"Mr. Halsin is helping me investigate the missing people. He's from the city."

"Maybe you should be the one helping him," she said acidly. "Seeing as how you haven't found a single person yet."

I cleared my throat and stepped up to the porch, casually putting myself between the two women. "Ms. Hill and I don't want to disturb you, but I would like it if you could make yourself available to answer some questions after we look at Henry's room." I let my irritation firm my voice a little. There were times when a firm voice and a little bit of looming helped cut through social bullshit, and this time it worked.

Mrs. Davis wilted. "I suppose. You don't look like a cop, though. Can I see your badge?"

"I'm not a cop. I'm a privately retained investigator."

The woman's scowl returned.

"If you would lead the way to Henry's room, please," I said firmly.

"Tammy!" Mrs. Davis yelled.

A moment later, Tammy appeared in the doorway. "Yes, Ma?"

"Show these two to Henry's room. I suppose you want coffee Mr. Halsin?"

"That would be good, thank you. I'll take it black, please. How about you, Harper?"

Harper shot a look at me that I couldn't decipher before she turned to smile at Mrs. Davis. "Cream and sugar for me, thank you."

Mrs. Davis grunted something under her breath and stomped back into the house. Tammy winced again and tilted her head. "This way," she said in a small voice.

Harper gestured for me to go first and I stepped up onto the porch and into the Davis homestead. The front door opened in a great room that was lined with bookshelves and filled with worn furniture. An ancient CRT flatscreen TV sat on a low table with bunny ears sticking up over it. A quilt hung on the wall, horribly clashing colors of blue and yellow polka-dots.

Tammy took a left and we followed her through the majority of the house to the most recently added wing. Up a flight of stairs, and Henry's room was the first door on the right. Tammy pushed open the door and revealed a predictably cluttered room that would belong to a young boy. Posters from video games were on the walls. He had a small TV on his dresser with a game console next to it that was two generations out of date. Clothes littered the floor around the hamper.

"Here's Henry's room," Tammy said. "My room is across the hall. If you don't need me for anything, I'll go get dressed."

"That's fine," Harper said. "We won't go anywhere until you get back."

Tammy ducked her head and retreated to her room. I saw a flash of pink, and posters of fashion models with flowing hair, then the door closed. I raised an eyebrow at Harper. "You run into this shit a lot?" I asked her softly.

"I don't really want to talk about it," Harper said stiffly. "Can we just get this over with?"

"Certainly. If you need my intervention, just say the word."

"I can handle it," she protested and shook her head. "The sooner we finish, the sooner we get out of here."

I shrugged. "If you say so."

CHAPTER FIVE

Henry's room didn't have much that was interesting. There was no sign of a struggle that I could see. His bedclothes were tossed back, left where they lay when he had gotten up earlier on in the night. I slid a hand between the sheets and found them cold. Tammy had discovered Henry's absence less than half an hour ago. If Henry had been recently asleep, his sheets should have still been a little warm.

Footsteps came from the hallway and I turned to see a tall, slender young man lean into the room. "I heard my brother's little slut was here, and what do you know." He stepped into the room and slapped Harper's ass with a confident grin. "Owen's not here, but if you're looking to get a quick fuck, I could oblige."

I straightened from leaning over Henry's bed and took two long steps across the room. "Hey! What the fuck is your problem?" I straight-armed the kid in the chest and knocked him back into the doorframe.

"Ryan!" Harper gasped.

"Hey, fuck you!" the kid yelled. "Who the fuck are you, anyway? This is my house, bitch!"

"Liam, just go away. Please." Harper's voice was tight, and I heard the edge of tears barely held back.

Cold rage swelled in me. Liam went to shove me back and I caught his wrist and twisted it up around behind his back. I slammed him face-first back into the doorframe, then leaned my weight on him, straining his arm close to the breaking point.

"Liam, is it?" I hissed in his ear. "If you know what's good for you, you little piece of shit, you'll walk the fuck away. Now." I shoved him out into the hallway.

Liam stumbled and caught himself against the far wall. He spun around and took half a step toward me. My hands flexed and I mapped out just how I would break this little fuck. Catch the punch and snap the arm at the elbow. Stamp on his knee, shatter the joint and cripple him for life. Ram that curled lip into the stairway bannister and snap out every tooth in the front of his stupid mug.

The kid must have seen the violence on my face because he drew up short. He leveled a shaking finger at me, and I took half a step forward, my arms spread in invitation. With a last wordless snarl, he turned and ran down the stairs.

"Fucking coward," I spat after him.

"Ryan!" Harper said, aghast. "What are you doing?"

"Putting a little fuck in his place," I said hotly. My blood was still up, and Harper took a step back when I turned to her.

"You're not helping me," she said, and her voice hitched. I could hear the fear and long-term suppressed grief in her voice.

The sound of her voice breaking sent my rage puddling out of me and I cursed under my breath. "Shit. I'm sorry, Harper."

I reached out gingerly and touched her shoulder. She turned her back to me and twitched her shoulder out from under my hand, but not before I felt a silent sob shake her.

"Can we just look at Henry's room?" she said quietly. The control was back in her voice, but she wouldn't let me see her face.

"Yeah. I... yeah."

I went back to examining Henry's room, and pretended not to notice when Harper took a tissue from the box by the bed to wipe her face. I pretty quickly got the impression that I was wasting my time. Henry had gotten out of bed sometime early in the morning and just... left. Walked out the door on his own.

Asking if the house had a security system was a waste of time. This whole town was living fifty years behind the rest of the world. Hell, the electrical sockets in the bedroom didn't even have a ground prong. And this was the 'new' wing of the house. I was as likely to find a Tesla in the garage as a security camera.

"What do you see?" Harper asked me a few minutes later. Her voice was back to normal, and when I glanced at her, her face was composed, if her eyes a little red.

"Nothing. Henry got out of bed a few hours ago and left on his own volition. Did you get a chance to look at Owen's room?"

"Sergeant Bunnings followed up on that call," Harper said shortly.

I nodded but knew enough not to comment. "We could look, but I suspect all we'll find is the same thing."

Tammy's door opened and she peeked out, her eyes wide. "Is everything okay?" she squeaked.

"Yes, everything's fine, Tammy," Harper said gently.

"Did you have a fight with Liam?"

"Just a difference of opinion," I said. "Hey, Tammy, do you think you could show us that overturned tree?"

She nodded. "Do you want to see Owen's room?"

"Maybe later."

"Oh. Okay." Tammy ducked back into her room and grabbed her jacket. "Follow me, then."

We went back downstairs. Mrs. Davis was in the kitchen. She had cooked oatmeal and was slicing fruit when we walked in. Mr. Davis was sitting at the long dining table, practically big enough to host a banquet. He was a mousey man with thinning blonde hair, slim shoulders and a bit of a paunch. He stood up when we walked in and came over to shake my hand.

"Mr. Halsin. Thank you for your prompt response. We're worried sick about Henry."

I shook his hand. "We're looking into it, Mr. Davis." To his credit, he actually did look worried sick. Where his wife was dealing with it by shoving her anger to the front, I could see that the grief of losing Owen, and now Henry, was taking a terrible toll on him.

"Thank you. Please. Bring him back home. Oh, hello, Harper. I didn't see you there."

Mrs. Davis cleared her throat and Mr. Davis flinched. He scurried back to the table and applied himself to his oatmeal.

"This is a working farm," Mrs. Davis said acidly. "Idle hands means no food during the winter. If you have anything else to ask, I'll answer the questions."

"Actually, Tammy was going to show us something in the woods that might be relevant to Henry," I said. "When we get back, I'm sure I'll have some questions."

Mrs. Davis grunted. "Tammy, you have your chores to do. Give them their directions, then get to them."

"Yes, ma'am," Tammy said.

The older woman dried her hands on a dishcloth. "I just realized I've got to go to the store. I should be back before you finish in the woods."

Mr. Davis watched his wife go, then got up from the table

again. "I've made you two coffee," he said quickly. "Black, as you like it, Mr. Halsin. And the way you take it, Harper."

"Thanks, Bill," Harper said with a tired smile.

I said my thanks and we took our mugs out onto the porch. The sun was just starting to pink the skies to the east. The woods across the hayfield looked dark and dense. We wouldn't find anything there until the sun came up. As much as I wanted to get out there right away and search for Henry, we needed light to see.

Tammy said something about feeding chickens while we waited and left us to our coffee.

The coffee tasted like shit, but I drank it steadily anyway. Five hours of sleep had left me feeling sluggish and my eyeballs grainy. The coffee might not taste great, but it had caffeine in it, and I could feel the rush in my system dragging me fully into the land of the living.

"I used to date Owen," Harper said, breaking the silence.

I glanced at her. Harper had a pensive, inward-looking frown on her face. There seemed to be more to her statement, so I stayed quiet, letting her get it out on her own.

"I think I loved him. This was in high school, senior year. He didn't care that I had native blood in me. Since he was the star athlete in basically every competitive sport our school participated in, nobody hassled him about dating me. And by extension, people left me alone."

"High school might as well be a four-year hazing ritual," I grunted.

"Yeah, well. It wasn't bad once I started seeing Owen. Then the day of senior prom came and he was meant to pick me up at my family's house. He never showed. I was left sitting on my porch until dark. He ended up going to prom with Cindy Stauffer, the lead cheerleader."

Harper gave me a watery half-smile. "I became the

laughing-stock of Kingfield overnight. Everyone knew. I found out later that Mrs. Davis threatened to kick Owen out of the house and disown him if he took me to prom. I believe her words were, 'No son of mine is going to breed a darky slut,' or something like that."

"Classy."

She coughed on her coffee and laughed ruefully. "He dated Cindy for a few weeks then dumped her. He never found another girlfriend after that. I think he regretted the way he treated me, but there was no way he could apologize. Not with his mom hovering in the background."

"And what about you? You find another boyfriend?"

Harper shrugged. "Nobody wants to be seen with Owen's darky slut. At best, I get propositioned like Liam did."

I put my mug down. I couldn't bring myself to keep drinking the Davis' racist brew. "I know it's not my place to say anything, but I'm a little surprised you've stayed."

"Me too, some days. But I like my job and I love these forests. I help people. And not everyone is as bad as Mrs. Davis. Besides, where would I go? What would I do? The only thing I'm really qualified for is being a Forest Ranger. I got a degree at U Maine Farmington, but it's a *tiny* college. My graduating class was less than a hundred and fifty people, across all degrees. I applied for a Ranger job in California and just got laughed at."

"I'm sorry."

"Don't be. This is my life, and I'm used to it." She glanced up at the sun. "If you're done with your coffee, there should be enough light to see by. Tammy's down at the barn."

I dumped my coffee into the flower planter next to the porch. "I'm ready to leave this whole farm behind." I grimaced and shrugged. "I know Henry is just a kid. But fuck these poisonous assholes. People like Mrs. Davis will just twist him into their image, and he'll conform rather than be outcast."

"There's hope for Henry. Tammy isn't so bad." We left our mugs outside the door and started following the footpath around the back of the house toward the barn.

"She's not. But she's terrified of her mother. Same with Mr. Davis. He's so henpecked if he tried to stand up straight his back would snap like a dry twig."

Harper gave an unwilling laugh and shook her head, but she didn't deny it. We followed the sound of chickens and found Tammy outside a large chicken coop built on wheels. She had several hundred chickens around her feet and they were frantically squawking and chasing after the handfuls of milled grain she was throwing from a steel bucket.

"Holy shit, that's a lot of chickens," I said.

Tammy looked up at my comment and grinned. "It's the summer laying flock," she called. "We'll cull the four-year hens in a few months when the days get shorter."

I glanced at Harper. Her expression suggested this was all perfectly logical, but Tammy might as well have been speaking Greek to me. "We can go when you're ready, it should be light enough to see now."

"Okay. I was just wasting time, really." Tammy flung the remaining contents of the bucket over the hens and they exploded in raucous excitement as they chased after the cascading grain. She hung the bucket on a nail and hopped the short electric fence with accustomed ease.

I was a little surprised when Tammy wrapped her arms around Harper and gave her a big hug. Harper saw the look on my face and shrugged. "I grew close to the younger Davis kids when I was in high school. You were nine when I started dating Owen, weren't you? And Henry was five."

Tammy nodded with a smile. Out of the house and away

from her mother, Tammy looked like a completely different person. The mousey, submissive demeanor was gone, leaving a vibrant, happy teenager. "I miss seeing you, Harper."

"Me too, Tammy."

The happiness coming off Tammy smudged out and she swallowed. "We should go look at that tree. I don't think Henry's there, but I can't think of anywhere else he could have gone."

The woods in back of the hayfield were tangled with blackberry vines. Tammy led us down a narrow footpath that gave us a route through the prickly mess. It didn't take long before the canopies of the trees closed in overhead and blotted out the sun.

In the early-morning light, it was hard to make out the path we were following. Tammy didn't seem to have any trouble making sense out of which way to go, though, and she led us confidently deeper into the woods.

"How much farther is it?" I asked.

Tammy glanced back at me with a knowing smile. "First time in the woods?"

"Contrary to my appearance, maybe, I am quite fond of the outdoors. I just haven't been in the Maine woods before. This is something else. How do you know where we're going?"

"We're just following the path," Harper said. She managed to keep a straight face, but I could hear the amusement in her voice.

Tammy took pity on me. "It's just up ahead, Mr. Halsin. Another minute and we'll be there."

"Your parents let you play out here?" I muttered, mostly to myself.

"It's not so bad as it seems, Ryan," Harper grinned. "Your parents let you play outside when you were young, right?"

My father had spent most of my youth training me to fight

monsters. What little free time I had was spent at the shooting range or reading through manuals on different fae species and how to kill them. Tammy was looking at me expectantly, and I gave her a grin and a shrug. She didn't need to hear that. "There's a lot less trees where I'm from."

"It's really just a matter of perspective," Harper said. "It only seems like a lot because you're not used to it. Kids around here grow up learning how to find their way in the woods. We develop a sixth sense about it, right Tammy?"

"It's not bad, Mr. Halsin, honest. And I've spent hundreds of hours out here. I couldn't get lost if I wanted to."

"I suppose the same thing goes for Henry? He wouldn't come out here and lose his way?"

"Oh, no. He's not a child."

I rubbed the back of my neck and shrugged. Henry was twelve. That sounded like a child to me. "If you say so."

Tammy slowed the pace and started peering into the woods on the right. Then she stopped and pointed. "There it is! I knew it was around here somewhere."

I followed her pointing finger and saw a massive pine tree that had fallen over sometime in the last few years. Its root ball had torn up and taken several smaller trees with it. The smaller trees had roots that were intertwined and had tenaciously clung together. The topsoil had come up in a thick layer, held in place by the roots, and made a damp cave.

"Ooh, nice," Harper said. "What a great hideout."

"It is pretty great," Tammy agreed. She stepped off the path and picked her way nimbly through the trees to the cave.

Reluctantly, I followed. The cave exuded the smell of wet soil. The big tree that had fallen over was thick with mushrooms that added a not-unpleasant earthy scent. It was pitch black in the cave. I was starting to get my phone out when

Harper's flashlight shone over my shoulder, illuminating everything in front of me.

"There's something there!" Tammy said.

"Hold on, Tammy. Let me go first," I said quickly.

She stepped aside and I got my phone out and turned the light on. I really needed to get me one of those little belt flashlights like Harper had. Sure enough, a spot of pristine white caught my eye, too pure to be anything made by nature.

I squatted down and crab-walked my way into the cave. The cave might have been big enough for two kids to play in, but I barely fit. My shoulders brushed the roots dangling from the roof and sent clods of cold, damp earth raining down on me. I snagged the bit of white with an outstretched hand and backed out of the cave.

It was a piece of printer paper folded into quarters, still new and crisp. I caught Harper's eye and shifted my gaze sideways to Tammy.

Harper caught on and stepped over to Tammy. She put an arm around the girl's shoulders. "How is school going? Are you going to be playing basketball? You're tall enough, girl! You grow like a weed."

I unfolded the piece of paper and found a note, scrawled in a sloppy print. *It has her.* I stared at it for a moment before folding it up and putting the note away in my jacket. I turned to Harper, trying to think of an excuse to get us out of the forest.

The human eye is an amazing thing. Beyond being an absolutely fantastic camera, far better than it has any right to be, the image processing part of our brain can do some truly remarkable feats of deductive isolation. There are whole structures in the brain seemingly dedicated to recognizing a human face. With a little training, anyone can learn to process a ridiculous quantity of information and pick out patterns or recognize manmade structures in the midst of the chaos of nature.

As I was turning toward Harper, some part of me recognized the unmistakable shape of a man standing in the trees. I did a double-take, and the man darted away.

"Hey!" I cried. "Stop!"

Then, without giving myself a chance to think, I broke into a sprint after the fleeing figure.

CHAPTER SIX

"Wait, Ryan!"

Harper's call barely registered as I ran. Ahead of me, I could see the man running through the trees. I only caught glimpses through gaps in the foliage, but he was undeniably there. I redoubled my efforts and found an extra burst of speed.

The trees grew thick around me. It was untouched, virgin forest, the trees so close together that in places I had to twist my shoulders sideways to fit. In a straight, unhindered sprint, I could have caught the fleeing figure in seconds. As it was, as soon as I started to build up some speed, there was a tree that I couldn't avoid or a sapling that whipped across my face.

The man was smaller than I was by nearly a foot, and probably a hundred pounds lighter. He was better at cornering than I was, and always seemed to stay just far enough ahead that I couldn't get a clear look at him.

Behind me, I could hear Harper chasing after us. She kept calling out for me to stop. I understood why. I had no idea where we were heading, what direction was north, or anything. The claustrophobic density of the trees threw off my perception of distance. We could have already run most of a mile, or barely traveled a hundred yards.

All I knew for sure was there was someone ahead of me who was trying as hard as he could to avoid being caught. Harper was too far behind, and growing farther with every passing minute. She couldn't see what I was chasing, couldn't know how close I was to catching him.

And I was gaining. My breath came hard, but I had better endurance than most, and the strength to drive myself forward. Through the trees, I caught a glimpse of a shirt flapping behind the running man. It was a light color, but I couldn't make out if it was patterned or if the fabric was just dappled by the sunlight that managed to filter through the canopy.

No matter. In another minute I would catch him up, and then we were going to have words. I couldn't comply with Harper's demands to stop running. I just needed to close the distance by a few more yards and then I would be able to get a clear look at him. Kingfield was small enough that I could pick the man out of a lineup easily enough, if I just managed to get a clear look.

Ahead of me, I saw the man climb over a partially fallen tree. He got a foot up on the tree and jumped, then kept running. I bared my teeth in a fierce grin. There was my chance to close the distance. Rather than taking the time to carefully climb over the tree, I leapt into the air and vaulted over the four-foot high trunk.

On the other side of the tree, a narrow gulley had been cut through the ground by a shallow brook rather than the flat ground I had been expecting. I hit the far side of the gulley hard and barely kept from falling backward into the brook.

Adrenaline got me out of the gulley and I took two steps before I realized I'd had the wind knocked out of me. Abruptly, my legs refused to carry my weight and I fell to my knees, wheezing and gasping after breath. Through the trees, I saw the man I was chasing pause and look back, before he ran onward and disappeared into the trees.

Behind me, I heard running footsteps and Harper called out, "Ryan! Wait! Don't keep running!"

"Harper!" I gasped. "I'm here!"

"Ryan?" She came out of the forest behind me and pulled up at the fallen tree. She climbed up and jumped over the same as the man I had been chasing, then knelt down next to me. "What happened? Are you hurt?"

"No. Just... fuck! I was so close. Jumped the stupid tree and fell into the gulley."

"Close to what? What were you chasing?"

"A man. Someone was watching us by Tammy's tree."

"Henry?"

"No." I pushed myself up to my feet and winced as the abraded skin on my stomach objected. "An adult, or young adult. He was going this way. We're not far behind him."

I started limping in the direction the man had disappeared in, then Harper caught my wrist and dragged me to a halt. "No, we're not running through the forest after some unknown figure! Are you out of your mind?"

"He's going to get away, Harper!"

"Forget it, Ryan. He's gone. If there was even a man in the first place."

"What do you mean by that?" I demanded. "I definitely saw someone!"

"Did you get a clear look?"

"No, there were trees in the way."

She shook her head. "Listen to yourself. There's something in these trees that makes people disappear! What if it's some will o' the wisp that makes people think something vitally important is just ahead? I've had some experience with them, remember."

I gritted my teeth. I wanted to argue that I hadn't been chasing a wisp, but I didn't actually know that much about them. The fairy-tale image of a ball of floating light might just be one kind of wisp. I looked down at the ground. I didn't want to admit that Harper was right, but now that I wasn't in hot pursuit there wasn't any way to deny it.

"Harper."

"What?"

"Do will o' the wisps leave footprints?"

I pointed at the ground close to the gulley. The ground was disturbed there where I had botched my vault, and my own big boot prints made clear impressions in the soil. Harper's smaller boots were clearly identifiable as well, but there was a third set of footprints with the tighter treads of running shoes.

I got my phone out and took a photo of one of the clearer prints. Harper followed the prints a short way, examining them closely, then came back with a frown on her face.

"You're right. It's a man's tracks. Five-ten, a hundred and sixty pounds, give or take."

"You can tell that from the footprints?"

She shrugged. "I'm not an expert, but I took classes in it. It's part of search and rescue."

"Know anyone that's five-ten and a buck sixty?"

Harper swallowed. "Yeah. Owen."

I stared at her for a moment. "Ah, shit. Would Owen run from us?"

She shook her head. "No. I don't know. Why would he? Unless he thought you were law enforcement or something?"

"He would have been close enough to see you and Tammy. I don't know the Davis family. Would Owen have wanted to let his sister know he was alive?"

"Owen is a good man," Harper said, "despite what you saw

today." Her voice was tight and I saw the shimmer of moisture in her eyes before she turned away.

"Okay. Well, five-ten and one-sixty is pretty smack in the middle of the bell curve. Probably a third of the male population in the US fits that descriptor. It might not be Owen."

Harper laughed bitterly. "Maybe in other places. Have you seen the people around here? The gene pool is more like a mud puddle. Most everyone around here is related in some way or another. That doesn't lend itself to growing tall. Owen was by far the tallest kid at school."

I nodded, understanding another facet of Harper's social stigma. At five foot nine, she would be taller than almost everyone else. "I hadn't thought of that. Still, that doesn't mean we were chasing Owen."

"No. I suppose not. The tracks are pretty clear." She looked sideways at me. "I'm confident we could follow them."

I didn't need any more encouragement. "Lead the way, then."

"How are you doing?"

I took my hand away from my stomach and winced as my shirt stuck to the abrasions. "Good enough to follow him. I'm not bleeding much."

She nodded uncertainly. "I can take a look at it when we're out of the forest again. I've got first aid training."

"Yeah, me too. I'm fine. Let's get going before he gains any more ground."

Following the tracks was easy. Now that I wasn't sprinting headlong through the trees, there was plenty of time to look closely at the ground. We were in the middle of summer and the fallen leaves of the year before had mostly decomposed. What was left behind was soft and spongy, and took footprints easily. A few times we lost the trail when our quarry had charged through some undergrowth, but by following the broken stems and trampled ferns, we quickly found the footprints again.

We heard the sound of a big rig rumbling by and Harper glanced back at me, surprised. We picked up the pace and a minute later came out of the trees on the verge of a highway.

"This is the highway leading to the Davis homestead," Harper said. She turned and looked up the road and muttered a curse.

I followed her gaze and saw a truck pulled up on the verge. The last time I had seen it, it had been parked on the side of the Davis' house. "Is that Mrs. Davis' truck?" I asked.

"Yeah."

I caught Harper's arm as she started toward the truck and nodded at the ground. "Footsteps. Our man went that way."

Harper nodded grimly and pulled the service pistol from her holster. I reached into my jacket and loosened the strap on my own gun, but didn't draw it. I wasn't sure how the locals would react to seeing a drawn gun in my hands and I didn't need the cops being called on me. Harper would probably be able to talk me out of getting arrested, but it would waste time.

We approached the vehicle carefully and heard someone wheezing after breath behind the truck. Harper stepped wide, her gun raised, then quickly lowered the barrel and holstered it.

"Are you okay, Mrs. Davis?" she called.

"Christ as my witness," Mrs. Davis said angrily. "You go waving that gun at everyone you find stopped on the side of the road?"

I stepped up to Harper's side. "Sorry about that, ma'am. We thought we saw someone coming through the woods. A man, around five-ten. Did you see anyone like that?"

"See him? I damn near hit him," Mrs. Davis said waspishly. "Came running out of the forest, out of nowhere. God was with me, or I would have run him over. Practically gave me a heart attack."

"When was this?" Harper asked.

"Just a minute ago. I had to pull over and catch my breath."

"If you're feeling better, you ought to get home, Mrs. Davis," I said politely. "It's not safe if you're alone."

She eyed me for a moment, then evidently decided I was right. Mrs. Davis pushed herself off the rear bumper and walked around to the driver's door. Harper and I stepped back as she fired up the engine and drove off toward her home.

"She was sweating," Harper commented.

"A good scare will do that to you," I shrugged. "In her condition, I wouldn't be surprised if she really did have a minor coronary."

Harper's face was unreadable as she watched the truck vanish down the highway. "Wouldn't that be nice."

I snorted a laugh. "Remind me not to piss you off."

"You see the footprints around?" Harper changed the subject.

We backtracked until we found the running shoe imprints again, then followed them forward until they stepped out onto the road.

I looked over at Harper and frowned. "This seem weird to you?"

"What, you mean that Mrs. Davis said she nearly ran him over, but she had pulled off the road twenty yards ahead of the tracks?"

"I suppose our man could have doubled back into the woods. Let's go check that way."

For an hour, Harper and I combed the verge on both sides of the road, searching for the footprints. We could have covered more ground if we had split up, but neither of us wanted to be alone. We checked up the road past where Mrs. Davis had pulled over, but we didn't find anything. The grass grew thick there, and there wasn't much exposed soil that could take a footprint.

Finally, we had to admit defeat. We were sweating with the morning sun beating down on us, hungry, and tired from getting up early. The deeply shadowed forest on either side of the highway seemed to loom toward me, threatening and promising in equal measures.

"We're wasting our time, I think," Harper sighed.

"You're right." I stretched my back and winced as the abrasions on my stomach brushed against a damp patch of sweat on my shirt. "I can't believe that guy outran me."

"Speaking of. I don't think I've ever seen anyone your size move so fast. What's your deal? Were you some Olympic cross-country sprinter or something?"

"Nothing like that. The Halsin family has a history of... being tough and strong. Should we head back to your truck?"

"Nothing else out here for us," Harper agreed. "But don't think you're getting out of the conversation so easily. Are you, you know, human?"

"I'm not djinn, if that's what you're asking. Our working theory is that at some point in the long-distant past, one of my ancestors was a Nephilim."

"I don't think I've heard of that."

"Not surprising. A Nephilim is half-human, half-angel. My... sister, adopted sister, is a Nephilim. Her mother is... powerful. Alex has powers like you wouldn't believe. She's scary strong. Terrifying, actually, but she's a good person."

"Really? Who is her mother?"

"That isn't important. If you ever meet Alex, that would be her story to tell. My point, though, is that if I have any of the light in my heritage, it's diluted to being almost nonexistent.

Other than being a little faster than your average human, there's nothing special about me."

"Wow." Harper looked sideways at me, a small smile playing around her lips. "So how did you become a monster hunter, Mr. I'm-just-a-normal-human?"

"Family tradition, more than anything. Believe it or not, monster hunting isn't that hard. There are creatures I wouldn't tangle with, but with a little foresight and a lot of training, there's not much I can't handle."

"And humble, too." She grinned at me, taking the sting from her words. "Are there a lot of people in the Chapter?"

It was my turn to grin at her. "You know it's a secret society, right?"

"You'd tell me, but you'd have to kill me?"

"For your own protection," I nodded. "Seriously, though, it's dangerous. My father was assassinated. We still don't know by who or what. It's something I intend to find out someday."

"Revenge."

"I think of it more like taking out the trash. Something that would kill Chapter members isn't out to help society."

"And what if it's a person? Ah... you've killed people?"

I snorted. "I did four years in the army. Yes, I've killed people."

Harper laughed. "Okay, now I know you're lying. You can't be a day over twenty-five."

"Actually, I'm forty-two."

She stopped walking and stared at me. "No. How?"

"That Nephilim blood I was talking about. My father was nearing ninety when he was killed, and he looked like he was in his forties."

"Holy shit. That's, like, biblical aging."

"Genesis 5:5, And all the days that Adam lived were nine

hundred and thirty years: and he died," I quoted. "Makes you wonder how much Nephilim blood they had."

"So, your sister, she'll live to be a thousand years old?"

"If she doesn't get herself killed first, yeah. Which is more and more likely the better I get to know her."

"People want to kill her?"

I laughed. "Alex has a special way about her. She makes enemies with things that would give you nightmares. The people she pisses off are the least of her worries."

"You sound like you're proud of her." Harper gave me an odd look, but she smiled as she said it.

"I guess you'll have to meet her. She also makes friends easily. She's... different. A magnetic personality. Things in Los Angeles are complicated, to say the least. LA has always been a focal city. Lots of big things happen there. In the last year, the balance of forces in the city got all messed up. Now it's just Alex holding the city together. She's doing a good job so far, but she needs help."

"Well, why aren't you there, then? Helping her?"

"Because I have to catch this damn monster first." I waved a hand at the forest on either side of us. "The Chapter is a political body as much as it is a monster hunting one. Politics brought me to Maine, and until I find whatever is out here disappearing people, politics will keep me here."

Harper wrinkled her nose. "Politics. I run into it in the Forest Rangers too. Being part native makes me something of a diversity hire, which is a double-edged sword. I'm just as qualified as anyone else in the local service, but to some people I'll always be 'the native girl'."

"There's not really any diversity hires in the Chapter. Either you can do the job or you die."

"What kind of requirements does the Chapter have for its new recruits?"

"Why, are you interested?"

"I'm just wondering if everyone there is the distant descendent of an angel. Which I totally believe and don't think you're delusional at all."

I did a double take and she smiled sweetly at me.

"Are you making fun of me?"

She laughed. "I think you're telling the truth as far as you know, but old Mr. Douglas will swear on a bible that if you go out fishing on Gilman Pond at midnight during a full moon, the aliens will come and butt-probe you."

I nodded. "You believe in wisps?"

"Sure. But I've seen them with my own eyes."

"But you don't believe in angels?"

"I grew up going to church along with everyone else, but in the last few years, religion has seemed more and more like a crutch for people who don't want to think for themselves. I guess if I had to label myself, I'd call myself agnostic."

"Wait and see, huh."

"It's reasonable."

"What if I told you that there are angels in the fae?"

"What, along with the boogeyman and werewolves?"

"They retreated to the fae after Jesus died on the cross. Those that didn't go insane, at least."

"So, your great-great-whatever was fooling around with an insane angel and oops?"

"Look, forget it, all right? I'm not interested in playing the convince-Harper-of-the-truth game. Either you can stay oblivious of the truth or you can learn from what I'm trying to teach you."

We walked for a few minutes before Harper muttered, "I'm sorry, you're right. I'm the one who asked. I do want to learn the truth about the world. I'm thinking like a local and I shouldn't be."

"That's understandable. I'm not trying to ice you out, here. I just don't have the time or resources to explain everything to your satisfaction."

"I know. And I appreciate your candor. Let's just rewind a bit and pretend I wasn't being skeptical."

I snorted. "Fine. To answer your question, no, not everyone in the Chapter is djinn or non-human. There aren't many humans who can keep up, or even want to, but they are there."

"So, hypothetically speaking, if I wanted to join the Chapter, how would I do that?"

I stared at her for a long moment, really looking at her closely for the first time. There was a quiet desperation in her eyes that she was trying hard to hide. Life in Maine had not been kind to her. Despite the cheerful face she showed the world, I thought there wasn't much she wouldn't do to escape Kingfield.

"Well. Hypothetically speaking, once someone proved themselves in some way, either in their own efforts or as part of a team, then all they would have to do is ask. Whether they get accepted or not is another question. These days, there isn't that much activity from the fae, so we don't need hundreds of active hunters. But people get old, or they want out, and new hunters are constantly being added."

Harper nodded. "I see."

She fell silent after that, and we walked all the way back to the Davis homestead without exchanging further words.

CHAPTER SEVEN

At Harper's insistence, we went to her place for a late breakfast or early lunch. She lived by herself in a house that was far too large for one person. The inevitable clapboard siding was peeling in places where she hadn't had time to give it the attention it needed. But the roof was in good repair and she had long rows of firewood stocked up under tarps on one side of the yard.

"Excuse the mess," she said as she kicked her boots off in the entryway. "I haven't had time in the last few weeks to properly clean up."

I didn't comment. Other than a few streaks of dust on top of furniture too high for Harper to see easily, the place was as clean as any hotel I had been to. I took my boots off and followed her into the kitchen.

"What are we making for lunch?" I asked.

"Before we do that, let's get your front seen to."

I glanced down at my stomach. "Honestly, it's not a big deal."

"Sit on the couch," she said, ignoring my protest. "I'll be right back."

She headed upstairs and I sat down as instructed. Then I got up and went to the bookshelf next to the TV. She had a handful of photos on the shelves of her family. Young Harper had needed braces, I discovered. As she grew older, she seemed to slowly evolve into an awkward teenager, then abruptly turned into a young woman.

In one photo she was all lanky limbs in a track jersey, braces showing in her smile, her hair in a tight braid. Then, in the next, the braces were off and puberty had hit her like a truck. Gone was the teenager and in her place was a young woman with more curves than her professional work clothing had suggested. There was a photo of her and a red-headed young man, their arms around each other, love on their faces plain as day.

Then there was a candid shot of her mother, hair tucked back behind one ear, intent on the gardening she was doing. It wasn't a great composition, but it had the magic glow of life that some candid shots managed to capture.

"She died of cancer the next year," Harper said quietly behind me.

I put the photo back on the shelf. "Sorry. Curiosity got the better of me. That must have been hard."

Harper shrugged. She had a hard-backed first aid kit in her hands the size of a lunch box. "It was a long time ago. Sit."

"Is your father still alive?" I went back to the couch and sat down, trying not to bend my stomach much.

"Shirt. No, he died when I was in high school. Logging accident."

I shrugged out of my jacket and shoulder holster, then pulled my shirt up over my head. I had scrapes all up my stomach that had started to scab over. I must have hit the gulley harder than I'd thought. Harper had frozen in place after I pulled my shirt off, and then she gave herself a little shake and bent to the first aid kit.

"That's not nothing, Ryan. Those scrapes will get infected." She came up with a bottle of rubbing alcohol and a box of gauze pads. "Lie back, this is going to sting."

I reclined back against the cushions and folded my arms up behind my head so they would be out of the way. Harper got a gauze pad wet with alcohol and leaned over me. I tried not to flinch as she rubbed the cold alcohol into my cuts, but it stung like a motherfucker. I clenched my teeth shut and tried not to whine out loud.

Harper got a new pad and fresh alcohol and went back to rubbing away the dried blood on my stomach. The pain was starting to merge together into a dull ache that hurt worse than the original injury did. Then it plateaued and endorphins started to take over. By the time Harper switched to applying an antibiotic cream, the ache had faded to a distant throb.

"There," she said. "That's done with. Let me get some bandages."

It wasn't practical to wrap my whole chest in bandages, so she settled for sticking a few big patches over the worst of the scrapes. Her touch was gentle, and when she finished smoothing out the last bandage, her fingers lingered, brushing against a scar on my shoulder.

"I was expecting you to have more scars," she said softly. She looked up and met my eyes, then cleared her throat and stepped back. "I'd say change the bandages tomorrow, but they'll scab over and be fine by then."

"Thanks," I said.

"Sure." She ducked down and picked my shirt up off the couch, then handed it to me.

It had been close enough that I could have reached it, but I took it from her without comment. She spun around and walked away to the kitchen. I looked after her, my eyes lingering on her ass. She had an unconscious swing of her hips when she walked that I hadn't noticed before.

I tugged my shirt back over my head and slipped the shoulder harness back on. The weight of the handgun in its holster reminded me of why I was in Maine. I was here to hunt a monster, not to fuck an admittedly attractive Forest Ranger.

Still, I mused, maybe one didn't have to cancel out the other. I joined Harper in the kitchen and she gave me a quick smile before opening the fridge and bending over to examine its contents.

"It's feeling better already," I said.

"That's good. How do you feel about a Reuben?"

"A what?"

She clucked her tongue. "Reuben it is."

Harper started pulling ingredients out of the fridge. My attempts to help were turned down with cheerful insistence, so I ended up leaning back against the counter and watching her cook. A Reuben, I discovered, was a hybrid corned beef sandwich and grilled cheese on rye, with sauerkraut and horseradish, served with an over-easy egg on top.

It was an unlikely combination of flavors that just seemed to mesh together perfectly. I found myself eating hungrily, and cleaned my plate before Harper was halfway through hers.

"I take it you approve," she grinned.

I leaned back in my chair and gave a contented sigh. "You're an excellent cook, Harper. I don't usually get to eat a home-cooked meal."

"Thanks. Always nice to hear. Why no cooking? Too busy traveling?"

"Between you and me, I'm a lousy cook. I can't remember the last time I had a meal that wasn't from a restaurant. We should talk about what's next."

"Oh, I totally forgot! What was in that note you found?"

"Let me grab it." I got up and went to my jacket on the couch, then returned with the folded paper. "It's not much." I flattened it out and slid it over so Harper could see it.

"It has her," she read aloud. "That's Henry's handwriting. You think he saw whatever has been killing people? Is Henry…"

"I'm sorry, Harper."

"But, you can't know that for sure." She stared down at her plate, her Reuben completely forgotten. "He could still be alive!"

I reached across the table and touched her hand. She grabbed my hand and squeezed it tightly, and sudden moisture swam in her eyes.

"It's hardest when children get involved," I said gently.

She dashed the back of her free hand across her eyes. "When I was lost in the woods, the search party didn't give up on me. I won't give up on Henry!"

"Good. We're not giving up on him. Not until we know for sure one way or the other."

"So, what do we do? Go back and search the Davis farm? We could comb the woods around that fallen tree, try to pick up a track."

I frowned, but nodded. "Okay. That might be a possibility. How long would it take to search through the forest?"

Her face fell and she pulled her hand free of mine. "A week, maybe. A space that large…"

"What about dogs? Do the local police have a K9 division? Search and rescue dogs?"

She laughed bitterly. "No. You've seen this place. No towns around here have that kind of budget. We'd have to go all the way to Portland to find rescue dogs, probably."

"We don't have a week. Henry doesn't have a week. We

have to continue with our investigation. If we can find the monster, we might be able to find Henry."

Harper nodded reluctantly. "I suppose that makes sense. So, what do we do next?"

"There wasn't anything we could find at the Davis homestead, so we go back earlier. Who went missing before Owen?"

"Wait, that's it? We're just done with the Davis house? What about dusting for fingerprints? Searching for stray hairs?"

"The fae aren't human, Harper. We don't care about fingerprints because we're not going to haul some bloodthirsty creature before the local judge and a jury of its peers. We find it, and we end it." I made a cutting motion with my hand.

Harper swallowed. "What if we make a mistake? What if an innocent gets killed by accident?"

I frowned. "That's not really an issue. But if you want to be sure, press some iron against their skin. To a fae, that burns like a hot coal."

"Oh. That's... good to know."

"So, how about it? Who went missing before Owen?"

"Um." She pressed a hand to her forehead and collected herself. "The midwife. Cathy Holsten."

"Tell me about her."

"She's an older lady, in her sixties. She was a pediatrician before she moved out to Kingfield."

"An odd move for a doctor."

"She grew up here. She moved back to take care of her father when he grew ill. After he passed, she stayed on."

"I see. How is she liked in the community? Does she live on the fringes like Mrs. Wilson?"

"Oh, no. Cathy lives in town. She's a pillar of the community, everybody likes her."

"You know, we should really have a map. Lay out where and when everyone went missing."

"That's a good idea. Hold on, I've got just the thing."

Harper got up from the table and cleared away the dishes, then came back with a folding map of the area. The map was centered on Sugarloaf, but the whole of Kingfield and the surrounding forest was included on the bottom right. With a silver sharpie, Harper went over the map, putting dots where people had gone missing and writing in the date next to them with a black ballpoint.

There were a lot of dots.

When she finished, I frowned down at the map, trying to make a logical connection to the various points. It was an exercise in futility. As much as I looked, there didn't seem to be any coherent link. The sequence of abductions jumped all over the map. I had thought there were going to be mostly people missing on the edges of the town, but there were a roughly equal number in the middle of Kingfield.

"And which one is Cathy Holsten?"

Harper put her finger on a dot not too far from where we were.

"Is there going to be an issue with us looking around her place?"

"No, she lived alone."

"Then that's where we're going next."

Cathy Holsten only lived two blocks away, so we decided to walk. The noon sun was warm on my shoulders, almost too hot to wear my jacket. Whenever a cloud passed over the sun or we stepped into the shade of a tree, the temperature seemed to drop twenty degrees.

Still, it was a nice day. Walking down the quiet street next to Harper and listening to the gentle wind in the trees, I could almost convince myself twenty-eight people hadn't gone missing from this tiny town. Twenty-eight men, women and children just… vanished. No signs of struggle. No evidence that Harper and Sergeant Bunnings had been able to find. No ransom notes.

It was no wonder the sergeant had abandoned himself to drink. Twenty-eight! I still couldn't believe that number. If only Harper had reached out to the Chapter a month ago. And damn John Baptiste for his shitty intelligence that put the monster threat in Portland. He had me searching for fae a hundred miles from the real threat.

Tires squealed behind me and I spun around, my hand leaping to the holstered gun under my jacket. A pickup truck swung out onto the road we were walking down. It idled for a moment, then the driver revved the engine making the diesel motor roar and black smoke billow from the stacks. There were two men in the truck bed, holding onto the mounted light bar and leaning out over the side.

Harper muttered a curse.

The truck dropped into gear and gravel flung up from its tires as it roared toward us. I saw metal in the hands of one of the men, glinting in the sunlight. I took two steps toward Harper and launched myself at her, bowling her over with my weight and crashing to the ground.

A shotgun boomed and a revolver cracked. I kept my weight on Harper, preventing her from getting up, and counted the revolver shots. On the sixth shot, the truck's engine roared again and gravel showered down around us as the driver fishtailed away.

I levered myself off of Harper and looked after the truck. The men in the bed jeered at me and waved. The shotgun-wielding man fired another shell off into the air and roared with laughter. Harper rolled onto her stomach, coughing and trying to get her breath back.

"Sorry, Harper," I said. "Didn't mean to squash you."

"That was Liam at the wheel," she wheezed. "That little prick! I'm going to have him arrested!"

"You'd be wasting your time, I think." I climbed to my feet and offered her my hand to pull her up. "This is just a distraction. I think I hurt his feelings this morning."

"You think? Kid's fucking unstable, if he thinks he can just ride around and shoot guns into the air."

"They weren't shooting at us?" I hadn't looked toward the truck. I had been too busy expecting a bullet in the back.

"No, but that doesn't make it any better. Let's see if he thinks it's fucking funny when his mom hears about what he did."

"She'd probably buy him ice cream." I shook my head and brushed bits of grass from Harper's back. "Assuming she didn't put him up to it in the first place. Forget it, Harper."

She swore again and stomped away. I had to lengthen my stride to catch up to her. She speed-walked in angry silence for a minute before the dam burst.

"I hate this fucking town!" she hissed. "All I do is help these stupid fucking hicks, and this is the treatment I get!"

"Hey, easy there, Ranger Hall. Weren't you just telling me a little while back how you were happy with your life here? It's not all bad, right? Sure, Liam is being a racist little cockring, but he's just one man."

"There were four in that truck," she growled. "I know exactly who they are. Little fucking wannabe gang pieces of shit."

I held up my hands. "Look, Harper, if you want to gun these kids down in the street, I totally understand. But I'm here to kill a monster, not some bored teenager, however much he might deserve it."

She glared at me, then her shoulders sagged. "Fuck."

I gave her a gentle punch in the shoulder. "I like that fire, though! That's the kind of spirit I like to see."

"Asshole," she muttered, but she gave me a reluctant smile.

Cathy Holsten's house was at the end of the block, and we made it there without further incident. The only thing unusual about Cathy's house was it hadn't been expanded upon since its original construction. It was a square two-story cube with a forty-five-degree pitch roof perched on top. It was about as basic a house as could be built. It looked like a child's crayon sketch made real by the world's least creative architect.

"What is it with Maine and white clapboard siding?" I asked. "Was there a sale on white paint a century or two ago, and everyone just kind of stuck with it?"

Harper rolled her eyes without answering and walked up the short flight of wooden steps to the door. She tested the knob, found it unlocked, and pushed the door open.

The front parlor of the midwife's house had been converted into a professional space. There was a small waiting area furnished with comfortable-looking armchairs, and a door with a large window in it that led to an office. Medical posters hung on the wall, showing different stages of pregnancy, lactation aids, and various home-birthing options. It was a little bit of a shock seeing this isolated pocket of twenty-first-century technology. Everything else I've seen in Kingfield so far hadn't been updated since the mid-nineties.

Harper crossed the waiting area to an unobtrusive door hung with a poster showing different pregnancy-related exercises, and led the way further into the house. I found myself plunged back into the fifties once again. I half expected to see a Bakelite rotary phone hung on the doorframe. I had to glance back at the office space to convince myself I hadn't hallucinated it.

"There's no cleanroom here?" I asked.

"Cathy was a midwife, not an obstetrician. She helped

people with home births and education, mostly. If they needed to go to a doctor, there are hospitals in Franklin and Skowhegan, not thirty minutes away."

I grunted and looked around the kitchen. The details of pregnancy and childbirth were subjects I usually avoided if I could. The last thing I needed these days was a child to take care of. I would make the world's worst father, or even more damning, end up like my own dad and pull my children into the life I had.

There weren't many decorations in the tiny kitchen and eating nook, but there was a quilt on the wall that struck me as impressively detailed and well-made. Enough so that I commented on it. "That's some fine needlework there."

Harper came to stand beside me. In the cramped space she had to stand well inside my personal space, close enough that she leaned against my arm. I felt the soft swell of her breast pressing against my arm and the heat of her breath on my neck. I tried not to shift away. The close contact was fine by me.

"Didn't know you were a connoisseur," she said.

"I'm not. I've seen my share of quilts, but nothing with this level of detail."

"It's the local quilting club," she explained. "They're constantly trying to one-up each other."

"I wonder if Mrs. Davis is part of that club," I mused. "She had a quilt in her living room."

"I wouldn't be surprised. Most of the women in Kingfield are. Once the winter sets in hard, there isn't much else to do but find a hobby that doesn't involve going outside."

"But not you?"

She pulled away from my side and shrugged. "I wasn't invited. Besides, just because there's snow on the ground doesn't mean my work stops."

"True enough."

"So, what are we looking for?"

"I'm not sure. Maybe we're asking the wrong question. Instead of why did these people leave, what if we asked why were these people picked out as targets?"

Harper nodded thoughtfully. "In the beginning, that was easy. They were all isolated, or went missing when they were far away from human habitation. But Cathy is, well…" she turned around gesturing at the house. "She's right in the middle of town."

"Maybe that's where her house is, but she could have gone missing when she was out on a call. Is the office unlocked? We could check to see if she had a day planner or itinerary."

She blinked then smacked her hand into her forehead. "Why didn't I think of that?"

We went back to the waiting room and Harper tried the doorknob. It was locked.

"Let me try."

"It isn't a pickle jar, Ryan, being bigger than me won't—"

I stepped up to the door as she backed up, and drove my elbow through the glass window. The safety glass exploded into the office in a glittering rain of little cubes. Through my jacket, the impact stung.

"Huh. Safety glass. That's convenient."

"What the hell, Ryan?!"

"Relax. Cathy's dead, she's not going to mind. And if she's not, a broken pane of glass will be a low price to pay for her rescue." I reached through the gaping window and flicked the lock on the door knob over. I tested the knob, found it unlocked, and pushed the door open. "You coming?"

I led the way into the office, kicking a path through the safety glass. There was a fairly old laptop on the desk. I knew how to use a computer, but hacking my way through a Windows security screen was beyond my ability.

I crossed my fingers and hit the power button. The laptop booted out of hibernation and went directly to the desktop. "We're in luck! Thank god for small town trust, huh?" I waved at Harper to come over. "Are you just going to stand in the doorway, or do you want to find out what happened to Cathy?"

"You can't just break into people's houses!"

"Technically, I broke into her office. Why are you being so difficult about this? The door's open, isn't it? What's the difference between walking into an unlocked office and breaking a window to get in?"

"The difference is I'm here on official business! I can't just break windows!"

"Not a problem. I broke the window. If it makes you feel better, you can bill me for it. Now get in here and let's save some lives! That's what's important, right? Who cares about a stupid window?"

She glared at me, but then she sighed and walked in. "Just don't break anything else, okay?"

"That's my girl." I pointed at the scheduling app I had pulled up on the computer. "Cathy was busy. None of these names mean anything to me, though. She had four appointments the day she went missing. Do you see any connection here?"

"Um. Let's see... Ruth isn't pregnant. I wonder if she's trying some fertility drugs or something. Lisa is expecting, but not for months yet. I don't know, Ryan. This feels like we're violating doctor-patient confidentiality."

"I don't care if they're pregnant or expecting or having quintuplets, Harper. Look at the names. Where do they live? Any of them live out on the fringes?"

"No, well... hold on. Lisa Barson lives next to the widow Chase. Amy Chase went missing almost two weeks ago now."

I straightened up. "Is that right?"

"I mean, it isn't much."

"Not much? Harper, this is the break we've been looking for!"

"What do you mean?"

"How does a detective investigate a murder?"

"I don't really know, I'm not a cop, but—"

"It's a rhetorical question. More than half of murders are committed by someone known to the victim. It's the first thing the police look at. That's useless for us, because whatever is killing people isn't human. The first thing we do when hunting a monster is figure out how it operates. What are its motivations? Why is it killing? And then we go from there."

Harper bent her head in thought. "So, if the monster was still around Amy's house, it could have seen Cathy and decided she was an easy target?"

"Yes. That tells us our monster is an opportunist. An ambusher."

"Is that helpful?"

"Sure. It means we're not dealing with a more overt fae. We'll need more information before we can make a positive identification, but it's something. We need to speak with Lisa Barson."

"Why Lisa?"

"She might have been the last person to see Cathy alive."

CHAPTER EIGHT

L isa Barson's house was a neat little one-story with a shingled roof that sat near the south edge of town. Unlike every other house I'd seen in Kingfield, this one had broad vinyl siding and was painted a light cream with tan trim.

I liked Lisa without having met her, just for being daring enough to not have white siding on her house. We pulled into the gravel driveway and Harper parked off to the side so she wouldn't be blocking the car in the garage. We got out, and I stood behind Harper as the Ranger knocked on the front door.

"She might not be home," Harper said. "She works at the hotel."

She hardly had the sentence out of her mouth before the door opened and a slender young woman with a shawl wrapped around her shoulders looked through the screen door at us.

"Hello, Harper. Who is your friend?"

"Lisa! I'm glad you're home. This is Ryan Halsin. He's helping me investigate the missing people."

"Oh. How do you do, Mr. Halsin? Are you a specialist or something?"

"Something like that," I agreed. "I'm fine, thank you for asking."

She nodded and tightened the shawl around her shoulders. "I was about to put a kettle on for some tea," she said to Harper. "Would you like to come inside? I hope nobody else has gone missing."

Lisa's eyes were sunken and the skin on her hands seemed translucent. She struck me as being ill, though there wasn't anything obvious I could point to. She was heavily pregnant.

"That would be nice, thank you. We won't be long."

I followed Harper's lead, and we went to sit on the couch in the living room. There was some daytime soap opera playing on the TV. It was muted, and the subtitles stacked up as the transcriber tried to keep pace with the shouting match among a colorfully dressed group of angry women.

Lisa puttered around the kitchen for a few minutes, then came out with a tea service and a packet of frosted biscotti. "Sorry," she muttered as she set it down on coffee table. "I've been having some difficulties lately. I'm afraid I'm not the most graceful pregnant woman. I feel like a grounded blimp."

"Nonsense," Harper said. "You look radiant."

"I look like I've thrown up every day for the last two weeks," Lisa said with a wry smile. "But thanks." She poured us tea and the scent of peppermint filled the living room. "How can I help you, Harper?"

"Don't worry, Michael is fine."

The tension in Lisa's shoulders dropped away. "Oh, thank God."

"We're actually here to ask about Cathy."

"Oh, poor woman," Lisa sighed. "I hate to complain, but the nearest OB/GYN is all the way in Madison. Michael's been driving me every few days. It's been hard for him at work."

"When was your last appointment with Cathy?" I asked.

"Last Wednesday. It was just a routine checkup."

"Did Cathy keep the appointment?" Harper asked.

"She was running a little late, I think, but she showed. We were discussing my nutrition intake."

"You can keep the details of your meeting private," Harper said hurriedly. "We're just trying to trace where Cathy went that day."

"Oh. Sorry. Yes, she did come by."

"How did she seem to you?" I asked. "Did she say anything strange? Act weird in any way?"

"Oh, I'm sure she was normal," Lisa said. "I don't recall her saying anything out of the ordinary."

"Do you have a security system? Outdoor cameras?"

"What for? We don't have crime here like in the big city. But... now that I think of it, Michael mentioned one of the chickens had been killed by something and he put a game camera out. I don't know if it will be of any use to you, but you're welcome to take a look at it."

"That's very kind of you, thank you, Lisa," Harper said.

"If you don't mind, I'd like to take a look at the footage now," I said. "Where did your husband put the camera?"

"Around the back of the garage where the coop is. I'm not certain exactly where he put it."

"We'll look for it," Harper assured her.

"I hope it's some use to you," Lisa laughed. "Michael never catches anything on it. Between you and me, he's a lousy hunter."

I drained off the rest of my tea. "I'll go see if I can find the camera. Do you want to come, Harper?"

"You don't need to stay here to be polite," Lisa said. "I know you're busy."

"I'll come back and visit with you properly once all this is over," Harper promised. "Take care of yourself, Lisa."

Back outside, we circled around to the rear of the garage. Unlike the Davis chicken operation, Lisa and her husband only kept half a dozen hens in a little coop and run painted to look like a barn. There was a scattering of feathers in the grass where a chicken had fallen victim to a predator.

"So, you two seem friendly," I said. A game camera would probably be set up somewhere where it could get a wide-angle view of the coop. I walked through grass that was ready to be mowed again to the tree line at the edge of the property and started searched the saplings for a camera.

"Lisa and I were in the same class in school. We've been friends since Elementary."

"It's nice that you're able to stay in touch with your old friends."

"What, you don't have any friends from school?"

I snorted. "None to speak of, and they're all married with families. It would freak them out to see me looking twenty years too young. Besides, what would I talk about? Hunting monsters? Maybe tell combat stories from the Middle East? Nah. Not worth it. Got to have something in common to stay in touch."

"You're probably right. Lisa and I are friendly, but I'll be honest, all she talks about these days is being pregnant. It wears on me. Is that the camera?"

I followed her pointing finger to a little camouflaged box Velcro-strapped to a stumpy pine. "Good eye. Being friendly is different from being friends. Have you told her about the will o' the wisp?"

Harper shook her head. "I haven't told anyone about that."

I nodded, unsurprised. "You know, when we finally find this monster, you won't be able to tell people what you've done."

"I... why not?"

"Think about it." I waded through the uncut grass to the tree and got the lid on the camera open. I fished around the edge until I found the slot for the memory card and popped it free. "You wouldn't be able to tell them about the monster. And without a relatable culprit, nobody would believe you when you say it's safe again."

Harper was silent for a moment. "I hadn't thought about that."

"The more time you spend dealing with the supernatural, the less you'll be able to relate to average people. Like me, with no friends outside of the Chapter except the odd djinn here and there."

"You make it sound lonely."

I shrugged. "It is, but I'm used to it. Shall we go see what's on the card?"

Lisa's husband had their laptop with him at work, and she insisted we take the memory card. Harper didn't have a home computer, so I suggested we return to my room at the bed and breakfast to use my laptop.

It was starting to get late in the afternoon and storm clouds were rolling in from the north when we pulled into the gravel parking lot next to my rental car. Wind gusted by, bringing with it a biting cold that felt more like it belonged to January or February than the middle of June.

"Is this normal?"

"Is what?"

"This weather. It's looking like a storm."

Harper looked up at the sky and shrugged. "Seems normal. Last year we had snow in May."

"Bloody hell." I looked up at the sky and shivered. "No thanks. Let's get inside."

The front desk was empty, and we didn't run into anyone on the way up to my room. There was a covered tray sitting outside my door and I realized I hadn't told Sylvia about my early-morning adventure.

"More muffins?" Harper asked.

"Maybe. Grab it and we'll find out." I unlocked the door and stepped aside to let Harper in first.

The rooms were cold, and I felt a draft blow across my face. I looked into the little sitting room and saw one of the curtains was billowing in the wind.

"You leave a window open?" Harper asked.

"Not me." I did a quick turn about the two rooms, but didn't find anything missing. My laptop was still in my duffel where I had left it. The sheets had been changed out, though. "Maybe just housekeeping? Nothing was stolen."

"Odd. I would check with Sylvia. That doesn't seem like a mistake she would make."

"I'll ask her next time I see her if I remember. In the meantime…" I took another circuit around the room and made sure all the windows were locked. "That should do it. You ready to see what mysteries await us?"

Harper set the covered tray on the coffee table in the sitting room. She had taken her shoes off, and now sat on the couch with her feet tucked up under her. I joined her with my laptop and took a moment to run the power cable before sitting down.

"You see what I missed for breakfast?"

"Smells like more muffins." Harper lifted the cover and revealed the same meal I'd had the day before. Without waiting, she snagged one of the blueberry muffins for herself and settled back. She waved a hand in my direction. "Entertain me!"

I laughed and opened the laptop. It booted up, and I fed the memory card into the slot in the side. The game camera had been focused on the hen house, but the left side of the frame caught a look down the driveway and the highway leading to Kingfield. Every car that drove by had triggered the camera and the memory card was completely full. I scrolled to the end of the folder and checked the date stamp. The last image had been taken sometime last night. At least the card probably included Cathy's visit to Lisa.

"Ah, shit," Harper muttered. "We're going to have to look at every single one of these?"

I sighed and rubbed the back of my neck. "Looks like it. You want a drink?"

"I don't usually drink on the job, but for this, I will make an exception."

"Sounds good. Let me see what this place has in stock."

I got up and went to the little kitchenette. In a top cabinet, I found a dusty bottle of scotch, the label illegible from water damage. I showed it to Harper. "Feeling brave?"

"Jesus. How old is that?"

I unscrewed the cap and gave it a cautious sniff. "Smells like it could be okay." I got a snifter from the cupboard and poured myself an inch. I swirled it, sniffed it again, then sipped. "Oh. Yes, this will do." I grabbed an extra glass for Harper and joined her on the couch again.

She accepted my offered glass and sipped. "Oh, damn. Should we be drinking this?"

"It's good, huh? If they didn't want us to drink it, they shouldn't have put it in my room."

I took another sip and felt the smooth alcohol slip down my throat with hardly any burn. I could feel the warmth begin to spread in my chest. It wouldn't take much of this blend to make me tipsy. I'd have to pace myself, and maybe eat a muffin before I got too much further into my glass.

"Mm. Now it's a party," Harper grinned. "Let's get that slideshow rolling!"

I had a moment's regret that I hadn't packed an HDMI cable to connect my laptop to the TV, then realized the TV probably only accepted coaxial or composite, or some other archaic input type. I pulled up the first image, set it to play as a slideshow, and leaned back.

It was going to be a long afternoon.

This wasn't the first time I had found myself watching slideshows from a trail camera and I knew what to expect. Initially, Harper and I were vigilant. We focused on each image that went by, pausing the slideshow whenever one of us saw something that needed a closer look.

Unsurprisingly, there wasn't much to see. The road didn't get much traffic, and what cars did go by were often the same half-dozen or so that had regular business to the south.

About an hour in, we discovered another problem. Most laptop manufacturers were quite proud of the viewing angle on the screen and it was one of the focuses of the advertising. When flatscreen technology first was introduced, users could only see the screen clearly when they were sitting directly in front of the monitor. As the technology got better, the user became able to see the screen from the side, and now, with the latest screens, you could see the image even if you were looking from almost ninety degrees off.

Considering what I typically viewed on my laptop, I had gone through a lot of trouble to find a screen with as narrow a viewing angle as possible. I didn't want someone coming up behind me and seeing something they shouldn't. Consequently, Harper had to lean pretty close to me to see the screen. After trying a few different positions, I ended up putting my arm up over the back of the couch and she moved as close to me as she could without actually touching.

That worked for a few minutes. We were going through early morning images when Harper thought she saw something and leaned forward to pause the slideshow. After going back, it turned out to just be a white van.

"Ugh!" Harper groaned and slumped back onto the couch. She leaned her head back to stare up at the ceiling and found my arm with the back of her head. She tilted her head sideways to look at me. "Is it always like this?"

"Like what?" There was a sudden frisson in the air and I felt my heartrate pick up a notch.

"So boring! Not your company, but this digital stakeout."

"At least we're not doing it in real time. How'd you like to hang out in an old Lincoln town car for a week straight, eating cold fast food and peeing into our old coffee cups?"

"Well, when you put it like that." She dropped her voice an octave and put on a terrible Boston accent. "All we had were cigarettes and a need to know. One of them was going to give out first, and I would be damned if I had to wait for Nine-Finger Joe without a smoke."

I laughed. "You missed your calling."

She grinned at me and smacked my thigh. "Speaking of, I've got to use the ladies."

Harper got up and I wiped the disappointment from my face before she could see it. She left to use the restroom and I resumed the slideshow with a sigh. Lisa came out, carrying a trash bag. I could see her waddle even in the still images. There had been nothing so far, but we had reached the day that Cathy had visited her. If there was anything worthwhile on the camera, we would find out soon.

Rain started, a gentle susurrus against the tin roof. I heard the toilet flush, and the sink run for a few minutes, before Harper came out with her jacket in her hand. She had taken her hair down and it fell loose around her shoulders, wavy from being in a braid. She tossed her jacket onto a chair, shot me a small smile and came back to the couch. When she sat down, she was close enough that our hips pressed together and I could smell the conditioner she had used in her hair.

"Sounds like it started raining. Did I miss anything?"

"Lisa took out the trash. Riveting. You want me to rewind?"

"Ugh. No thanks." She shifted around, trying to find a comfortable spot, then muttered, "Ah, fuck it," and leaned into me. I felt her breast press into my ribs and her head laid into the hollow of my shoulder.

I froze, uncertain of what her intentions were. After a moment, she twisted her head around to look up at me, and I stared into her green eyes from a few inches away. This close, I saw there were flecks of gold in them.

"You're not watching the slideshow," she said, her voice throaty.

"Um." I cleared my throat and looked back at the laptop.

Harper's hand came up and brushed across my chest before sliding down and finding a comfortable resting place across my stomach. "Mm. That's better," she said softly. "This isn't a problem, is it?"

"Uh, no. Not at all."

"Great. My neck was going to seize if I kept holding it at that awkward angle."

"Don't want that," I murmured. Having Harper lying against me was infinitely more interesting than the slideshow. I could feel her warm breath on my neck. Every time I tried to focus, she would shift a little. The worst of it was, I still had no real idea what Harper wanted. Was she just being friendly? Was this a prelude to having sex?

Harper was a lonely woman, I knew that much. Her options for finding a boyfriend were slim to none, which was strange, considering how she looked. Was she interested in having some fun, or was she just happy to have some human contact? She wasn't drunk, or rather, she didn't seem drunk. If I accepted her overtures, would that be taking advantage of her?

Hell. She was a grown woman with full awareness of what

she was doing. I took my hand off the back of the couch and brought it down to her shoulders.

"Mm," she sighed. "Took you long enough. I was beginning to think I had misread you, Ryan Halsin. You're not gay, are you? Not that there's anything wrong with that if you are."

"No," I said. "I'm not gay."

"Good," she said. I felt her head turn up to look at me, and her breath moved from my neck to my ear.

I cleared my throat and glanced down at her. "Where are we going with this, Harper?"

"Wherever we want."

"And where do you want it to go?"

"What, you're going to make me say it?"

"That's the polite thing to do, right?"

"Ryan, I haven't had sex in five years, ever since I finished college and came back to Kingfield." She straightened up and swung a leg over my hips so she was straddling me. "Now will you stop being so damn nice and just fuck me?"

Well. If she was going to put it like that, who was I to refuse? I brought my hands up over her hips, up the curve of her back and tangled my fingers in her hair. I felt the dampness at the base of her skull where her braid had kept her hair from drying out all the way, and I pulled her head down to me.

Her lips were hot and her tongue tasted of blueberries and brandy. Her hands were all over me, wherever she could reach, tugging at my clothes. My jacket and shoulder harness kept getting in the way, and I could tell she was getting frustrated with it.

I shifted my hands down to her hips and grabbed the tight muscles of her flanks, then stood up with a grunt. Harper gasped and wrapped her arms around my neck and her legs around my waist. I carried her into the other room and dropped her onto the bed.

As fast as I could, I stripped out of my jacket and shoulder harness and pulled my shirt off. Harper threw her own shirt to the side and pulled her supportive athletics bra up over her head. Without the bra, she had larger breasts than I'd expected.

I leaned forward and kissed her again, and filled my hands with her tits. Her nipples were hard and dragged against my palms, and she groaned into my mouth as I caught them between my fingers. I felt her fumble at my belt and then her hot hand slid down into my pants.

It might not have been five years for me, but I hadn't had the time or opportunity to date someone in Portland. Harper found me hard and ready. With a decisive tug, she got my pants and boxers down to my knees. She grabbed the base of my prick with one hand, her fingers gripping hard, and with the other she gently caressed up and down the length of my shaft.

The conflicting sensations pulled a growl from the back of my throat. Harper grinned into my mouth, her breath coming in tight pants. For a girl that hadn't had sex in five years, she hadn't forgotten how to make a man excited. She already had me on the brink of coming.

As good as her hands felt, I wasn't ready to finish yet. We had barely even started. I leaned my weight forward and pushed her down onto the bed. I gathered her hands together and lifted her arms up over her head, pinning her hands as far away from me as I could. She started muttering a protest, then broke off in a gasp as I found her nipple with my teeth.

"Yes, more of that," she groaned.

I was happy to oblige, and shifted my attentions back and forth between her breasts, sucking and using my teeth, and not being particularly gentle about it. With my free hand I found the button on her jeans and got her pants opened up. She wasn't wearing underwear. I glanced up at her and got a broad grin in response.

"Left them in the bathroom."

I slipped my hand between her thighs and found she was shaved smooth, recently enough that there was only a hint of stubble. Either she shaved regularly, or she thought she would be getting laid.

The velvety softness of her outer lips were warm against my fingers and I stroked her gently, and she shifted her knees wider, giving me better access. I found the slick heat of her opening and slowly pushed my middle finger inside her. She was tight, and despite being wet, I could only get to the second knuckle.

Harper stiffened and flexed her hips upwards. She tried pulling her wrists free of my grasp and I tightened my fingers, holding her pinned in place. I rubbed around the top of her mound with the ball of my thumb until I found her clit. When I brushed against it, a tremor ran through her and her legs clamped down on my hand.

"Fuck, Ryan," she groaned.

I released her nipple from my teeth and moved up to kiss her, leaving my other hand buried in her. I fought the pressure of her thighs and started working my finger back and forth inside her. "Too much?"

"Just... go a little slower."

"I can do that." I kissed down the side of her jaw and caught her earlobe with my lips.

Her legs relaxed and she started moving her hips in time with the motions of my finger. "Yes. Like that."

Too many of my previous partners expected me to somehow read their minds. It was refreshing to have Harper make it perfectly clear what she wanted. I kissed my way down her neck, lingered for a minute around her breasts, then had to release her hands as I went even lower to her navel.

I knelt between her knees and pulled her pants down and off all the way. Her low moan caught in her throat as I kissed the top of her thigh. I licked and nibbled my way around, teasing her. Harper's nails scraped over my scalp and pulled me close, and I finally relented. I sank my tongue into her with my nose pressed into the top of her mound.

She tasted warm and slightly salty, and her legs trembled as I delved deep inside her. I withdrew from her and shifted my focus upward to her clit, taking my time and being gentle with her. I pushed my finger back into her, and found she had relaxed and was even wetter than before. My finger slid in all the way to the base, and Harper gave a little yelp.

Her fingers didn't unknot from around my skull, so I guess that yelp wasn't a bad thing. I added a second finger after a minute, and she pushed her hips into my hand, trying to get them deeper. She was ready, and I didn't think I could hold off much longer myself.

I kicked off my boots and pushed my pants off, a little awkward with one hand and my mouth still firmly attached to her. Then I climbed up between her legs and braced myself above her. Harper's hair was tussled from her writhing around on the bed, her face flushed. She levered up at the waist as I crawled up to her, and the taut muscles in her abdomen were clearly visible beneath her skin.

Harper's hands reached down to grab my dick, and she pulled me toward her, no patience left for foreplay. She guided me straight into her, a look of tight concentration on her face. After preparing her with my tongue and fingers, I slid in to the base in one thrust. She was tight, and I could feel her muscles clamping down on me.

"Fuck yes," Harper whispered. Her hands locked onto my hips and held me tightly in place. Her hips ground against me, the motions ragged and uneven.

I kept myself braced above her and watched her face twist as she fucked herself onto me. Her eyes were unfocused and her mouth open slightly as she panted. Finally, her grip on my hips relaxed and I was able to pull out of her slightly and push back in again.

The motion caused her to focus on me. For a moment she stared at me, then she lunged upward and kissed me. Her arms wrapped around my neck and she did her best to push her tongue as far into my mouth as it would go.

The sheer hunger in her made me want to pin her to the bed and just fuck her as hard as I could. Instead I kept my rhythm and slowly built up speed. I was rewarded a minute later when she pulled her mouth away from mine and tucked her chin down. Her breath was coming hard through her clenched teeth, and I felt the trembling begin in her thighs.

"Don't stop," she gasped. "Just, keep…"

I held my rhythm steady, and a few seconds later the muscles in her stomach locked up and the grinding of her hips against mine froze. I pulled back far enough to see her face. Harper had her eyes tightly shut and a flush colored her cheeks. Her arms around my neck squeezed, and then her growing orgasm crested.

Harper threw back her head and let out a long, shuddering moan. Spasms went through her stomach, and I felt her rippling around the head of my dick. That was it for me. My own orgasm blindsided me out of nowhere and I erupted inside of her with a groan of my own.

She pressed herself against me and her mouth found mine. Her kiss this time was gentle, and the motion of her hips against mine were slow. She milked me through my orgasm, and only after I had softened and slipped from her did she release her grip from around my neck.

We fell to the bed, panting after our breath. Harper reached up and ran a finger across the stubble on my jaw.

"That was intense," she said with a small grin.

"What can I say, you inspire the best in me."

"Yeah? I'm just a backwoods Forest Ranger. What did I do to earn that kind of sex?"

I kissed her and brushed the tangled hair away from her forehead. "You're not 'just' anything, Harper. And you gave just as good as you got." A thought occurred to me and I pushed myself up on an elbow to see her face clearly. "Shit. Are you safe?"

"You mean am I on the pill? Yeah. I take it to control my period."

I let out a sigh of relief and fell back against the pillow. "That's good."

Harper shimmied over and climbed on top of me. She leaned low and tips of her breasts dragged across my chest. I could feel the wetness between her legs on my thigh and I stirred, already reacting to the sheer sensuality of her. She kissed me, and the hunger was back, tempered, perhaps, but no less eager.

I caught her shoulders and gently pushed her back. "Easy there, Harper. Too soon. Besides, we have work to do."

She glanced toward the other room and pouted. "Whatever is on that camera can wait."

"I'm not going anywhere, Harper," I grinned. "Tell you what. We finish watching the slideshow, and if there's nothing on it, we can come right back to bed. I need a few minutes to recharge anyway."

"I suppose you're right. In that case, I need a shower. I'll make it quick."

Harper rolled off me and quick-stepped to the bathroom. I stared at her ass as she went, then got up off the bed. I really hoped there wasn't anything of interest on the memory card. I had a whole list of things I wanted to do to Harper.

She wasn't the only one that needed a shower. In the interest of expediency, I took a minute to give myself a sponge bath in the bathroom sink then pulled on my boxers. I almost didn't wear anything, but I suspected sitting on the couch naked would just be an invitation to Harper to jump me the moment she came out of the shower.

While we had been otherwise occupied, the slideshow had finished. It took me a minute to find where we had left off, but I got the slideshow started back up without having to look at more than a dozen repeat slides.

The shower turned off and after a bit, Harper came out wearing nothing but a towel. The bottom of the towel barely covered her ass, and her legs seemed to go on forever. I couldn't pull my eyes away from her as she crossed over to the couch and sat down next to me. There was nothing shy about her now. She curled up on the couch and leaned her head on my shoulder.

"I never thought I'd get turned on by looking at Lisa's driveway," she murmured in my ear.

"Easy now," I laughed. "Let's finish watching the slides."

She sighed and didn't push the issue, though she did keep playing with the bit of towel folded over in between her breasts that kept it closed. It took some effort, but I pulled my eyes away from her cleavage and went back to watching the screen.

The rush of morning traffic southbound occupied the next few dozen slides. Then in the following slide, the sun was higher in the sky, just before noon. Cathy pulled up and freeze-framed her way up the driveway.

"Here we go," I said. If there was something worth watching from the camera, it was about to happen.

I reached forward and paused the auto-progression on the slideshow. The next image showed Cathy's back as she walked out of Lisa's house. The sun had skipped forward and was casting a harsh glare across the camera lens.

"What's that? On the right?"

I zoomed in on the image and panned over so the little blob on the edge of the image filled the screen. It was a person, standing hunched over. I couldn't make out any details of the face. After looking at it for a minute, I advanced to the next slide.

The figure had come up the driveway a little further, and Cathy was mid-stride, running toward it.

"Holy shit," Harper said softly.

"What?"

"That's Amy Chase." She sat up and leaned forward to get a closer look.

I glanced up at the top of the screen and verified the filename. "That can't be right. This is from Wednesday. Amy disappeared on the Thursday before, six days earlier."

"No, it's definitely Amy. See how her back is twisted a little? Amy has a light case of scoliosis."

"Could she still be alive, then?"

"Maybe." The playful sensuality was gone from her voice. She was back to being the professional once more. "We better get dressed. Amy's house isn't far."

CHAPTER NINE

I stepped out of the shelter of the roof of the bed and breakfast and pulled the collar of my jacket up higher. The rain was absolutely pissing down, falling in sheets and blown by gusts. It also wasn't what I typically associated with a summer storm. The rain felt only a few degrees above freezing, and it bit into my skin wherever it found an opening.

Harper started making a run for her truck, and I called after her, "I'll meet you there, I need to grab something first."

I jogged across the parking lot to my rental car and swung around to the trunk. I popped the hood and lifted up the mat to expose the wheel well. I'd taken the spare tire out when I had rented it and put a flat, nylon case in its place.

The rain ran under my collar when I bent forward to unzip the case. Inside I had a short-barreled military carbine with a folding stock. I'd kitted it out with a holographic sight, a flashlight, and an infrared laser. The laser wasn't any use without the low-light goggles sitting under the carbine, and I decided to leave them where they were for now.

I grabbed a small pack that had spare magazines and a few other tools, then zipped the case back up and covered the wheel well. Headlights swung over me as Harper pulled around. I waved and jogged over to her. She unlocked the door when I got close, and I joined her in the cab with rainwater streaming off my head and shoulders.

"Nice gun," she said.

"Thanks."

"I thought it was strange you were monster hunting with only a pistol, but now it makes more sense. This is Maine, Ryan, you don't have to hide it. Strap it to your forehead. Nobody cares."

"It might be legal, but sometimes its better if the monsters don't know you're coming into their territory packing heat."

She pursed her lips, then nodded. "There's that, too. Ready to go?"

"Onward," I nodded.

Amy Chase lived a quarter-mile down the road from the bed and breakfast. Harper pulled off the main road onto a bumpy dirt track closely hugged by trees. She had to slow down to a crawl, but even so, the roots and bumps in the road threatened to shake the teeth loose from my head.

After a few dozen yards, the trees opened up somewhat and a house came into view. It might have been a nice house at some point, single story with tall, gabled windows, but it was all but falling down now. The primary structure was mostly intact, but the second wing was missing half the roofing tin and the walls were sagging badly out of plumb.

Harper coasted to a stop and we stared at the building for a moment in silence.

"Someone actually lived here?" I asked.

She nodded stiffly. "I hadn't realized it was so bad."

"You want to come back in the morning?" I asked.

"Why? Are you scared?" Harper gave me a challenging grin, but I could see the disquiet in her eyes.

"Of course. I'm not stupid. But not so scared that I'm going to run."

She swallowed. "Okay. Good. Can't have you chickening out on me."

"Harper." She had started reaching for the door handle, and now she looked back at me. "Stay close to me. Don't go off on your own. Be ready for anything, and check your targets before you shoot."

I got a nod, and we got out of the truck. I unfolded the stock on my rifle and flicked the light on. It had a red filter over the lens that would keep my night vision from being ruined. Rain filled the cone of light as I snugged the gun to my shoulder. Harper circled around the front of the truck. She had pulled the lever-action hunting rifle from the rack in the truck, and was holding a flashlight awkwardly alongside the forward grip, but she hadn't turned it on yet.

Time to investigate the house. Despite seeing Amy Chase on the camera alive and well, my gut told me there was something wrong with it. I didn't know what we were going to find inside, but I doubted it would be Amy and Cathy playing Yahtzee in the dining room.

I moved forward, my weight on my back foot, and stepping on the outside of my foot with the ball first and rolling the rest of my foot down. It was slow, but it made my footsteps silent. I kept my gun pointed at the ground. I didn't want lights sweeping across the windows alerting anyone, or anything, that might be inside.

We got to the front door and I eased up onto the porch. The boards squeaked a little under my weight, but there was nothing I could do about that. I glanced over at Harper and made sure she was close.

"Stay tight on my six."

She nodded and I reached for the doorknob. It was loose in

my hand, the internal mechanism disconnected from the knob. At my touch the door sagged inward. I gave the door a little push, then snapped my rifle up to my shoulder and swung into the room. I panned my light across the room rapidly, scanning for threats, all my senses straining.

I cleared the close quadrant then pivoted around to check the half of the room behind the door. Behind me, I felt more than heard Harper slip into the room, her rifle pointing at the floor at her feet. I took a few short steps and cleared the space behind the couch, then gestured toward the kitchen.

With Harper on my heels, we swept the house, moving silently and swiftly. The last place we checked was the door that led to the addition. Water damage had made the wood sections delaminate and the hinges were rusted over. One of the upper panels was missing and I could see through into the ruin of the next room.

Most of the drywall had fallen from the studs in chunks, giving a clear view to the far side of the house. A pair of bedrooms and a bathroom were visible. Rain fell through the roof in a dozen places, turning the floor into a marsh of gypsum and insulation.

At some point in the recent past, someone had smashed in the door where the handle had been. Splinters of fresh wood there hadn't yet started to mold. As much as I didn't want to go into the addition, I knew it had to be done.

I gestured for Harper to get behind me, and I pulled the door open. The hinges squealed and opened about halfway before they stuck. I tried pulling a little harder and the door fell apart in my hand. The sound of the wooden panels hitting the floor seemed deafening. I snapped my rifle up to my shoulder again and froze, listening intently.

For a long minute I waited, but besides the patter of rain falling through the roof, there was no noise in the house. I grimaced and rose back up into my half-crouch. I tilted my head at Harper, telling her to follow, and stepped out into the addition.

The dissolved drywall under my feet made the floor slippery. I stepped carefully, keeping my balance, and cleared the rooms in the addition. After checking behind the last bed, I straightened up and nodded at Harper.

"All clear. This place is a dump."

"Yeah…" She looked around and shook her head. "I had no idea Amy was living like this."

"Well, she wasn't living in the addition," I grinned. "Come on, let's get in out of the rain and see what we can find in the rest of the house."

Back in the house, I flipped up the red filter on my flashlight and unclipped it from the barrel. I didn't want to have to point my rifle where I wanted to look. The unfiltered light made me squint for a moment until my eyes adjusted.

"So, what are we looking for?" Harper asked.

"Anything out of the ordinary."

"That's not very helpful."

"Remember, we're hunting a fae. They're not human, and they don't act like it. We're looking for anything that seems weird. Cans of food smashed open instead of opened with a can opener. Beds made into a nest instead of made properly. Places set with only knives, or eating without dishes. That sort of thing."

Harper nodded thoughtfully. "I think I understand."

"I think we're alone in here, but stay close anyway. You never know if something might return."

We started in the living room and took our time examining the furnishings. As far as I could tell, there wasn't anything strange there. We moved on to the kitchen. Besides the mess and unwashed dishes in the sink, there wasn't anything that struck me as unusual. Harper opened the fridge and checked inside.

"No vegetables," she commented. "Just butchered meat in the freezer. Looks like Amy did a lot of hunting."

"That's strange, isn't it? Do many people around here live entirely off what they can hunt?"

She shrugged. "Amy was poor. It might have been the only food she could get. There's probably a garden out back where she grows her greens."

I looked into the fridge over Harper's shoulder. It was full of plastic-wrapped bundles of red meat. I wasn't an expert, but it all looked pretty lean. "A deer?"

"There's a lot for a deer. Maybe an elk?"

"What's the hunting limit like?"

Harper shrugged. "There's the law, and then there's what is enforced. For a local like Amy, who's hunting to feed herself, we don't care much."

I grunted. That seemed awfully level-headed for a government agency. Then again, this was Maine. "Shame it's all going to go to waste."

"Yeah. I'll let Sergeant Bunnings know. He might be able to distribute it to people who are in need."

"That's a good idea. Let's keep looking."

We went to the master bedroom next. The bedding was scrunched up at the foot of the bed and stained with mildew, but it just looked like a slob lived there, not necessarily a fae. Strangely, the floor looked like it had been recently scrubbed clean. In a house that was otherwise a total disaster, a bit of clean floor was out of place.

"What do you make of this?" I asked.

"Weird," Harper shrugged. "Maybe something spilled?"

"Yeah." I looked around, frowning. "Look, there by the dresser. The wear patterns on the floor are wrong. It was moved recently. And someone cleaned the walls as well. I would bet money that it wasn't Amy who did the cleaning."

Harper sighed. "I don't want to talk her down, but the rest of the house makes it seem like she wasn't big on hygiene. Why would someone scrub down the bedroom and rearrange the furniture?"

"Hold that thought."

I slung my pack off my back and dug through the outer pocket before coming up with a stubby flashlight. I clicked it on and turned the blacklight onto the floor and walls. The remnants of blood spattered up the walls and stained the floor.

"Holy shit," Harper whispered.

I stepped backwards off the stain on the floor so I could get a better picture of it. The gore had spread in a wide pool initially, and I could see where the secondary stains had spread when someone had cleaned the floor. A drag path stretched out the door and down the hallway outside toward the kitchen.

"Harper," I said, "I don't think that meat in the fridge is elk."

She looked at me blankly for a moment, then darted for the bathroom. I heard her throwing up in the toilet. My own stomach felt sour and I focused on the abstract puzzle the glowing stains represented to keep my stomach where it was. I frowned to myself, trying to understand what I was seeing.

Someone had been murdered here, then cut into steaks and put in the fridge. Was it Amy that was all neatly packaged up? There seemed like a lot of meat to belong to only one person, especially an older lady with limited mobility.

If Kingfield had a proper police department, I might suggest getting the meat DNA matched. It would be nice to know who exactly had been butchered, but maybe not especially useful. In the end, it didn't change anything. We knew that people were going missing. Finding out where they were being stashed didn't materially change the nature of the investigation.

Harper came out of the bathroom. Sweat was beaded on her face, and she had her phone in her hand. "I'm going to call it in," she said hoarsely.

"Hold on."

"What? Madison might not have a huge police force, but they have a proper CSI department."

"Think it through, Harper. What will that accomplish? They'll turn this place into a crime scene. By morning, the Butcher of Kingfield will be all over the news and our quarry will disappear. It might take weeks to find it again, and by that time, God only knows how many more people will be dead."

Harper stared at me, her phone held in a white-knuckled grip. "It's the right thing to do!"

"If we were hunting a human murderer, I would agree," I said, trying to keep my voice level and calm, "but we're not. The police won't find fingerprints. They won't find DNA other than from the victims. The police won't be able to help us find the killer, Harper."

"So... we just... leave Amy there?" She gestured vaguely in the direction of the kitchen. "And then what? We try to catch the murderer when it comes back?"

I shrugged. "If it comes back at all. Or, it might get close, realize its stash is discovered, and abandon it. I suppose it wouldn't hurt to set up a game camera or two and see what we can find that way, but we can't stick a hunting blind out in the woods and wait."

She pressed her fingers against her forehead and took a few deep breaths. "I understand where you're coming from," she finally said, "but it's totally fucked."

I nodded. "It is. But that's how we catch fae. We can't think like policemen. The murderer won't act like a human, so

120

it's not predictable. For all I know, the freezer full of meat might be the equivalent of a squirrel storing nuts for the winter."

"Jesus Christ." She turned away, one hand pressed to her stomach. "Then what do we do?"

"I don't know yet." I shook my head. "I guess we can start with following the blood trail and seeing where it leads. Hunting fae has more in common with hunting animals than humans."

Harper's face was pale, but she nodded. The disgust and horror were starting to be replaced by anger. I could see it in the way her spine stiffened and in the squint of her eyes. "Okay. I know how to hunt animals, Ryan. We can do this."

I nodded. "Damn right, we can."

We followed the blood trail out of the bedroom and into the kitchen. Surprisingly, there was very little blood spatter, really only some staining on the floor in front of the sink. Dead bodies don't bleed very much, and Amy must have bled out in the bedroom.

"I think I see something. Bring your flashlight over. Here, on the floor."

I went to where Harper was pointing and shined my blacklight at the ground. There were drips of blood on the floor that hadn't been wiped away.

"Good find," I grunted.

"The bones," she said, having a realization. "There are no bones in the fridge."

"Wait, Harper!"

She stopped and looked back at me impatiently. "Come on, Ryan!"

"No. Damn it, stop! Listen to me. We go carefully. What if this was a bear's den? Would you go running in just because you saw a blood trail?"

The eagerness dropped from Harper's face and she winced. "No."

"Think of this thing like a very intelligent bear. Smart enough to set a trap and use tools. Maybe even smart enough to speak. Except this bear eats human flesh. We may be hunting it, but it is also hunting us. Never forget that."

Harper swallowed. "Sorry."

"It's okay. No harm done this time. But if you're going to be a monster hunter, you will have to learn quickly. Most times, the first mistake you make will be your last."

"What makes you think I want to be a monster hunter?"

I grinned at her and shrugged. "Or not. Up to you, of course, but right now, you *are* a monster hunter. Besides, what would I tell John Baptiste if I got his backwoods protégé killed?"

I walked past her, following the dotted drips of blood on the floor. Harper stared after me, conflicting emotions rolling across her face.

She jogged to catch up to me. "Wait, John said that? Called me his protégé?"

"I thought you didn't want to be a monster hunter?"

"I mean, I never said I didn't," she muttered.

The trail of drips led to the addition and we stopped at the doorway. The rain hadn't let up while we were investigating the house. If anything, it was coming down even harder than before. The trail disappeared into the puddled water.

I shone the blacklight around, but if there were any traces of blood on the soggy drywall, I couldn't make them out. I looked over my shoulder at Harper and got a determined nod in response. I couldn't very well back out now. I put the blacklight away in a pocket and snapped my flashlight back onto the barrel of my rifle, then I stepped out into the rain.

It took maybe fifteen seconds for the rain to find its way past my jacket collar and start running down the back of my neck. I sloshed out into the addition with my light pointing at my feet. The water was ankle-deep and clotted with debris from the collapsed walls. Beneath my feet, clouds of gypsum mud from the dissolved drywall kicked up in blooming gouts of grey.

"What are we looking for?" Harper asked from behind me.

"Bones," I grunted.

I went into the first bedroom and walked around, dragging my feet through the slop. With Harper at my side, we covered the area quickly. I even flipped the twin mattress up on its side so we could feel our way through the crap beneath.

Nothing. We gave it up and moved to the little bathroom. It only took fifteen seconds to determine there was nothing in there, and then on to the larger of the two bedrooms in the addition. As we walked, I kept expecting to feel my foot come down on a femur or a rib. I dreaded it, but also hoped it would happen quickly so I could get out of the damned rain.

We finished pacing out the room and found nothing.

"Damn it," I sighed.

"What about under the mattress?"

It was a queen-sized mattress and half-submerged in the water. Lifting it up was guaranteed to cover me in nasty slime.

"Fuck."

I bent down and found the bottom edge of the mattress. With a grunt, I heaved it up off the floor. It sagged in the middle and rank, black water ran down over my hands and up my sleeves. I could feel the icy water soaking into my shirt and running down the side of my chest. Cursing under my breath, I gave up on trying to stay clean and threw my weight into the mattress.

With my shoulder pinning the top of the mattress to the wall and my hip keeping the middle from sagging out, I managed to clear the way for Harper.

"All right! Just hold it there for a minute while I check underneath."

Harper started pacing over the floor that the mattress had been covering, her eyes down at her feet. Not that she could see anything. The rotting mattress and floorboards had turned the water into reeking black soup. She started at the foot of the bed and made her way to the head, then turned around and started back again, dragging her feet with every step.

As she drew close to me, she looked up and smiled at me. It was a smile that promised an interesting rest of the evening once we finished searching the house. Then she stumbled, her eyes opened wide, and she dropped through a hole in the floor.

CHAPTER TEN

Harper let out half a scream before she plunged into the black water. I reached out for her, but I had myself braced to hold the mattress against the wall and I couldn't reach her. She splashed down into the hole in the floor and sprawled forward.

"Harper!" I cried out.

She caught herself on the far edge of the hole. Water sloshed around her shoulders and into her face. She sputtered and coughed, and struggled to find her footing. Harper finally found something to stand on and straightened up. The hole was only hip-deep and she leaned against the rim.

"God, that's foul." She spat to clear her mouth and wiped some of the black sludge from her face.

"Are you okay?"

"Fine, just... ugh. There's something down here."

Harper squatted down in the water and fished around at her feet. The water came up to her chin, and she kept her lips tightly pressed so a stray splash didn't get more water in her mouth. I watched the quizzical expression on her face change to recognition, and she straightened up, pulling something round and smooth from the depths.

I knew the shape even before it crested the water, and I didn't need Harper's look of horror to confirm my suspicion. It was a human skull, still covered in patches of rotting flesh and clumps of stringy hair. Harper threw it away from her and it splashed down a few feet away, grinning up at the open sky.

"Hold on, Harper," I said. "Let me get this mattress out of the way."

I dug my fingers into the bottom of the mattress, punching through the rotten fabric and grabbing onto the metal mesh that held the springs in place. With a grunt, I lifted it up and threw it to the side. Harper turned her back against the wave of water that rushed over her.

"Asshole," she muttered.

"What," I said as I leaned down and offered her my hand, "would you rather I dropped it back where it was?"

She shuddered and let me pull her from the hole. "No thanks. There are more bones down in that hole," she said.

"How much?"

Harper shook her head. "A lot."

I grimaced, sighed, and handed her my rifle. "All right. Keep an eye out."

I felt forward until I found the edge of the hole and dropped down into it. I felt something crush beneath my boots as I landed and my stomach turned over. That had felt like a rib cage. I bent down and felt around at my feet. Unlike Harper, the water only came up to my shoulder. That didn't make it any more pleasant, though.

My fingers snagged on something and I pulled it up. Sure enough, it was half a rib cage with most of a spine attached. There was a twist in the spine, and several of the ribs were recently broken where I had landed on them.

"Amy," Harper confirmed, her voice tight. "That's the same scoliosis."

There were still bits of flesh clinging to the bones. The monster hadn't done a thorough job picking the skeleton clean before disposing of it.

"There's more," I said, feeling around with my feet.

I ducked back down and came up with a femur. The long bone had been split and the marrow scraped out with something sharp. Bit by bit, I came up with most of the larger bones that had once been Amy Chase.

As I felt around, I discovered the hole was actually a tunnel. About three feet below the surface of the water, an opening in the ground had been dug out. The dirt walls had partially collapsed, and I could tell there was something else in the hole, I just couldn't reach far enough.

"There's more, but it's deep," I said.

"No. No, no. Don't go under, Ryan. Please."

I held Harper's eyes. "I'll be fast. In and out."

She shook her head, but didn't protest. I took a deep breath, steeled my nerve, and ducked down under the black water.

I could tell right away that the thing in the hole was another skeleton. It seemed more intact than Amy, like the monster hadn't finished eating the scraps of flesh yet and had stored it underground where the cold earth would keep it somewhat preserved. The tunnel had collapsed and now the skeleton was pinned in place.

The skull was the most exposed, and I dug away some of the fallen earth until I could get my fingers hooked into the empty eye sockets. Then I pulled, using my back and my legs. There was a dull crunch that I felt through my numb fingers and the skull broke loose of the spine.

I straightened up out of the water, gasping for air. Harper bit back a cry of relief and rubbed the back of her hand across her cheek, smearing the slime on her face.

"I found something," I said. I made sure my fingers weren't still dug into the eye sockets of the skull, and pulled it from the water.

Rot and the water hadn't done the skull any favors. The flesh was mostly gone, but enough of the hair was left to tell that the dead person had closely-cut blonde hair. It was male; scraps of the flesh still on the jaw had stubble sprouting from it.

Harper fell to her knees in the water and let out a low keening whimper. "No... damn it, no!"

I set the skull on the edge of the hole and climbed out. Black water streamed from my clothes as I crouched down next to Harper. She turned to me and pressed her face into my shoulder. I wrapped my arms around her and held her as she cried silent tears.

When her shoulders stopped shaking, I rubbed my hand across her back, trying to soothe her. Crying women always made me uncomfortable. I didn't know what to do. I didn't know what they expected from me.

"I'm sorry," I said. "It's Owen, isn't it?"

She nodded and drew in a shaky breath.

"Shit."

"Is he... the rest...?"

"Buried. The hole collapsed."

Harper pulled back from me. "Thank you. For looking."

We stood and I collected my rifle from her. For a moment, we stared at Owen's skull sitting in the water, then Harper reached out with her foot and nudged it back into the hole. It disappeared with a plop and she shivered.

"Better he's just missing, than eaten by a monster," she said softly. "For Tammy and Henry. Oh, God. Henry."

"We don't know what happened to him," I said quickly.

"Not yet. He left a note. It's possible he escaped and is hiding in the forest somewhere."

Harper looked up at me and shook her head. "I'm not a child, Ryan. Henry is dead."

"You don't know that," I insisted. "Not yet. Maybe we'll find his body, but until we do, he's still alive."

She ducked her head and dropped the argument. "I don't think there's anything else in this house."

"You're probably right. We could come back in the morning, maybe we could find some other clues we missed in the dark."

Harper swallowed. "Maybe. What do we do with all this?" She gestured at the piled remains of Amy Chase. "I don't like the idea of just leaving her out in the rain."

"She deserves a proper burial. So does Owen."

"They can be put to rest once the monster is dead," Harper said grimly. "You were right. We have to stop it from killing any more people. That's the priority."

She crouched down and shoved the piled bones back into the hole. They disappeared into the water with little splashes, and a few seconds later, it was as if we had never disturbed the grave at all.

I sighed. "Help me pull the mattress back into place. It won't fool the monster if it looks closely, but it might pass a casual glance."

Harper nodded, and together we wrangled the floppy mattress back over the hole. Once we finished, we trudged back into the main house, soaked to the skin and starting to shiver. Neither of us spoke, and we both headed straight out to the truck.

The unexpected synergy sparked something warm inside me. It reminded me of working with my dad before I had left to join the military. Harper started the truck up and made a three-point turn to get us going back up the bumpy road.

The heater was on, but the engine had cooled while we were in Amy's house and all it was doing was blowing cold air. I flipped the vents closed and tucked my hands into my armpits.

"I'll drop you off," Harper said quietly once we hit the main road and the ride smoothed out again.

"Thanks."

We rode the rest of the way to the bed and breakfast in silence. Harper pulled into the spot next to my rental car and killed the engine. I stared out at the rain drumming against the windshield and tried to work up the motivation to get back out into it. Everything I had on was drenched already, but I had just started to warm up again.

"Ryan," Harper said, so quietly I almost didn't hear her.

"Yeah?"

"I don't want to be alone tonight."

I reached out and took her hand. "Me neither."

"Can I…"

"Sure."

I got out of the truck and Harper joined me at the back of my rental car. I put my rifle away and gave her a tight smile. "Ready to go in and get out of the rain?"

"Very."

We hurried inside and stopped in the entryway, shaking the worst of the rain from our clothing. Sylvia was at the desk and she greeted me with a smile.

"Oh, Mr. Halsin, I've got another message for you."

I detoured to the desk and she handed me an envelope. "Thank you."

"Of course. Are you and Ms. Hill working together?"

"She's being my guide," I nodded.

Sylvia sniffed. "I'd have thought she would be too busy. You've heard of the missing people?"

"She mentioned it. Very odd."

"Hmph. Well, I won't keep you."

"Thank you for the message," I said. "Oh. Is there a laundry here than I could use? I'm afraid I'm not as good at balancing over the river as I was five years ago."

"Down the hallway there, at the end on the left."

"Perfect. Will I need quarters, or...?"

"Oh, no. It's free for guests."

"Great. Thanks again, Sylvia."

We didn't speak until we had my door closed and locked behind us.

"I don't know about you, Harper, but I need a shower."

She wrinkled her nose at me. "Yeah, you do. You smell like the inside of a leg cast."

I laughed. "Ouch. You don't smell like roses either." I raised an eyebrow at her. "Join me?"

"Mm. I think I will."

I got the hot water running, and when I came back out, Harper was peeling her shirt off over her head. I leaned against the door jamb and admired the play of muscle in her stomach and the swell of her breasts as they were uncovered.

"You just going to watch?"

"I'm enjoying the view." I unzipped my jacket and shrugged out of it. The heat of my body had warmed up the swamp water and the smell hit me. "Oh. That's bad."

I finished undressing quickly. Harper found a laundry basket in the closet and we dumped our damp clothing into it before hurrying into the bathroom. The water was running hot and steam fogged the mirrors. We climbed in under the stream of water and gave a synchronized sigh of relief as the heat hit us.

There was only one washcloth. I reached for it first and got it nice and soapy with the bar, then I put my back to the showerhead and pulled Harper to me by her waist. She leaned her head back, offering her mouth to me, and we kissed.

I began washing her, starting with her back and shoulders before dropping both hands to her ass. Harper leaned into me, pressing her chest against mine. Through the kiss, I felt her breath catch as I gave her a squeeze with both hands.

"Oh!" she breathed, pulling back for a moment. "It's going to be *that* kind of shower."

"Damn right." I turned her around so her back was to me. The suds covering her made her skin slick against mine and her ass pressed into my crotch. I felt myself behind to stiffen in response, and brought my hands up to cup her breasts.

The washcloth in my hand reminded me that this was not just a foreplay shower; we also had to get clean. I could only use the washcloth with one hand, which left the other free to explore her body. Harper reached back with one hand and wrapped strong fingers around my dick. She stroked me to hardness while I played with her breasts, and rubbed the head of my cock up and down the soapy cleft of her ass cheeks.

I washed her arms, and the soap on the washcloth was rinsed away by the time I finished. Harper plucked the cloth from my hand.

"My turn."

We switched places so she could stand directly under the stream of water and she loaded the cloth up with soap again. Then she gave me a thorough scrubbing, probably getting me cleaner than I had been in my adult life. Which isn't to say she didn't have wandering hands of her own. I hung onto the curtain rod and relaxed, enjoying the attention she was giving me.

Eventually it became obvious that there wasn't anything left to clean on me, and the repeated applications of soap were for sole the purpose of providing lubricant to her hand working like a piston up and down my dick.

"You keep that up, and I'm not going to be able to hold back."

Harper flashed me a grin and redoubled her efforts. "Come for me!" She abandoned all pretense of cleaning me and used her free hand to lightly stroke the head of my dick.

"Ah, fuck," I groaned.

It didn't take much longer before I felt the inevitable building, and a few seconds later I flexed my hips forward and let the orgasm crash over me. Harper gave a victorious gasp as my dick throbbed in her hands and spattered a long rope of cum up onto her breasts.

This soon after the last time I'd had sex, I was surprised I had that much left in me. The subsequent pulses weren't nearly as strong, and after a last half-hearted spurt, she had milked out everything I had to give.

Harper stretched up on her toes and kissed me. "That was fun," she said breathily.

"I'm going to get you back," I promised her.

"Mm. I like the sound of that."

She turned to the water to wash off her front again and I wrapped my arms around her. "I don't think I've ever enjoyed a handjob before," I mumbled against her neck.

"Did you enjoy that one?"

"Very much."

"Well, let me wash my hair, and we can get to a more comfortable place."

"I'll run the laundry down to the washer, then. You'll be okay by yourself?"

"Just don't be long."

"I'll be back before you know it."

I got out of the shower and dried off quickly before putting on a loose pair of sweatpants and a long-sleeved shirt. My boots were still soaked so I left them were they were and decided to go barefoot. I grabbed the laundry basked full of our foul clothing and stepped out. I made sure to lock the door behind me and hurried down to the laundry room.

The laundry room had a pair of washers and dryers, and I loaded our clothes into one of the washers, doing my best to touch them as little as possible. Harper's clothes looked like they were sturdy, so I just threw them in with mine.

I was adding detergent to the washer when a footstep scuffed behind me. I spun, one hand reached for my shoulder holster before I remembered I had left it on the bed. A young woman stood in the doorway, a basket of rumpled bedclothes on her hip. She gasped at my sudden movement, then pressed her free hand to her chest.

"Oh! Mr. Halsin, you scared me!"

I eyed her and slowly relaxed. The monster probably wouldn't look like a slender fifteen-year-old girl. "Sorry. I'm a little on edge. And you are…?"

"Sorry, I'm Sherry Toole. Sylvia's daughter."

"Oh." I gave her a smile that I hoped would look reassuring. "For some reason I thought Sylvia didn't have any children."

Sherry laughed. "Sometimes I feel like an employee, not a daughter. I help with the cleaning when Mom has visitors. Normally that's only during the snow months."

"I see. I suppose it's good to help with your parent's business."

"They certainly think so." She walked past me to the other washer and loaded in the bedding. "Are you finished with the soap?"

I glanced down at the box in my hand and realized I hadn't got the washer started yet. "Oh. Sorry." I handed her the box and spun the dials around on my washer, then hit start.

"If you like, I can switch your clothes over to the dryer and bring them to your room when they're finished?"

"You don't have to do that. I can do my own laundry."

"It's okay, really." She looked up at me with a conspiratorial grin. "I know you have the Ranger with you. You probably have better things to do than babysit the dryer."

"Does your mom always gossip about her guests?" I asked dryly.

Sherry giggled. "Nothing like that. I overheard you when you arrived. Come on, go relax. I've got your laundry covered."

I found a grin on my own face. "All right, Sherry. I appreciate it."

"Leave the basket and I'll have it up to you in about an hour."

I gave her a wave and headed back up to my room. I let myself in and locked the door behind me. I found Harper in the sitting room, crouching in front of the fireplace. She was wearing one of my shirts, and it looked like a dress on her.

"Oh, a fire! I should have thought of that."

"I washed our shoes out," she said. "They'll dry overnight and hopefully not smell like death in the morning."

"One can hope." I knelt down next to her and ran my hands over her shoulders. I could feel the tension in her and gently kneaded the tight muscles. "You miss me?"

"Mm. Do more of that."

"Hold on, let me sit." We arranged ourselves so we were sitting on the thick throw rug in front of the fireplace, with Harper sitting between my legs.

The position let me work over Harper's shoulders, and I dug my fingers into the knots, starting gently and gradually working harder. After a few minutes of it, she groaned and leaned forward, folding herself in half at the waist. I worked my way down her spine, taking my time and staring into the crackling fire.

I reached her hips and discovered the shirt she was wearing had pulled up from under her butt. I got my hands underneath it and started working my way back up. The shirt came up as I worked higher until I had my hands on her shoulders again and the hem was bunched up under the fall of her breasts.

When I let my hands slip down her sides, she gave a happy groan and guided my hands to her breasts. Her nipples were hard and she tightened her hands over my own, urging me to increase the pressure of my fingers. She straightened her back and lay against my chest, then she reached up and ran her nails through the hair on the base of my neck.

I tugged her shirt up higher, and then with an abrupt motion, she tugged it all the way off. Harper twisted around in my arms and pressed her mouth against mine. We kissed and she leaned her lithe body against me. I let her weight push me over backwards and she crawled on top of me. She lifted her breast up and fed the nipple into my mouth.

I could feel Harper's moans vibrating in her chest. I caught her nipple in my teeth and flicked my tongue over the tip. She grabbed onto my head and pulled me tight to her. I reached down and grabbed onto her ass. Harper let out a surprised gasp, then an excited groan as I lifted her higher up onto my chest.

Harper shifted her knees up past my shoulders and settled down over my face. I sank my tongue into her and found her damp with arousal. She let out a moan and her hips began slowly gyrating. I looked up past the flat plane of her stomach and saw her cupping her breasts her with hands and pinching her nipples. Her head was tilted forward, her mouth open, her eyes half-closed.

I briefly regretted letting her finish me off in the shower, then lost myself in the joy of driving Harper mad with my mouth. She was an expressive lover, and it didn't take much trial and error to find the spots that gave her the most pleasure. I brought her slowly up to the brink of orgasm, only to let her down again. Then, before she could do more than swat me on the top of my head, I put my mouth over her clit and brought her swiftly to a finish.

Her legs clamped on either side of my head and I could feel the long muscles in her thighs trembling. She fell forward to catch herself on her arms and let out a long, shaky groan. I hung onto her hips so she couldn't escape from me and kept lightly, delicately, working on her clit until she finally wrenched free with a shuddering cry.

Harper collapsed to the side and sprawled out on the rug. Her chest heaved as she panted after breath. She was flushed, her eyes only open a bare sliver. I gathered her up in my arms and lay with her pressed against me from shin to shoulder as she slowly came down from her orgasm.

We lay in front of the crackling fire for a long while. Finally, she shifted and let out a sigh.

"Was that getting me back for the shower?"

"Are you satisfied, or do I need to do it again?"

"Oh, God, no. I'm all worn out. With a mouth like that, I'm surprised you're not married."

I chuckled. "Not many women want a man without a home. Mouth or not."

"Don't you get lonely? Or want to just stop and enjoy what life has to offer?"

I shrugged, awkward with her lying on my chest. "Sometimes. But the world needs the Chapter, whether they know it or not. I can't leave the Chapter behind, so I have to find my satisfaction in stolen moments, like this night."

She made a sound in her throat, too soft for me to tell what she thought of my rationale. Her hand came up to trace lazy circles across my chest. I felt my eyes sagging closed, the rigors of the day and short sleep the night before making me tired. The combination of the fire and the soft weight of Harper started to drag me to sleep.

Suddenly, Harper made a vexed sound and shifted off my chest. "Shit."

"What?" I asked, blinking back awake.

"Our clothes. We'll need to change them over to the dryer."

"Don't worry about it." I reached out and brushed a lock of hair out of her face. "There's a girl who works for Sylvia, she said she would switch it over for me."

Harper stared at me and pulled herself into a sitting position. "What girl?"

A tremor of unease went through me at Harper's reaction. "She was in the laundry room doing a load of sheets. Fifteen years old, give or take, skinny, blonde. Had a cute nose and shoulder-length hair. She said she was Sylvia's daughter."

She sucked in a breath. "Did she give a name?"

"Sherry, I think? Yeah. Sherry Toole. Harper, what's wrong?"

"Ryan, Sherry Toole went missing almost three weeks ago!"

CHAPTER ELEVEN

"What?" I sat up, cold goosebumps racing up my back.

"It's why Sylvia was giving me the cold shoulder at the door. She wants the whole town out combing the woods, looking for her daughter and the other missing people."

"That's impossible. Sherry was right there in front of me. We talked, it wasn't much, but she seemed like a normal person. There must be someone else that Sylvia hired. Some local kid who was playing a prank on me."

Harper shook her head. "You described Sherry perfectly. That was her."

"But... I don't understand." I reached for my boots and stuffed my feet into them. The insole was still soggy with water, but I laced them up anyway. I might get a blister or two if I had to do any running, but I wasn't about to go down to the laundry room barefoot again.

"Where are you going?"

"To get our laundry," I grunted. "I don't know what's happening, but we'll need our clothes in any case."

"I'm going with you."

"Good. Sherry mentioned knowing you were with me. I would feel better if you weren't alone."

I found Harper some gym shorts to put on under my shirt. She was probably a size four, and the amount of slack she had to take out of the shorts with the drawstring was comical. She put her boots on while I strapped into my shoulder harness. The comforting weight of my handgun helped calm my nerves somewhat.

"What if Sherry is the monster?" Harper asked as she tightened her boot laces.

"A fifteen-year-old girl isn't going to chop an adult into steaks," I said bluntly.

She flushed. "I mean, what if the monster only appeared as if it was Sherry?"

There were numerous fae that liked to appear as something else to lure unsuspecting mortals into traps. I took a deep breath and nodded. "Sorry, I didn't mean to be pissy. I'm listening."

"There are old Native American legends of monsters that would take the form of their victims. They're only supposed to attack at midwinter, though, and it's in the middle of summer."

"Huh." I checked the draw on my handgun, inspected the mag, and holstered it again. "Tell me more."

"That's about all I know. It was a story told to scare children. Sorry."

"Nothing like a spot of existential paranoia to lull children to sleep with. Your dad tell you that one?"

"My mom was the one with Native blood."

"Nice."

She shrugged. "It made midwinter into a sort of holiday. We had short pins that we would prick people with. If they were a monster, then they weren't supposed to feel the prick."

I grinned. "Okay, I take it back. That does sound fun."

"Fun for the kids, maybe. I distinctly remember the adults not finding it amusing."

"Well, if we see Sherry again, I'll be sure to stick her with a pin."

Harper finished tying her boots and rolled her eyes at me. "I'm ready."

We stepped out into the hallway and I made sure to lock the door behind me. I didn't like the idea of the monster possibly roaming around the bed and breakfast able to disguise itself as anyone. There was something about the encounter with Sherry that didn't make sense to me. Why would the monster expose itself to me? Was it that confident? Was it playing with me? Taunting me?

After the toasty comfort of resting in front of the fire, the chill of the hallway bit at my skin. I pushed my wandering thoughts away and focused on the present. The lobby was empty, and I brushed my knuckles against the knurled butt of handgun before forcing myself to let my hands hang at my sides.

The hum of the dryer came from the laundry room up ahead, and I gestured for Harper to get behind me. Moving as silently as I could with my wet boots squeaking around my feet, I edged up to the doorway and peeked inside.

The laundry room was empty. There was a little folded note propped up on the dryer. In Sylvia's handwriting, it said, *I moved your wash to the dryer -Sylvia.*

I sighed and showed it to Harper. "I don't know what I would have thought about a monster that helped people do their laundry."

She forced a smile, but I could see the nerves behind it. "Now what?"

I popped open the door and stuck my hand inside. I could feel some dampness in the heavy canvas of my jacket, but everything else seemed nearly dry. "It's done enough that it can finish air drying in our room."

Harper grabbed the laundry basket and we loaded our clothes into it. We moved quickly, and then all but ran back upstairs. We laid out our clothes over the backs of chairs in a ring around the fireplace, then retired to the bedroom.

"I'm totally beat," Harper groaned.

I grabbed my laptop and climbed into bed. "Come on, then." I patted the pillow next to me.

Harper slid in under the covers still wearing my clothes. "What's the laptop for?"

"I've been thinking about the open window," I said. "I'm sure I had my door locked. It's possible Sylvia left the window open after housekeeping, but I doubt that."

"You think it was Sherry?"

"Or whatever is wearing Sherry's skin," I shook my head. "I'm worried it might have a key. I'm going to stay up and do some research while you sleep. After you get some rest, I'll grab a few hours. I'd like six, but four will have to do."

"Four hours of sleep after I woke you early? You're going to be exhausted tomorrow."

"Not as much as you might think. I've got enough lilin in me that I can be comfortable with six hours of sleep. Four is just an inconvenience. A perk of the Halsin blood."

Harper frowned, but didn't dispute it. "If you say so." She made herself comfortable and pulled the covers up over her shoulder. "What are you researching?"

"I think you may be on to something with your Native American myth."

"Really?"

"The fae usually only exist in the mortal where there are humans that remember them. What is the name of your shapeshifting monster?"

"The wendigo," Harper said.

I raised an eyebrow. "Is it now? I originally came to Maine hunting a wendigo, but that was nearly six months ago. The information we had on it was quite different."

"Different how?"

I shrugged. "The fae, in some ways, is a reflection of human belief. People from different places have slightly different beliefs and myths. That could mean there are different individual wendigo in the fae, or they could completely different monsters that humans call by the same name."

"It sounds complicated." She yawned and snuggled close to me. "It must be hard to sort the facts out from all the rest."

"If all you had was the normal internet, absolutely. But I have all the Chapter Archives to refer to, as well as private forums in the supernatural community. I'm bound to find something, somewhere."

I didn't get a response. I looked down at Harper and saw her eyes were closed and her chest rose in even breaths. She was asleep. I watched her for a minute then turned my attention to my laptop. What I had told Harper was true. I was certain I would find something on wendigos online, but I had done a lot of research already and had come up with nothing.

I did have new information, though. Harper's suggestion that the wendigo could be impersonating its victims opened fresh avenues of search. First, I needed a review.

I logged into the Chapter Archives and pulled up the incident reports. For over a thousand years, the Chapter in its various forms had kept detailed records of every supernatural encounter. There were scrolls and papyrus leaflets, and notes scribbled in the margins of other books. There were hand-drawn sketches, in various degrees of skill, showing a visual representation of the encounters. In recent years, it had all been painstakingly photographed and translated into a dozen different languages.

As technology had advanced, the handwritten reports turned into typewritten sheets, the ink faded but still legible. Early daguerreotypes were replaced with black-and-white photographs, then Polaroids. Grainy, low-framerate videos started being added. And then, with the advent of digital photography technology, the Archives abruptly transitioned into largely multimedia content. There were still written reports that were appended to the images and videos, but there were also transcribed voice logs.

There were terabytes of data stored, all of it cross-referenced and tagged. The entries were grouped by location, but also by type. There were lists of keywords, folders of articles collected with obscure connections, clips of relevant anecdotes from the news and other sources. The Archives were huge, complex, and still didn't contain everything there was to know about the fae.

Out of deference for the sleeping Harper, I kept to the transcripts and written reports and avoided audio files and videos. I had already compiled a collection of incident reports that mentioned a wendigo, and I pulled them up now. There were few elements in the reports that matched what I was running into.

The main thing that was dramatically different, was that the wendigos always appeared in the dead of winter. I was only a couple months past the last frost, but in Maine, late June was about as solidly into summer as one could get.

In the reports, a wendigo would always appear during a winter famine. Desperation among isolated communities led to slow starvation and eventually to cannibalism. The cannibal was overcome by the spirit of the wendigo, and a change to the monster would take place.

Once the wendigo had fully transformed, they were ravenous, insatiable creatures, continually in a state of near-starvation. The only thing they could eat was human flesh, but no matter how much they consumed, it never was enough.

Wendigos weren't the only consumers of human flesh out there. It seemed like most of the wild fae took great pleasure in murder and mayhem, and eating humans was just a part of that. But there weren't many that exclusively ate human flesh. The giant from Jack and the Beanstalk, the rakshasa, and Baba Yaga, to name a handful, but they were few and far between.

An oddity about the wendigo was that it seemed to retain some vestige of humanity. It hated that it had to consume flesh. The longer they lasted, the stronger the hunger grew, until it could no longer resist the urge and had to gorge itself again. Eating would give them a respite from their urges, but the hunger never grew less or went away.

Inevitably, they could no longer resist the hunger and had to kill once more. The time between killings grew shorter as time passed. Weeks, rather than months. But the incident logs usually concluded with the wendigo being killed shortly after that.

The creature I had on my hands was killing a lot more frequently than that. How long had it been alive? Without anything to compare it to, I could only guess. Six months? That thought gave me pause. Those skiers had gone missing around six months ago.

Moving carefully so I didn't disturb Harper, I grabbed my phone off the side table and opened the photo gallery. I had a few pictures of the bones in that cave, and I zoomed in on the one I had taken of the broken femur.

There were tooth marks on the bone from whatever had gnawed off the cartilage. I had assumed the marks had come from whatever animal had eaten the dead skiers, but now I took a closer look. I was no forensics expert, but I saw none of the fine scrapes that were evidence of canine chewing as from a wolf. What I did find were broad scrapes, like those I would expect from human teeth.

Immediately, my theory about what had happened in that cave changed drastically. In my mind's eye, I imagined the four skiers in the cave. Their fortune at finding such a perfect place to hide from the storm turning into horror when they realized they were trapped.

How long had it been before one of them died of starvation? Or had one of them been overcome with despair and taken their own life? What had the others done when faced with the choice of inevitable death or maybe, just maybe, surviving long enough for a rescue party to find them?

A healthy adult human would have nearly eighty pounds of meat on them, but it would have been much less after the long period of privation. Reduced by half, maybe more. Forty pounds of meat wouldn't last long, split three ways. And then what? Back to starvation again? Or desperation? Had one of the survivors turned murderer? Forty pounds split three ways wasn't much, but what about a hundred and twenty pounds all for one person?

And then, after the choice meat was gone, and the survivor had consumed the livers and kidneys and other rich organs, what then? They had cracked the bones and sucked the marrow out. Gnawed the cartilage from the joints. Scraped what fat remained from the skin. Chewed even the skin for what little nutrients it contained. Until nothing was left but bones and knotted hair.

Somewhere during that time, the wendigo had come from the fae, drawn by the self-loathing and racking hunger, and possessed the survivor. Wendigos in their natural state were emaciated, barely more than skin-wrapped skeletons. They were also immensely strong, maybe strong enough to shift the fallen tree just far enough to squeeze free of its prison.

And then it had gone hunting, desperate for more human flesh. I wagered Harper would know of someone having gone missing in the area around Sugarloaf. And then the wendigo had traveled south to Kingfield. From there, its actions were well-documented, if not well-understood.

My new theory rang true. The Chapter hadn't been wrong about there being a wendigo in Maine, they just had the wrong part of the state. I had been chasing my tail in Portland while the wendigo's long starvation in the cave played out.

What was the best course of action now? There were three incident reports describing the killing of a wendigo. They had all been recently created, and it was noted that they grew stronger the longer they lived in the mortal. In all reported cases, it had been enough to simply shoot the monster. One report had a notation that the locals had claimed wendigos would be vulnerable to flint arrowheads. That claim was unverified, though.

I really hoped it wouldn't come down to stalking the wendigo through the forest with a bow and arrow. That sounded like a sure way to get murdered.

Harper shifted against my side and rolled over in her sleep. Moving slowly, I got out of bed and stretched. I had been sitting in one spot for hours, and my eyes were feeling heavy. A little exercise would get my blood flowing again. I dropped to the floor to do a few pushups.

I counted out ten pushups, then held the plank position for a count of twenty. Movement caught my eye and I looked up. There was nothing in the room. I felt the hairs on my neck lift as some primordial instinct screamed at me, demanding action. I climbed to my feet, moving silently, and collected my handgun from the bedside table.

A board creaked in the hallway outside my door and I froze. The dim illumination of the hallway light coming under the door was partially blocked as something moved in front of it. After a moment, I heard footsteps retreating, but something still blocked the light.

I shifted over to the bed and put my knee up on the mattress so I could lean over to Harper. I nudged her shoulder without taking my eyes off the door. Harper blinked awake, then sat upright as she saw me with my gun pointed at the door. I put my finger to my lips.

"What?" Harper mouthed at me.

"Door," I pointed, and slowly shifted my weight off the bed so the springs wouldn't squeak.

I tried to remember if the floor in the bedroom creaked at all, but couldn't recall. I could tell by the shadow that there was still something outside the door. Whatever it was, it wasn't moving anymore. The suspense was killing me. Part of me wanted whatever it was to burst in so we could just get it over with.

I took a step toward the door and Harper made a sound in her throat. I ignored her and eased forward until I had crossed the room and stood next to it. I glanced back at Harper and she shook her head. I shrugged, reached for the doorknob, and yanked the door open. With the same motion, I swung out, gun at the ready.

The hallway was empty. Or mostly empty. In front of the door was a covered tray, the smell of hot blueberries wafting from it.

"Shit," I muttered. I glanced out into the hallway just to make sure it was actually empty, then picked up the tray and nudged the door shut behind me. "Breakfast," I said with a wry smile.

"Damn it," Harper sighed and flopped back into the bed. "You had me so worried. Asshole."

"Woops." I juggled the gun and the tray for a second and got the door locked, then headed back to the bed. I slid the tray onto Harper's side table. "Can I make it up with some food?" I lifted the lid and found double the normal size of breakfast. "Looks like Sylvia made enough for two."

Harper buried her face in her hands and laughed. "Oh, God. I'm so embarrassed."

"Oh, come now. I'm not that bad looking, am I?"

She spared me a glance and rolled her eyes. "By midday, everyone in town is going to know I spent the night with the private investigator from out of town."

"Ah." The people in Kingfield who already gave Harper a hard time would only see it as a confirmation of their bias. "Sorry about that."

"You know what, screw them." She grabbed a muffin from the tray and bit into it. "I'm going to eat breakfast in bed."

"That's the spirit."

"I take it you haven't slept yet?"

"No." I grabbed a muffin of my own and went back to my side of the bed. I checked my phone and was surprised to find it was a few minutes after five in the morning. "I did find some interesting information, though."

"Tell me." She sat up and brushed a few wild strands of hair back from her face.

"You were right. It is a wendigo." I gave her a brief rundown on what I had found in the Archives. "The skiers we found in that cave, I believe the fourth one turned into the wendigo."

"Poor bastard. So, it's like a spirit?"

"When it first comes to the mortal, yes. But then it takes up residence inside the host and transforms it into a creature of skin and bones, and unnatural strength."

"I… see. And what about appearing as other people?"

"I don't know. I didn't see anything about that in the Archives. You heard about the wendigo from your mom?"

"Yeah, she told me the stories when I was little."

"I really would like to hear the full story."

Harper frowned. "It's been so long, I'm not sure I could do it proper justice. And what I was told was sanitized for children. Sticking a wendigo with a pin probably isn't the real method of killing one."

"If only it were that easy," I agreed. "Well, do you know anyone who does know the full story, then?"

"Maybe," Harper said reluctantly.

"Oh?"

"My grandmother."

I raised an eyebrow. Harper did not sound enthused. "Bad blood? Or none of my business?"

She wrinkled her nose. "Not exactly. Not with her." She sighed and popped the last bit of muffin into her mouth. "We can go visit her tomorrow. Or today. Whichever."

"All right. I'm sure she's a lovely person."

Harper snorted. "Just wait until you meet her."

"I'm down for an adventure. I just need to get a few hours of sleep first."

"Oh, of course. How do you want to do this? After waking up to you holding a gun on the door, I don't think I could go back to sleep again even if I wanted to."

I gave her a tired smile. "Just stay awake. If something happens, wake me up. Otherwise, let me get four hours of sleep and I'll be good to go."

"You sure? Grandma isn't exactly a morning person. In fact, she'd probably skin us alive if we showed up before noon."

"Six hours, then."

Harper nodded and climbed out of the bed. She stretched, then padded barefoot into the other room. A minute later, she came back fully dressed and carrying one of the chairs we had used to dry clothes on. She set the chair down at the foot of the bed, sat in it, and crossed her legs.

"Sleep," she said. "I'll keep watch."

"Thanks, Harper."

She waved a hand at me, dismissing it, and turned back to face the door. "Less talking, more snoozing."

I grinned and lay back against the pillow. With my thoughts full of the wendigo, I expected to have a hard time falling asleep, but I still hadn't found a comfortable position when unconsciousness dragged me under.

CHAPTER TWELVE

I jerked upright, sweating, a shout halfway up my throat. Harper was leaning over me, her expression concerned.

"You okay?"

"A… nightmare. I think."

"You think?"

I shook my head and wiped at the beaded sweat on my forehead. "It's already gone. Something about being trapped in darkness."

"Sounds like a nightmare to me." She grimaced. "I had my own share last night. Anyway, it's noon. I gave you close to seven hours of sleep. I called my grandma, she knows we're coming."

"Thanks. I hope you weren't too bored." I rolled out of bed and padded into the bathroom to brush my teeth. My head felt like it was stuffed with wool, and my mouth tasted like the inside of a shoe.

"Not at all. You left your laptop open. I… browsed the Archives."

I leaned out of the bathroom and eyed her for a moment before going back to spit.

"I hope that isn't going to get you in trouble or something."

"Normally we try to keep straights from exposing themselves to that kind of stuff because it just gets them in trouble. It's a little late for you." I shrugged. "For you, the more you know, the better. Find anything interesting?"

She ignored my question and asked, "Is it all true?"

"The Archives? More or less. You probably saw the supposition annotations. If something is proven to be false, it gets purged. Too many lives depend on the contents of the Archive for it to have lies muddying the facts. We're very careful of what gets added."

She hugged herself and nodded, her face troubled. "I had no idea there are that many fae still interfering with mortals."

I started getting dressed. The fire had burned out hours ago but my boots were nice and dry. "There are a few dozen active Chapter teams right now. We're never bored. You leave me any breakfast?"

"Ah… oops." Harper gave me a guilty look. "Those muffins are like crack. We'll get something on the road. It's lunchtime, and I need something with protein in it anyway."

I made sure my gun was secure in its holster and shrugged into my jacket. It was a little stiff after air drying, and still damp in places. "I'd prefer that, myself. Too many carbs makes me feel cranky anyway."

We headed down to the parking lot. The front desk was thankfully empty and we reached the cars without Harper having to confront anyone, or I having to explain why we were leaving the bed and breakfast at noon. I retrieved my rifle from the trunk of my car. With the stock folded down, it could fit into my pack. I got it all zipped up and joined Harper in her truck.

"Feel like a sandwich?" she asked.

I shrugged. "Good as anything, I suppose."

She nodded and pulled out of the parking lot. Two minutes

later we were pulling into the gas station at the center of Kingfield.

"I've got to fill up," Harper said. "Order for me?"

"Sure, what do you want?"

I took her order and headed inside. The lady at the counter gave me a polite smile and took my orders without comment, though her eyes kept flicking out the window to where Harper was leaning against the side of her truck as the tank filled. I paid for our food and took a seat near the door to wait for it to be made.

The bell over the side door jingled and I looked up to see Liam Davis step inside. He had three young men with him around his age. His gaze swept over the deli and settled on me. An unpleasant smile spread across his face, and he swaggered over to my table.

"Well, well. If it isn't the private investigator," he said loudly.

"I don't want any trouble with you, Liam," I said quietly. I wasn't particularly worried about him picking a fight by himself, but if his friends joined in, I'd have to do damage.

"Aw. That's too bad." He pulled the chair out across from me and slumped into it. "What's your game, flatlander?"

"Sorry?"

"I said, what's your purpose here?" He kept talking loudly, as much to me as to his loose gaggle of friends. An older lady on the other side of the deli folded her unfinished sandwich into its wrapper and left.

I waited for the door to swing shut behind her before putting my hands flat on the table in front of me. A ripple of tension went through the young men. "I'm in Kingfield investigating the missing people."

"Yeah?" Liam swiped his sleeve across his nose and leered

at me. "Seems to me like you're spending more time investigating in the inside of Harper's underwear."

"Why, are you jealous? She's too old for you, kid."

Liam started standing up and I kicked out under the table. I hit his shins and knocked his feet out from under him. He fell forward and caught himself on his elbows on the table. I grabbed his wrists as he started to get up and held him tightly. He snarled at me, our faces only inches apart.

"Let go, you fuck!"

"Liam, I am going to tell you this one time, and one time only." I squeezed until his snarl turned into a pained gasp. "While I'm here, leave me and Harper the fuck alone. Do you understand?"

The bell over the door chimed and Harper stepped into the deli. Her voice rang out, sharp and commanding. "Liam Davis!"

I let him go and he reeled backward, anger, embarrassment, pain, and fear twisting around on his face. "Now fuck off, kid," I said.

"Get out of here before I arrest you for being a public nuisance. That goes for the three of you, too. Out!" Harper pointed at the door, the picture of outraged authority.

The four kids left, trying to maintain their tough swaggers while all but running for their truck. The engine roared to life and they peeled out of the parking lot, swerving into the street before roaring off down the road.

"Sorry about that, Anni," Harper called.

The lady behind the counter glared at Harper and finished bagging our sandwiches with more than the necessary amount of force. "There'd be no trouble if the two of you weren't here," she said irritably.

Harper opened her mouth and I put a hand on her arm. "You're right," I said soothingly. "My apologies." I got an extra twenty out of my wallet and put it on the counter as I picked up our food. "We'll be heading out."

A lot of the irritation faded from Anni's face as she picked up the tip. It was twice what our sandwiches had cost. I gave her a pleasant smile and steered Harper out of the door.

"What the hell was that about," Harper growled at me.

"Liam tried picking a fight," I shrugged. I took her sandwich out of the bag and handed it over.

"It looked to me like you had him pinned."

"It wasn't much of a fight."

There was a picnic bench off the side of the parking lot in the shade of some trees. I led the way over to them and sat with my back to the table so I could see the traffic going by. I wasn't about to let Liam get the drop on me while I was eating.

The only thing remarkable about the sandwich was that there wasn't anything to complain about. We ate quickly, in silence. Something seemed to be bugging Harper, but she didn't broach it until we had finished eating and were on the road once more.

"I live here, you know," she said abruptly, her voice tight with anger.

I raised an eyebrow at her. "I know?"

"When you leave, and go off to wherever the Chapter has you going next, I'm going to still be here. There's less than two hundred people living in this town, Ryan, with another few hundred scattered about the area. Everyone knows everyone else. It isn't like a big city where you can pick a fight with someone and never see them again."

Ah. That was why she was upset. "To be fair, I didn't start the trouble."

"That doesn't matter! It might be easy to mock Liam and humiliate him in front of his friends, but he won't forget that. Ten years from now, he'll still be holding it against me. He's a miserable little prick, don't get me wrong, but I'm going to have to live with him for the rest of my life."

"Okay, I get that. But what would you have me do? Ignore him sexually harassing you? Let him and his idiot friends pull me out into the parking lot and beat me up? He's a bully. You let him have an inch and he'll take a foot. It's how people like him work. The sooner he's put into his place, the easier it will be for everyone."

"That's easy for you to say. You're a man! I don't doubt that you could take all four of those kids in a fight. But once you're gone, all the animosity you're creating will be directed right at me."

"How bad could it be? I felt his arms. Liam's a little shrimp. You could take him with one hand tied behind your back."

"Maybe, but he's only nineteen. What about in five years after he's put on some muscle? What if all four of them jump me some night when I'm alone?" There was a tightness in her voice, and I glanced over at her. To my surprise, her eyes were glistening with tears and her knuckles were white on the steering wheel. "I can't fight all of them at once, Ryan. I'm a Forest Ranger, not an Army vet like you are. I don't know how to fight. Not really."

"Harper…" I trailed off, unsure of what to say to her. This wasn't the happy, confident, woman I'd come to know. There was something else going on here, something from her past. "Look, I'm sorry. I'll try to de-escalate next time. But I won't let him bully you, either."

"I don't need you to defend my honor."

"What, then? You want to go through the rest of your life hiding from them? Liam isn't ever going to stop being an asshole to you, not until someone stands up to him. People like him only understand fear. Unless he's afraid of you, he will do whatever he wants to you, treat you however he feels like."

"No! I—it's not like that, Ryan! I just want to live my life. I want to do my job and help people."

"And what happens when Liam doesn't let you? He was harassing you before I came to Kingfield. I might have brought things to a head, but you can't blame it all on me."

She was silent for a while. I was afraid I had pushed her too far, but in a fit of pique, decided to let her stew. I was certain that I was in the right in this argument. It might be uncomfortable for her, but if Harper was going to stay in Kingfield, eventually she would have to confront Liam and his bullshit.

Eventually, Harper cleared her throat. "You're an asshole, Ryan."

"Thank you."

"But you're also right."

"I know."

"Shut up. I'm not finished. I'm helping you search for this monster because I care about my community. This isn't just a job for me. The people going missing are my friends and people that I've known my entire life. I can't tear apart my town in the process of trying to save it. Liam might be an immature jerk, but he's part of this town just as much as I am. Even if he doesn't appreciate the efforts I'm going through on his behalf, I'm still going to keep trying to save him, and every other person who lives here, no matter how cantankerous, unpleasant, antisocial, backwoods, bullshit-filled, and racist they might be."

That was more like the Harper I knew. "Okay."

She took her eyes off the road long enough to glare at me. "That's it? Just okay?"

"Yep. I understand, and I'll support you. I might just be some flatlander outsider, but the only reason I do this job is to help save people from things they don't understand and can't fight on their own. Kingfield might not be my home, but I'll fight to save everyone here as hard as I can. Including Liam and his dickhead friends."

She grunted and eyed me sideways. "But?"

"But I won't put up with some stupid kids getting in the way of that. Liam might be acting out because he has some personal vendetta against you, but he's actively putting his entire community in danger whether he realizes it or not. I can't afford to have my local contact put in the hospital because he feels like he has to defend his turf. There's no way I'm going to catch the wendigo without you. If it's a choice between keeping things smooth with Liam and killing the monster, I will step all over him to save everyone else."

"And leave me to deal with the consequences when you're gone," she growled.

"There's an alternative."

"What?"

"Leave Kingfield. Come with me back to Portland and join the Fourth Chapter."

She glanced at me. "Are you out of your mind? What do I know about fighting monsters?"

"More than most who join," I shrugged. "Like you said, you're a Forest Ranger. You know the wilderness. You know how to track wild animals. You have survival and safety training. You know how to shoot. That's ninety percent of the way there. The rest is learning about the fae, and you're no fool. You could pick up the basics quickly."

"But... leave Kingfield? Would I ever come back?"

"If you wanted to, sure. You would get a chance to travel, though. See North America and all its wild beauty. Everyone joins with a five-year provisional period. After the five years, if you decide it's not your cup of tea, you can quit, and no hard feelings. We even set people up with jobs that suit them, and vouch for background experience. If you want to be a Ranger, but not in Maine, you do your five years with us and you could have your pick of the national parks to work in."

She swallowed. "I don't know. I haven't ever considered leaving. This is my home!"

"If at the end of the five years, you decide you want to come back, you could do that too. Except you could come back as a higher position. Slate looked like he's near retirement age. You want his job? You could still work in the area, but you'd have an income that would let you buy a house in Madison."

"Wow. You're really selling me hard on this."

"I'm just giving you options. But don't let fear hold you back."

"Let's say I did join the Chapter. Would I work with you?"

I grinned at her. "It's possible. I don't have a partner right now, and I haven't trained a new recruit in years. That would be fun, right?"

"I'm not sure I would call it fun. Is it always like this? Staying up into the early hours, sleeping in shifts, always on guard?"

"Only when we're being hunted by a shapeshifting wendigo. Seriously, most of the time it's nowhere near as sketchy. The wild fae aren't usually very smart. We locate them, track them down, and eliminate them."

"Like your zombies?"

I shrugged. "Sure."

"I read your report of what happened in the Archives. And saw the entry on your sister. She's really the *daughter* of Mahlat?"

"Ah... yes." I looked at Harper and saw she was back to gripping the steering wheel again. "Alex is an amazing person. Funny, smart."

"Extremely dangerous."

161

"But also caring and kind," I countered. "If there is anyone I trust to watch my back, it would be her."

"So long as she doesn't seduce you and turn you into a mindless slave."

"You read the report. She hasn't accepted the offer. She's still human, with all her morals and scruples intact."

Harper frowned. "If I was your partner, would I have to work with her?"

"If that's where the Chapter puts us, I don't see why not."

"Jesus." She blew out a sigh. "Maybe I should withhold judgement until I meet her."

"I think you'll like her."

"What, just because we're girls we automatically like each other?"

"Isn't that how it works? I'm kidding. No, I think you'll like her because you have a lot in common."

She looked at me askance. "I doubt that. Besides, you seem to just assume I'll abandon my life here. I still don't think joining the Chapter is an intelligent career path."

I nodded. "Well, the offer's open. It would certainly solve some of your more immediate problems."

"That's the thing, though. It'd be just running from one bad situation into another."

"It's your decision, of course. I'll stop trying to sell you on it, but if you have questions, I'll be glad to answer them."

She sighed. "Thanks. I guess. Though I wouldn't have to run from Kingfield if you would just stop fucking with my affairs."

I grinned. "That's fair. I haven't asked. Where are we going?"

"To my grandma's camp. It's a bit of a drive."

CHAPTER THIRTEEN

arper's definition of a 'bit of a drive' turned out to be around an hour. We took the 27 north, and soon passed beyond even the regular signs of civilization. Both sides of the road were an unbroken wall of trees. Other than the occasional dirt road turning off from the highway, there weren't any signs of human habitation.

I had felt like I was in the middle of nowhere before, now it felt like I had gone back in time. If we weren't driving on a rather decent road with telephone poles marching alongside it, I might have thought we had gone back in time to the early settlement years. I half-expected to see someone paddling a canoe piled high with beaver pelts whenever we passed by a lake.

The conversation with Harper wandered all over the place, from random childhood anecdotes to old family stories. She seemed to get a lot of amusement out of my stories about my dad's adventures in Egypt in the 1920s when he was just out of his teens. In return, she told me about obscure fae stories passed down in verbal tradition over the centuries.

Eventually, Harper slowed and started calling out the mile

markers. I didn't see our destination road until Harper was already turning onto it. It was little more than a set of tire tracks. A long time ago, someone had dumped a bunch of gravel down in an attempt to fight the seasonal mud, but all it ended up doing was creating deep ruts that had the same approximate consistency as hardened concrete.

Harper dropped us into first gear and slowed to a crawl. Still, it felt like I was in a human-sized rock polisher. I braced myself against the dash and kept my tongue out from between my teeth.

The land started to climb and the road evened out. Talking became possible once more.

"Sorry about that," Harper said with a grin. "I keep telling grandma to put new gravel down. I think she sees it as a convenience. Nobody wants to drive up here to harass her, so she's happy."

"I mean, she already lives in the middle of nowhere," I said. "To get any more alone, she'd have to move to the moon."

"Oh, she's not alone."

We turned a corner and the trees opened up in front of us to reveal a glittering blue lake. A large clearing had been cut through the trees to make room for a few dozen log cabins. Children stripped down to bathing suits ran through the grass, playing a game with a wooden hoop. A few adults were visible, chopping wood, hanging laundry, or engaged in some other housekeeping chore.

"This is a camp?" I asked. I had expected a bushcraft shelter or maybe a canvas tent, not a little village in the middle of nowhere.

"Welcome to Nebeske Odana," Harper grinned at my expression.

She pulled to a stop in the shade of a tree at the edge of the village and climbed out of the truck. Someone waved at her, and she waved back.

"Come on," she said. "They don't bite."

I got out of the truck and left my pack in the footwell. One of the children spotted Harper and shrieked out her name. A second later, we were surrounded by excited children, all trying to get Harper's attention by being the loudest.

A man came out of a nearby cabin and shouted something in what I guessed was the native language. The children reluctantly dispersed and the man came over to us with a scowl on his face. He was as tall as I was, with the dark skin and hair of a Native American.

"Why are you here, Harper?" he demanded. "And why did you bring this white man with you?"

"Hello, uncle," Harper said pleasantly. "This is Ryan Halsin. I've come to speak with Nokemes Kawinse."

Harper's uncle glared at me. "He is not welcome here. You may speak with Nokemes, but he must wait in the truck."

"Actually," she said brightly, "I brought Ryan to speak with her."

He growled something in the native tongue.

"Maybe," Harper replied, "but she did, and here I am. Now, are you going to stand there like an asshole, or are you going to get out of the way?"

He snarled something that was identifiable as a curse even through the language barrier, spit toward my feet, and stormed away. I watched him go then raised an eyebrow at Harper.

"What happened to playing nice?" I asked.

"He called me a light skinned bastard, and blamed my dad for my mom getting cancer," she said. "Fuck him."

"Ah. I take it this isn't the first time you've had this conversation."

Harper rolled her eyes. "No, this is familiar ground.

Besides, he doesn't live in Kingfield. I only see my extended family on my mom's side once every year or so. Come on, let's go meet my grandma."

Her uncle wasn't the only one in the camp who seemed to have a problem with Harper. As we walked through, most of the adults looked our way with varying degrees of hostility. It wasn't until I locked eyes with a young man around Harper's age that I realized they were glaring at me.

"What's their problem?" I asked Harper softly.

"You're white. That's more than enough to condemn you in their eyes. If you thought the people in Kingfield were racist, just wait. Remember, if you pick a fight, we're done here."

"I'm not the one who is going to be doing the picking," I muttered.

"Doesn't matter. They only need half an excuse to throw us both out. Don't give them one."

We crossed the village and went uphill away from the lake. The cabins here formed something approximating a street, with an especially large cabin at the top. Harper brought us to the front doors of the large cabin and hauled open the heavy wooden door.

I wasn't sure what to expect. Maybe hand-woven rugs, headdresses hung on the walls, maybe a totem pole or two. I knew barely enough about Native American culture to know I was hopelessly scrambling different tribes together.

What I didn't expect was a common area with a faded green carpet on the floor and strip lighting. There was a pool table tucked in one corner, and a large flatscreen TV hung on the wall with around twenty folding chairs in front of it. A handful of elderly residents were watching a soccer game playing on the TV, with the sound muted. A pair of teenagers were at the pool table, idly knocking balls around.

Harper caught the look on my face and snickered. "What

did you expect? A smoke lodge? Come on, we're going this way. Grandma's probably in the lounge."

The lounge was on the ground floor on the other side of a communal eating area. Through a side door, I saw a large kitchen filled with fairly modern stainless-steel appliances. Harper gestured for me to be quiet, then gently pushed open a hand-hewn oak door.

The walls here were paneled in polished wood, the floor covered in overlapping hand-woven rugs in muted browns and greys. The furniture had been re-upholstered with deer skins and an impressive bearskin hung on the wall above a river stone fireplace large enough to crawl inside. The walls were decorated with historic memorabilia, taxidermy, and hand-carved wooden statues. Light was provided by wall sconces, the bulbs giving off a dull yellow-orange light barely enough to illuminate the center of the room.

Sitting in an armchair with a pile of leather in her lap, was an ancient Native American woman, her face deeply creased and her hair more salt than pepper. She was stitching a seam in the material, her gnarled fingers pushing a thick bronze needle through layers of leather with the help of a carved bone tool.

Harper caught the door behind us and eased it softly shut. She cleared her throat. "Nokemes, it's me, Harper."

The old lady grunted. "I heard you coming. My eyesight might be shit, but the ears still work. Is Catah still giving you a hard time?"

"Nothing I can't handle," Harper said evenly. "I brought a friend with me."

"The Chapter hunter," she grunted. "Heard him, too."

I exchanged a look with Harper. She looked as surprised as I did. "It's a pleasure to meet you," I said. "My name is—"

"Why have you come, hunter?" she cut me off brusquely.

She lifted her head and looked in my general direction, and I saw her eyes were milky with cataracts.

Harper gave me a helpless shrug and I decided to just cut to the chase. "There's a wendigo in Kingfield."

The old lady clucked her tongue and bent her head back to her stitching. Her fingers felt along the leather seam until they found the punched holes, and with a deft movement, she drove the needle through. "A wendigo, is it? I felt the ley lines tremor in the early months of the year. Late March, I believe it was. Still in the depths of winter."

"There was a group of skiers trapped in a cave," I nodded. "They cannibalized each other to survive."

"As it goes. And what, you wanted assistance? The aid of the braves to track it down?"

"Actually, Nokemes," Harper cut in, "we only desire knowledge."

The sightless gaze lifted to me again, and she lifted a gnarled hand to beckon to me. "Come, hunter. Sit by me."

I stepped into the room and my feet sank into the thick layers of carpet. I made my way through the furniture and knelt by the armchair. She reached out and found my shoulder. Her blunt, cool fingers fumbled their way up to my face. The tips of her fingers brushed across my features as she muttered to herself.

"You're a handsome fellow, aren't you? Are you fucking my granddaughter yet?"

I choked out a laugh and Harper buried her face in her hands. "Ah. Yes. She's a beautiful woman."

"I will skin you if you repeat this, but there is something to be said for mixing blood with outsiders. You won't find tits like hers among my people."

"Nokemes!" Harper gasped.

"What? It's true. You ask me, Catah is so hard on you

because he wishes to be with you. You've seen his wife. Naja has these tiny little tits, less than a handful. Not like Harper's, which are more like two handfuls. If you have big hands." She leered at me, and patted my cheek with a leathery hand.

"Oh, good lord," Harper groaned. "They're not *that* big. Can we please stop talking about my breasts? We're here for the wendigo, remember?"

"They're worth talking about," I grinned. "But you're right. We are here for a reason."

"Very well." The old lady gave my arm a last pat and went back to her stitching. "What do you wish to know? You are already aware of the wendigo. That is half the battle."

"We only have partial information," I admitted. "The Chapter Archives describe how they are made, but the one we face is not like anything recorded."

"Tell me."

"It appears to be taking on the appearance of its victims. We saw it as an old lady at one point, and it spoke to me while wearing the appearance of a young girl who had gone missing weeks earlier. I want to hear the full story about them, from you."

"The full story…" She drove the needle through the leather a few times, gradually stitching her way around a curve. With all the leather bunched up in her lap, I couldn't tell what it was she was making. "I suppose I could tell that tale. But go sit on the couch. I don't want you breathing on me the whole time."

I got up and moved over to the couch. The upholstered hide cushions had been tanned with the hair still on them, and they were slippery in one direction and coarse in the other. Harper joined me, but sat on the far side of the couch, out of arm's reach.

"We're ready, Nokemes," Harper said.

The ancient woman sniffed. "You sit too far apart. There is

no shame in your intimacy. We are not like the Christians, preaching chastity before marriage."

Harper gave me an embarrassed look and shifted over to my side of the couch. I lifted my arm up and she leaned in against my chest. Her more-than-a-double-handful breast pressed against my side and I felt myself start to get an entirely inappropriate boner. I put my arm around her shoulders and gave her a little squeeze.

"There. That's better, isn't it? Much more comfortable."

"I guess," Harper sighed.

"I told you." She stitched for a minute and finished the seam she was working on. She nipped the leather cord off with her teeth, then started feeling around through the leather, searching blindly for the next pair of edges to join together. I found it fascinating to watch. Doing it visually would have been hard enough. All the leather was the same color, and she had it all piled up in her lap. I couldn't tell one piece from the next. She found a corner, and after a bit more digging, matched it up to another corner and started stitching again.

"Nokemes," Harper said gently. "The story?"

She tsked. "It's been nearly seventy years since I heard the story, child. My mind may not be as nimble as it once was, but I'm not doddering yet. I need to organize it in my mind before I begin to speak."

"Sorry." Harper leaned her head back against my shoulder and stared up at the ceiling.

"Patience. It is a lesson you never learned properly."

I saw the muscles in Harper's jaw clench and she closed her eyes. After a moment, I felt the tension ease out of her shoulders. She twisted around and put her feet up on the couch, and leaned against me. I put my back against the side arm of the couch and half-turned so she could lay across my lap.

There wasn't anywhere I could put my arms that would

keep things appropriate for the setting. Still, it wasn't like the old woman could see where my hands ended up. I wrapped both arms around Harper and gave her tit a quick squeeze before moving down to her stomach.

Nokemes cackled to herself and nodded. "Good. More comfortable now, Harper? And how about you, Chapter hunter?"

Harper gave my wrist a swat. "We're fine, Nokemes."

"Yeah, this is comfortable," I said, and grinned at Harper. She rolled her eyes.

The old woman nodded and went back to her stitching. With Harper lying on my lap, my boner seemed to take it as evidence that it would be required soon and grew harder. Harper shifted and looked back at me with a puzzled expression. I shrugged. She reached around behind herself and groped at my waist. It didn't take her long to find my dick. Her expression went from curious to angry.

I gave her a wide-eyed look and shook my head. She glared at me for a few seconds more, then sighed and relaxed back against my chest. I tried to put my thoughts anywhere other than the warmth of the woman lying on me. With my arms wrapped around her, the soft weight of her breasts settled over my forearm and I could feel the beat of her heart through my palm. If there wasn't an overly-perceptive old lady sitting on the other side of the room, I might have tried to get Harper interested in a repeat of the night before.

When Nokemes finally cleared her throat, it startled me. "I believe I have the thread of the story now. Are you ready to hear it?"

"Yes, thank you," I said.

"Good. It has been many years, and I am translating from the original language, so do not interrupt." Her hands worked the needle through the leather without pausing as she began telling the story. "This is a tale about Azeban, the raccoon trickster spirit. Long before the white man came to these shores, the Abenaki were a prosperous people that lived along the coast. We spent our days hunting, fishing ,and living just as Kloskurbeh, the All-Spirit, had taught us.

"It was a good time to be of the Alnobak. But not all were happy. Amasec was a man of more intellect than wisdom. He was fond of the thick syrup obtained from boiling the sap of the maple tree, and every spring he would gather buckets of it to make into candy. He would make crystals of the refined sugar, formed around the long thorns of the locust tree. So enamored was he of the sugar that he would eat nothing else whenever the season was right.

"Amasec was never satisfied with how much sugar he could make in a season. The maples where he lived were few, and did not have a strong sap flow. Amasec was always searching for new maples, often hiking for miles through the woods around his home.

"Azeban came to the Alnobak one night during the dead of winter and bragged about an area far inland where the maple trees grew thick as weeds, and produced enough sap to float a canoe on. Amasec listened in jealous greed. He laughed at Azeban, accusing him of lying, and dared him to show where this maple grove was.

"Azeban was not lying, and he took great affront to the accusation. He agreed to show Amasec where the grove was located, but only if they would leave immediately, and on foot. Amasec, greedily imagining all the sap he could collect, had his three children come with him, all of them burdened with as many buckets as they could carry."

I exchanged a look with Harper. I knew where this story was going.

"For three days and three nights, Amasec and his children

followed Azeban deep into the west. On the dawn of the fourth day, Azeban brought them to an enormous grove of ancient maple trees. There were hundreds of trees, and all of them eager to give up the sweet sap by the bucket-load. Feeling generous, Azeban offered Amasec the opportunity to collect one bucket of sap from each tree.

"Without a word of thanks to Azeban, Amasec ordered his children to begin tapping the maples, and he himself went to cut down a locust tree. For twenty days, Amasec was only interested in producing as much syrup as possible and hardening the maple sugar onto the locust thorns.

"On the dawn of the twenty-first day, Azeban returned to his grove and found the woods surrounding the maples had all been chopped down to provide firewood for rendering the sap. His beautiful maples had all been drained dry by the greed of Amasec and were in danger of dying.

"Azeban flew into a rage and ordered Amasec to leave the grove immediately and to abandon all the sugar he had created. Amasec laughed in Azeban's face and continued to render his sugar. He had amassed so much of it now that it was nearly as much as he and his children could carry.

"In retribution, Azeban summoned an unseasonal blizzard, and warned Amasec that it would arrive in three days. Amasec was not afraid. It had taken three days to reach the grove, and it would be easy to return to the village before the blizzard arrived. In fact, he could wait for the next batch of sugar to finish. It might cut the time close, but Amasec and his children could hike through the night and be safe.

"And so Amasec did not leave the grove, and cut down more trees to build his rendering fires even higher. Azeban could not let that insult go unpunished, and whenever Amasec was not looking, he would add water to the rendering pots. By the end of the first day, the sugar was no closer to being finished.

"Amasec still did not leave. He was certain it would only be a few more hours before the sugar would be finished. Since all the nearby trees had been cut down, he cut down one of the maples to fuel the rendering fires. Again, Azeban added water to the pots, and on the dawn of the following day, he warned Amasec that the blizzard would be upon them in two days.

"Amasec was beside himself with anxiety. The sugar was almost ready, but the storm was coming. Greed kept him in the grove, and he cut down more of the maples to fuel the fires. Still, Azeban would not allow the sugar to finish rendering. At the end of the second day, Amasec knew that the sugar would not finish in time. He had his sons gather all the sugar they had created and started the long run for home.

"At the end of the third day, they had only covered half of the distance to the safety of the village. They had been running non-stop, burdened by many buckets full of pure sugar, but they knew they did not dare rest.

"In the middle of the night, the blizzard found them. Out of desperation, Amasec and his children took shelter in a cave. Snow fell until it formed a solid wall blocking the cave entrance. Snow fell for twenty-three days and nights, one day for each day Amasec had spent in the grove stealing from Azeban.

"When the snow finally stopped falling, Amasec and his children were starving. They had consumed all the sugar they had created, and they were trapped in the cave beneath snow that buried even the trees outside. Sugar might be a fun treat, but consumed on its own is unhealthy, and one by one, the three children of Amasec fell unconscious and died.

"Out of desperation, Amasec consumed the bodies of his children. When the last of morsel of meat from his youngest son was gone, Amasec went mad. The snow melted the next day, and Amasec emerged from the cave without knowing who he was. Azeban sent the spirit of the wendigo to possess Amasec.

"For the next ten years, Amasec wandered the woods, creating sugar-coated locust thorns and luring people away from the village with the treats. Once he had them alone, he murdered them and ate them. It was impossible to catch him. Because he did not know himself, Amasec changed himself to be the people he consumed.

"Amasec was finally caught when he pricked himself with a locust thorn and Azeban restored to him all his memories. Out of horror of what he had done, Amasec threw himself from a cliff into the ocean and killed himself."

Nokemes fell silent. Harper and I waited, abiding by her earlier caution to not interrupt. The old woman finished the seam she was stitching together and grunted to herself. "That is the end of the story. On the surface, several good morals to teach children. Don't be greedy. Don't eat too much sugar. Respect other people's property. Don't eat dead people."

I snorted a laugh and Nokemes favored me with a broad, gap-toothed smile.

"It was a great story. Thank you for telling it to us," Harper said. "The one my mom told me lacked a lot of detail."

"I can't help but notice the similarity between the accident that trapped the skiers and what happened to Amasec," I said. "It was a freak accident; a tree fell and trapped the skiers in the cave."

"It is a favorite trick of Azeban," Nokemes nodded. She nipped the cord with her teeth and started searching around for the next seam to stitch. The leather was starting to take shape in her lap, and I recognized it now as being a piece of clothing, maybe a long jacket or a dress.

"The skiers were being greedy and ignored the warning of

the blizzard," Harper added. "Ryan, you told me how parallels between the mortal and the fae draw the fae into this world. Do you think Azeban caused that tree to fall over the cave entrance?"

"It certainly seems that way. Poor bastards." I sighed. "Does the story give us a way to catch the wendigo?"

"Prick it with a locust thorn," Nokemes suggested. She seemed to have lost interest in us, and was focusing on her stitching.

"Mom gave us thumb tacks to prick people with," Harper reflected. "I suppose they were easier to come by than thorns. Not many locusts grow around here anymore. Now that I think about it, pricking people was supposed to make them reflect on their actions."

"I can't imagine that worked very well," I grinned. "People these days don't have the wisdom of the Alnobak."

"Or maybe it was to teach me that my actions had consequences," Harper mused. "Stick a pin in old Mrs. Teatle and get whacked with a wooden spoon."

"All good lessons have multiple meanings," Nokemes said.

"Focusing on a more practical approach," I said, "causing the wendigo to introspect might be how to bring about its destruction."

"Or failing that, recognize it in its guise as a missing person and fill it with lead," Harper said darkly.

"Full metal jacket would be better," I said. If it's tough enough, a copper or lead round might just piss it off. Iron and steel are the best way to fight the fae."

"Wonderful," Harper sighed and sat up. "Well, we better get back to Kingfield. If we stay any longer, we'll have spent the whole day."

Nokemes grunted. "Very well. It was good to hear your

voice again, Harper. Chapter hunter, give me a moment with my granddaughter."

I got up from the couch and twisted my back to work the stiffness out of it. The old woman's story had distracted me from Harper and thankfully my boner had given up on embarrassing me. "It has been an honor, Nokemes. I very much appreciate your time and memory."

"Yes, yes." She waved a gnarled hand at me. "You are welcome. Now go."

"I'll be right outside," I told Harper, and ducked out into the dining room.

A couple kids were racing around the tables, competing on who could lay out silverware next to the place settings faster. Judging by the number of places, meals were a community activity here. I leaned against the wall next to the door and mulled over the story I had just heard.

As a folk tale, the only really remarkable aspect was how accurately it had described the fate of the skiers. They had been a bunch of young adults on vacation. I didn't doubt they were engaged in some sort of excess, alcohol, drugs, or something else. Or maybe Azeban had picked up on the chocolate-covered protein bars in their pockets and equated it to Amasec's abuse of the maple grove. God knew they had enough sugar in them.

Ultimately, though, I couldn't think of a way to make practical use of the story. Despite my suggestion to the contrary, getting a homicidal monster to introspect was likely going to be impossible. The wendigo might feel guilt over its victims, but I seriously doubted sticking it with a thorn was going to suddenly make it commit suicide.

The door opened and Harper came out. She had a bundle of leather in her arms that I recognized as what Nokemes was working on. There was a strained look on her face.

"Everything okay?" I asked.

She flashed me a quick smile and gave herself a shake. "Yeah." She cleared her throat and held out the bundle to me. "This is for you."

"It is?"

I took the leather from her and it unfolded into a hooded trench coat. The stitching holding the various panels together was simple, but perfectly executed. "Wow. Seriously?"

"She made it for you."

I turned it around and found the inside of the leather had been worked over with a branding iron in intricate patterns. Simple, repeating geometric shapes were worked around stylized animals that reminded me of totem pole figures.

"I can't accept this. Are you kidding? This must have taken hundreds of hours to make."

Wordlessly, Harper pointed to the collar. Branded into the leather were my initials.

"How?" I asked, at a loss for further words.

"She wants me to take your invitation to join the Chapter," she said tonelessly. "She had joined the Chapter in her own youth and wants me to do the same."

I raised an eyebrow. "Really? Did you tell her I asked if you wanted to join?"

"No. She... has always had some degree of prescience. Try the jacket on."

I have never liked leather clothing. Unless it was custom fit, it never seemed to be comfortable. It bunched in places and was too tight in others. Still, it seemed churlish to refuse to try it on. I took off my jacket and handed it over to Harper. I slipped an arm into a sleeve of the leather coat and felt the roughness of the branding that extended down the full length of the sleeve. That seemed elaborate decoration for an area that wouldn't ever be seen.

"Do I have it inside out?"

"No, the design goes on the inside."

"If you say so." I got my hand down the other sleeve and shrugged the coat onto my shoulders. The fit was perfect. "Okay. This is amazing, but I'm also weirded out."

Harper gave me a helpless shrug. "She said she had been working on it since the wendigo came through the ley lines. It's supposed to be protection of some sort."

I ran my hands down the front of the coat. I could feel the way it narrowed at my waist then widened again to give my legs room to move if I had to run. The front panels had knotted thongs and wooden closures instead of buttons.

It was conspicuously free of iron of any description, and had probably been crafted without use of iron tools. Even the needle to do the stitching had been bronze. I wouldn't be surprised to learn that the branding had been done with hot stones. If I had commissioned a leatherworker to make the coat, it would have been tens of thousands of dollars, assuming I could even find one that would work without iron or steel tools.

"I don't know what to say. This is an incredible gift."

Harper nodded. "She said you would need it. Well!" She gave herself a shake. "I don't know about all that. Still, hard to disbelieve the evidence of your eyes." She reached out and tugged a lapel fold straight. "It looks good on you. Very imposing."

"I feel like I should go back in and thank her."

"No, she isn't looking for thanks. It would just embarrass her. Come on. Let's get back to the truck."

CHAPTER FOURTEEN

W e got back to Harper's truck without running into her uncle. I was a little worried that if he saw me wearing the coat, he'd lose his shit. It was mid-afternoon and while the leather might have been comfortable in the air-conditioned community building, I was sweating by the time we got to the truck.

I shrugged out of it and folded it as neatly as I could, then climbed into the truck. "Well," I said. "That did not go as I had envisioned it."

"It went better than I thought it would," Harper admitted.

"That's what I mean. I thought we'd get laughed at for thinking there was a wendigo hunting people. Instead we get welcomed. Maybe not by your uncle, but your grandmother was more than accommodating."

"Not to mention that she used to be a Chapter member. I can't believe she kept that secret!"

We hit the rough part of the dirt path leading to the village and talking became impractical for the next slow mile. It gave me time to think, but my mind seemed content to run in circles.

When we got to the highway, I was no closer to figuring out a next course of action.

The ride smoothed out and Harper broke the silence. "I've seen clothing like that coat before."

"Yeah?" I unfolded it a bit so I could see the branding on the inside and ran my fingers over my initials. "You mentioned it was for protection?"

"That's a guess. I… am not as fluent in my pictogram translations as I should be, but I recognized warding patterns."

"I'll admit, I've never seen branding done like this in Native American art. Not that it means anything. I'm largely ignorant of the culture if it doesn't have to do with the fae."

"A lot of the animals depicted in totem poles or in art are requests for the attention of spirits. The raccoon in the center of the coat is a call on Azeban, asking him to protect you."

I felt a chill crawl up my spine. The fae weren't called upon lightly. The best you could hope for is they wouldn't respond, particularly any manifestation of trickster spirits. "If that's true, then this coat is dangerous to wear."

"I certainly wouldn't wear it clubbing," Harper shook her head seriously. "Azeban doesn't look favorably upon substance abuse. I mean, look what he did to Amasec for eating too much sugar."

"No kidding. Do the pictograms say anything else?"

"I'd have to look at them more closely. I didn't have a chance to examine it."

"Maybe when we get back to my room."

Harper sighed. "Speaking of that… I think I ought to sleep in my own bed tonight."

I glanced at her and saw she had a pensive frown on her face. "Certainly, if that's what you want. I've no claim on you. Though I have to ask if I did something I need to apologize for."

She shook her head and gave an exasperated huff. "No, nothing like that. You're fine, though you could use a bit more discretion. I like a sneaky feel as much as the next girl, but Nokemes was *right* there!"

"Aw, I mean, she's blind. I bet she never realized."

"Did you see her stitch together a coat for you or not? She knew who you were before you introduced yourself. Does that sound like a woman who is fully reliant on her sight to experience her surroundings?"

I pursed my lips. "All right. You may have a point."

"But it's not even that. She probably got a vicarious kick out of it. It's just that we're… it's all moving too fast, Ryan. Part of me wants to pull over at the next passing turnout and fuck your brains out."

"I mean, I'm not much for display sex, but—"

"*But*," she cut me off, "that part of me always has the worst ideas. So, I'm going to keep driving. And tonight, I'm sleeping in my bed. Without you in it."

"If that's what you want, I'll respect it."

"Thanks."

"Well, there's still a few hours of daylight left. Before we retire our separate ways, there's time to do some investigation."

"Of course. Do you have any idea what to do next?"

"Honestly, I was hoping you did. Try as I might, I can't think of a way to turn what we learned from Nokemes into an action plan."

"There was something we never followed up on."

"Oh?"

"We know the wendigo takes on the guise of its previous victims in order to lure the next ones. I think if we look, we can find connections between the missing people. We might be able to make an educated guess at which person it's currently impersonating."

"Wait, you think it's taken over its victim's life entirely? And is just hiding in plain sight?"

"In the story, Amasec forgot who he was. It would follow that wendigo was the same way. Without a sense of self, I think it would hang onto an identity that it felt was still safe."

I grimaced. The implications of that were unsettling. "So, it could be Sylvia? After eating Sherry, it could have just been waiting and watching from plain sight?"

"Maybe?" Harper shook her head. "It doesn't sound right, though. Henry was the last one to go missing. Henry was staying at home, so it would be a stretch if Sylvia went all the way out to the Davis homestead to target him."

"No, you're right." I let out a sigh of relief and gave Harper a weak smile. It was bad enough knowing that the wendigo knew I was staying at the bed and breakfast. I didn't like thinking it was feeding me breakfast every morning as well. "Okay, Henry was the last to go missing, and Owen before him. If Henry never left the homestead, odds are, someone in the Davis household is the wendigo."

Harper muttered a curse. "Liam?"

I thought back to our interactions and reluctantly shook my head. "No. I felt his strength when I pushed him. He's still human."

"That leaves Tammy and her parents. Do you think Tammy is the wendigo?"

"You know her better than I do. Did she seem like she was acting out of character?"

Harper thought for a minute before sighing. "I don't think so? Two of her brothers have gone missing in the last week. I don't know how she *should* act in a situation like that. Would you still be acting normal?"

"No, I suppose not. She seemed scared and worried to me

when we spoke with her. My gut tells me it isn't her, but we can't rule her out yet."

"Mrs. Davis, then?"

"Huh." I replayed back what had happened at the Davis homestead. "She was unpleasant, but from what you said, that wasn't out of character for her."

"I was more thinking about how she was out of breath and hiding behind her car after we came out of the woods," Harper said darkly.

"Holy shit. It was the wendigo we were chasing through the woods, and then it changed into Mrs. Davis once it reached the road!" I smacked my hand into my forehead. We had been so close to the monster. If only we had known what we were looking for at the time.

"Then we know where we're going," Harper said. "To the Davis homestead."

I heard the truck engine pick up an octave as she pressed the gas pedal down. "We still don't have a plan on how to confront it," I objected.

"Doesn't matter. If we can scare it away, maybe we can prevent it from killing Tammy. It already got Owen and Henry. I won't let it kill Tammy too." There was a fixed glare on Harper's face and her hands were tight on the wheel.

"So, we scare it off, then what? It changes back into Cathy Holsten and makes a house call somewhere else in Kingfield? How many pregnant women are there in town? What if it goes back and kills Lisa? We could lose the trail for days before it kills again."

Harper slammed her hand against the steering wheel. "Damn it, Ryan! We have to do something! You said it's vulnerable to iron. I know a gunsmith who can make me solid steel reloads for my rifle. Let's see how it likes a half-inch of steel punched through it."

"You're angry," I said.

"You're God-damned right I'm angry!"

"Okay," I said, keeping my voice mild, "but shouting at me isn't going to help anyone. And simply scaring off the wendigo won't be enough. I want to save Tammy too, but I won't endanger countless others to do so."

"All right, mister big shot Chapter hunter with all the answers. What do we do?"

"Rather than driving off the wendigo, what if we got ahold of Tammy and snuck her away from the homestead? She could spend the night with you."

The fury slowly drained away from Harper and her furrowed brow softened into a thoughtful expression. "It won't be easy, and we'll need a good excuse to get her to leave. Mrs. Davis is nothing if not controlling."

"Okay, how hard could it be? We've got an hour to come up with an excuse. Can we call her now and tell her to get ready?" I reached for my phone, and Harper shook her head.

"Don't bother. You won't have a connection out here."

I finished the motion and checked my phone. I'd hardly used my phone except for as a flashlight the last couple days. Harper was right. I had no bars. I held it up anyway, trying to find a signal. Harper snorted a laugh.

"I was serious about not bothering, Ryan. There aren't any cell towers out here. Depending on your carrier, you won't find much of a signal in Kingfield either."

"No cell signal?" I suddenly remembered the notes Sylvia had handed me. I muttered a curse and reached into my jacket pocket. The notes had been through the washing machine and the envelopes were little more than nuggets of paper mâché stuck to each other. "Shit!"

"What is that?"

"Probably Baptiste trying to get in contact with me. I'll have to give him a call from a landline and find out what he wants."

"You seriously didn't notice you had no signal?"

"I've been focused on the monster," I grumbled.

She shook her head and smirked. "Once we get closer to town, we can try and get ahold of Tammy with my phone. The reception is spotty, though."

"All right. That's the plan, then."

We lapsed back into silence. I was trying to not take Harper's rejection of my nighttime company personally. I thought we had been hitting it off rather well, and I know she had been satisfied with the sex. I wondered if her change of attitude had been from what her grandmother had told her.

The ride back to Kingfield dragged on. Without being able to look forward to another night spent with Harper, the business of eliminating the wendigo moved up to the forefront of my thoughts.

I was surprised to find myself impatient. I just wanted to finish with this backwoods shithole and return to civilization. Some place where I could get a meal without having to suffer dirty looks. A proper hotel room rather than a bed and breakfast. A city with more than one attractive, available woman in it.

I sighed. Damn my standards were low right now.

"Everything okay?" Harper asked. "You've been quiet."

"Just thinking ahead," I shrugged. "Looking forward to finishing this job."

"Can't wait to get out of Kingfield, huh?"

I glanced at her. "Present company excluded, there's not a lot to like here."

"Do you really dislike it in Kingfield that much? It's beautiful here."

"Trees are nice. I won't deny that. But I can go somewhere that's not in the middle of nowhere and find trees too."

She frowned, but before she could follow up, I was rescued from the conversation by her phone chiming. "Hold that thought," she said, and pulled her phone from her pocket. "Voice mail," she reported.

Harper put the phone to her ear and listened, and the color drained out of her face. Without commenting, she replayed the message and put it on speaker.

"Harper, it's Tammy!" The girl's voice was tight with panic. "My mom has disappeared! Please, call me back. I don't know what to do. Dad's just staring at the TV and not saying anything. Liam got in his truck and is driving around the town looking for her vehicle. Please, please don't be missing too, Harper..." Tammy trailed off and the message ended.

"Well, shit," I said.

"I'm calling her back," Harper said. She hit redial and waited with her phone held up against the steering wheel so she could see the screen and drive at the same time. After a wait of several seconds, her phone dropped the call with a despondent beep.

"No signal," I sighed.

"Damn it," Harper growled. "We're going straight to the Davis homestead. It doesn't matter anymore. Mrs. Davis is gone. Maybe she wasn't the wendigo after all."

"Or maybe she was, and the monster has switched to someone else in the household in order to bait us in. Like Mr. Davis. Or it could have killed Tammy and taken her place."

"No. I won't believe that."

I shrugged. "Well, you're the one who's driving."

"How can you be so callous?" she demanded angrily. "Do these people mean nothing to you?"

"You know they do. That's why I'm here. If I didn't care, I'd get a job where I'm not putting my life in constant danger.

Get a gig being a bodyguard for some movie star and spend my days hanging out in a mansion. Or something."

"A mansion?" Harper asked dubiously, her anger fading as quickly as it had come.

"I don't know. Something. That was just the first thing that came to my head, okay?"

"I think you would get bored being a bodyguard."

"Yeah, well, I haven't put a lot of thought into alternate career paths, okay? I do this job because I can't imagine doing anything else."

There was a truck approaching us on the highway, notable in that it was the only other car we've seen on the road all day. I turned my head as I was speaking, following the truck idly as it passed us, and sudden recognition hit me.

"That's Liam!"

Harper did a double take, then looked into the rearview mirror. "He's driving Mrs. Davis's truck."

I leaned over so I could look out the side mirror. The brake lights came on and the truck screeched to a halt in the middle of the road.

"Harper…" I warned.

"I see it." She stepped harder on the gas, but she was already pushing her old truck near its limits. The engine got louder, but the speedometer didn't move much.

Liam did a three-point turn behind us. He was nearly out of sight around a bend in the road when he got turned around. For a minute afterward, I couldn't see Liam. I twisted around in my seat and watched behind us. We reached a straight part of the road, and before it started to bend again, I saw Liam again.

"He's gaining on us," I called out.

"Maybe he just came out to search for us because his mom went missing," Harper said.

I didn't bother refuting it. By the tone of her voice, even

Harper didn't believe that. Over the next minute, Liam closed the distance to us until he was riding on our bumper. Through his dirty windshield, his face seemed set and emotionless.

"The hell does he want?" Harper muttered. She kept glancing out the rearview mirror, paying more attention to him than the road in front of her.

"I don't know. Roll your window down." I pulled out my handgun and checked the chamber, verifying it was loaded and ready to shoot, then I moved the gun down out of sight. "He's not trying to run us off the road," I said. "Not yet, at least."

As if Liam could hear me, as soon as I finished talking his engine revved and he swerved out into the oncoming lane. He pulled up alongside us and I shifted in my seat, giving myself room to pull my gun up and shoot if I had to.

"Stay leaning back," I warned Harper. She glanced at me, her eyes wide, and nodded.

For a few seconds, Liam stared straight ahead, then he turned and stared directly at me, his teeth bared in a rictus that had no humor in it. I was a heartbeat from lifting my gun and shooting him, but I couldn't. Having a creepy smile wasn't enough for a death sentence, no matter how much of an asshole the guy was. Until I was certain it was the wendigo I was aiming at, I couldn't pull the trigger.

Then Liam floored his truck and it surged ahead of us. He pulled over into the right lane and in a minute, was gone down the road ahead.

"Okay, that was fucking creepy," Harper said.

"I'm guessing Liam doesn't smile like that normally?"

"You're damn right." She swallowed. "He's the wendigo now?"

"If I was sure, I would have shot him," I said grimly. I flicked the safety back on and holstered my gun. "But let's say he's suspect number one."

Harper sighed. "Of course, now that he's out of sight, the wendigo could turn back into any of its earlier victims. Fuck. So, Liam is dead?"

"It would seem so."

"We've got to get Tammy out of that house."

"No argument here. How's your cell service?"

She checked her phone and her face brightened. "We're getting close to Kingfield. I've got a bar." Her smile flickered and went out. "And it's gone. I'll check again on the next rise."

Harper kept her phone in her hand as she drove and glanced down at the screen every few seconds. The road followed the valleys in the rolling hills, but the surveyors tried to keep it going in as straight a line as possible. The next rise came a minute later, and Harper slowed a little as we neared the crest.

"There! Got a bar." She hit dial on her phone and crossed her fingers.

I was looking at the phone screen too, and almost didn't see a flicker of something metal catching the afternoon sun. I turned my head, searching for what had caught my eye. Whatever it was, the angle of the sun was different now, and the reflection didn't repeat. It had been in the road, though, and I lifted a hand to shield my eyes against the sun.

Harper's phone started ringing, and almost immediately was picked up. "Harper!" It was Tammy, her voice filled with relief. "Did you get my message?"

I could see something ahead of us, but it looked like a mirage. It had been warm during the day, but not hot enough to make mirages. Or so I thought. I squinted, trying to make out detail. We crested the rise and I suddenly got a better look at the road.

"I got it, Tammy. I'm driving, so I might lose the connection. You've got to get out!"

There was a metal chain lying across the road, pulled taut.

Metal spikes had been welded to the chain, turning it into a homemade STD device.

"Harper!" I shouted, "The road!"

Harper looked forward and gasped. She slammed on the brakes, but it was too late. We ran over the chain, and it was severe tire damage all the way. I heard, and felt, all four tires get blown out. Harper's truck surged like a stallion trying to buck us off. The bare rims of our wheels screeched on the asphalt and Harper wrestled with the wheel, trying to keep us straight.

Then the front left rim caught in the road and we skewed sideways. Instantly, the forward momentum of the truck threw us over on our side, and the truck flipped. I braced one arm against the roof and gritted my teeth as we rolled down the hill going far too fast.

The windshield exploded and the driver-side airbag deployed, enveloping Harper in an abrupt marshmallow. I clenched my eyes shut against the safety glass flying around the cab and tried to brace myself for the inevitable impact.

Harper screamed, but there wasn't anything I could do for her. I opened my eyes just in time to see a flash of green, then we slammed into a tree. Wood splintered, and metal shrieked and tore. I was slammed forward and felt the seatbelt lock around my shoulders. Pain exploded across my chest where the belt brought my momentum to a sudden halt.

We had stopped. I opened my eyes fully, but felt dizzy and disoriented. The seatbelt had knocked the wind out of me.

"Harper," I gasped. I pushed the deflating airbag out of the way and saw Harper was slumped against the driver side door, her eyes closed. My perspective swung around and I realized the truck was on its side and I was dangling from my seatbelt.

I struggled with the belt for a moment, trying to get the buckle to release. Then it popped free and I almost fell on top of Harper. I caught myself on the side of her seat and the steering wheel, and leaned down to press my outstretched hand against her throat.

It took me a moment to calm down enough, but I felt her pulse under my fingers. I let out a sigh of relief. She wasn't dead, just knocked out. I got her seatbelt undone and pulled her awkwardly into a sitting position. The hole where the windshield had been was blocked by a tangle of smashed branches. Above me, my door had been crumpled by the crash and was jammed shut. The passenger window offered the only escape.

"Come on, Harper!" I growled and tapped her on the cheek. "We need to move!"

She stayed unresponsive. I swore under my breath and climbed up the seats to stick my head out of the window. I scanned the area, but couldn't see anyone immediately visible. We had tumbled several hundred yards from where the chain had stripped our tires off. If our attackers had been at the chain, it would take them a few minutes to reach us on foot. Less if they had a vehicle handy.

I ducked back down into the truck. I could only hope that Harper didn't have a neck injury, but leaving her in the truck wasn't an option. The truck was likely to catch on fire after a tumbling crash like that, and whoever had set the trap wasn't coming to invite us over to dinner tonight.

I caught her under the arms and hauled her upright. She was limp in my arms, and heavier than I would have thought. Blood smeared the side of her head, but it didn't seem to be bleeding too badly for a scalp wound. I hiked her up and got my knee between her legs to help support her weight, then pushed her head and shoulders up through the window overhead.

It was awkward, and I probably gave her a couple extra bruises in the process, but I got her out of the window and lying across the side of the truck. I climbed out after her and swung her up into a one-armed fireman carry. Then, moving as fast as I could, I climbed down the side of the truck to the ground. I found a spot free of broken branches and put her down, then ran back to the truck.

There were a few things I wasn't going to leave behind. I grabbed Harper's rifle from the rack behind the seats, my pack, and my gifted leather coat, and climbed back out of the truck. Acrid smoke was starting to billow from under the hood and I coughed as a plume wafted over me.

An engine roared to life up the hill and I saw a truck pull out onto the road from where it had been hidden behind some trees. It was the truck that Liam had been driving when he had shot at us the day before, but even at a distance I could tell it wasn't Liam behind the wheel.

I tossed the coat down off the side of the truck and checked over Harper's rifle. It seemed undamaged from our crash. I worked the lever and saw a round get fed into the breech. It was a big cartridge, like half a carrot in size, and I remembered Harper's comment about it being chambered for bear rounds.

Well, I wasn't about to let these assholes chase us down in their truck. If they wanted us, they could catch us on foot. I lifted the rifle to my shoulder and lined up the iron sights on the front grill of the truck. I pulled the trigger and was deafened by the roar of the rifle. The stock punched me in the shoulder and almost knocked me off balance. I had been expecting a big kick, but that was absurd.

Sparks erupted from the front of the truck and it immediately lost power. Smoke started boiling out from under the hood and the distant whoops turned into furious cries. I grinned, scooped up my coat, and dropped down to the ground.

Harper was sitting up, looking at me with a dazed look on her face. "What happened?"

"Oh, thank God. Can you walk?" I bent down and hauled her up to her feet.

She touched the side of her head and winced. Her fingers came away bloody. "I think so? Did we crash?"

"Later. Right now, we need to move. It isn't safe."

Her eyes shifted over my shoulder and widened as she took in the sight of her truck lying on its side. "Holy shit!"

"Yep. I hope you had insurance. Now, come *on!*"

I grabbed her hand and dragged her away from the truck, and deeper into the forest. I didn't know where I was going, but I was damn sure I didn't want to be around when our attackers reached the crash site.

CHAPTER FIFTEEN

"What happened to my truck?"

It was about ten minutes later when I finally let Harper pause to catch her breath. If the kids from the truck were chasing us through the woods, they were being too quiet for me to hear. Unless they had a dog that knew how to track with them, I was fairly certain we were safe for the moment.

"How much do you remember?"

"I... was on the phone. I think? We were trying to get ahold of Tammy."

I nodded and leaned against a pine tree to catch my breath. Short term memory loss like that wasn't uncommon after a hit to the head. At least it was only a few seconds worth of lost time. "Liam and his friends stretched a spiked chain across the road. Blew out all our tires. I shot out their engine when they started chasing after us."

"I heard the shot. It's what woke me up." Harper swiped at the blood still oozing from her head with her sleeve, and grimaced at the clotted mess that came away on her clothes.

"Hold on, let me help you with that."

I took off my jacket and stripped out of my shirt. I folded the torso into a thick pad and used the sleeves to tie the whole thing around her head. I adjusted it so it kept her vision as clear as possible, then tightened the knot hard so it wouldn't slip.

"Ack," Harper said.

"Sorry. Too tight?"

"Nah, you just caught a hair. No, leave it, the damage is done now. Thanks." She patted around her pockets then sighed. "I don't suppose you grabbed my phone?"

"There wasn't time," I shook my head. "We could go back and ask them nicely if they found it."

She gave me a flat look. "You're not as funny as you think you are."

I shrugged. "I was more concerned with saving your life. Next time, I'll grab the phone too."

"That would be nice, thanks. At least you didn't forget my gun."

She reached for it and I handed it to her. "How are you feeling? Dizzy at all? Trouble focusing your vision?"

"Just a headache. I don't think I got a concussion."

"Good." I straightened up and squinted up toward the sky. "I know you've warned me about running into the woods, but it was the only thing I could think to do under the circumstances. I don't suppose you know where we are?"

Harper looked around herself then shook her head. "I've never been in this part of the forest before. But that's not that bad. I know where we went off the road. All we have to do is go south and we'll hit a stream before too long. Then we follow it east until it brings us back to the highway. So long as we don't crest a hill going west, we'll be back on the road in an hour."

"And, if we did crest a hill?" I tried to think back on the lay of the land. We had been going up and down rolling hills the whole way. The sun barely made it through the thick branches overhead and I couldn't tell north from south. Did we cross a hill going to the west? I couldn't say one way or the other.

"Then we still go south. It will be a longer trek, though. So long as we weren't running due west, we should be okay. And if we were... well, we'll be in the forest until after nightfall."

"Shit." The idea of being lost in the forest at night with a wendigo hunting us was not enticing. I handed Harper my jacket. "Put this on."

"You're going to go shirtless?" she asked dubiously.

"No, I'm wearing the leather coat. I'd offer it to you, but it'd drag on the ground if you wore it."

"You're probably right." She put my jacket on and zipped it up. It looked enormous on her and the sleeves went six inches past the tips of her fingers. She had to roll the cuffs up, and the bottom of the jacket came down to mid-thigh.

"Looks good on you," I grinned.

"Yeah, right."

I put my leather jacket on. The branded leather felt rough against my skin. If I started sweating, it felt like it might chafe. Still, it would be better than getting scratched to hell by all the low branches. I knelt by my pack and pulled my folded-up rifle from within it. It snapped it open and socketed in a full magazine. I shrugged into the single-point harness and got the rifle hanging from it properly.

"All right. I'm all set. Which way is south?"

Harper pointed, off to the left of the direction we had been traveling.

"Are you sure?"

She shrugged. "Unless I can get a clear look at the sky, no. If we start going uphill too much, we should swing left. It doesn't really matter. So long as we don't start going in circles, we'll find a road or a stream eventually."

"Okay. You're the one who knows this land best. You take point."

"Right. Stay close."

Harper set out, walking quickly and easily. I kept an eye on her for a while to make sure her head injury wasn't going to become a problem, but I needn't have bothered. Her footing was surer than mine, and pretty quickly I had to focus on keeping up with her.

After nearly an hour of hiking, I was hot and sweaty. Every inch of skin that was exposed was covered in scratches from tree branches. Despite the weight of the leather coat, I was thankful for the protection it offered. In front of me, Harper's footsteps were starting to slow, and I could tell she was getting tired from carrying the heavy rifle.

"Harper, I don't know about you, but I could use a break."

She paused to balance against a tree and looked back at me. There were circles forming under her eyes and she looked drained. "It can't be that much longer. There should be a stream just up ahead."

"I've got iodine tablets and a canteen in my pack. If we can find water, I can make us some electrolytes to drink. It's not Gatorade, but it'll keep us moving."

Harper swallowed. "That sounds amazing. I think I might be in love with you, Ryan."

I grinned. "I won't hold you to that. One step at a time. Let's find the water first, then we can talk about how many kids we want."

She laughed and set off again with a fresh spring in her step. "I was resigned to just drinking straight from the stream and rolling the dice with dysentery."

"Take my word for it, that is a gamble you'll only want to make once."

"And thus, the emergency pack with tablets." She glanced

back at me. "I forget how old you are sometimes. You look like you're my age, or a few years older."

I shrugged. "I guess."

"Can I ask you a question?"

"I don't see why not."

"Why did you leave the army?"

"My four years was up."

"What rank were you?"

"Look, if it's all the same to you, I'd rather not talk about the army. I signed up, did some shit, and left."

"Sorry."

"It's okay. I did say you could ask a question."

"I was just curious. Most guys who come back can't stop talking about their time in the service, but you haven't said more than ten words about it."

I shook my head. "Most of the people who like to brag barely left the barracks, and when they did, they just sweated it out in their Kevlar while tucked into the backseat of a Humvee, and were scared the whole time."

"That sounds like personal experience."

"Let's just say it wasn't like what they show you in the brochure."

"Then, what did—" she cut herself off and froze, listening intently. "I hear water!"

She broke into a run and I followed after her, holding my free arm in front of my face so I didn't lose an eye from a branch. A minute later, we came out onto the bank of a chuckling stream. There was a gap in the canopy overhead and we were able to see the open sky for the first time since going off the road. It was getting to be late in the afternoon, and we had maybe an hour of good sunlight left.

The stream was a little too wide to jump across without a stepping stone, and looked clean and clear. I swung my pack off and got out the canteen. Harper hovered over my shoulder as I filled it from a deep spot, then dropped in an iodine tablet.

"Five minutes," Harper read off the packet. She sighed and slumped down to sit on the bank. "This day sucks."

"Let's take a look at your head," I suggested.

She gave me a tired look, but didn't protest as I squatted down next to her. She looked like a child, bundled up in my jacket with the sleeves rolled up. I checked under the folded-up pad of my shirt and found all the blood had dried. Her hair was glued to the fabric of the shirt, and she winced.

"We're going to have to get it wet to get it off." I gave the canteen a shake and unscrewed the lid. The iodine hadn't had time to dissolve into the water fully and it stank. Still, it was better than using raw stream water.

I splashed water onto the pad and into her hair, then added more until it started dripping down the side of her face. Harper gave me a miserable look, but didn't move.

"Sorry." I used the end of the sleeve tied around her head to wipe at the overflow. "How's the head?"

"Feels like I was in a car accident. I don't suppose you have any painkillers in that magic pack of yours."

"Oh. Yeah, I do. I wish you had asked earlier. Let's wait for the water to finish, and I'll give you a few."

"Thanks," she said, and gave me a weak smile.

We sat quietly and watched the water until the five minutes were up. I added a packet of electrolytes to the water and handed it over to Harper along with a few tabs of ibuprofen from a blister pack. She drank thirstily, then returned the canteen to me.

I gave it a little shake. She had drained over half the canteen. I took a pull, then handed it back for her to finish.

"Are you sure?"

"I'll make another batch. You need it more than I do."

She nodded gratefully and finished the rest of the canteen. I got up to refill it and added another iodine tablet.

"Let's test that pad again."

Harper tilted her head toward me and I checked under the pad. The water had softened the blood again, and I was able to get the pad lifted free with only a few hairs getting stuck. I balled my shirt up and stuffed it away in my pack.

"It doesn't look bad," I assured her. "Just a small split. Won't even need stitches." '

"That's good."

"So, what do we do now? Head downstream?"

"Yeah. Not too close. We don't want to have to fight the underbrush. As long as we stay close enough to hear it, we're close enough for it to guide us."

"Okay. Are you ready to keep moving, or do you want more of a break?"

"Better to keep moving. If I wait any longer my muscles are going to stiffen up."

"Sounds like a plan." I got up and offered Harper my hand.

I hauled her upright and we gave each other a sober look.

"Things are going sideways, aren't they?" she asked quietly.

"The wendigo is playing us against each other. It has Liam now, and with it his little gang. Tell me the truth. How bad was it between you and those boys before I came to town?"

"What do you mean?" She turned away and started walking, heading up the bank a bit away from the stream before turning to follow it.

"I might have stirred the hornet nest, but it takes time to weld up an STD chain like that. Dozens of hours of work. And normal people don't have plans in place to string spiked chains across highways. Who are these kids, really?"

Harper walked in silence for a minute before responding. "They never had any personal beef with me, specifically. But you're right, they are a gang. We never had any proof of it, and they always acted in the large cities a few hours away. Small time robberies, for the most part, though the police suspected they were working up to something larger."

"What were they going to do with the STD chain? Hold up an armored car?"

"I have no idea, honestly."

"Well, we've got all the evidence we need now to put the whole group away in prison for years. Attempted homicide, at the very least."

"Will that work to contain the wendigo?"

I laughed ruefully. "Not at all. Could you even imagine what it would do to a prison population? Besides, it would never allow itself to be caught. The moment Liam's appearance is pulling too much attention, it'll abandon the likeness and find another victim."

She sighed. "I'm beginning to really hate this wendigo."

"It's looking rough at the moment, but we've got it on the run, now. It's desperate. It'll start making mistakes."

"Mistakes like attacking us in broad daylight and totaling my fucking truck," Harper grumbled. "I've got insurance, but my truck was old and the payout is barely going to break four figures. A reliable replacement is going to cost ten times that amount! I'm going to be in debt for years trying to pay off a car loan on my salary."

"Ah. Yeah, that sucks. I'm sorry about that."

"Nothing that can be done about it now. I'll figure it out. I always do."

We lapsed into silence after that and concentrated on hiking. This close to the stream, the underbrush was lush and thick, with more vines and brush underfoot than before. The break hadn't been a long one, but I found my muscles had stiffened. I ached from head to foot. Now that the adrenaline had time to settle out of my system, my body was letting me know it disapproved of the rough treatment.

Harper was feeling it too. She was putting on a tough façade, but I could see the way she favored her right side. She was limping a little, and every few dozen paces she paused and braced herself against a tree for a moment.

I didn't want to keep pushing Harper, but there wasn't anything else we could do except get out of the forest. If we took a break long enough to make a difference, darkness would be on us, and our task of getting out of the forest would be monumentally more difficult.

The effort of putting one foot in front of the other had a hypnotic, lulling rhythm to it. That, combined with the shell-shocked state I was in, put me into a semi-conscious state. I stirred out of it when we crossed over a small stream that ran off to merge with the larger one we were following, then fell back into it immediately afterward.

At some point during our interminable march, the sun finally began to set. The gloom thickened until I could hardly see my hand in front of my face. Above us, the tops of the trees still caught the last rays of the sun, but none of that light managed to make it down to the forest floor.

Ahead of me, Harper muttered a curse and stopped. "I can't see a thing. Just got poked in the eye from a branch."

"Here." I unclipped the flashlight from my rifle and turned it on. The red-filtered light turned the green forest into muted blacks and reds, but we could see.

Harper took the flashlight from me with a muttered thanks and kept pressing forward. She had no enthusiasm left, just raw determination to finish this forced march and get to the road.

I always believed you find the true worth in a person by the way they reacted during a crisis. It wasn't until all the chips were down and you were staring peril in the face that you truly found out who you were. Most women I knew would have broken down a long time ago. Hell, most would have been hysterical after the accident.

Besides a bitter complaint about losing her only vehicle, Harper hadn't let a single negative word slip from her lips. She hadn't protested the necessity of the march, hadn't whined about having a headache or being in pain from the car accident. She was putting up with the rigors of the day better than most of the soldiers in my squad would have.

Any doubt that she would be fit to join the Chapter was gone in my mind. I could already imagine working with her and training her how to fight the fae.

"Oh, thank God."

I blinked out of my thoughts and looked around. Ahead of Harper, the forest abruptly opened up. It took me several seconds to process the fact that we had finally made it to the highway. Harper staggard forward, laughing out loud.

"Wait, Harper!"

She turned to look back at me, giddy relief on her face. "What?"

"Maybe we should stay under cover. At least until we're closer to town."

The happiness on her face dried up and she glanced up the road to the north toward where the accident had happened. She clicked off the flashlight and sighed. "Yeah, you're right."

"If we see a car coming that is definitely not Liam or his friends then we can flag them down, but until then, we stay out of sight."

She grimaced. "This late at night? That's not likely."

"We can always hope. How much farther is it to town?"

"An hour? Hour and a half, maybe?"

"The moon is full. That will help us walk, but also make us

more visible. You watch down the road to the south, and I'll keep an eye behind us."

"Okay. What am I looking for?"

"Any movement. Don't wait to identify what it is, the moment you see anything move, we take cover."

She swallowed and nodded.

"We'll be okay. We're almost to safety. It's just a little bit longer. First house we see, we go and ask for a ride in to town."

Harper took a deep breath and gave me a single nod. "All right."

"You're doing great, Harper. I'm proud of you."

She flashed me a smile and turned southward to start walking. We walked in the weeds in the ditch, with the trees brushing our right shoulders. I kept my head on a swivel, looking behind us as much as I could, and only glancing forward long enough to avoid branches that stuck out into the ditch.

The heavy rain from the day before had mostly dried up, but there were low parts of the ditch that were still marshy. The mud clung to our boots, weighing down every step we took. The sun finally dropped beyond the horizon and darkness plunged down on us. I didn't dare use the flashlight. Even with the red filter, it would be visible for a long way.

Fortunately, the sky was clear of clouds, and the starlight was enough to keep us from tripping over our own feet. Then, half an hour later, the moon rose in the east and flooded the road with its pale light. After straining to see in the starlight, it seemed as bright as day.

A few minutes later, we were in a valley where a stream passed under the road through a series of culverts. We were about thirty yards from the culverts when I heard Harper suck in a breath. I immediately ducked into the gap between a pair of pines and dropped to the ground. She joined me a moment later, and together we lay in the prickly grass and dried pine needles, barely daring to breathe.

From where we were lying, I couldn't see down to the culvert. Whatever had spooked Harper wasn't in sight. When she looked at me, I shook my head and touched a finger to my lips. She nodded and went still.

If Harper had seen a deer or something, she would have said something. I told myself that, and I waited. My rifle was partially under me, but I didn't want to shift my weight to clear it. It was a stupid mistake to make, and it dug at me as the minutes dragged by. If I had cleared the rifle immediately after lying down, I would've had plenty of time.

I counted my heartbeats and controlled my breathing so it was slow and deep. Then, with nothing else to do, I rehearsed in my mind the exact motions needed to get the rifle up into firing position. I was fairly confident I could get something in my sights in less than a second if I had to. For most things, that was fast enough, but the wendigo was supposed to be wickedly fast and strong.

I was still going back and forth on whether it would be worth the risk to clear my rifle when movement caught my eye. A figure came loping up the road, moving in an odd, hunched over run. Every few paces, it ran on all fours before pushing back up into a bipedal lope.

The wendigo had discarded its stolen appearance. It was naked, emaciated, its limbs shrunken and skeletal. There was zero fat left on its body, and I could see every surge of muscle, every strain of tendon, as it ran. It was bald, its eyes sunken and dark in its gaunt face.

There was a rustle of pine needles next to me and I glanced over to see Harper slowly bringing her rifle around to aim at it. I gave her a wide-eyed look and shook my head just the tiniest amount. I could see the protest in her eyes, but she relented and let the barrel of the rifle settle back into the pine needles.

The wendigo jerked to a halt and straightened up. Its head swiveled about, the pits of its eye sockets shadowed by its heavy brow, making them look like they were empty. Abruptly its flesh filled out and clothes appeared out of nowhere to drape over it.

Liam Davis stood in the road, scanning along the solid wall of trees, squinting in the moonlight. I froze and held my breath, cursing the uncertainty that had left my rifle pinned under me. For a long moment, the wendigo stared in our direction, then it turned away. The flesh melted from it until it was skeletal once more. The clothes shriveled up, turned into wisps of smoke, and were gone.

It dropped to all fours and continued its rapid lope to the north. I waited until it was gone from sight, then counted to a slow hundred. Then counted back down to zero again to be sure. Only then did I creep forward one slow inch at a time until I could see up the road.

The wendigo was gone.

I let out a sigh of relief and gestured the all clear to Harper. She stood and brushed the pine needles from the front of my jacket.

"Why did you stop me?" she whispered. "I had the shot."

"Did you? It was a hundred feet away, in uncertain lighting. The moment you worked the lever on your rifle, it would have heard it. You would have had time for one shot, then it would have been on us. Or worse, it would have run. And then it would have stalked us through the dark forest and struck when we were distracted."

"I could have made the shot," she said doggedly.

"Maybe," I sighed. If I'd had my rifle in the right position, would I have tried for it? I thought back to the speed it had reacted to the slightest crunch of pine needles under Harper's rifle, and I wasn't sure. I rubbed the back of my neck. I couldn't trust my own judgement right now. I was exhausted and in pain, and Harper must be feeling the same way. The thought of killing the wendigo and ending this whole cat-and-mouse game was like a drug. "I don't know, Harper. You might be right. Still, I would have made the same call again."

"Damn it," Harper swore bitterly.

"We'll have another chance at it. And next time, we'll make the shot a sure thing."

"And how many people will it kill before that chance comes?"

"Harper…" I didn't have an answer for her.

She read it in my face and turned away. "That's what I thought. I think I know where we are, now. Come on. There's a house just over the next rise."

CHAPTER SIXTEEN

Harper gave the elderly gentleman who had given us a ride a wave goodbye and turned to walk up the short set of brick steps to her front door. I hitched my pack up onto my shoulder and followed. Harper hadn't been interested in conversation since I had stopped her from shooting the wendigo, and she ignored me as we walked to her door.

She stopped at the door and reached for her pocket before aborting the motion. "Fuck!" She bit back further expletives and her shoulders slumped.

"What?"

"My keys are in my truck." She turned around to sit down on her doorstep and buried her face in her hands.

It hurt to see her indomitable spirit finally start to crack. "Maybe we can go around to the back door?"

"No, I locked all the doors and all the windows the last time I left. And don't you dare go breaking any of my windows!"

"I wasn't…" I pressed my lips together and let out a sharp sigh through my nose. She was hungry, tired, in pain, and physically exhausted. I reminded myself of these things and did my best not to snap back at her. "Okay. I'm just trying to help, Harper."

"Yeah? Maybe I'm done with your help. You ever think of that?" She lifted her head up and glared at me, her eyes swimming with tears.

There was a scuff on the other side of the door, then a rattle of the lock disengaging. Harper turned her head, scrubbing the rolled-up sleeves of my jacket across her eyes. The door swung open and Tammy Davis stood in the opening, clutching an aluminum baseball bat in a white-knuckled grip.

"Harper?" Tammy said, her voice shaking.

Harper scrambled to her feet. "Tammy! What are you doing in my house? I mean, I'm glad you're safe, but how did you get in?"

The girl held up a key. "I found it in Owen's things. I was going to return it… I just, I forgot when you were over last time."

Harper made a sound that was half-laugh, half-sob, and wrapped Tammy up in a hug. "It's fine. I'm so happy to see you!"

The two of them moved deeper into the house and I followed behind, making sure to lock the door behind us. It wouldn't stop the wendigo, but if it had to break a window to get inside, it might give us time to react. I reached into my coat and drew out my handgun.

"Harper, let go of her."

Harper looked over at me and her eyes went wide as she saw the barrel of my gun leveled at Tammy. "Ryan? What the hell are you doing?"

"Step away from Tammy," I said grimly.

She released Tammy from her hug, but then grabbed the girl's arm and pulled Tammy behind herself. "This is too far, Ryan! Put the gun away!"

"No." I thumbed back the hammer. "Move."

"I won't let you shoot her!"

"I'm not going to shoot Tammy," I said, starting to get angry. "But how do you know that's Tammy?"

Harper glanced over her shoulder at Tammy, then back to me. "She's not the wendigo!"

"How do you know? Now, *step aside!*"

"You asshole," she hissed, but she moved out of the way.

"Harper?" Tammy whispered. Her voice was tight and high with fear.

"Sorry, kid," I said. "I'll explain everything in a second. But first, walk over to the coffee table."

I kept my gun centered on Tammy's chest and followed after her, keeping my distance. Tammy walked into the living room and stopped next to the coffee table. It was made of hand-forged cast iron rods, hammered into whimsical curlicues and topped with a heavy piece of tempered glass.

"Thank you. Now reach down and grab the iron."

Trembling, Tammy did. As soon as her hand touched the iron I pulled my gun up and let out a sigh. "Shit. Sorry, Tammy. I had to make certain."

Tammy ran over to Harper and buried her face against Harper's shoulder, sobbing quietly. Harper wrapped her arms around Tammy and glared at me. I gave Harper a helpless shrug and put my gun away.

"Was that necessary?" Harper demanded.

"You know the answer to that yourself," I retorted. "Unless I've gravely misestimated you."

"What's going on, Harper?" Tammy asked. She threw a glance over her shoulder at me, confusion and fear swirling across her face. "Why did I have to touch the table?"

"Maybe we should all get something to eat," I said, and

made calming motions with my hands. "This is going to be a lot easier on a full stomach."

"I'm not hungry," Tammy muttered.

"Maybe not, but Harper and I haven't eaten since lunch, and we spent most of the day hiking through the woods after we got run off the road."

"You got run off the road?" Tammy looked up at Harper in surprise.

Harper gave me an unreadable look, then gave Tammy's shoulder's a squeeze. "We're fine. A little shaken up, but not badly injured. Ryan might be an ass, but he's right. I'm starving. You want some ice cream? I think I've got some in the freezer."

Tammy nodded and the two went off into the kitchen. I gave them a minute before following. Harper was busy at the stove cooking something. Oil hissed and the smell of bacon filled the air. My stomach growled.

"That smells good," I said quietly.

"How many eggs do you want?" Harper asked without looking at me.

"Five or six," I said.

Wordlessly, Harper started cracking eggs into a bowl. I walked around the kitchen and drew the curtains. Tammy stood in a corner of the room with a bowl of ice cream, watching me with wide eyes. I gave her a tired smile and went to sit down at the dining table.

"Do you want something to drink, Ryan?" Harper called.

"I have my canteen," I said.

She glanced at me and rolled her eyes. "Don't be ridiculous. I'm not going to let you drink stream water in my house." She grabbed a beer bottle from the fridge, the kind with a flip top. There were homemade labels pasted to the bottles. She set one down on the table next to me, along with a glass, and went back to the stove.

I popped the top on the bottle and poured a rich, brown ale into the glass. There was a layer of yeast on the bottom of the bottle, a sure sign of the beer being from a local microbrewer. It was mellow and full-bodied, and smelled vaguely of caramel and hops. I took a sip and rolled the beer around in my mouth. It had a warm, nutty flavor with a complex, almost fruity undertone.

"Huh. This is good!"

"You like? I brew it myself."

"No shit?" I took another swig. "Why are you a Ranger, again? You could make a killing with this stuff."

"It's just a hobby," she said, and gave me a smile that looked more like the normal Harper. "If I did it all day every day, I would hate it."

"That's fair."

"Can I have a beer?" Tammy asked.

Harper started shaking her head, then shrugged. "Why not. But only if you eat some real food first."

"This is real food," Tammy said, and waved her ice cream spoon at Harper.

"Nice try." Harper forked some bacon out of the pan and set it aside on some paper towels. "Get the bread out of the fridge and make some toast while you wait."

A few minutes later, Harper brought the food to the table and served out portions for all of us. My plate was piled higher than both of the girls' combined. We tucked in, and Harper showed Tammy how to pour the beer without disturbing the sediment.

My plate was empty faster than I thought possible and I sat back with what was left of my beer. "Thank you, Harper. I needed that."

"Sure. You want another beer?"

"Yes, but I better not."

Harper's eyes flicked to the closed curtains and nodded. "I've got a pitcher of cold water in the fridge."

"That would be perfect, thanks."

Harper got up and came back with the pitcher and fresh glasses for everyone. She poured for us, then sat down again. She took a deep breath and let it out. "All right. I guess it's time."

I tossed back the last of my beer and picked up the water. "Go ahead. I'll jump in if you get stuck."

Harper nodded and sighed. "Tammy, your mother is dead."

I winced, but didn't interrupt. Sometimes it's best to just rip the bandage off, hair and all.

Tammy flinched, but nodded. "Okay." There was weary acceptance in the girl's eyes, and a distinct lack of grief. "I think I knew the moment she went out to collect the chicken eggs that she wasn't coming back. What happened to her?"

I cleared my throat and gave a tiny nod when Harper looked at me.

"There's a... monster that is hunting people and eating them," Harper said carefully.

Tammy covered her mouth with her hand and stared at Harper.

"It's called a wendigo. It kills people, then takes their likeness and pretends to be them. The reason Ryan had you touch the table is because it can't stand contact with iron. He wanted to make sure you were still you."

"What?!" Tammy cried out in a choked voice. "That's insane!"

Harper looked to me and I leaned forward. "Let me introduce myself properly, Tammy. I'm Ryan Halsin, descendent of Erik Van Helsing. I'm a hunter for the Chapter, an organization that has hunted monsters since the early sixteen hundreds, first in England and Europe, then in the Americas."

Predictably, she latched onto the only thing that she understood. "Van Helsing was real?"

"Quite. Harper called the Chapter for help when she realized that the people going missing wasn't normal."

"Then, all the people that went missing…"

"Are dead," Harper finished for her and nodded.

"Owen?"

Harper reached across the table and gave Tammy's hand a squeeze. "We found him. I'm sorry, Tammy."

Tears sprang into Tammy's eyes that had been conspicuously missing when she'd learned of her mother's death. "Oh, no. No, no. Henry, too?"

"We haven't found him yet," I said. "We're hoping that Henry ran when he realized your mom was really the monster. That's what we think the note he left meant. It's possible he's still alive and hiding in the woods."

"So, Henry's alive?!"

Harper got up and went to wrap her arms around Tammy from behind. "We're hoping he is."

I met Harper's gaze over Tammy's head and saw the helpless rage in her eyes. "Tammy," I said, "we're doing everything we can to find this thing and destroy it."

"I want to help."

"I know you do, sweetie," Harper said. "But right now, the best thing you can do is be somewhere safe so I don't have to worry about you."

"How is that helping? I'm a good shot, Harper. I can shoot as good as any of the boys. I don't want to just go home and hide in my room!"

"Actually," I said, "your home isn't safe either. We think the wendigo is currently using Liam as its disguise."

"What about my dad? He's all alone, now!"

"We'll figure something out," Harper said.

"In the morning, when it's light out. We'll check to make sure he's still your dad, then the two of you can go to Farmington and get a hotel room for a few days." I held Harper's eyes and the impotent fury faded some. At least we'd be able to save two people.

"Speaking of the morning, I'm exhausted," Harper announced. "Tammy, do you have clothes to sleep in?"

Tammy shook her head. "As soon as you said to get out, I came straight here."

"No worries. You can borrow some of mine. Let's all go upstairs and we can figure out sleeping arrangements."

Harper's bedroom had more lace and doilies than I would have expected. But then, I could tell it was essentially unchanged since when it had been her mother's bedroom. I looked around at the keepsakes that were too old to have belonged to Harper, and wondered what it must have been like to grow up with a stable family and home.

My dad hadn't been a bad parent by any legal definition, but we never had a place to call home. I did my schoolwork in the passenger seat of my dad's '79 Bronco as we drove from one town to the next. I learned how to fight monsters along with my fractions.

The few short months I spent in public school, I couldn't find anything to connect with my classmates over. I was aloof, smelled of gunpowder, and had weird stains on most of my clothes. The girls shunned me and the boys respected my athletic ability, if from a distance.

When I grew older and reached the junior and senior years of high school, that dynamic flipped. I had better clothes, then, and knew how to wash away the various scents of monster hunting before going in to school. The girls saw me as a titillating, dangerous newcomer, and I always had dates. The boys mocked me for refusing to play football, and probably for stealing a few of their girls.

None of the school drama mattered to me, because I knew in a few weeks my dad would be moving on to the next job. Finishing high school was a relief for both of us. My dad didn't have to worry about keeping up appearances any longer, and I was just happy to be done with algebra. We still constantly moved around, and I found my hookups in bars instead of the school cafeteria.

"Ryan."

I looked around, realizing I'd lost track of what was happening around me. Something in Harper's voice told me she had been calling my name for a while. "Sorry. Memories. What's up?"

"I have my old mattress in the other room, if you want to sleep there," she said.

Tammy and Harper were both sitting on the queen-sized bed, which told me they intended on sharing it. "Oh. I was going to sleep in my room. It's just down the road, not more than a five-minute walk."

Harper hugged herself and looked uncertain. "What about staying together?"

I shrugged. "I don't want to impose."

"Don't be an idiot," Harper said. "We might have a disagreement, but that's hardly enough for me to send you out to walk to Sylvia's alone, in the dark. Besides, I need you here."

I raised an eyebrow. "Why?"

"Because," she scowled, "as much as I hate to admit it, you know what you're doing. I'm not even a gifted amateur. You made the right call in the woods. I might have been able to hit the shot, but if I missed or only wounded it, we would probably be dead right now."

I glanced toward Tammy and saw she had a horrified look

on her face. I cleared my throat. "Maybe. But we can talk about it later. I suppose if I'm going to sleep here, the floor will be fine. I'll sleep against the door so nothing can enter that way."

Harper looked doubtfully at the hardwood flooring. "Are you sure?"

"I've slept on worse, though I wouldn't say no to a spare blanket and a pillow."

"Yeah. Of course. Ah, check in that bottom drawer over there. I think I still have one of Owen's shirts. It might be tight on you, but better than nothing. I'm going to take a shower before bed. Do you want to?"

"Sure. After you finish." I grinned at Harper's blush and winked at Tammy.

Tammy giggled and Harper threw a pillow at me before going to the bathroom and shutting the door behind her. Tammy waited for the shower to start before shifting over to the foot of the bed so she could sit closer to me.

"Do you really fight monsters, Ryan?"

"I do." I pulled open the drawer Harper had indicated and found a neatly folded Metallica t-shirt.

"Is Harper part of your Chapter?"

I glanced toward the bathroom and shook my head. "No. She learned of the Chapter when she got lost in the woods a few years back."

"I remember her telling me that story. She never mentioned the Chapter or monsters, though."

"She wouldn't have. It's hard to believe if you haven't lived it yourself. Usually people are much safer if they don't know there are monsters outside of movies and fairy tales." I pulled the shirt on. It was a large, and it was pretty tight across the shoulders. It felt like if I breathed in too deep it would split across the back. Still, it was better than nothing.

"But you're telling me?"

"Because for you, it is safer if you know. The wendigo has been eating through your family for the last week. If you had stayed at home, you might not be alive right now."

"We should call my dad, then! He could drive us down to Farmington right now!"

I held up my hands, gesturing for Tammy to slow down. "I don't know your dad very well, but answer me honestly. If we called him and told him a monster was pretending to be his wife or Liam, would he believe you?"

Tammy opened her mouth, then her face fell. "No."

"The worst thing that could happen, is if he went to Liam and told him our suspicions. Once the morning comes, we can talk to him in the light of day. But until I bring up monsters, we keep that to ourselves, okay? If your dad thinks it's just a serial killer or something, it might be easier to convince him to take you both out of town."

She nodded and bit her lip. "Will you test him to make sure he's still my dad?"

"Of course. Though I'll be a little more circumspect about it. I only pointed a gun at you because Harper would have been in danger. I am sorry about that. Truly."

She nodded and slumped back on the bed. "I don't know if I'm going to be able to sleep. My life doesn't even seem real right now."

"I know. I wish that you didn't have to experience any of this. Nobody deserves to have their world turned upside down. It sounds trite, but therapy can help."

Tammy gave a sour laugh. "Yeah. If I tell my therapist I can't sleep because my mom was a cannibal monster, they'd throw me in the loony bin."

"You might be right about that. The Chapter has counselors who could help, but the closest one is in Portland. If you went to a straight counselor, you'd have to speak in allegory."

"You mean lie."

"You can tell the truth without saying it was a monster. Given the number of people that went missing, I suspect you won't be the only one who needs therapy after all this is said and done."

She was silent for a long minute, and I thought she had fallen asleep, then Tammy spoke again. "Why did God let this happen to us? Did we not pray hard enough?"

Tammy wasn't looking at me, so I didn't have to hide my grimace of distaste. Religion had its uses, but the way some people thought life was all according to God's Plan irritated me. God wasn't around anymore, and the Plan, if He ever had one, had long since been derailed by the greed of humans.

The real answer to Tammy's question was someone in the Chapter fucked up and sent me to the wrong part of Maine. If I had been sent to Sugarloaf when the wendigo had first entered the mortal, I could have had it sent back to the fae before more than a handful of people had died.

Instead, I had been left chasing nothing while the wendigo slaughtered its way south to Kingfield. I was going to have words with whatever pencil pusher was responsible for that screwup. And maybe use my fists to do the talking.

"I don't know, Tammy," I said. "But I'll promise you one thing. I'll find the one responsible, and I'll make them pay."

CHAPTER SEVENTEEN

The night passed without incident. I slept on a hair-trigger with my rifle loaded and ready next to me. A dozen times during the night, I woke to the creak of the house settling. Every time, I'd force myself to come fully awake and listen until sleep dragged me under once more.

When the sun came up, I gave up on trying to sleep. My back was done with lying on the floor, so I moved over to sitting in the chair. I held my rifle slanted across my lap and let my thoughts drift. I kept working at the puzzle of the wendigo, trying to figure out how to kill it.

We had to know for certain someone was the wendigo in disguise. Only then could we act to kill it. And I wanted it to be on my terms. I needed room to take several shots, and I couldn't let it escape. Every fae was different, but it was safe to assume the wendigo would focus on hunting me once it knew I was trying to kill it.

Bait, then? What would draw the wendigo? The story Harper's grandmother had told offered some hints. It was a ravenous creature, always starving no matter how much it ate. Food, then, would be the obvious bait. But it only ate human flesh. I couldn't exactly go down to the Portland coroner's office and ask them for a corpse they weren't using.

But, then again, maybe I didn't need to. In Amy Chase's house, there was a freezer full of human flesh. That suggested the wendigo likely had stashes around Kingfield. We had found one of them, but there were likely more. If we found all the stashes and collected the flesh, the wendigo would be desperate. That would make it dangerous. A desperate creature was unpredictable.

"Did you sleep at all?"

I glanced up and saw Harper was awake and looking at me with a bleary smile. "Yeah, woke up about half an hour ago. How about you?" I kept my voice soft to keep from waking Tammy.

She rolled out of bed and stretched. I didn't bother trying to hide staring at her breasts. She came down off her toes and caught where my gaze was directed. Harper looked over at Tammy, ensured the girl was still sleeping, then lifted the hem of her shirt up to her shoulders. She gave me a long look at her tits then pulled her shirt back down.

"I feel much better today," she whispered with a wicked smile. "You're lucky Tammy is here."

"Yeah?"

Harper swayed over to me and straddled my hips. I moved my rifle out of the way and she sat on my lap. The soft firmness of her breasts pushed into my chest as she draped her arms over my shoulders. "I've put some thought into the future of our relationship," she breathed.

With the way she was pressed into my crotch, she probably knew exactly the effect her proximity was having on me. "Did you now?" I set my rifle on the ground so it was propped against my knee, then brought my hands around to squeeze the firm globes of her ass.

She sucked in a breath. "Mm. Yes. I haven't decided if I'll take your offer and join the Chapter. But while you're here, I don't plan on wasting opportunities."

"I see. There's sense to that."

"I was mad at you yesterday."

"I could tell. But not anymore?" The way she was sitting on me had my dick trapped at an awkward angle. I lifted her a few inches and got myself adjusted, then set her back down.

"I was taking my frustrations out on you, which wasn't fair. I hate to admit it, but realizing Liam was dead was an enormous relief."

"I think I understand."

"I need to brush my teeth. My mouth tastes like a track shoe insole."

She climbed off my lap and headed for the bathroom. I shook my head, trying to get rid of the image, and watched Harper lean over the sink to brush her teeth. I glanced back at Tammy and saw she was still asleep.

"Fuck it," I muttered, and followed Harper into the bathroom.

I nudged the door shut behind us and Harper looked up in the mirror with a questioning look on her face. I stepped up behind her and pressed my hips into her ass. I brought my hands up under her shirt and caught the weight of her tits in my hands.

"Hmmg," she mumbled through her toothpaste.

"What's that?" I leaned in closer and let go of a tit long enough to brush her hair to one side so I could nip her earlobe. "You want me to fuck you?"

"Ynnh." She nodded, and spat her mouth clear. "You fucking better."

I knelt down behind her and yanked her sleeping shorts with me. I nudged the inside of one of her thighs and she lifted her leg up, putting her knee on the counter. She was all the way opened for me now. I didn't know how much longer I had before Tammy woke up, so I didn't bother teasing her this time. I pressed my face into the juncture of her thighs and went to work with my tongue.

Harper gasped and muttered something under her breath. While I was busy with my mouth, I undid my pants and kicked them off. Harper tasted faintly musky and salty, and as I buried my tongue up inside her I could taste her rising arousal.

My dick was more than ready. I stood and stripped my borrowed shirt off, then lined up and pushed into her in one thrust. Harper let out a gasp, then clapped a hand over her mouth, muffling her moan. I grabbed the hem of her shirt and pulled it up over her head. She tried to get it off, and ended up getting tangled.

I pinned her hips in place with one hand and grabbed a swinging breast with the other. Harper got her shirt mostly off and her eyes met mine in the mirror. She mouthed the words, 'fuck me!' and her eyes went unfocused as I obliged.

There was an urgency driving me as I pounded into her. It was more than just knowing Tammy was in the other room. I felt a need to get close to Harper, some primal instinct to make her mine. She braced herself against the mirror, panting and mewling her pleasure. Her hips worked against mine, doing her best to match me thrust for thrust.

It didn't take long before her hips started losing their smooth motion. She trembled, let out a long, moaning, "Fuuuck!" And came hard.

I gave her dozen more thrusts then felt my own orgasm rush over me. I pressed deep into her, enjoying the feeling of her ass cheeks pressing into my hips. We held still for a few breaths, then I pulled out of her.

She turned around and pressed her mouth to mine. She still tasted like toothpaste and her cheeks were flushed. "You keep fucking me like that, and I'll join the Chapter just to keep you handy."

I chuckled. "I appreciate that, but you should have a better reason than a good fuck to join the Chapter."

From outside the bathroom, I heard Tammy clear her throat. "I can hear you, you know."

Harper winced then laughed. We cleaned up and got dressed. I squeezed back into Owen's shirt and got my pants back around my hips. Harper led the way out of the bathroom and gave Tammy an embarrassed wave.

"Hey, sorry. Did we wake you?"

"It's cool," Tammy said. She had a broad grin on her face and a slight flush on her cheeks.

"So, ah, you heard us?" I asked.

"All of it," she nodded. "You're going to join the Chapter?"

"Oh, I don't know. That wasn't really a promise, just a..." Harper shrugged, her cheeks pink, and struggled to find the words.

"What Harper is trying to say," I jumped in, "is that she enjoyed the sex. That's all."

"Ryan!"

"What? Was I wrong?"

"No, but you don't... You can't just tell someone that!"

Tammy laughed. "It's okay, Harper. I hear my parents having sex sometimes. Though my mom never makes noise like you do."

"Oh my god," Harper groaned and covered her eyes with a hand. "You're just a kid. I'm the worst influence ever."

"I'm fifteen," Tammy pointed out. "Lots of kids my age are having sex."

I cleared my throat. "Well, this was a fun talk."

"Do not tell your dad about this," Harper said with a mock growl.

"Ew, no. Besides, he'd totally have an aneurysm if I told him. And Mom would—" She cut herself off and her face went white.

The mood in the room went from embarrassed amusement to shocked silence in a split second. After a moment, I cleared my throat. "Let's get some food," I said gently.

Tammy nodded silently and slid off the bed.

Harper put an arm around Tammy's shoulders and gave her a hug. "You want waffles?"

"Okay."

I started for the door, then doubled back to get my shoulder holster and rifle. The girls were halfway down the stairs when I caught up to them.

"Tammy, what time does your dad usually wake up?" I asked.

"With the dawn," she said. "Lots of chores to do around the farm. Oh. The chickens! We can't just leave the farm for a week. Who will take care of the chickens?"

"That is not what you need to worry about right now," I said. "We'll make sure a neighbor is around to look after them or something. Right, Harper?"

"Of course. Most important thing is your safety. The chickens will be fine."

Tammy nodded. "Okay. I guess Mrs. Miller can look after them. She's done it before."

"Perfect." Harper nudged Tammy with her elbow. "See, it'll all work out. Now, let's get those waffles made!"

We made waffles and carefully steered the conversation away from Tammy's problems. We ate quickly from paper plates as fast as they came off the waffle iron. The girls put syrup on theirs, but having dessert for breakfast always made me grumpy later in the day, so I found some fresh blueberries in Harper's fridge and used those as a topping instead.

Then, with the sun just peeking over the tops of the trees to the east, we locked Harper's house behind us and set out on foot to the bed and breakfast. I didn't feel safe splitting up, so we all went upstairs to my room so I could get a proper change of clothes.

There was a folded-up note slid under my door, and I realized that I hadn't called Baptiste yet. Inside the note was Sylvia's handwriting, with a transcribed request from John to call him back. No doubt Sylvia's translation was much more polite than John's original message had been. I checked my phone again and saw I still didn't have any bars, even this close to Kingfield.

Stupid backwoods town.

I dressed in a shirt that actually fit me, changed my underwear, shrugged into the leather coat, and rejoined the girls in the hallway. I would have worn my jacket, but after the hike through the woods it needed another visit to the washing machine. Harper unslung the rifle from her shoulder and held it out to me, barrel first.

"Touch the iron," she said.

At least she didn't have her finger on the trigger. I reached out and grabbed the barrel, and held it for a few seconds before letting go. Harper sighed and slung the gun back up onto her shoulder.

"I'm glad you checked," I said. "Though I like to think I would put up enough of a fight for you to hear it through a door if the wendigo attacked me."

"You never know."

"Yep. Okay, Tammy. Ready to go get your dad?"

She nodded and we all went down to my car. After driving around in Harper's truck all week, getting into my little economy car felt like a massive downgrade.

"This is what you drive?" Tammy asked doubtfully as she buckled her seatbelt.

"It's a rental," I said. "I don't actually own a vehicle."

"You don't?" Harper asked.

"I mostly fly to new cities," I shrugged. "I was in California before I came to Maine, and I'll probably be going back to the west coast after this. I'd much rather fly than drive for four days all the way across the country. And I usually get a better car than this. The Portland Hertz rental didn't have a huge selection."

"Sorry, not trying to make you feel defensive," Harper grinned.

I rolled my eyes at her and pulled out of the parking lot. My car's shocks were not designed for driving over ruts in gravel roads, and the ride was pretty shaky until we reached the pavement. The drive through town to the Davis homestead took only a few minutes.

I pulled into the drive and killed the engine in front of the house. Mrs. Davis' truck, and Liam's, were both missing. I remembered the shot I had put into the grill of Liam's truck and took some satisfaction in knowing Harper wasn't the only one who had lost a vehicle yesterday. Of course, Liam was already dead, and wouldn't care one way or the other about the fate of his truck. All I had accomplished was temporarily depriving the wendigo of transportation.

Nobody was getting out of the car and I looked in the mirror back at Tammy. "I got the right house, didn't I?"

"This is my house," Tammy acknowledged in a small voice.

"Ryan," Harper said. I glanced at her and she tilted her head. "Outside."

I got out and shut the door, wondering what I had done this time. "Yeah?"

"Have a little compassion," Harper chastised me after she

had shut her own door. "Tammy just lost most of her family. She's about to go in and find out if her last family member is dead too."

"Shit." I sighed. "You're right. I'll admit, I'm not the best at dealing with people all the time." I opened my door again and leaned down to look at Tammy. "Hey, kiddo. Do you want to stay here? With the doors locked, you should be safe enough. We'll come out with your dad as quick as we can."

Tammy nodded silently and scrunched down in the seat.

"All right. I'll lock the doors and set the alarm. You see something, just bang on a window. It'll set the alarm off."

I shut the door and locked the car with the key fob. It beeped, letting me know the alarm was set, and I gave Tammy a thumbs up. She didn't return the gesture. I looked over at Harper and gave her a little shrug.

"Come on," Harper sighed. "Let's get this over with."

"She's a tough kid," I commented as we walked toward the front door. "I'm not sure I would have held up as well as she is when I was her age."

"I hope so. How are we going to test Mr. Davis?" Harper asked.

"You know him best. How do you think we should proceed?"

"You're asking me?"

"Why not? You've got as much experience with the wendigo as I do. I'll be your backup. Just don't get too close to him. The stand-your-ground distance is twenty-one feet for a reason. This thing is faster than any human. Until we're sure of Mr. Davis, try to keep a piece of furniture between you and him."

"I don't know, Ryan," Harper said nervously.

"Alternately, we can throw a handful of iron nails at him and see how he reacts."

"You mean, other than being pissed? What exactly happens when a fae touches iron?"

"They don't catch on fire, if that's what you're asking. It's extremely painful. They welt instantly, like brushing against stinging nettle or a bad reaction to a bee sting. But it has to touch skin."

"And it has to be iron?"

"Or steel. It has to be bare metal, though. Any plating like with galvanized steel or chrome blocks the contact. As a rule of thumb, if it can rust, it can harm a fae. Stainless steel works too, but the reaction isn't as strong."

"Maybe we better find some nails, then."

We were almost to the door. I glanced back at my car and saw Tammy peeking out at us over the frame of the door with just the top of her head visible. "I don't want to leave Tammy alone longer than we have to. She would get worried if we ran off to the barn to look for nails."

Harper nodded uncertainly. "And you want me to go first?"

"Mr. Davis knows you."

"Okay." She swallowed and gave herself a little shake. "Let's get this over with."

She shifted her rifle slung over her shoulder to a more comfortable position, then stepped up to the door and rapped it with her knuckles. "Mr. Davis!" she called. "It's Harper Hall. I need to speak with you! It's about Tammy."

Through the curtains, I saw movement in response to Harper's yell, and I backed off a few feet. I had my rifle on its harness, and it hung down by my side. I had my hand on my hip, near enough to the grip that I could grab it and swing it up into firing position in less than a second.

The rifle was chambered in .223, with steel-core rounds. At this range, the bullets would rip right through the target without fragmenting, which meant the steel core would never come in contact. If I wanted a lethal shot, it would have to be a vital organ or a headshot. Anything less would only wound a human. For a wendigo, at best I would just piss it off.

Someone shuffled up to the door and I heard the deadbolt slide open. The door swung open and revealed Mr. Davis. He was unshaven, his eyes surrounded by dark circles. He was wearing work clothes from the day before, still marked with sweat stains. His eyes seemed to hold no life in them as he stared at Harper.

"She's gone, then? My little Tammy?"

"Actually," Harper said brightly, "she's in the car."

Mr. Davis took a moment to react to Harper's words, then he swung his gaze up to where my car was parked. Something changed in his face, and he slowly sunk down to his knees. Tears trickled down his face, and his hands braced against his thighs trembled.

"She's alive! They're not all gone!"

"Tammy is safe," Harper said. "We want to make sure she stays that way. Have you seen Liam or Mrs. Davis today?"

"No. My wife has left me. I called all of Liam's friends, but none of them have seen him. What is happening, Harper? What happened to my family?"

Harper started lifting a hand toward him and I made a sharp hissing noise. Her hand froze and she glanced at me. "The test," I said firmly.

"Test?" he asked. "What test?"

"Before you can see Tammy, I need to do a quick test," Harper said, her voice abruptly professional. "If you would step inside, it won't take long."

"I don't understand," Mr. Davis said querulously. "I want to see my daughter!"

"In a moment," Harper said. She gestured back into the

house, and Mr. Davis got up to obey, glancing over his shoulder toward my car.

I followed, keeping my distance, with my hand hovering near my rifle. Mr. Davis didn't seem like he was the wendigo to me. Unless it was an incredible actor.

Harper pointed toward the kitchen. "Maybe we should get some coffee."

Mr. Davis nodded and set about making coffee with a mechanical disconnect in his motions. He took the sack of beans from the cupboard and scooped out a couple ounces into a grinder. The scoop was unmistakably stainless steel. I met Harper's eyes and nodded.

The tension in Harper's shoulders sagged away and she sighed. "Can you tell me where you were last night?" she asked.

Mr. Davis kept the grinder going for another few seconds, then released the plunger. "Here. At home. Waiting for my family to return to me." He nodded toward the living room. "I can't prove it, if that's what you're looking for."

"I see. Then, you're okay to see your daughter," Harper said.

"I can?" He abandoned the grinder and made for the front door, brushing past me blindly on the way.

I stepped aside and let him go, but followed closely after him. "Mr. Davis, before you go out, we need to talk about what is going to happen for the next week or so."

"What do you mean?"

"It isn't safe in Kingfield."

He stopped at the door and looked at me. "You know what is happening to people?"

"Yes."

"You know what happened to my wife? My sons?"

"I do."

"Then. Then, tell me. Please. Where are they?" Mr. Davis

may have spent the better part of his adult life in subservient misery to his wife, but there was no doubting the anguish in his eyes. The last week had broken his spirit and crushed what hopes and dreams he had left. He might have been on the brink of giving up everything, but now his daughter had returned. He had something to live for again, and the fire that had been lacking before was coming back.

"They're dead."

The bluntness of my words shook him. He blanched. Glanced at the rifle hanging at my side and flicked sideways to Harper. Swallowed. Squared his shoulders in determination. "What killed them?"

"There's something in the forest that is hunting people. Ranger Hall and I are on its trail, but we can't do our jobs if we have to worry about you and Tammy. I need you to take your daughter and leave town for a week or two. Farmington might be safe, but it would be better if you could get farther away. Do you have family out of state?"

"Yes. A brother in Virginia."

"Perfect. No, hold on. You don't have time to pack a bag. You got your car keys?"

"By the door."

"Good. You'll go from here to your car. I'll walk Tammy over, then the two of you will leave for Virginia. Don't stop in town. Don't stop driving until you have to get gas. Do you understand?"

He nodded jerkily. I could tell he had a million questions, but the brisk tone of command in my voice overrode his natural objections to taking orders from a stranger. "Yes, sir."

"All right. You've got a chance to protect yourself and your daughter. Don't mess it up."

"I won't."

I clapped him on the shoulder. "Good man. Let's go."

He took a set of car keys from the row of hooks on the wall by the door, grabbed the jacket hanging below, and stepped outside.

"Straight to your car," I reminded him. "I'll get Tammy."

He complied, and I jogged over to my car. Tammy sat up as I got close, and I beckoned for her to get out.

"Is my dad...?"

"He's fine. Come on, we're going to his car. You guys are going straight to Virginia to your uncle's place."

"Oh, thank God," she cried, and then she was off.

I had to run to keep up with her as she bolted for her father's car. Mr. Davis saw her coming and got out of the car to wrap her up in a bear hug. I slowed to a walk to give them a moment, but when I got close, I cleared my throat.

"There will be plenty of time to catch up on the drive," I said gently. "You better get going."

Mr. Davis turned to me and held out his hand. "Thank you, Mr. Halsin. Thank you for saving my daughter."

I shook and clapped him on the shoulder. "Take care of her. Remember. Don't stop for anything. Even if you think you see one of your family on the road."

"I'm not going to just drive by one of my sons if I see them," he objected.

"Listen to me, man. The thing that's killing people, it can look like anyone."

"What, like a costume or something?"

"Yeah. It might look like Liam, but it's really not. And if you pull over..." I trailed off and fixed him with a hard look. "You and your daughter will die. Do you understand?"

He swallowed. "No, but I will keep driving like you say."

"Good man." I fumbled for my wallet and found a business card giving my cell and a contact number for the Chapter. It was still damp and the ink had smudged a little, but was legible.

"Here. If you do see something, call one of these numbers and report it. I'll investigate and find out if it really is one of your family or if it's... not."

"Thank you."

Mr. Davis got into his car and it rumbled to life. I stepped to the side and waved, and he pulled out into the road. Tammy looked over her shoulder at us until they were out of sight. Harper stepped up next to me and sighed.

"That went better than I was afraid it would."

"Sometimes you have to scare a straight with something that's within their worldview, even if it isn't true." I reached out and gave her a one-armed hug. "But at least they're gone, right? If nothing else, we saved two people."

She leaned against me for a moment then pulled away. "We better get to work."

"I had some time to think this morning. It's time we started being active in hunting the wendigo. And unless I'm mistaken, this farm is where we start looking."

CHAPTER EIGHTEEN

The Davis farm had a handful of outbuildings in addition to the sprawling house. There was a detached garage and a large workshop, along with an assortment of sheds and animal shelters. It would take time to search all of it.

"We're sticking together?" Harper asked.

"Absolutely. Until the creature is dead, we don't leave each other's sight. Why don't we start with the house?"

"Works for me. What are we looking for? Other than the wendigo."

"We need to arrange an encounter with it on our terms. The best way to do that is to set a trap."

"And for a trap we need bait." She nodded thoughtfully. "The meat we found at Amy's house would work."

I chuckled. "And you say you aren't cut out for this job. It took me a bit to think of that angle, and you had it in just a few seconds."

"I mean, it's how you trap an animal, right? Lure it in with a meal." She shrugged. "I don't see why this would be any different."

"You're not wrong, but remember this is an intelligent being. Smart enough to carry out a convincing conversation and drive a car. We can't just put a chunk of meat in a box trap and expect it to walk in. Not unless it has no other choice." I paused to see if Harper would make the next logical leap, but she just looked at me expectantly. "We have to find all its stashes and either destroy them or collect them to use as bait. That way it has no choice but to come to us."

"Or kill again," she said quietly.

"Well… yeah. But I think it will want to recover its stashes if it can. The fae are predictable once you know what to look for. They are immutable, and their nature drives their actions. They can't stray from the core of their being. The wendigo is no exception. We can use that to our advantage."

"What is the wendigo's nature?"

"You heard the story from your grandma. What drove Amasec?"

"Greed, I guess?"

"Yep. Insatiable greed. It isn't enough to just have enough to eat. In the maple grove, he had to have *all* the syrup, even though staying put him in mortal danger."

"Would it be enough to recover only some of its stashes, then?"

"Maybe. But it might take it days to get around to checking on them. The more we find, the quicker it will respond. I don't know about you, but I want this thing dead. I don't want to hide out watching a pile of meat for days."

Harper grimaced. "No argument here. So, we look for a stash here on the farm?"

"It operated out of this place for several days. I'd be surprised if it didn't make a stash somewhere nearby."

"All right. Should we start inside the house?"

"It's as good a place as any."

We went back inside. The house was cool and dark, and somehow felt empty. It was more than just that the residents weren't here. The threshold was gone. I wasn't particularly sensitive to magic or other psychic phenomena, but even I could tell this building was no longer a home. The Davis family, what was left of it, was not coming back.

Harper looked around the entryway and rubbed her arms as if she was cold. "I'll check the kitchen."

I followed after her, taking in the remnants of the lives that had been lived in this place. Framed photos on the walls. Hunting trophies mounted over the fireplace. Well-worn sofa cushions. A china cabinet filled with heirloom dishes, inlaid with gold leaf.

"Nothing in the freezer," Harper called.

I gave my head a shake and pulled my gaze away from the quilt hung on the wall. The kitchen was a large one, cluttered with little ceramic figurines of chickens. There were two refrigerators, one near the stove that was your typical household fridge, and a second one with a single door that was off near the pantry.

"Did you check the other one?" I asked.

"It's full of chicken," she shrugged.

"It is?"

"They raised their own flocks of meat birds and butcher them for their own personal use."

I blinked. It hadn't even occurred to me that it was an option to raise your own meat. "Fascinating."

"I checked in the back just to make sure there wasn't any… meat. Back there."

"Brawn."

"Sorry?"

"The word for human meat is brawn."

Harper frowned and gave a little shudder. "Great."

"Fijian tribes called it *bakolo*, the Hebrews *adambasar*. I just find it easier to refer to it as brawn."

"Well, there's no brawn in the freezer. I—"

She cut off as the phone in the living room burst into raucous proclamation. We shared a look. It was still pretty early in the morning to be calling people. Maybe there were different expectations on a farm. I ducked back out into the other room and followed the ringing to a side table that had been pushed up against the wall. The phone had caller ID, and a little LCD screen on the receiver displayed the name of the caller: Harper Hall.

"Ah, shit. Harper, get in here!"

Harper came running. I put a finger against my lips, asking for silence, and put the phone on speaker. I swallowed to clear my throat, and put on a tone of polite curiosity.

"Hello, who is this?"

Harsh breathing. "Is Harper there?" It was Liam's voice.

"She is. Is this Liam Davis?"

"I wish to speak with Harper."

I met Harper's eyes and gave her a nod. Harper's face was pale, but there was a flush rising in her cheeks, and her eyes were narrowed in anger.

"I'm here," she growled. "Who are you?"

"Harper…" The voice deepened, took on a more rounded, mature tone. "I've missed you, you know. I still dream about you, your thighs rubbing against mine."

The breath caught in Harper's throat. "You bastard," she whispered hoarsely.

A low laugh. "I saw what you did with my sister and father. That was smart. I was going to take them next, you know. Collect the whole family. Oh well. There are so many delicious options in this town. Who shall I take instead? Maybe Lisa

Barson. She's got that baby growing inside her. There's something delectable about a fetus, don't you think?"

Harper stood frozen, anguish and shock on her face. A tear rolled down her cheek.

"We found your stash in Amy Chase's house," I said into the charged silence. "I'm going to drive nails into every square inch of meat. Let's see how much you enjoy picking iron out of your teeth."

"Stay out of this!" the voice switched to an old woman, her voice quivering with sudden fury. "Whoever you are. My business is with Harper!"

"No, it isn't," I persisted. "You have no business in this world at all."

There was a long silence, then, a young girl's voice, the one I recognized from the laundry room at the bed and breakfast. "I was called here. I'm needed! I have a right, as much as anyone else!"

"I will drive you forth from the mortal by iron or by fire," I promised it, "You are not welcome here."

"I will strip the skin from your flesh," it shrieked, the young girl's voice rising in frenzied hate. "Chew your meat, gnaw the sinew from your bones, suck the marrow—"

"Look to your stashes," I cut it off. "By this time tomorrow, you will have nothing. If you want your meat back, follow the directions we give you."

I hung up the phone. Almost immediately, it started ringing again. I reached around to the back of the table and ripped the cord from the wall. The phone went dead and I stared at it, surprised to find I was panting and adrenaline was thumping in my veins.

There was a grin on my face as I turned to Harper, then I saw the misery she was in and my triumph vanished. I stepped up to her and wrapped her in a hug.

"I'm sorry, Harper," I muttered.

She buried her face in my shoulder and a sob ripped through her. I didn't know what to say, so I just held her and let her cry.

"That... fuck!"

"It's just trying to get inside your head," I said soothingly. "None of it meant anything."

"But how did it know? How *could* it know?"

"I don't know, Harper." I gave her shoulder a squeeze. "Was it common knowledge that Owen still had feelings for you?"

She pulled back and dashed the back of her wrist across her eyes. "No. I wasn't even certain of it myself. Could it, I don't know, somehow eat Owen's memories too?"

"I... maybe? Magic isn't really my forte, but there's not really any limit to the things that are possible with it. The wendigo has some natural magic ability. It's possible that it can gain knowledge its victims had by eating them. It would explain why it was able to drive a truck and operate a cell phone." I snapped my fingers. "Wait, was your phone password protected?"

Harper shook her head. "Why would I bother with that?"

I coughed out a laugh and looked at her incredulously. "Why would you bother? Don't you have any concern for privacy?"

"Sure. That's why I don't leave my phone in strange places. Besides, if someone in Kingfield found my phone, they would just return it."

I grinned and shook my head. "Oh man. We're definitely going to have to work on your paranoia. At any rate, at least it can't steal your memories simply by touching your possessions."

"You lock your phone?"

"Sure. Biometrically and with a twelve-digit pin that I change twice a month."

"But… what do you have on your phone that's worth protecting like that?"

"Credit card information, emails, my identity. That wouldn't be great to have stolen, but worse than that, what if someone used my phone to infiltrate the Chapter? There are hundreds of humans and djinn that could be compromised. So, yeah. I take security very seriously."

"Well, shit. I hadn't thought of all that."

"Don't feel too bad. If you do join the Chapter, you'll take a course on operational security before you go out into the field."

"Wait, the Chapter has courses?"

"Sure. How else would newcomers learn the ropes? There's too much people have to know before they can be let out into the wild. It'd be chaos otherwise."

"I suppose that makes sense. I hadn't really thought about it. So, there's like a classroom or something? I'm picturing some crotchety old djinn that's been around since the Chapter was formed, pacing down the rows of student chairs with a yardstick and rapping on knuckles when people snooze off."

"It was like that when I took it," I laughed. "Now there's an internet course. No knuckle-rapping at all. You ready to go check the outbuildings? The wendigo said it saw us send the Davis family away, which means it was nearby."

"Yeah. If I remember correctly, there are more freezers in the barn for holding game kills. Let's go there first."

"All right. Keep your guard up. The wendigo could still be nearby."

"Not likely. There's no cell signal here. The closest place you can make a call is about half a mile closer to town."

"Huh. Okay, that's good to know."

We went out the back door and headed toward the barn. Without having to worry about scaring civilians, I held my rifle at the ready. Despite Harper's assurances about how far away the wendigo would have to be to make a cell call, I wasn't going to take any chances.

Harper must have been feeling the same, because she slowed to a stop outside the barn door. "You want to clear it? I have no idea what I'm doing."

"Yeah. What's the inside look like? One big room? Partitions?"

"It's one big room, unless they renovated in the last ten years."

"Okay." I stepped up to the door and settled my rifle against my shoulder. "Throw the door open at my nod."

She put her hand on the doorknob and looked at me. I gave her a nod and she pushed the door open. I swung inside as it opened, cleared the near corner, then pivoted about to cover the rest of the barn. 'Barn' might be the wrong term for the building. It was timber-framed, with no internal dividers or stalls. A tractor was parked in the middle, with various hay-making attachments neatly set to one side. There was a stainless-steel silo near the large rolling door, probably for holding the hay seed mix. A pair of snowmobiles, a riding mower, and other miscellaneous machinery filled the rest of the barn. In the back, a pretty comprehensive metal fabrication station had been set up, likely to facilitate repair of equipment.

I held my position for a long minute, listening intently, every sense cranked to the maximum. Nothing. I unlocked my pose and cat-footed along the wall until I could see around to the far side of the tractor. The barn was empty.

"Clear," I called.

Harper joined me in the barn and pointed toward the back wall. "The freezer is over there. Under that stack of tarps."

The tarps she indicated looked old and worn, but the dust that had settled on them looked freshly disturbed. Harper helped me move them to the ground, then I put my hand on the lid to stop her from opening the chest freezer.

"Are you sure you want to look in here?"

She swallowed, then met my gaze. "Yes. I need to see."

I nodded and lifted the lid. Cold air poured out and fog sprang up, but it wasn't thick enough to hide the hastily plastic-wrapped bundles of red meat. Harper took a deep breath and pressed her hand to her stomach, but she didn't throw up or turn away.

"I haven't done a lot of hunting. Does this look like deer meat to you?"

"It's not."

"Okay." I shut the lid again.

Harper looked to me, disgust and horror warring with anger on her face. "Now what? We use it to bait a trap?"

"Yes. Grab that cooler over there. I need to get something."

She nodded and went to the shelves of camping supplies for a cooler, and I headed toward the metal working corner. It didn't take me long to find what I was looking for. There was a heavy lathe to one side, an industrial machine that must have weighed several tons. Behind it, against the wall, a drift of tiny steel chips and curls had accumulated.

I grabbed a leather glove from a workbench and slipped it on, then scooped up a heaping handful of the metal fragments. The older bits were rusting, but that didn't matter for my purposes. Now I needed a container to hold the filings in. I felt like I was going to get tetanus just looking at it. After a quick search of the workbench, I found an old coffee can holding oily rags. I dumped the rags out and filled the can with iron filings and shaved whorls.

When I got back to the freezer, Harper was loading the last of the wrapped packets of brawn into the cooler. She looked up as I approached and brushed a stray lock of hair back behind an ear.

"What'd you find?"

I tipped the can over so she could see inside. "A little seasoning for our friend. A dusting with this and the wendigo won't be able to eat the meat, no matter how hungry it is."

"Good." Harper shut the lid of the cooler and picked it up with a grunt. "Are we done here?"

"Almost. We need to leave a note so the wendigo knows where our trap will be."

"What, 'meet me outside the saloon at second bell?' Isn't that a little obvious?"

"We probably need a place a little less populated than the saloon, but yes. Some place open, were we can see it coming."

"Like an empty field?"

"Sure. You know where one is?"

"Maybe better than that… there's a gravel dump outside of town to the north. Good sightlines, lots of open space with nothing in the way. And no people around, too."

"What about the owner?"

She shook her head. "He went missing almost a month ago."

I nodded. "All right. Let's leave a note for the wendigo to find."

Harper found a scrap of paper and a pencil, and wrote 'You want your meat, come get it', along with the address for the gravel dump. "What time?" she asked.

"Uh. Let's go with three in the afternoon. That gives us time."

She added the time and laid it on the bottom of the empty freezer. "There. Can it even read?"

"Yeah. If it can drive, it can read. Let's get back to my car. It might be too late, but we should check on the stash at Amy's house."

"I've got the cooler. You watch our backs."

"Aren't you supposed to let the guy do the lifting?"

"I can carry thirty pounds of meat. Stop being chivalrous and let's go."

I grinned at her. "Not going to lie, I think I could get used to having someone around to do the heavy work."

She narrowed her eyes at me. "Har har."

"Everyone's a critic. Here, hold this too." I put the can of filings on the cooler lid and led the way out of the barn.

The bright sunlight made me squint and I paused in the doorway to give my eyes a moment to adjust. Despite the clear skies overhead, the air was still crisp and cool. Rather than suffering under the weight of the leather coat, I felt comfortable.

Once I could see without wanting to shade my eyes, I headed around the side of the house toward the front where I had parked. When we reached the corner of the house, I slowed and held a hand up for Harper to wait.

I peeked around the corner and scanned the cleared lot in front of the house. I was about to step out into the open when movement down the road toward town caught my eye. A figure was running on the road coming toward us, and though I couldn't make out detail at the distance, I knew at a glance that it was Liam.

"What is it?" Harper whispered.

"It's coming," I said softly. "You want your shot? I'll let you take it."

Harper sucked in a breath and set the cooler down on the ground. "I won't miss," she promised.

She unslung her rifle from her shoulder and I stepped back to give her the corner position. She leaned out around the edge of the building and hissed out a breath. The wendigo was still five or six hundred yards up the road, moving at a rapid clip.

Harper racked the lever on her rifle and chambered one of the enormous .444 rounds, then braced the rifle against the corner of the house. I raised an eyebrow. If she was going to take the shot now, that was some Olympic-level shooting. Hitting a stationary target was one thing, but a running man, up a thirty- or forty-foot rise? That wasn't a shot I was comfortable making.

She let out a slow breath and I lifted my hands to plug my ears. The rifle boomed and a second later I saw the wendigo stagger, but I couldn't tell where it was hit. Then, without moving the gun, Harper cycled the action smoothly and fired again. The shots were measured, deliberate, but also as fast as I could have aimed and fired with a semi-automatic rifle.

On the road, the wendigo went down hard. Red bloomed on its front, but it was too low to be a lung shot. It tumbled, then rolled to a crouch with surprising grace. I saw at least one more shot hit it high in the shoulder, knocking it briefly off balance, then it turned and bounded for the woods on the side of the road.

Harper's rifle clicked on an empty chamber and she rotated the rifle sideways and started feeding fresh rounds into the magazine.

"Do that later," I said urgently. "We need to get in the car and get moving!"

"I hit it at least three times," she protested, but she stopped reloading and slung the rifle back up onto her shoulder. "Its bleeding out. We should just finish it now!"

"Its not like an animal, Harper," I shook my head. "If it isn't dead, it'll recover very quickly. We need to be gone before it does."

"It can just heal?"

I grabbed one handle of the cooler and Harper took the other. Together, we started jogging toward the car. "Not as such. I'll explain once we're in the car."

We reached the car and I popped the trunk. We hastily loaded the cooler inside and wedged the can of filings in next to it. We climbed inside and I pulled out of the driveway fast enough to make my tires skid in the gravel. I took us toward town, and slowed when we reached the spot where the wendigo had gone down.

There were splashes of blood on the asphalt, but nowhere near the levels of gore three hits with a .444 round should have caused. If it had been a human that had been shot, the shock would probably have killed it on the spot, and blood loss would have ensured the job before it had crawled more than a few yards.

"Jesus Christ," Harper muttered. She sat back in her seat and put her seatbelt on. "Okay. Tell me why it didn't die."

I pulled away and got up to a speed that I was fairly certain was faster than the wendigo could run. Only then did I relax a little. "The wendigo is fae."

"Yeah, I got that part."

"Let me finish. It might be here, in the mortal, but that's just, like, an echo. Or maybe more like a standing wave."

"I don't understand."

I rubbed the back of my neck and tried to think of an analogy that would communicate. "All right. Well, maybe I better back up. A creature from the fae doesn't really travel to the mortal. It doesn't come through a portal between dimensions physically, it is a projection of its true self still in the fae. So, what is out there eating people is less the creature itself, and more a manifestation of it."

"I... think I understand what you're saying, but I don't get how that's possible."

"It's magic," I shrugged. "The fae believe they can manifest in the mortal, so they can. And no, I couldn't explain to you how that works. At any rate, when you pumped a few rounds through the wendigo, you definitely wounded it, but you didn't totally disrupt the manifestation. Because the original source is still intact, the monster returns to its normal condition rapidly."

"How rapidly?"

"It depends on how much iron is in your bullets," I shot her a tight smile. "If you were shooting copper and lead at it, probably a minute or two. The fae cannot stand contact with iron. It's enough to make them abandon the manifestation entirely if enough iron is used. I've seen fae get disrupted by shooting them a few times with a nail gun."

"Shit." She pulled out one of the rounds she had been loading into her rifle and held it for me to see. "Copper jacket over lead. How much damage would it need to take to, uh, disrupt the manifestation?"

"Kill it dead. A shot to the head, heart, spine, like that. It might just be a manifestation and not the actual fae creature, but it's still a mortal body, with mortal requirements for life. You may not have killed it, but that was some impressive shooting."

She sighed. "But not good enough. Damn it. If only I had steel rounds. I can get some, but I'll need to special order it from Walter."

"Who's Walter?"

"My gunsmith. He's an old guy who lives outside of Kingfield to the east. He does my reloads for me."

"How fast does he work? It might be worth it to pay him an extra few hundred dollars if he can make you some now."

"Sure, but I don't have that kind of money, Ryan."

"Maybe not, but I do. I'll expense it to the Chapter. Just tell me where to go."

CHAPTER NINETEEN

We stopped off at the local bank so I could draw some cash, a cute little one-bedroom house that had been converted into a bank. I couldn't help but think of how easy it would be to rob. Just drive through the wall with a pickup truck, put a winch on the safe door, and rip it open. Probably take about five minutes.

Then again, the big payoff would be ten or twenty thousand dollars, all in small bills. It wasn't like a town the size of Kingfield had any use for stacks of hundreds. The residents here likely had to drive down to Madison if they wanted to get bills to make a large cash purchase.

I followed Harper's directions across the Carrabassett river, then south to a little scattering of houses. Walter's place was set back from the road down a bumpy dirt path. The house itself was a tiny two-bedroom, well-maintained with fresh paint on the walls. A garage twice the size of the house was attached by a covered walkway. A riotous garden took up the rest of the cleared land.

I parked and we got out of the car. A high-pitched squealing was coming from the garage, loud enough to make me want to cover my ears.

"He's working in the garage," Harper called out the obvious.

I didn't feel like raising my voice to shout over the squeal, so I gestured for Harper to take the lead.

I've met my fair share of gun nuts. Most people who spend any length of time hunting monsters end up with a weapon fetish of some description. My father had a thing for a World War One Ithaca 37 shotgun, a slam-fire trench broom with which he had developed a relationship with more depth and meaning than he ever showed the various women in his life. Needless to say, he loaded all his own shells for it, and had invented a dozen different payloads for various situations.

My dad's shotgun fetish wasn't the weirdest weapon obsession I had witnessed. After forty years spent around Chapter hunters and soldiers in the military, I had seen all kinds of weapons and the men that used them.

I knew the moment I walked into Walter's garage that here was a kindred spirit. The walls were hung with paraphernalia from at least two wars, a broad collection of Native American weaponry, and a battle-tattered American flag. Long workbenches lined the walls, neatly organized with tools and containers. I saw the gleam of brass casings everywhere.

Walter himself was leaning over a metal lathe, from which the squealing sound was coming from. He had on ear protection, and hadn't noticed our entry. Harper gestured for me to wait in the doorway, which I was happy to do. I knew more than a few weapon aficionados that would react poorly to being surprised in their own home. Walking up and tapping Walter on the shoulder would likely result in getting shot.

We waited until there was a pause in the lathe work, and Harper called out, "Hi Walter, it's Harper!"

At first I thought he hadn't heard us, and was prepared to wait again. He made a few more passes at the lathe, then flicked the machine off. He turned around to face us and slipped the hearing protection down to around his neck.

"Harper! You should have called ahead, I would have waited for you."

"It's okay, Walter. I'd like you to meet a friend. Ryan, this is Walter. Walter, Ryan Halsin."

Walter stood up and walked over to shake my hand. He was in his sixties, if my guess was right. Tall, a little stooped, with glasses perched on his nose. He had a thick, iron-grey handlebar moustache and was wearing a leather apron.

"Halsin. That name sounds familiar but I can't place it. You from around here, Ryan?"

"No, sir. You might know my father, I suppose. Nils Halsin?"

"Nils…" he narrowed his eyes at me thoughtfully, then shrugged. "Nah. Not unless your old man had you when he was in his seventies."

I laughed along with him, wondering if he had actually met my father at some point. "This is an impressive shop you've got, Walter."

"Well, thank you, son. You strike me as a man what would appreciate such a place."

"I like to think so. A little surprising to find a place like this in Kingfield."

He chuckled. "I haven't been here my whole life, and it's hard to beat the wilderness out here. You can hike out into the woods and not see another man for days. Now, I know you two aren't here to make a social call and keep an old man company. What can I do for you, Harper?"

"I was hoping you could help me with a special order, Walter."

"Looking for something for your Marlin? How's she treating you?"

Harper patted the butt of the rifle slung over her shoulder. "That adjustment you made to the trigger worked perfectly," she said. "But I don't need work done on the gun. I need some special ammo."

He raised an eyebrow at her and tilted his head forward so he could look at her over the top of his glasses. "Special ammo? Tell me."

"I need steel rounds."

"Steel." He frowned and looked over at me. "What are you hunting that needs a steel bullet? Or should I say, 'who'? No animal in Maine has bone thick enough to need that kind of penetration. Not unless you were taking a trip south to go hog hunting."

"It's a what," I said. If this man knew my father, it was likely he knew something about the fae. Halsin was an uncommon name, but it wasn't *that* uncommon. "And what we're hunting isn't from around here."

Walter's frown deepened and I saw a calculating look in his eyes. "Maybe you better speak plainly. I don't look well on strangers making trouble around here."

"It's okay, Walter," Harper said. "He's not making me do anything I don't want to do."

The old man's eyes didn't leave my face. I shrugged. "There's something killing people. I'm here to make it stop."

He nodded slowly. "Something. Not someone."

"If it was a human that was doing the killing, the cops would have caught them by now."

"You may have a point." He eyed me for a long moment, then turned back to Harper. "Steel rounds, you say?"

"If you could, Walter."

"Yeah. I can do that. I should warn you, though, without a

jacket, they're not going to be accurate for very far. The bullets won't conform to the rifling and you'll get bad tumbling after a few dozen yards. Once that happens, God only knows where it will go. You'll get about the same accuracy range as a pistol. You still want them?"

Harper glanced at me and I nodded. "It will have to do," she said. "How much will I owe you? And can you load them now?"

"Well." Walter puffed his cheeks out and his moustache twitched in a sudden smile. "Funny thing about that. I thought the old lady was batty. Steel rounds? Who wants their bullets made out of steel? Useless as a rifle round, and it will mangle the hell out of your barrel. Still, she paid me in cash, so who am I to refuse? Said someone would be along to pick them up."

He turned back to the lathe and grabbed what he was working on with a pair of rag-wrapped tongs. He released the chuck and dropped the bit of metal into a bucket of water.

"I've already made the bullets. Been turning them all week. I'm not going to lie to you, they've been a right pain in the arse to work. This here was the last of the batch. If you want to grab a sit, I'll have them loaded into cases for you in a jiffy."

"Wait," Harper said, "who ordered the steel bullets?"

"Old Native lady. Blind as a bat, had her grandson with her to guide her around. You know her?"

Harper nodded. "She's my grandma."

"Well, well." Walter frowned thoughtfully and stroked his moustache. "Now I want to know how she knew you would want the bullets. You didn't tell her?"

"I didn't know I'd need them until about half an hour ago," Harper said, and gave me a sideways look. "But my grandma is thoughtful like that."

He harrumphed. "Thoughtful my arse. Downright spooky, if you ask me. What kind of powder load do you want?"

257

"Low," I suggested. "Ideally the bullet lodges in the target."

Walter clucked his tongue. "The Marlin uses a big brass. I can maybe add some wadding, but if the charge is too low, you'll get misfires."

"Make it safe, then."

"Safe would be a full powder load."

I shrugged. "You're the expert. Do what you think is best."

He grunted. "Best would be a lead or copper round that would bite into the rifling and give it some proper spin. But steel will do the trick, if it has to. Now let me work."

Harper and I stood on the far side of the garage and watched as Walter set about loading the rounds into shiny new brass shells.

"How did your grandma know we'd need steel bullets?" I muttered.

"Same way she knew how to brand your name into your coat a month before she met you." Harper shrugged. "Like I said, she sees something of the future, and of the fae."

"Well. I'd be lying if I said I didn't appreciate it. I'm a little surprised I haven't met her earlier. The Chapter isn't that large of an organization. If there was a seer in the Chapter, I would have heard about her."

"From what she said, she didn't stay past the probation period. The Chapter bought the land for Nebeske Odana. She did do some consulting with them every now and then, but not as a regular activity. She was more interested in preserving her ancestral culture."

I nodded. "That makes sense."

"The land is hundreds of acres, and surrounds the entire lake. It must have cost a small fortune. The Chapter really gave her all that for five years of service?"

"It varies, and degree of service is rewarded. I imagine five years as a seer was more valuable to the Chapter than five years of occasional monster hunting. But even so, we do try and make the transition back to civilian life after five years a comfortable one. Nobody regrets joining the Chapter."

"Nobody?" Harper asked doubtfully.

I hesitated, then decided to tell the truth. Harper deserved that much. "It's dangerous. Not everyone who goes into it is mentally prepared for the necessities of the job. A second's hesitation at the wrong moment can cost a life. A lot of new members die before their five years are up."

Her jaw tightened and she looked down at her feet. "How many?"

"Half. More or less depending on the number of fae incursions we have to deal with."

Harper jerked her eyes up to my face. "So many?!"

"Imagine trying to hunt our current target without knowing what you were doing."

"But... surely they don't go into it alone?"

"Of course not. I..." I trailed off as Walter finished the last of the rounds and turned around, rattling the little plastic bin in his hand.

"All finished! These lot are beauties, if I do say so myself."

"That was fast, Walter! Thank you." Harper left my side and went to join him at the bench. "Did my grandma pay you enough for your work? I'd feel bad if you had to go out of your way."

"Don't you worry your pretty head about that. If she hadn't paid my price, I wouldn't have done it." He put the newly loaded rounds into a plastic caddy, then the caddy into a little cardboard box. "One or two of these won't hurt your gun too badly," he cautioned her. "But if you fire the lot, you'll probably need to replace the barrel entirely."

"It's a good thing I know a quality gunsmith, then," she grinned. "I'll let you know if it's needed."

Walter nodded. "Be safe, Harper. Even with your killer friend watching your back. I don't know what you're hunting, but too many people have disappeared already. I'd hate to see your name among the missing."

"I'll be careful," Harper promised.

"And you," Walter said, looking to me. "You protect her. With your life, if you must."

"It won't come to that," I said. "I'll find the thing and end it so nobody else goes missing."

He grunted. "No promises for life, only for death. I know your type. Just don't drag Harper down with you."

I nodded. There wasn't any point in arguing with the man. "Thank you for the ammunition."

Walter's moustache twitched, and he turned away. "You know where the door is, killer."

Harper caught my eye and gave her head a little shake, warning me not to engage. I rolled a shoulder, trying to slough off my own irritation, and followed her back out into the sunshine. Behind us, the whine of the lathe started up again.

"Sorry," Harper muttered. "He's a little protective. He taught me how to shoot, you know. Back when I was just a little sprout."

"Yeah. You know, I think he actually did know my father. Small world, isn't it?"

We got into the car and Harper set about unloading the old rounds and loading the new steel ones. I took one from her and held it up to the light. You could see the lathe marks spiraling down the bullet, but when I brushed my finger over it, it felt smooth as glass. It was odd to see the shine of fresh steel sticking out the end of the casing. Even my own steel rounds had a copper sheathe over them to protect the barrel of the gun.

"Will these really work?" Harper asked.

"Believe me, you put one of these into the wendigo, and it

will feel it. I don't know if it would be enough to kill it on the spot, but it won't go running off into the woods afterward."

"We just have to let it get close enough to hit," she sighed. "Will shooting steel rounds really wreck my gun?"

"Not immediately, no. It's a matter of metal hardness. Normally people use copper or lead because it deforms under the firing pressure and engages with the rifling of the barrel. Steel won't do that, and will wear out the rifling over time. My dad used to go through shotgun barrels almost once a month, it seemed."

"Shotguns don't have rifling, though."

"Yeah, but considering the crazy shit he shot through it, he's lucky it was just the barrels that wore out."

"Your dad sounds like he had been an interesting guy."

"That's one way of putting it."

I got us back onto the road and headed back to town. It was nearing lunchtime, but I was conscious of the cooler full of meat in the trunk. It had been frozen, but that wouldn't last forever.

"Where are we going now?" Harper asked.

"To Amy's. We don't need to take that stash with us, just give it a sprinkle with the iron filings. The wendigo won't go anywhere near it after that."

Harper nodded and swallowed. I could tell talking about human meat was upsetting to her. It was something she'd have to get used to. While not many wild fae ate humans as their primary diet, most wouldn't turn down a meal of brawn.

"Can we, ah, talk about something else?"

"Sure. I think I was in the middle of answering your question back in Walter's workshop before he finished loading the rounds. What was it again?"

She winced. This wasn't an easy topic either. "The new Chapter recruits. They don't get assigned…"

"Incursions," I supplied.

"Yes. They don't have to deal with an incursion by themselves, right?"

"Of course not. All new recruits are partnered with experienced members of the Chapter. But there's no end to the weird that comes out of the fae and even an experienced hunter might make a mistake."

"But… half? That's an insane amount of loss."

"Are you personally worried?" I asked.

"I mean… the wendigo *eats* people! It doesn't get any worse than that."

"I'd love to say you were right. But in terms of actual, physical danger, the wendigo is fairly low on the list. It's fast and strong, but at least it's not an ogre. Or a minotaur. Or a dozen other things that are even more dangerous. Or an angel."

"An angel? Angels are real?"

"As real as anything else. And no, they're not friendly. They're all completely, totally, batshit insane. Even the ones who have managed to regain some degree of self-control are unpredictable and incredibly dangerous. They are without master or purpose, and only live to fulfill echoes of their lost divinity. To make things worse, they're not really fae, they just live there. When an angel comes to the mortal, it is really present, and it doesn't give two shits about iron or salt or any other tricks we have to fight the fae."

"You know," Harper said after a pause, "I don't think I've ever seen you afraid. But you're afraid of angels, aren't you?"

"You're goddamn right I am. Let me give you a piece of advice. If you ever see an angel, fallen or otherwise, run." I gripped the wheel and took a deep breath. "Look, as long as you stay close to me and do what I say, you'll be fine. I wasn't kidding when I told Walter you would be safe. I've been hunting fae for almost thirty years. We'll be okay."

"Well, at least that makes one of us that's certain," Harper laughed nervously.

"If everything goes to plan, we'll have this fucking wendigo back in the fae before nightfall."

I slowed as we neared the turnout that led to Amy Chase's house. The last time I was there, it had been dark and raining, and I wasn't sure where exactly the dirt road was. The trees lining the road all looked the same to me.

"Here," Harper said.

A moment later, I saw the narrow dirt path that dove into the trees. I couldn't stop in time, and pulled off onto the shoulder of the road. I threw the car into reverse and bumped back until I could see down the path. I wouldn't be able to drive down it without scratching the shit out of the car. It was a rental, but the Chapter bean counters would be less than thrilled if they got a body repair bill when I turned it in.

"Maybe we should walk," I suggested.

"Really? You want to walk? What if its waiting for us?"

"Then it will find us whether we walk in or drive," I pointed out. "If we walk, we might surprise it."

"No fast getaway on foot, though," she protested.

"You've been driving in the same car I have, right? Hell, I can *crawl* faster than it will drive down that path."

"Yeah." Harper made a face then laughed. "You made your point."

I shut the car off and we got out. There was a heaviness to the air that wasn't there half an hour ago, and I looked around at the sky. It was still bright and clear.

"Summer storm," Harper said with a knowing nod. "Smells like there's going to be a real downpour tonight. We won't get clouds rolling in for another hour, though. Lots of time to spring our trap."

"I'll take your word on that." I put the container of metal

filings in my pack, then locked the car and we headed for the path.

Neither Harper or I felt talkative, and we made our way down the overgrown road in silence. I kept all my senses stretched out, searching for any sign of the wendigo in the forest around us. I couldn't see more than a dozen feet through the trees. The wendigo could be watching us go by, and we would never know it.

"I hate this forest," I muttered.

"Shh," Harper replied.

And that was it for conversation. After almost five minutes of walking, I saw the damaged roof of the house ahead of us through the trees. I nudged Harper and pointed, and she nodded with a tight smile. Twenty feet further on, we both came to a stop at the same time. There was a truck parked outside the house.

It wasn't one I had seen before, and I looked the question to Harper.

"It's Mason's truck," she whispered. "One of Liam's friends. Is the wendigo here?"

"I don't know."

I thought about the story Harper's grandma had told us, and how the monster was driven by insatiable greed. I was certain it would have checked on its stash on the Davis farm, but what would it have done after that? What would its course of action be? Would it want to check up on all of its stashes? Or would it want to recover the one that was lost?

I had threatened to destroy all of its stored human flesh, but would it take my threat literally? Or would it assume I was bluffing? Maybe it would check on a few, find them undisturbed, and race around urgently, checking on them all before going to the gravel dump. It was all conjecture. I had no real way of knowing. But if it was the wendigo in the house, it wouldn't stay there for long.

"Let's hide for a few minutes," I suggested softly. "If it's the wendigo, it won't stay inside for long."

Harper nodded, and we stepped off the path into the woods. The ground was soft with spongy mulch and piled leaves, and the air filled with the rich, earthy scent of leaf mold in our wake. We crouched down behind a bush, and this time, I made a point of having my rifle ready to fire.

A minute into our wait, a light turned on in the kitchen. I heard Harper's breath catch next to me and she shifted her weight.

"Easy," I muttered. "Stay still like you were hunting a deer."

The next several minutes dragged on. I started counting my breaths so my nerves wouldn't throw off my perception of time too badly. After a hundred slow breaths, I knew something was wrong. If the wendigo was in the house, it would have left by now.

I nudged Harper and leaned close. "I'm going in. Come with me, and watch our backs."

She gave me a wide-eyed look, but didn't argue. I got up out of my crouch and took a moment to stretch the kinks out of my joints. I wasn't as limber as I had been when I was young. I set out toward the house, taking care to swing wide of the front windows.

I crept silently to the front door and tried the handle. The knob was locked, but the door swung inward at my touch. Freshly broken wood from the doorframe was scattered across the floor. From inside the kitchen, I heard the slurping and noisy chewing of someone, or something, eating hungrily.

A glance back at Harper told me she was ready. Her face was set in concentration, her rifle was up and ready. I knew I wasn't going to be happy about hearing Harper's Marlin firing indoors, but I'd deal with a little tinnitus if it meant the wendigo would be dead.

I took a few careful steps out into the living room. I knew of the one target in the kitchen, but I didn't want to be surprised by a second threat. There was someone standing in the kitchen, bent over the sink. He had a knife in one hand that he was using to carve strips of partially defrosted raw flesh from a big hunk, and was using the other hand to shove the strips into his mouth. Blood foamed around the figure's mouth and its cheeks bulged with meat.

At this range, I couldn't miss. I had the thing clear in my sights, and there was no cover for it, nowhere to run but directly toward me or directly away. Still, something about the way the figure was choking down the raw meat made me hold my fire. Despite the frenzy with which it was eating, it was gagging as it tried to swallow.

"Mason?" Harper called softly.

The figure froze, and I nearly put a round in its head right then. Its head swung toward us and it swallowed convulsively. Its mouth was so full it had to swallow a few times. On the last swallow it gagged and almost threw up, but managed to get his mouth clear.

"Harper?" Its voice was ripped. "What are you doing here?"

"Ryan, I don't think this is the monster," she told me.

"Don't move," I warned it, ignoring Harper. "You take one step, and I will put two rounds in your head, then the rest of the magazine in your chest. These are steel-core bullets. Trust me, you *will* feel them."

The figure raised his hands slowly. Mason was a man not older than twenty, around five-nine, maybe five-ten, with a skinny, rangy look to him. His sandy-brown hair was starting to thin with early-onset male-pattern baldness. The shirt he was wearing was damp with sweat and clung to him, showing that his stomach was visibly distended.

I glanced around the kitchen, searching for something made of steel or iron. There was a cast-iron pan hanging above the stove. I twitched my gun barrel toward it. "Pick up that pan."

"What the fuck, man," Mason whimpered. "We weren't shooting at you on the street. It was just a prank! You don't need to freak out about it."

I shifted my aim a few feet to the side and shot the refrigerator. The clap of the report hammered out into the room and Mason flinched hard.

"Fuck!" Harper gasped.

"Do it!" I snarled. "Grab the pan!"

Mason reached up and grabbed the pan by the handle, and pulled it off the wall. "I did it, okay? Chill the fuck out, man!"

There was a latex grip on the handle so whoever was cooking didn't have to use an oven mitt to grab it. "The metal," I barked. "Touch the metal!"

"The fuck? Why would I—?"

"Just do it, Mason," Harper said urgently.

"Fine, Jesus. Fucking psycho." He switched his grip around until he was holding the metal in both hands. "There. Happy?"

I lowered my rifle part way, but still kept it at the ready. Mason wasn't the wendigo. He was human, but that just gave me more questions. What was he doing here? Why was he stuffing his face with raw brawn? Where was the wendigo?

Harper beat me to the obvious question. "Mason, why are you eating that? Don't you know what it is?"

He looked over at the sink, spattered with blood and juices, and the half-carved hunk of flesh in it. He looked suddenly sick, like he was going to throw up. Then his expression firmed with fresh determination. "I know what it is. Who it is."

"Then... what the fuck?" Harper asked.

It was a fair question. "Answer her," I growled.

"You don't understand!" There was a sudden fire in his eyes, an almost fanatical desperation. "I have to!"

"You have to stuff yourself with human flesh?" I asked. "Why? How can you possibly think that's a good idea?"

"It's the only way." Mason looked back toward the lump of meat with renewed hunger. "To be strong like him."

"Oh my God," Harper gasped. "You're trying to *become* one of them?!"

"We would be unstoppable," he said. Then he broke into sudden laughter. "Liam showed me! Cut himself to the bone and it healed right over! What fear would we have of the law? Bullets would mean nothing!"

"Bet he didn't cut himself with a steel knife, though," I said grimly. "I know what it sounds like, but inviting in the wendigo spirit is not a good idea. You would destroy yourself in the process!"

"Liam is still himself," Mason argued. "He proved it. And it's like being a superhero! Liam can lift a car, jump up onto a roof from the ground. If I have to eat the remains of old Mrs. Chase to be like him, then I'll do it!"

"Don't do this, Mason," Harper pleaded.

"You're just scared," Mason countered with a sneer.

Mason reached for the hunk of brawn in the sink and Harper took a few steps toward him. "Stop! Mason, Liam is dead! What is walking around in his skin is not human!"

For a second, Mason hesitated, then he grabbed the chunk of meat and brought it to his mouth. He started chewing at it, tearing pieces free with his teeth and bolting them down.

"Harper," I called, "get back!"

She looked at me, torn with indecision. I could see the care in her eyes. Even though Mason had all but killed her yesterday, she was still concerned with his well-being. Personally, I didn't care if Mason died. But while he was still human, I couldn't kill him myself. I mean, I could. It would be so easy; just a little more pressure on my trigger finger and Mason would be a cooling corpse. But it would be wrong. I killed monsters, not humans.

Mason choked on the meat he was forcing down his throat and started to gag. Then he recovered and finished swallowing. He clutched at his stomach and groaned. A sudden gust of wind rattled against the windows and thunder boomed.

"Harper!" I shouted. "Get away from him!"

A sibilant whispering filled the air, coming from no direction in particular, just too soft to be intelligible. I clutched my rifle tight and drew a bead on Mason's forehead. Harper was backpedaling away and fighting with her rifle strap trying to get the weapon into position. She seemed to be moving through honey, even the drift of her hair about her face was moving in slow motion.

"Mason! This is your last chance!" I cried.

Mason shuddered. A tremble ran through him from head to toe. The chunk of flesh fell from his hand and hit the floor with a wet splat. Lightning struck the house. The brilliant flare of coruscating light threw the room into stark contrast.

My vision was clouded with the after-images, but I saw a ripple in the air behind Mason suddenly surge across the kitchen and impact into Mason's back. He started upright, straining on his toes with his back arched, his mouth open in a silent scream.

I watched in horror, unable to believe what I was seeing. In all my years as a hunter, I had never even heard of someone witnessing a fae coming into the mortal. Mason seemed to be suspended in the air, every tendon straining against some horrible force. Another gust of wind hit the house, and this time the windows in the kitchen shattered. Howling wind swirled around me, tugging at my coat and hair.

Mason's eyes met mine, and I saw the understanding and panic there. Then he threw back his head and the scream finally tore free of his throat. He twisted around, still suspended in the air, thrashing wildly as the fae spirit bound itself to his body.

The healthy flesh of his face was the first to go. His cheeks went sunken, like he was starving in fast-forward. His eye sockets darkened and drew back into the depths of bone. His hair was stripped away by the gusting wind. Mason's arms shrunk down to just bone and tendon. The only thing that remained of his previous physique was the bulging in his stomach where he had gorged himself on flesh.

The sibilant whispering grew louder, then it and the wind cut out abruptly. In the suffocating silence, Mason floated in the air, his back arched, his face twisted in horror. The he dropped to the floor and landed on his feet. The black eyes of the wendigo stared at me, and it shrieked in sudden, ravenous fury.

A flash of light burst and a thunderous boom deafened me. The wendigo's head vanished in a spray of clotted gore. Harper worked the lever on her Marlin and took a step forward, her rifle never shifting from its aim. She put another round in the wendigo's chest, dead center on its heart, and racked the lever again. The second shot punched the wendigo backward and it slammed against a kitchen cabinet, leaving a smear of blood behind.

Once the worst of the ringing was gone from my ears, I stepped up next to Harper and surveyed the damage. The wendigo was very dead. The massive 444 round had obliterated its skull and hollowed the soft tissue out. The second shot hadn't been necessary, but I didn't blame her for it.

"Oh my God, Ryan!"

"Yeah. Holy shit."

"Did he… Is that how…?"

"Watch." I pointed, directing her attention back to the dead monster.

The corpse on the ground seemed to sag and become insubstantial. The gore that was splashed across the kitchen turned clear and evaporated away, then the body itself collapsed into nothingness.

I sighed and shifted my rifle up onto my shoulder. "It's done."

CHAPTER TWENTY

Harper stared at me, her eyes wide in shock. She still had her rifle pressed tight to her shoulder. "I killed him," she said hoarsely. "I killed Mason!"

"No," I told her firmly. "He was already dead. You killed a fae monster, nothing more."

She nodded uncertainly. "Is that what happened, there? The spirit of the wendigo took him over?"

"Do not doubt your own eyes, Harper. You saw the transformation, and that's what prompted you to take the shot. That was cleanly done, too. You should be proud of that. No everyone can keep their cool under pressure."

"And I suppose humans don't just fade away into nothing," she laughed, and it was like a sudden dam of tension burst. She flicked on her rifle's safety and finally lowered it from her shoulder. Harper took a deep breath and turned away from the kitchen. "Now what do we do?"

"Now… I'm worried. The original wendigo is recruiting members of Liam's gang. We caught Mason in the act of giving in to his greed, but there were more young men in that truck that shot at us."

"Travis and Oliver. Those are his other two friends. There aren't any others that would be close enough to agree to something that… extreme." She nodded toward the bloody sink.

"Three wendigos." I sighed and shook my head. "And I thought we had it hard with one."

"Did we do this?" Harper asked after a moment.

"What do you mean?"

"I guess, well, we threatened the wendigo. Did he send Liam's friends to the stashes as a reaction?"

I frowned thoughtfully. "Maybe. But it doesn't change anything. Our plan stays the same. We spike the meat with the iron filings, then set up at the gravel dump. We have to gain the initiative somehow. Unless we can find out where the damn thing made its den, provoking it is the only option we have."

"Oh, I didn't even think of that. Where would a wendigo make its den?"

I shook my head. Nothing in the Chapter Archives or the story suggested where the monster would make a den. "I don't know. It could be anywhere. An overturned tree, a cave, a house of one of its victims."

"Oh. Well, there aren't many caves around here, just one or two down the river a bit."

"Maybe something we can look into if our trap doesn't work. For now, I think we should stick to the plan."

"Yeah. Okay." Harper flipped her hair back and got her rifle slung up onto her shoulder again. "You got the filings?"

I slung my pack off my back and tossed it to her. "You can do the honors. I'll watch our backs."

She got the coffee can out and gave it a little shake. "How much should I use?"

"Like you were seasoning a steak."

Harper set about spiking the flesh. Other than making a few disgusted faces as she worked through the bags in the freezer, she didn't complain or object to the grisly task. I was impressed. I knew seasoned Chapter hunters who would have bitched about it the whole time.

When she was finished, Harper popped the cap back on the coffee can and washed her hands in the sink. She scrubbed at them with soap all the way up to the elbows like she was preparing for surgery.

"It's like butchering a deer," she said grimly as she scrubbed. "I don't mind how dirty I get, because I know I can always clean up afterwards."

"That's a good way of looking at it," I agreed. "You all set? We've been here too long."

She wiped her arms dry with a dishtowel and tossed it into the sink. "I guess we don't need to hide that we've been here this time."

"Nope. The wendigo would figure it out pretty quick anyway," I grinned. "I almost want to see its face when it tries to eat this flesh."

We headed outside. The sky was blotted with heavy clouds, a dramatic change from ten minutes earlier. Even Harper was surprised.

"I take it this isn't a normal weather pattern?" I asked

"It shouldn't be this bad for a few hours at least," she said with a puzzled frown.

In the distance, thunder growled. The first drops of rain started falling and splashed against my upturned face. The day had taken a turn for the worse. I just hoped it wasn't an omen.

The gravel dump was just outside of town. Three or four acres of trees had been plowed down and a few thousand tons of gravel had been dumped in their place. A dozen different grades of gravel had been piled up in towering windrows, following some organization pattern that wasn't readily evident.

It was strange being able to see in a straight line for more than a hundred feet. Other than the roads, there wasn't an open space in all of Kingfield larger than the parking lot outside the general store. Here, though, there were piles of gravel scattered all about, but there were good shooting sightlines down the lanes left clear for heavy equipment.

The rain was starting to come down in earnest now. It wasn't heavy enough to cut visibility much, but that could change soon. I parked near the entrance and we got out of the car.

Harper wasted no time in going around to the back of the car. She popped the trunk and hauled the cooler out. "Should we season this meat too?" she asked.

"Yeah. No reason to give those things any flesh. Just sprinkle a layer across the top. That should be enough. But set a piece aside to use as bait."

She did as I suggested and put the can back in the trunk. It was mostly empty now, with only a handful of the steel shavings left inside. I set the reserved chunk of flesh on the lid, grabbed a handle on the cooler, and together we hauled it out into the gravel dump.

As we walked, I looked around at the piles of gravel, trying to calculate where a good spot would be. I wanted the cooler somewhere clearly visible from the road, and I wanted a vantage point where I could see anyone approaching from the road or the woods.

It didn't take me long to realize the futility of finding the perfect spot. The piles of gravel might offer good oversight positions, but they also provided cover for too many approaches.

"We're going to have to split up," I said. "Not too far. I'll be up there on that pile, and you'll be over there. We'll be able to protect each other and we'll double the number of sightlines we can cover."

Harper wiped rainwater from her face and squinted up at the pile I had indicated for her. It was around twenty feet high at the peak and backed up on the property line. From the top, she should have a clear line of sight down the main truck path between the piles.

"You want me up there?"

"Yeah." I set the cooler down in the middle of the intersection where anyone approaching from the street would see it clearly. From Harper's position, she would have direct sight of it as well. "I hope you're feeling patient. We might be lying in the rain for a while."

She grimaced, then shrugged. "I'm already soaked. What's an hour more in the rain? If this means we end the wendigo now, I'll sit out all night."

"That's the spirit. Let's get into position and see what happens."

Climbing the pile of gravel was easier in my head than it turned out to be. The pile I had picked was three-quarter minus, basically whatever was left after granite rubble had been crushed and all the bigger bits were sorted out. Every step I took, my feet sank into the pile halfway to my knees. The gravel had been stacked as steeply as possible, and I kept triggering little miniature avalanches that threatened to knock me backwards.

I persisted, and after a few minutes finally made the peak. I paused to catch my breath and looked over at Harper to see how she was getting along. She was sitting on the top of her pile comfortably, and apparently had been for a while.

Harper gave me a silent round of applause and shifted around so she was laying on her stomach, with her body on the far side of the ridge. From the ground, you'd have to be paying close attention to spot her. I did the same, grumbling to myself about having picked the harder pile to climb.

Behind me, there were a few smaller piles of different-sized river rock, ranging from pebbles to rocks the size of my head, and behind that was the tree line. If someone were to approach me from behind, they'd have to navigate over the tricky piles of rock to reach my pile, and then arduously climb up the slope to reach me. I was safe enough.

I got myself into as comfortable a position as I could and pulled my coat lapel up to cover the back of my neck. The rain wasn't as cold as it had been the other day, but that didn't make it any more enjoyable.

The rough gravel dug into my knees and elbows, despite the leather. I got my rifle into position and checked the various angles, making sure I had a clean line of sight to cover the approaches. The spot I had picked was perfect. There was no way the wendigo would be able to make it to the cooler without me being able to shoot it, and the awkward angles were covered by Harper. After seeing her shoot today, I had no reservations about her ability to hit a target.

Now all we had to do was wait. And hope that the wendigo showed up before nightfall.

I've found there's a trick to waiting. In the build up to a combat situation, long waits can be hard on your nerves. Always expecting something with big teeth and poor dental hygiene to jump out at you from the shadows wears you down. Then, when it *does* jump out, you get startled, your adrenaline has been wasted hours before, and your reactions are delayed.

You have to disengage. You can't let yourself get distracted by daydreams, or even worse, fall asleep, but you can't stay hard focused for hours on end. Nobody can. There's a middle ground to be found, where you're aware and mentally present, but not riding on a hair trigger.

I shifted my knees and elbows around a little so there weren't sharp rocks actively digging into my skin, then I just let my thoughts shift into neutral. I wasn't waiting. Waiting implies expectation, and with expectation comes worry and thoughts about the future or the past. I was just... being there.

It's hard to teach someone the trick, and harder to learn it, but I'd had plenty of time to practice over the years. The rain falling on my head and slicking down my hair shifted out of importance and turned into just another facet of my existence, no more important than the need to remember to keep breathing.

On the other pile, I saw Harper shifting around every few minutes, trying to be comfortable. Every movement she made sent little rocks tumbling down the pile she was on. Eventually she found some Zen state of her own and settled into silence and stillness.

Time passed. The rain lightened and grew heavier, back and forth, before finally settling down into a steady shower. Visibility was cut down to a few hundred yards, but I could still see the road and the occasional car driving past. The rain wouldn't affect the accuracy of my shots, so I ignored it.

I didn't know how much time had gone by, but eventually a pair of headlights going down the road slowed, then swung in toward the gravel lot. It was not quite night yet, but the heavy clouds overhead turned the evening into an extended twilight. The peace of my neutral wait vanished and adrenaline thumped in my chest. Almost immediately, I became aware of how cold I was. I wasn't freezing, or even cold enough to shiver, but I could feel the stiffness in my muscles.

It took an effort not to shift my weight in an attempt to get circulation flowing better. I remembered how even the smallest movements from Harper had sent gravel sliding down her mound. If the same thing happened to me, my position would be given away instantly.

The headlights bounced as the vehicle drove onto the uneven ground of the lot, casting cones of light ahead that bobbed and swayed with the shocks. It was a truck, I could tell that much, but the details were washed out in the glare.

The truck slowed to a stop around twenty yards from the cooler. At this range, I was confident I could put a half-dozen rounds inside a silver dollar as fast as I could pull the trigger. If the wendigo was the driver, it was dead.

Anticipation made my heartrate pick up. I had my sights centered on the driver, and I was just waiting to confirm it was actually the wendigo. If Liam stepped out of the truck, I wasn't going to let him get away again. The rounds my rifle fired might not be as destructive as Harper's Marlin, but they would more than suffice.

For a long moment nothing happened, then, instead of the driver's door opening, the passenger door swung open. Glare from the headlights prevented me from making out who was sitting in the driver's seat when the cab light went on, then my attention went to the figure getting out of the passenger door.

It was a boy, shorter than I was expecting, and he stumbled out in front of the headlights. He shaded his eyes against the headlights and did a slow turn-about, peering up at the piled gravel.

"Harper?" he called in a wavering voice. "Harper, are you there?"

Ah, shit. I knew who it was before I heard Harper's call.

"Henry?!" Gravel cascaded down the gravel pile from where Harper was hiding and I saw her rise up into a kneeling position.

Fuck. Giving her some kind of signal would only give away

my own position. All I could do was hope she had sense enough to stay back. If that was truly Henry Davis down there, and not a wendigo wearing his skin, the kid was in serious trouble.

"That you up there, Harper?" The voice calling from the truck was not one I knew. "Why don't you come on down so we can talk?"

"Fuck you, Travis!" Harper shouted. "Let Henry go!"

"Henry, show Harper, like I told you," Travis said.

Henry lifted his hand, and I saw a short length of rebar clutched in his fist. "I want to go home, Harper!" he cried. "I'm scared!"

I swallowed against a tight throat. The kid was alive. He had managed to hide from the wendigo for a time, but that game of cat and mouse was over. The memories stolen from its victims had told the wendigo that Henry was more valuable as bait than as a meal. Now Harper was halfway into the trap, and there was nothing I could do.

"It's okay, Henry," Harper called. "Just walk away from the truck. Climb up to me and you'll be safe. I know where your sister and your dad are."

"I can't," Henry whimpered. He reached down to his waist and held up a thick nylon rope. I hadn't been able to see it earlier because of the headlight glare.

"Don't bother, Harper," Travis mocked. "I've seen through your little plans. There's only one way Henry walks free. You want to know what it is?"

I shifted my sights over to the rope. It would be tricky to hit it. Henry wasn't staying still and the rope was swinging. There would be a stationary point where it traveled under the door of the truck, but the glare of the headlights washed out my vision and I couldn't see it clearly. Besides, even if I managed to hit the rope directly, it was too thick to be cut clean through.

"Damn you," Harper cried.

"Oh, stop whining," Travis laughed. "Here's the deal. You come on down and get in the truck, and I'll let Henry go."

It took a physical effort for me not to call out to warn Harper. If she got in the truck with a wendigo, she would be screwed. I swung back to examine the windshield again, searching for any hint of where the wendigo might be. I could just start shooting, but if I missed, the wendigo would reverse out of the lot and drag Henry along with the truck. The kid wouldn't live through that. I could try and disable the truck, but without the ridiculous penetrating power of Harper's Marlin, I doubted I'd be able to wreck the engine fast enough.

"Do you promise?" Harper asked.

I gritted my teeth and willed Harper not to make that mistake.

"Would you trust me if I said so?"

"No."

"Then why ask? For what it's worth, I do promise. Now stop wasting time and get down here."

Harper was silence for a moment, then Henry called out, "Please, Harper, don't leave me with them!"

I could see the decision come over her. The wendigo must have recognized it too, because it said, "And leave your rifle up on the pile."

She was halfway through standing up, and now she bent back over and set her rifle down on the gravel. Harper tested the slope with an outstretched foot, then shied back as the face of the pile collapsed.

"Hurry up!" Travis called.

Harper got on her butt and started sliding down the slope, bringing a cascade of gravel with her in a building hiss. The growing noise gave me an idea, I just had to time things perfectly. She reached the ground and jumped forward out of the rush of gravel following on her heels.

The racket wasn't going to get any louder, and if I was lucky, it would be enough to muffle my rifle's report. Or at least make it hard to tell where it was coming from. I took aim at the right headlight and squeezed the trigger. My rifle barked and the light went out with a crack. I swung my aim over a few feet and shot out the other headlight.

The gravel lot was instantly plunged into gloom. Through the windshield, I could finally see the outline of a man leaning over the center console so he could watch Harper slide down the gravel pile. The man's head flinched around, and I saw the sudden emaciation pull his cheeks in as the wendigo resumed its true form. Henry squealed; he was close enough to the headlight that he might have caught some flying glass.

No more hiding. I shifted my sights up. The wendigo was trying to get back into position where it could reach the pedals, shifting back and forth between its natural form and Travis. Just as I pulled the trigger, something landed in the gravel next to me.

I twisted away and saw a figure lunge toward me, moving faster than any human could. I got my arm up to shield my face, and a foot crashed into my stomach. The impact knocked the wind from me and threw me from the top of the pile. I landed on my back and started sliding down the back side, away from Harper and Henry. The figure leapt after me, sending gravel skittering down to pelt me in the face.

Instinct sent my hand diving into my coat. The rough grip of my handgun filled my palm and I ripped it free. The wendigo recoiled and tried to dodge, but couldn't find footing in the sliding gravel to leap away. I got a shot off, but had no idea where the bullet went.

I started pulling the trigger as rapidly as I could, doing my best to keep the sights lined up in the general direction of the wendigo. I reached the ground first. By the time my shoulders hit the bottom of the pile, my handgun's slide was locked open on an empty magazine.

I rolled to my feet and reached into my coat for a fresh clip. I didn't know if I had hit the wendigo during my slide down the gravel pile, but my hands flew through the automatic motions of reloading. The wendigo reached the ground and stumbled, somehow keeping its balance. Then, with my feet firmly planted, I put three rounds into the wendigo's center mass.

The wendigo slammed to a stop, its mouth hanging open in silent shock. It lifted hand to touch its chest, long, bony fingers feeling for the holes my bullets had punched through it. I could see the confusion in its eyes, surprised denial that anything mortal could hurt so bad.

On the other side of the pile, I heard the deeper bark of Harper's revolver, then her voice raised in a pained cry. The wendigo in front of me shifted back to the form of a young man. He coughed up blood, then skinned his teeth at me in something vaguely resembling a smile.

"I had a hard time finding you," he hissed. "But it's too late. You won't—"

I shot it in the face, then turned and was running down the path before the wendigo had hit the ground. The gravel pile was thirty yards across at the base, and it took me an agonizingly long time to sprint back around to the far side.

The truck started up and the engine roared. I rounded the pile in time to see the truck skidding through a puddle as it gunned for the exit to the lot. Harper was nowhere to be seen. I lifted my gun, but couldn't risk taking a shot. Then the truck screeched out onto the highway and roared off toward town.

"Fuck!"

A quiet sob caught my ears and I turned. There was a length of nylon rope snaking through the puddles. I followed it around to a hollow in the pile of gravel. Henry was crouched down out of sight, his arms wrapped around his knees.

His head twisted around when I came into view and he flinched so hard he fell back onto his ass. "Who are you?" he gasped.

"A friend of Harper's," I said gruffly. "What happened? Where's Harper?"

Henry gave out a racking sob, then dissolved into tears.

Shit. I took a deep breath and tried for a gentler tone. "Sorry. You must be Henry Davis. I'm Ryan Halsin. Harper asked me to help her find the missing people. We've been looking all over for you, you know?" I squatted down in the puddled rain and touched his shoulder. "Harper was sure you were still alive. I'm glad she was right."

"I couldn't stop them," he said in between sobs. "It took Harper!"

"Yeah." I looked back toward the road where the truck had left. "I don't suppose you know where they're going?"

He shook his head. "Somewhere dark, that's all I know." His sobs were winding down some. Not from relief, more because he was just too exhausted to keep up the effort of crying.

"All right, Henry. You're doing great. Was it dark like inside a building? Or was it a cave?"

"A cave, maybe? I don't know. The floor was dirt and rocks."

"Okay. I'm going to get Harper back, I promise. But first, we need to get you somewhere safe. Do you know where you could go?"

He just looked up at me with wide eyes and shook his head.

I sighed and nodded. "Right. I guess you can come and stay with me. Would that be okay?"

"Is Tammy alive?"

"She is! But she and your father have gone south to your uncle's house. They're both safe, and I'll make sure you get back to them." I knelt down next to him and untied the rope from around his waist. "Okay. Stay here. I have to find my gun and Harper's. You see anything coming, give a shout. I won't be long."

I hated leaving Henry there, but it would take too long if I tried to get him to follow me as I clambered over the gravel piles. I went to find Harper's gun first. I knew where it was, for one thing, and if another wendigo showed up, I wanted the firepower of the Marlin in my hands.

Harper's pile was a lot easier to climb than mine had been, and I found her Marlin where she had left it. I checked it over to make sure it was ready to shoot if I needed it, then tried to spot where mine had gone to. In the dark and the rain, it was difficult to see anything clearly, but after a minute my eyes picked out the straight line of the barrel among the tumbled confusion of the gravel.

It was full dark by the time I made it down from my gravel pile with both rifles. Henry was where I had left him, now soaked to the skin and starting to shiver. He gave a low cry when he saw me and ran over to throw his arms around my waist.

I shifted the guns around so I had a free hand and patted him on the shoulder, awkwardly trying to comfort him. "It's okay, Henry. I told you I'd be back. Come on, let's get to my car."

CHAPTER TWENTY-ONE

We rolled into the parking lot of the bed and breakfast a few minutes later. The car hadn't had time to warm up and the heater was still blowing lukewarm air. Getting out into the rain once more wasn't fun, but the thought of a dry change of clothes got me moving.

I walked Henry into the lobby and Sylvia looked up from behind her desk with a bright smile. "Mr. Halsin! I'm glad to see... Henry? My goodness, Henry Davis, you're alive?!"

She came out from behind the desk and hurried toward us. I stepped forward, putting myself between Henry and Sylvia. "Mrs. Toole, please. Henry's had a hard couple of days."

She drew up short and understanding washed over her face. She wrung her hands together and nodded. "Oh. Of course. What can I do?"

I was fairly certain Sylvia wasn't a wendigo. After abducting Harper, they were likely in whatever cave they were hiding in, doing something nefarious. They wouldn't be trying to ambush me at the bed and breakfast on the off-chance I returned there. Still, I couldn't be too careful, especially when it was Henry's life on the line.

"You know how to use a gun, Sylvia?"

A hard look came over her face and she nodded, the façade of the cheerful hostess vanishing in an instant. "Is Henry in danger?"

"As much as anyone else in this town. Here, take this." I unsnapped the flashlight from my rifle's barrel and held the gun out to her. I watched closely until she grabbed it by the metal of the barrel. Not a wendigo, then.

Sylvia checked the breach, ejected the magazine and confirmed there were rounds still in it, then socketed it back together with a familiarity that spoke volumes. "Henry will be safe with me," she said fiercely.

"Good. Get him something to eat if he wants, then I bet he'll want to sleep. Maybe my rooms?" I knelt down next to Henry. "How does that sound? Mrs. Toole will watch over you until I can get back."

"Okay," he said in a small voice.

"Good lad. Don't you fret. I'll be back with Harper before you know it."

"Is Harper…?"

"I just came by to drop Henry off. Harper needs me."

"Okay. I'll get him fed and up to your rooms. Don't you worry about Henry."

I nodded, relieved that Sylvia had stepped so willingly into the role of protective mother. "Good. Thank you, Sylvia."

She put her arm around Henry's shoulder and started steering him toward the back where the kitchen was. Then she paused and looked back at me. "You aren't here to do a wildlife survey are you?"

I shook my head. "No."

"You know what is happening in this town? Where the missing people have gone?"

I nodded.

"Then. Is Sherry… is my daughter…" She trailed off, unable to complete the thought out loud.

I held her gaze and gave my head a tiny shake.

Sylvia let out a sharp breath and went pale, then gritted her teeth with renewed purpose. "Thank you for letting me know," she said, and her voice came out tight with grief.

"I'm sorry," I said.

"You're going to stop… whatever is happening?"

"Yes." It was a simple response, but it seemed to give Sylvia renewed strength.

"Okay. I've got this. Go do what you have to do."

I gave her a nod and a last wave to Henry, then I turned around and headed back out into the rain. Dry clothes could wait until Harper was safe again. Maybe I would get lucky and Harper was still alive.

Still alive, and still Harper. The thought of a wendigo using her appearance to confront me made me sick to my stomach. I would pull the trigger if that happened, but I knew it would break something inside me to do so. I had grown close to the small-town Ranger, and being forced to kill her, or a likeness of her, would hurt more than I wanted to admit.

I stopped on the porch and watched the rain coming down. The leather coat Harper's grandma had given me hung heavy around my shoulders. What now? How was I supposed to find the wendigo when I had spent a week wandering around this forgotten corner of the world with nothing to show for it?

There were a few hints. Henry had been held in some place with a rough dirt floor that was dark. That could be a cave, or maybe a redneck survivalist shelter. If it was the latter, there was no way I would be able to find it. People paranoid enough to build underground shelters usually weren't open about sharing their locations with strangers.

That was an avenue of investigation that would take too

long. If Harper was being held in some survivalist bunker out in the woods, she was as good as dead. That left the cave option. Harper had mentioned the existence of a cave along the river. I didn't have time to wander up and down the bank looking for a cave entrance, which meant I needed a local to show me where it was.

I discarded the idea of turning around and asking Sylvia if she knew the location. She needed to stay with Henry. The problem was, I didn't know anyone else in this damn town. Maybe Miles or Slate, the two Rangers who discovered the missing skiers, could help but I had no way of contacting them, and waiting for them to drive from wherever they were would take too long.

There was only one person in Kingfield who might help: Police Sergeant Willard Bunnings. I had an address this time, at least. I stepped off the porch and into the rain. I didn't have much of a plan. Find Harper. Kill the remaining wendigos.

The two killed so far had been freshly created. The one I had killed in the gravel dump hadn't been more than a few hours old, but it had already been incredibly fast and strong. If it hadn't been for a lucky series of accidents sliding down the slope, that encounter could have turned out very differently for me. The original wendigo had been in the mortal for five months. It would be even stronger than the ones new to the mortal.

I stopped at my car's trunk and swapped out the spent handgun magazines with loaded ones. I grabbed my pack then got into the car. The box of steel 444 rounds was sitting on the passenger seat where Harper had left them. It was a little awkward reloading the Marlin with its long barrel inside the cramped car, but I got its magazine refilled and stuffed a few more rounds into a pocket.

There wasn't a single other car on the road as I drove across town to Sergeant Bunnings' house. It was raining out, but it wasn't that late. Even in a small town like this, I would have expected to see a few people around, running errands or visiting with friends. But this felt as if Kingfield was a ghost town. If I failed tonight then in a few weeks it would be one in truth.

The police sergeant's house was two stories and surprisingly not painted white. It was something of a shock to see the slate-grey siding and blue trim among the uniformity of the houses. An old police cruiser was parked out front, a sedan from the eighties, probably surplus from a larger city.

I parked next to it and got out to bang on the front door. "Sergeant Bunnings!" I called. "Sergeant! This is an emergency!"

Through the thin curtains hanging over the windows next to the door, I saw a hunched figure get up from an overstuffed armchair and shuffle toward the door. There was the rattle of a chain, then the door creaked open a few inches.

Sergeant Bunnings must have been tall and strong in his youth. There was still an echo of that physique in the old man, but that was all. A month or two of drink and despair had done more to ruin his health than the last ten years had. The watery, red eyes behind circular glasses held no more interest than if I was trying to sell him a fancy new vacuum cleaner.

"There are no emergencies in Kingfield," he said dully. "If someone is missing, come by in the morning."

He started to shut the door and I stuck my foot in the crack before he could get it all the way closed. "I need your help, Sergeant. Harper is in danger."

"Harper?" The name brought a flicker of interest, then horror and fresh despair washed over him. "Oh no. Not her, too." His arms went slack and the door sagged open again.

"No! Listen to me, Sergeant. She's not dead yet. I know where she was taken, I just need direction!"

"You don't speak sense. Who are you, anyway? I don't know your face."

I gritted my teeth, and refrained from reaching into the doorway and shaking the old man by the shoulders. "My name is Ryan Halsin. Harper called me in from Portland. I'm a specialist in dealing with situations like what you've been experiencing in Kingfield, but we can talk about that later. Harper is in a cave by the river, but I don't know where the cave is. I need you to show me where it is."

"The Carrabassett caves?" he mumbled. "Why would she go there? Those aren't safe."

"It wasn't by choice," I pointed out, trying to keep the frustration out of my voice. "She was taken there against her will."

"Who would do such a thing?" he asked querulously. "There aren't kidnappings in Kingfield! We're a law-abiding folk around here."

"Does it matter? What is important is that Harper is there now, and she needs our help. She needs *your* help."

He stared at me for a long moment, and I saw the understanding finally filter through the alcohol. "I'll get my keys."

"Ah, a moment, Sergeant. Should you be driving right now?"

Bunnings huffed, glared at me sideways, then rubbed a hand over his face. "No. You're right. I suppose that's your car there? Didn't peg you for a Civic guy."

"It's a rental," I sighed.

We got into my car and I started driving back toward the bed and breakfast. Bunnings smelled like he hadn't showered in over a week and reeked of stale alcohol. If I didn't need the man's cooperation, I would have kicked him out of my car. As it was, my eyes started watering and I had to crack the window despite the pouring rain.

Bunnings, for his part, seemed too drunk to notice. The cold wind must have started taking the edge off his buzz, because he started speaking and sounded almost sober. "It's not far, now. There's a bend in the river where the current started digging through a soft spot in the rock. Then the water level dropped and the cave drained out. The whole system is a few hundred yards deep, with a handful of branches. Local kids get lost in there every few years and we have to rescue them. Are you sure that's where Harper is?"

"No, it's just my best guess. Are there any other caves near town?"

"Nah. Not for a couple miles, at least. Up here, the next turnout is the one we want."

I slowed and turned off the highway onto the side road. At one point the road had been maintained, even covered in asphalt, but now the surface was completely broken up by weather and tree roots. I had to slow down to a crawl to make any headway, and my car's shocks still had my teeth banging together over the rough bumps.

"This isn't going to work," I grunted, and pulled off the road into the first clear space I could find big enough to fit my car. "I'm going the rest of the way on foot. Give me directions?"

"I'll go with you," Bunnings said.

"Forget it. It would be too dangerous, even if you weren't drunk. You stay here with the car."

"And what happens if you don't come back?"

I gave him a sour smile. "Just hope that doesn't happen. But if it does... We found Henry Davis. He's with Sylvia Toole at her bed and breakfast. Make sure Henry gets to his father down in Virginia."

"And what about whatever is making people disappear?"

I shook my head. There wasn't anything I could tell him that would be a comfort. "Like I said, let's just hope I make it back with Harper. Where are the caves?"

Bunnings frowned at the dashboard then sighed. "I don't know if I'm happy with you going there alone, Mr…?"

"Halsin."

"Yeah. You're not from around here, and I don't trust you."

I pushed down the flash of rage before it got properly started. "I don't have time to argue with you, Sergeant. Harper needs my help, and to be blunt, you're a liability. I'm sure you mean well, but I don't have time to babysit a drunk old man who has already abandoned his town." Maybe I hadn't pushed the rage down as far as I had thought.

The muscles in Bunnings' jaw flexed as he clenched his teeth, then his shoulders drooped. "I won't claim I've handled things well. But I did try."

I gripped the steering wheel and told myself that I would already be on my way if I had used a bit more diplomacy and less anger. "I know you did. I can only imagine how hard it's been. But this is the *only* chance we have to make it right. I don't have time—Harper doesn't have time—for you to feel sorry for yourself. Now, where is the god damn cave?"

He flinched and I cursed at myself silently. Real good diplomacy, Ryan. Then, reluctantly, Bunnings nodded down the busted-up road ahead of us. "A few hundred feet ahead, the road turns to follow the river. There's a footpath there that leads down to the bank. The caves are another twenty or thirty feet further on."

"Okay. Sergeant…" I waited until he looked at me, anger and self-hatred written all over his face. "Thank you."

Bunnings turned his head to look out his window. "Yeah."

Fuck it. I got out of the car and left the old man to his sulk. I had no patience for people who got offended by swearing. Oh no, he said a bad word! Grow the fuck up. I didn't quite slam my door, and flipped my collar up against the rain. I checked the chamber on Harper's Marlin and made sure it was loaded and ready to fire.

I wanted the initiative in my hunt for the wendigo, but I didn't think it would turn out quite like this. In any other circumstance, I would turn around and return to the bed and breakfast. Give John Baptiste a call and request backup. For a wendigo this old, they'd send every hunter in a hundred miles. I could storm the cave with a squad of a dozen seasoned Chapter hunters. We'd bring enough firepower to slaughter it several times over.

But by that time, Harper would be dead. Belatedly, I wondered if Baptiste's repeated attempts to contact me were efforts to offer me reinforcements. Or maybe just checking to see if I was still alive. Maybe I should have returned one of his calls earlier. Oh well, it was too late now.

I walked down the road, stepping carefully so I didn't turn an ankle on the fissured surface. The rain was pelting down, soaking my hair and running down the back of my neck. With nightfall, the rain had turned cold and I could feel the stiffness in my muscles.

I came around a bend in the road and saw a truck pulled to one side. The windshield and headlights were shot out and I felt a surge of relief go through me. It was the truck that had been driven by the wendigo. Harper was here. My gamble on the cave had paid off.

The truck still had its keys in the ignition and a faint dinging came from the cab, a digital protest over the doors being left open. I circled wide around the truck and saw the footpath Bunnings had mentioned. It was steep and craggy, with partially rotten wooden planks giving some structure to the stairs.

One step at a time, I worked my way down the path. I didn't dare use my flashlight to illuminate my way. The only advantage I had going for me was the element of surprise, and swinging a light around would be the surest way to ruin that.

The rush of the river filled my ears before I drew close enough to see it. Then the trees opened up and I saw the river going by, dark and cold-looking. The last stretch of the footpath dropped almost straight down the rocky bank, and I had to inch my way along. The granite was wet with rain and slippery with moss.

By the time I got to the bottom of the bank, I was out of breath and my hands were numb with cold. The footpath continued along the edge of the water, with only a foot or two of walking room. The river curved to the left up ahead, swinging wide around a rise in the land. At the base of the turn, I saw a dark splotch in the steep granite bank. It was the cave I had been looking for.

It took me a few more minutes to make my way to the base of the bank under the cave. Hundreds of years ago, the level of the river had been higher. The force of the water being turned around the rise in the land had beaten on the rock relentlessly, wearing away a softer seam in the granite. The cave was the result. What little experience I've had with such erosion caves wasn't much help. They were all different, depending on the structure of the surrounding rock. The only thing for certain, was the interior was going to be cold and damp.

Someone had chiseled a few shallow footholds into the granite years ago to give access to the cave from the footpath. The rock face was wet with rain, but the rough stone gave me a sure grip. I slung the Marlin onto my back and climbed up to the cave opening.

It was pitch black inside the cave, without even moonlight or starlight to shine inside. A cold draft wafted out of the entrance, spiked with a faint hint of decay. Any doubt that I was at the wrong cave was gone. Still, I couldn't bring myself to step inside the overhang and enter.

Azeban, the trickster god, liked to trap people inside caves. I didn't know enough about him to know how to mollify him if he was watching. The leather coat around my shoulders was a comforting weight, though. I might not know anything about him, but Nokemes did, and the coat had her protection burned into it. It would have to be enough.

I had come this far under the cover of darkness, but now I had no choice but to turn on my flashlight. I flicked the flashlight on and deep red light filled the mouth of the cave. There wasn't a practical way to hold a flashlight and aim a rifle at the same time, and Harper's gun didn't have mounting spots for it the way mine did.

Still, nothing a little duct tape can't handle. I got the tape from my pack and fixed the flashlight to the barrel with a few turns. It wasn't a permanent solution by any means, and the light was canted off at an angle to the barrel, but I could see and shoot at the same time.

I took my heavy-bladed hunting knife from my pack and hung it from my belt, then swung the pack up onto my back. There wasn't anything else holding me back from entering the cave now but my own fear. The air coming from inside seemed to whisper muted promises of horror within.

The last thing I wanted to do was enter the cave. If the wendigo heard or saw me coming, it would attack where I wouldn't have room to fight it properly. If it got to choose where we fought, I wasn't going to have a chance in hell.

For a long minute I hesitated. All my training, all my experience told me that going into the cave alone was a terrible idea. It was exactly the sort of thing I would have told Harper to never do. But Harper needed me. That thought was what made me take the first step forward, and after that my feet moved of their own accord.

The opening of the cave was a few feet taller than my head and roughly diamond-shaped, with a very narrow floor. Wind had blown in leaves and other debris, and there was clear, recent disturbance to the piles where someone, or something, had kicked a path through. The walls of the cave were tagged with graffiti and there were empty beer cans and cigarette butts mixed in with the leaves.

I kept my light pointed toward the ground as I headed deeper. The walls opened up into a small cavern, maybe fifteen feet across. The back walls of the cave closed together and I came to a stop, shining my light around at the walls. In the red light of my flashlight, the dark granite seemed to be glistening with blood. This was it? A dead-end not twenty feet from the entrance?

I backtracked a bit until I found the scuffing footprints through the debris again, then followed them deeper into the cave. After the junk around the entrance was gone, there wasn't much on the ground to show where someone had walked. It was all bare, seamed granite, with only occasional patches of sand and dirt. Still, I could tell that several people had walked through the cave. They were going somewhere, not just wandering around.

I lined my flashlight up with the footprints and pointed it in the direction they were headed, but all I saw were the uneven walls. I had to be missing something. Keeping my flashlight on the bit of wall where the footsteps were leading, I walked across the cave.

It wasn't until I was ten feet from the wall that I saw the changing shadows and realized there was a fissure hidden behind an outcrop of granite. The hidden opening was narrow enough that I had to turn sideways to fit in, and I flashed back to Slate's warning. Don't go through any areas you couldn't walk in easily. If I got stuck down here, help wouldn't be coming.

I couldn't point Harper's gun in front of me while making my way through the opening, so I had to feel my way in the darkness, testing every step ahead of me in case there was an abrupt drop. The tight passage didn't take long to get through, and it opened up again, wide enough for me to point the rifle around where I wanted to see.

The cave started dropping downward, below the level of the river. The walls became damp with humidity and water trickled downhill underfoot. The kids with spray paint had tried to tag these walls, but the damp made the paint patchy and inconsistent.

It never ceased to amaze me just how powerful erosion was. The water that had dug this cave out originally must have been extremely turbulent, and I could see the effects on the walls. There were no sharp edges here, and even the hard granite was rounded and smooth.

A sudden shriek came from somewhere deeper within the cave and I froze, the hair on the back of my neck trying to stand up. The shriek echoed and faded away, and then I heard Harper's low cry of pain. She was still alive!

CHAPTER TWENTY-TWO

The unsettling cry had locked my feet in place, but now I moved forward again, taking less care with my footing than I had earlier. The acoustics of the cave made it impossible to tell where sound was coming from. All I knew was that at least one wendigo and Harper were somewhere up ahead.

There was a branch up ahead and I eased up to the corner before swinging around it with the rifle held tight to my shoulder. The branch was a small cul-de-sac, ten feet across. A strangely sweet reek of decay hit me, and then I saw the piled human remains. There had to be at least ten bodies stacked up haphazardly, their meat and flesh stripped away without much care.

This far below the surface, the temperature was only a few degrees above freezing. The cold had slowed the decay, but the bodies on the bottom of the pile were clearly rotting. I held my breath and shone my light around the tangled bones until I was certain Harper wasn't there.

The smell lingered in my nose as I pressed onward. The scuff of my boots against the granite changed tone, and my straining senses picked up a large opening ahead. I kept my light pointed at my feet and crept silently forward.

It took another minute before I reached the opening. There was a steep drop down, then the cave opened up into a large cavern. Anchors had been drilled into the rock and an aluminum and nylon rope ladder had been installed. Judging by the wear on the rope, the ladder had been in place for decades.

At the bottom of the slope, I saw the little trickle of water that had been underfoot splash into a shallow pool. It took me a moment to realize I wasn't shining my flashlight down the slope and the light was coming from some other source. I reached down the barrel of the rifle and turned my flashlight off.

I wasn't mistaken. There definitely was a soft yellow glow coming from somewhere in the cavern. I crouched down and tried to see, but the steep drop made it impossible. Tactically, it was a terrible idea to descend a rope ladder into a hostile environment, but I didn't have a choice. I had to go forward.

I inched forward carefully until I could reach the first aluminum rung of the ladder with a foot. I tested it, putting my weight on it in increments until I was standing on it completely. The nylon ropes didn't so much as creak. They might be old, but whoever had installed the ladder had chosen the right materials to make it out of.

Moving slowly so I made as little noise as possible, I made my way down the ladder. When I neared the bottom, I searched for the next rung with my foot and didn't find anything. I leaned over to see past my feet and found the ladder didn't reach all the way down the slope and ended about three feet above the surface of the pool.

I twisted around to look into the cavern and saw a small camping lantern had been set on a stumpy stalagmite. There were two figures squatting near the lantern, both of which looked male. I couldn't make out any further detail, but I knew without a doubt that I was looking at the wendigos.

My heart thumped in my throat. So far, they hadn't noticed me, but there was no way I'd be able to drop three feet into water without making noise. I felt exposed hanging on the ladder. All it would take is for one of the wendigos to glance in my direction and they would see me. I had to drop.

There was a cluster of stalagmites sticking out of the water a few feet away. I had no illusions about being able to jump to them to avoid noise, but maybe I could hide behind them and still maintain an element of surprise. When the wendigos came looking, I might get the drop on them.

It was an awful plan, but it was better than just standing in the middle of the pool in plain sight like an asshole. Then, without giving myself a chance to second-guess myself, I jumped from the ladder.

The water was only about ankle deep, but it still made quite a splash when I landed. I darted for the cluster of stalagmites and crouched down behind them. The wendigos reacted almost instantly. I heard a surprised growl and the running approach of feet.

I got Harper's Marlin to my shoulder and froze. Too late, I realized that if they brought the lantern with them my hiding spot would be useless. The lantern light didn't move, though, and I heard the footsteps slow to a stop at the edge of the pool.

"What is it?" Liam's voice called.

"Nothing. A rock, maybe."

"Idiot! A rock had to come from above. There's an intruder here. You stay here and watch the mortal. I'll go and deal with it!"

The wendigo near me hissed something sibilant, too low to make out the words. Another set of footsteps approached, then splashed through the water to the base of the ladder. Liam came into sight, and he didn't even look my way. He reached up, grabbed the bottom rung of the ladder, then swarmed up it and was gone.

After a moment, the wendigo left behind stomped back to the lantern. I heard the scuff of his boot, then the thud of a kick landing. Harper yelped and coughed.

"I don't know why you bother with the mask," she rasped. "I know you're not Travis."

"You don't know anything," the wendigo growled.

I had never dealt with Travis in any meaningful interaction, and even I knew the wendigo's attempt at the impersonation was unrefined.

"Ryan is coming for me," Harper said. "Both of you are fucked."

There was another thud and she gasped. "Your boyfriend is dead. Oliver got the jump on him in the gravel dump."

"Yeah? Then where is he?"

"Oliver's probably stuffing himself to bursting. Lot of meat on that guy, and a bit more on the kid." There was a rough laugh. "Almost not worth it, but I suppose the young stuff is tender enough. He'll be down any minute now."

Moving carefully so I didn't splash, I crept out of the pool and stepped onto dry land. From my new vantage, I had a clearer view of the lantern. Harper was lying on her side, her hands and ankles tied together behind her back. The wendigo was standing over her, and as I watched, it kicked her in the stomach again. Harper couldn't bend forward to protect herself and the blow drove the wind out of her.

A hot flash of rage surged through me. I had seen enough. I would shoot the thing where it stood, but I needed to keep the other wendigo ignorant of my presence as long as possible. I slid the knife from my belt and crept toward the wendigo. My pulse was thundering in my ears so loud I couldn't hear my own footsteps, but I must not have been as quiet as I was intending.

The wendigo spun around and sank into a crouch. I froze, but it was hopeless. I was standing out in plain view of the monster, with nothing but uneven cave floor between us. The wendigo narrowed its eyes and tilted its head to the side like a puzzled animal. Then it grunted and turned back around.

What? I let out the breath I had been holding and flexed my fingers gripping around my knife hilt. It had looked directly at me and... didn't see me? I glanced down at myself just to verify that the lantern light reached me. I could plainly see the worked leather of my coat. Maybe its pupils were so shot from looking directly at the lantern that it couldn't see into the relative darkness?

Harper's eyes shifted from her tormentor and drifted up toward me. Her gaze snapped to meet mine and her mouth opened. Then she turned her head to face the ground and gave another pained groan.

I took another step and saw the wendigo's back stiffen. It spun around and lunged in my direction, the unconvincing façade of Travis' face melting away into emaciated tendon and bone. Its mouth gaped wide, the human teeth replaced with a snarl of razor-edges and serrated points.

It swung an arm at me, its hand hooked into a feral claw. I ducked back, even though I was out of what I thought was the wendigo's reach. The ragged nails passed through open air a full foot in front of where I had been standing. The monster hesitated, then lunged forward again, swinging wildly with both arms.

It couldn't see me. The realization hit me after I was already in motion. I met one of its swings with the barrel of the Marlin and the wendigo yelped in surprised pain. Then, before it could recover, I stabbed my knife into its gut. The steel blade ripped through the emaciated flesh and the force of my blow sent the knife carving clear through its stomach and out its back.

The wendigo threw itself away from me, scrabbling across the cave floor like a stepped-on spider; long, spindly limbs thrashing around madly. I stomped on its chest in an attempt to pin it down long enough to finish it off. My boot hit its chest and its hand snapped to my ankle with a grip like a vise. It yanked sideways and I lost my balance.

I hit the ground and the wendigo climbed up my body, dragging itself upward one crushing grip at a time. It was insanely strong. Now that it had ahold of me, I couldn't kick it free, and it ignored the battering I was giving it with my free foot.

Then it reached up and grabbed onto the barrel of the Marlin. It whimpered in pain and I could see the skin of its palm split and smoke under the prolonged contact with the steel. I pulled up on the gun and the wendigo let itself be dragged up my body.

The monster's face was transfixed with a snarl of hate and pain. The slavering jaws snapped on air as it blindly searched for the source of its agony. Then I brought my knife plunging down between its eyes. I felt the skull crack and the thick blade buried to the crossguard in the middle of its face.

A tremor ran through the monster and the strength in its clutching hands wilted away. I kicked the wendigo off of me and it flopped over onto the floor. The sunken eyes faded, the gaping mouth collapsed like it was a sand sculpture left out in the sun for too long. Then my knife dropped to the stone with a musical chime and the remnants of the creature faded away into drifting motes of dust.

"Ryan!" Harper called hoarsely.

I scrambled to my feet and scooped the knife up. I ran over to Harper and knelt down next to her. "Hey there, you had me worried." I grinned at her and reached over so I could get to the paracord tying her up. Then I paused. Was this still Harper, or was it a trap?

"Oh my god, I thought it had you," she choked out.

"Nah, wasn't even close." I pressed the flat of my knife against the back of her neck.

"What are you... oh."

That wasn't the reaction a fae would have to iron. I gave a sigh of relief. "Sorry, I had to check."

My knife cut through the paracord and she groaned as her limbs flopped back to a natural position. I rocked back on my heels as Harper threw her arms around my neck. I hugged her back tightly. "How are you doing? They didn't hurt you too bad, did they?"

She shook her head. "I'll live. How's Henry? Did he...?"

"He's fine. I left him with Sylvia. She's got my rifle. What were they doing down here?"

"They were trying to turn me," she said. There was a hundred-yard stare in her eyes that I recognized from my time in the army. It would be a while before Harper recovered from her ordeal. But she was alive, and with time, she would move past it.

"You're okay."

I released her and she sat back, rubbing her wrists where the paracord had dug into her. "We need to get out of here. Once the elder finds out there was nothing up the tunnel it will come back."

"Yeah, maybe. But I'd rather fight it here. There's space and light and we can set up a cross fire. Can you shoot?"

Harper hesitated, then shook her head. "Not my Marlin. The recoil..."

"No worries." I pulled my handgun from its shoulder holster and handed it over, along with a spare magazine. "If you get a clear shot, just mag-dump into it. Try for the center of its body. Don't worry about a headshot unless you're certain."

She took the gun and checked the chamber. "What is this, 45 ACP? The kick's going to be just as bad as the rifle."

"It's a big bullet, but a subsonic powder load. It won't kick as hard as you think."

"Huh. And copper-sleeved steel rounds? Your gunsmith is way fancier than mine is."

"Perks of being part of the club. If we make it out of here, I'll introduce you. How do you feel like being bait?" I shook my head at the horrified expression on her face. "Never mind. I'll stand out here by the lantern. You can go... maybe... over there, by that outcrop."

She followed where I was pointing and nodded. "I can do that. When do you want me to start shooting?"

"The second you get a clear shot. But make it count, Harper. I don't want it targeting you."

Harper swallowed and set her jaw. "And don't get yourself killed, Ryan."

She limped off to take cover and I set the Marlin to my shoulder. The cave was silent except for the patter of the stream trickling down the slope. Harper was crouched down out of sight around the corner of the outcrop. Her face was pale and drawn, but her expression was intent and focused. I gave my head a little shake. Damn, but that girl was tough as nails.

We didn't have long to wait. A few minutes passed, then I heard scuffing coming from up the passage. A little shower of pebbles and sand came over the slope. Then there was a grunt of pain and a figure went tumbling over the edge and crashed down into the shallow pool at the base of the slope.

I snapped the rifle around to focus on the man. He pushed himself up to his hands and knees, dripping water from his beard. It was Sergeant Willard Bunnings.

Bunnings groaned in pain and sat back on his heels. He peered around the cave, squinting into the darkness. He had lost his glasses at some point and blood trickled down the right side of his face from a gash in his scalp.

"Ryan? That you? There's something up there! It grabbed me, and…" He trailed off, gesturing helplessly up the slope.

I kept the Marlin's sights centered on his chest. I couldn't bring myself to feel sorry for the man. I had told him to stay in the car. In fact, to me, it was fitting that he would die at the hands of the wendigo after failing to deal with the monster himself.

"Stay where you are," I said grimly. "If you move, I will shoot you."

"What? No, I—" He twisted around to look up the slope behind him, and something came blurring down to splash down behind the sergeant.

The wendigo was making no effort to hide its true nature. It wrapped one spindly hand around Bunnings' throat and wrenched the sergeant's head up and back. The black eyes stared around the cavern, flickering past me and coming to rest on the empty ground where the other wendigo had faded back to the fae.

"There is another," it hissed. "Show yourself, mortal!"

I tried to draw a bead on the wendigo's face, but the monster was twitching and ducking, jerking its head from one side of the sergeant's head to the other, in constant motion.

"I can smell you. You are the Ryan?" it demanded.

"I am Ryan Halsin, Hunter of the Fourth Chapter," I called. "You do not belong in the mortal! Return to the fae at once, or I will send you back in agony."

The wendigo's empty gaze swung back in my direction. "Brave words, little hunter," it hissed. Bunnings tried to pull free and the wendigo effortlessly squashed the sergeant's struggles. The bony fingers dug deep into Bunnings' neck, gripping around the man's esophagus. The sergeant abandoned his escape attempt and clung to the monster's arms, wheezing in pain. "Show yourself, Ryan!"

"I think not. Let the sergeant go," I growled.

"You think me a fool," it rebutted. "I can smell the iron on you, hunter. Where is my spawn?"

"Back in the fae," I grinned. "I've sent all three fleeing this world in agony. Your scheme here has failed."

"A setback," it snarled. "But that is all." It started walking forward, dragging Bunnings along with it and holding the old man up like a shield.

How much was the old man's life worth? It would be easy to shoot through him and kill the wendigo, but I couldn't bring myself to pull the trigger.

Then the wendigo's black eyes met mine and a broad grin split its emaciated face. "There you are," it hissed.

And it tore out the sergeant's throat.

I yelled, anger, fear, and surprise at the abrupt death, all tearing free of my throat. I pulled the trigger and the wendigo twisted away, blindingly fast. I rocked the leaver action, chambered another round, and fired again. I knew how to use a lever-action rifle, but I wasn't intimately familiar with it like Harper was. I couldn't maintain the firing speed she could and keep any semblance of accuracy.

The wendigo darted to one side, then leapt in long, springing bounds toward me, moving on all fours like an animal. I racked the lever back again, then the wendigo hit me like a linebacker. I went flying backward and landed hard on my back. The rifle was knocked free of my grasp and I heard it go skittering away across the cave floor.

I saw flashing teeth and got my arm up in the way. The wendigo clamped down on my forearm and worried at it, throwing its head back and forth. I could feel the razor-sharp teeth trying to sink through the leather of the sleeve, but Nokemes' coat held.

With my free hand I found the hilt of my knife at my belt and fumbled the weapon free. Before I could get it drawn back for a proper stab, the flat of the blade brushed against the wendigo's side. It shrieked and flinched sideways, wrenching my arm around as it twisted away from the iron.

It kicked out and I felt my hand go numb from the wrist down. The wendigo swarmed onto my chest, pinning my good arm with its weight. Claws raked at me and scored parallel scratches down my chest. The leather tore and I felt hot pain as its claws drew blood. I heard Harper yell something, then the bang of the 45 echoed around the cavern.

The wendigo was knocked off balance by the impact of the bullet, and I flung the creature from me. It staggered upright, still managing to maintain its balance, and Harper emptied the magazine into the creature. The repeated gunshots were deafening.

The steel-core bullets blasted through the wendigo's withered flesh, leaving behind gaping wounds and raw craters. The wendigo screamed its agony and threw itself to the side. I heard the gun in Harper's hand lock open on an empty magazine. The wendigo scrambled to its feet and started limping toward Harper.

I saw the glint of my knife lying a few feet away and lunged for it. The hilt filled my hand and I threw myself at the wendigo. It spun around as I jumped the last couple yards. My blow was aimed to drive the knife through the creature's back, and it slammed through its shoulder instead. The wendigo slapped at me with its good arm and knocked me flying away from it.

The cave floor swept up and smashed me in the side of the

head. The iron taste of blood filled my mouth and my vision spun around, half blotted out with black. The echoing cracks of gunshots were ear-splittingly loud, but disconnected, like they were coming from down a long pipe.

The wendigo shrieked, but it wasn't a pained cry this time. Harper screamed. I lifted my head from where my cheek had been pressed into the gritty floor, and saw Harper dangling from the wendigo's grip around her throat. Its other arm was dangling at its side, nearly completely severed at the shoulder with my knife hilt still protruding from it.

Seeing Harper drove me to my knees and I cast about, looking for something I could use as a weapon. The lantern light caught against the barrel of Harper's Marlin, a dozen feet away from me. I crawled toward it and grabbed it by the wooden stock.

I rolled onto my stomach and got the gun to my shoulder. I got the wendigo's head centered in the sights and pulled the trigger. There was a click and I remembered I hadn't chambered a new round. I worked the lever and the spent casing pinged across the stone floor. The wendigo's head spun around and it snarled at me.

The wendigo dropped Harper and lunged toward me, moving awkwardly and favoring one of its legs. I brought the barrel up and fired. The roar of the Marlin crashed through the cave and the wendigo was thrown from its feet.

I got up to my knees and cycled the lever again. The wendigo was struggling to sit up. Half of its chest was a ragged mess of ruined flesh and splintered bone, but it wasn't dead yet. I took my time and got the sights centered between the black pits of its eyes.

It snarled, black blood bubbling up through its ragged teeth. There was something crazed in its eyes, and I knew it would never stop coming for me, never abandon its hunt. I needed to end it right here, right now.

I pulled the trigger and the Marlin punched me in the shoulder.

Bone shards and grey matter splattered out behind the wendigo as the massive 444 round all but took its head off. I cycled the lever again and found the gun was empty. I fumbled into the pockets of my pants and found the extra rounds. I fed another round into the magazine and cycled the action. Then I watched and waited, rifle at the ready.

The wendigo's limbs trembled. Despite the horrific damage dealt to its body, the fae spirit was still ravenous, and it clung to the mortal. Harper limped up next to me, handgun held in a white-knuckled grip, ready to pump even more steel into the monster if it was needed.

Slowly, the trembling stilled. I saw the moment that the spirit abandoned the mortal and returned to the fae. A final tremor ran through the emaciated body and then it went limp. The limbs shriveled even further then cracked and broke into chunks. The torso caved in, the ribs collapsing under their own weight. Then the pieces of bone crumpled into drifting ash. A cold gust of wind brushed past us, carrying away the last of the fading ash, and the wendigo was gone.

CHAPTER TWENTY-THREE

I sat on the steps outside Sylvia Toole's bed and breakfast, and watched Harper as she gave Henry a last hug goodbye. Tammy was in the front seat of her dad's car, her face streaked with tears. Our eyes met and she gave me a small wave. I lifted my hand in response, but stayed where I was. Henry climbed into the back seat and Harper gave Mr. Davis a firm handshake, then stepped back.

Mr. Davis looked over in my direction and I nodded at him. His mouth narrowed and I glimpsed a fraction of the raw terror he had been dealing with the last couple days. Having his two youngest children returned to him gave him something to live for, but he would never forget the loss of the rest of his family. He returned the nod and got into the car.

Harper stayed where she was, and waved until the Davis car had left the parking lot and was gone from sight. She sighed and walked back to the steps. She sat next to me and brushed a lock of hair back out of her eyes.

I looked at her sideways. "Mr. Davis didn't waste any time in driving back to pick up his son," I commented.

"Can you blame him?"

I shrugged. "No, I guess not."

I leaned back on my elbows and stretched out my legs. Besides a few stitches on my chest, I had come away from the encounter with the wendigo relatively unscathed. There were fading bruises on Harper's throat, and on her wrists and ankles, but she had fared better than I had in terms of severity of injuries.

But that was the physical damage. It was two days after I had gone after the wendigos in the cave, and Harper was still having a hard time sleeping at night. We shared my bed but hadn't had sex since then, and I didn't push her. For now, I was content to see her breathing and alive. In time, she would learn how to deal with the night terrors and move on.

"I guess it's over," she said after a few minutes.

I grunted. "I suppose it is."

"Are you going to leave soon?"

"John keeps calling," I deadpanned. "He probably wants a report in person."

Harper nodded. Her hands were knotted together, fingers clenched tight enough to almost draw blood with her nails. "Thank you, Ryan. For staying. I know you didn't have to."

"You can still come with me," I said carefully. "After what we went through, the Chapter will accept your application gladly."

Her jaw tightened and she swallowed. "I don't know. I can't imagine going through… all that. Again."

"It is hard," I said gently. "But we also saved hundreds of lives. For me, at least, that makes it worth it."

"Yeah." She turned her head to look back toward the town and didn't say anything else.

Kingfield was in uproar, at least as much as a sleepy town of a few hundred could be. The death of Willard Bunnings had created a panic that was only now beginning to fade. Nobody else had gone missing, but it would take weeks before people believed Harper's claims that the killer had been dealt with. If Harper wanted to stay in Kingfield, it would be a long time before things returned back to normal for her.

We sat on the stairs for probably close to an hour, just sitting in silence and enjoying the sun. Then I stood up and dusted off my pants. "Well, I think I'll head out now."

She looked up at me and I saw her squash down her surge of fear. "Oh. I'll help you get your things to your car."

I nodded and we headed up to my room. I had already packed my bags and I swung the big duffel up onto my shoulder. I could have carried my laptop bag as well, but I let Harper carry it. We walked back down to the front desk and found Sylvia waiting for us.

"Mr. Baptiste called again," Sylvia said with a small frown. "He is being very persistent."

"I bet. Well, he can wait until I get back in Portland and we'll have a face-to-face conversation. Better that way, I think."

She nodded uncertainly. "If you say so. I hope you enjoyed your stay, Mr. Halsin."

"Your establishment is a fine one, Mrs. Toole. If I ever come back this way, I'll be sure to stay here again."

Sylvia flushed a little and smiled broadly. "Aw, thank you. Don't take this the wrong way, but I hope you don't come back on business. For pleasure is fine," she amended hurriedly. "There is good skiing during the winter."

"You and me both. Though I think it will be a long time before I go skiing on Sugarloaf. I wish you the best, Sylvia." I gave her a wave and headed outside. I popped the trunk on my car and dumped my duffel. Harper was a little gentler with my laptop bag, and then she folded her arms and looked down at her feet.

"I can't believe you're leaving," she said softly. "It feels like I've known you forever, but I guess it's only been a week."

"Less, actually. I drove up on Saturday."

"Really?" She gave a small smile and rolled a shoulder. "I guess you're right. I'm going to miss you."

"This doesn't have to be goodbye," I said. "You have my number, right?"

She nodded. "Though I suppose I won't be able to call you until you're out of town."

"True. Don't be a stranger. Even if you don't decide to join the Chapter, I'd still like to hear from you."

Harper stepped up and gave me a quick hug, then retreated. So much for a goodbye kiss. "I'll let you know how things go out here. Don't forget Kingfield, Ryan."

"As if I could." I wished I could convince her to join the Chapter, but she was right. She needed time to think things through. It was a decision she would have to make on her own. "Take care of yourself, Harper."

"You too."

I got into my car and gave her a final wave before pulling out of the parking lot. She lifted a hand as I turned the corner, and then she was gone.

Another job complete. Another town saved whose residents would never know what I had sacrificed to keep the fanged horrors from their doors. Another lover, lost in the dust behind me.

I took Highway 27 down to Farmington, taking my time and enjoying the scenery. Now that I didn't have to search the forests for a man-eating monster, I could appreciate the beauty of the gently rolling landscape.

Already, my thoughts were shifting to the west. With the

wendigo dead, there was nothing keeping me from returning to Los Angeles. The west coast Chapter division was sure to keep me busy, but as long as I was in the area, I could make time to help Alex with whatever she needed.

Farmington came and went, and suddenly I had a burning desire to get the hell out of Maine. It took a serious effort not to floor it and find out just how fast my little rental Civic could go. The last thing I needed was to spend the night in a backwater clink while some yokel cop with a double-digit IQ played twenty-questions with the Chapter lawyers.

I kept my car within the speed limit and let the scenery flow by. The little towns came and went, most of them not much larger than Kingfield.

When I reached the outskirts of Lewiston, my phone suddenly went wild in my pocket. A week's worth of missed calls, emails, text messages, social media updates, and news alerts all came in at once. I got off the road and parked in a Starbucks parking lot to stretch my legs and use the restroom. Then I ordered a coffee and sat down at a table to find out what had happened in the world during the last week.

I had around twenty missed phone calls. Most of them were from John Baptiste, and I listened to the voice mails one at a time. They started out just asking for updates; John being the good controller and checking in on his hunter. Then things grew a little shrill.

"Ryan, listen, I don't know why you aren't calling me back, but the ley lines in Kingfield are going wild. Something powerful is up there! Watch your back, okay? And fucking call me!"

Beep.

"Ryan, I hope you're not dead. I saw traffic in the Archives entries on wendigos, so I'm assuming you're still alive. The noise in the lines split, we think there might be two of whatever it is you're hunting up there. I tried reaching you on the landline and the lady said you were fine. Call me, you asshole!"

Beep. That would have been nice to know. Maybe I should have returned one of Baptiste's calls.

"If you're not dead, I swear, I'm killing you myself when you get back to Portland. There's been some noise coming from the west. The Pacific Division thinks things are happening in Los Angeles. Lots of ley line fluctuations. Like an army is coming through. When you get back, you'll probably get your wish to go to California. Call me!"

Beep.

"Ryan! Hi, it's Alex. Listen, I could really use your help. Things have gotten weird and I need someone who can watch my back. I hope you get this soon. Thanks."

Beep. Woops. I hoped Alex was okay. That call had been missed at the beginning of the week. I'd have to call her back and make sure she was all right, but I needed some privacy for that. A Starbucks wasn't the right place to have open discussions about fae or whatever else it was Alex was running into.

I had another missed call from Alex, but she hadn't left a voicemail on the second call. I winced. I didn't want her to think I was a flake. I wanted her to feel like she could rely on me. I knew better than most how crazy things could get in a week. Still, there wasn't anything I could have done to help her. If I had abandoned Kingfield to the wendigo, dozens, maybe even hundreds more people could have died.

I flicked through my emails and found they were either echoes of my voicemails or routine Chapter business. I drained the last of my coffee and put my phone away. All of that could wait. I needed to get back to Portland.

The last hour of the drive into Portland was like coming forward through time. Gone were the mom n' pop diners, the no-name gas stations, the farm stands on the side of the road. I started seeing fast food restaurant chains and signs sticking up over the tops of the trees promoting businesses just off the highway exits.

Still, it wasn't until I was in deep into Portland that the ever-present walls of trees were finally replaced with sidewalks and parking lots. I was tempted to go back to my hotel and relax for the rest of the day, but it was only a passing thought. Even more than a well-deserved rest, I wanted to kick in someone's teeth for fucking up the ley line disturbance reports. Dozens of people were killed by the wendigo because of that mistake, and I intended to hold them to account.

So, instead of heading to my hotel south of the airport, I turned north to downtown Portland. The North-East Chapter House occupied the top two floors of a seven-story brick office building that overlooked the harbor. I parked my bug-spattered Civic in the parking lot out back and headed inside.

The cool air of the lobby washed over me. The building receptionist was a young man, slender, only recently graduated from high school. His name was John or Josh or something. I didn't care enough to remember.

He saw me coming and waved at me. "Mr. Halsin! You're back. That's good! Let me call up, I know they'll be wanting to hear from you."

"I'm sure," I grunted, and kept walking toward the elevators.

"Oh. Uh, they wanted me to—"

I thumbed the up arrow on the elevator and glared over my shoulder at him. "I'm not in the mood, Jack."

"It's Jason," he said hurriedly. "If you'll just give me a moment, I—"

"Save it, James."

The elevator dinged and the doors slid open. I stepped

321

inside and whacked the button for the top floor with my fist. There was a soft chime from above the door, and I looked up and locked eyes with the camera. After a moment, the red light next to the camera turned green and the doors slid shut again.

Out in the lobby, Jason was scrambling for the phone, calling my arrival ahead of me. Good. Maybe those suit-wearing assholes would sweat a little before my elevator arrived.

I reached the seventh floor and stepped out into a marble-inlayed lobby with expensive walnut furniture. Nobody was there to greet me. I got out of the elevator and started opening doors, searching through the meeting rooms.

The last room I checked was the main conference room. I pushed open the door and strode inside, then stopped dead in my tracks. The conference room had a massive hardwood table in it, sized to sit ten people on a side, more if they were feeling sociable. Every seat was occupied, and another twenty or so people stood around the edges of the room. It looked like the whole Chapter House was present.

A whiteboard was set up on the far wall with a map of the United States drawn on it. I recognized the pattern of ley lines sketched out over it. Some sort of presentation was going on, being delivered by an older gentleman I recognized as Elijah Moore.

The room fell silent and everyone in it turned to look at me. Elijah cleared his throat. "Ryan, I see you are alive after all."

John Baptiste got up from his chair. "Sorry, I'll talk with him."

"Very well. I'm glad you made it back, Ryan. I'll meet with you after this meeting is over."

I nodded, my anger suddenly puddling out of me. "Fine."

Baptiste grabbed my elbow and hustled me out of the conference room and into another, smaller room a few doors down. "What the fuck, Ryan? You don't return my calls for a week, then kick in the door during a meeting?"

I crossed my arms and reminded myself I had plenty of reason to be pissed myself. "Maybe if you ever left the comfort of the city, you'd know that the only cell tower in Kingfield is a jury-rigged piece of shit that has less range than a walkie talkie, and doesn't recognize any major cell carriers. Don't you fucking bust my nuts because you send your hunters out underprepared."

He blinked then backed off from the confrontation. "Shit. I didn't realize. Still, I left you messages with the bed and breakfast."

"I was busy," I growled. "You fuckups sent me after a six-month-old wendigo. It had been feasting on the locals for half a year! Do you have any idea how many people died? I almost died!"

Baptiste dropped his gaze and his lips pressed together. "Elijah already ripped us a new one for that."

"Yeah? Well, at least someone in this backwater shithole has their head out of their asses. What the fuck happened, anyway? Why was I sitting on my thumb in Portland for six months while that monster slaughtered people on the other side of the state?"

"You're upset," he said.

"No fucking shit, John. Answer the question!"

He raised his hands in a calming motion. "Look, things haven't been ideal, but—"

"Ideal?! John, like thirty people died!"

Baptiste blanched. "So many?"

"Yeah, a double-digit percentage of the population of Kingfield was eaten by that fucking thing! It even started convincing other humans to indulge in their greed. Three other wendigos were created. If I hadn't made it up there when I did, the deaths could have numbered in the hundreds!"

"Jesus Christ." He frowned pensively. "Okay. I understand why you're pissed. Are you sure you killed them all? You didn't miss any of the newly created wendigos?"

"Why don't you ask your scryer," I spat. "That's what their fucking job is, isn't it?"

"Ah. Well, that's the thing. Our scryer died and we had to call up reinforcements from the south. They were dealing with a Creole witch in Louisiana and didn't have the freedom to do any pro-bono work until last week. That's when we realized the original readings were off and sent you to Kingfield."

I held my scowl, but the rage I was feeling started to fade. "How did the scryer die?" People who were sensitive to fluctuations in the ley lines were rare, and they were closely guarded from harm. There was an apartment on the seventh floor in this building where the scryer lived, or had lived, and she had rarely left its safety.

"Heart attack. She was like eighty, Ryan. It was all unfortunate timing, but honest to God, we were trying our best to keep you and our other hunters as informed as possible."

I grunted and took half a step back from Baptiste, defusing the confrontation. "Damn it. I wish you had just told me. Would have saved everyone a lot of grief."

"In retrospect, I agree with you."

I suppose that was as close to an apology as I was going to get. "Have you had any luck finding a replacement scryer?"

"That's why Elijah is here, actually. He's briefing everyone on the current state of the ley lines in preparation for the hand-over. There's been some wild stuff going on. We've got a skilled scryer who is loaning us their talent until we can find a more permanent replacement."

I grunted. "Yeah? Who's that?"

"Nobody you would know. She was part of the Chapter a generation before you were around."

There was a commotion out in the hallway and Baptiste stuck his head out of the door, then beckoned to me. "You're just in time. Come on and meet our new scryer."

I stepped out into the hallway and saw the entire conference room had piled out to greet the scryer. From where I was standing in the back, all I could see were the tops of heads. I was the tallest person in the hallway, and I could see the crowd pressing in around someone, but the newcomer was too short for me to see them.

"All right!" Elijah said loudly. "Back inside! Where are your manners? There will be more than enough time to greet out new scryer personally. This way, if you would, ma'am."

There was some grumbling, but the Chapter staff started filing back into conference room. I lingered in the hallway, unwilling to stuff myself into an overcrowded room. Besides, I reminded myself, I would be on a plane to Los Angeles in a day or two. The new scryer of the North-East Chapter House was a curiosity, but wouldn't affect me much one way or another.

The last of the staff filed back into the conference room. I was turning back to Baptiste to suggest we go grab a bite to eat, when someone called my name. I did a double-take, and a broad grin split my face.

"Harper!" I crossed the hallway and swept her up into a bear hug. "What are you doing here?"

She swatted at my arm until I put her back on her feet. "It's only been like four hours since you saw me," she laughed. "And I came because my grandma asked me to. She showed up a few minutes after you left."

I looked toward the milling crowd in the conference room and caught a glimpse of Nokemes' hunched form near the head of the table next to Elijah. "Wait, your grandmother is the new scryer?"

"Hardly new," Baptiste said from behind me. "Hello, Harper."

"It's good to see you again, John," she said.

"I trust Ryan didn't give you too hard a time?"

Harper looked at me sideways and a smile tugged at the corner of her mouth. "I managed."

"Will you be staying?" John asked.

"Only long enough to make sure grandma is settled," she shook her head.

"Ah." There was disappointment on John's face, then he shook it off. "I'm assuming you're not going to drive back to Kingfield tonight? No? Then if you don't have a place to stay yet, the scryer apartment has a guest room."

"Thank you, but I believe I have a place for the night." She didn't quite look at me, but there was a lascivious twist to her smile that I recognized.

I cleared my throat. "Well. John, I believe we have a debrief to carry out and a next step to plan."

"Yes, we can do that. Harper, do you have something to do?"

"I haven't been to Portland since I was a child. It might be fun to walk around the city some."

"Oh. That sounds good. Do you have a phone yet?"

"Yeah, we found my phone Travis' truck."

"Oh, that's good. Does it get a signal here?" I asked.

She checked and nodded. "I'll go busy myself for an hour or so. Then dinner?"

"Perfect. I'll call you when I'm finished with John."

Harper gave a wave and headed for the elevators. I watched her go, then tilted my head back to the small conference room. "Shall we get to business?"

John snorted. "You're fucking her?"

I grinned. "What's it matter?"

"You are! You sly dog. That was fast work, even for you."

"Jealous?"

He looked after Harper and pursed his lips. "She's definitely hot. I've no idea how you get so lucky with the ladies. Shall we get started?"

CHAPTER TWENTY-FOUR

A post-action debrief with the Chapter was focused around creating a new entry for the Archive. We went through the week step by step, reviewing my impressions and checking facts. It was strange, running through it all again. When it had been happening, I had been so focused that I hadn't really had a chance to look at events from a distance.

I left out the details of my relationship with Harper. That wasn't relevant to an Archive entry, but John got the gist of it anyway. He might be a bit of an asshole, but he wasn't stupid.

By the time I got around to describing the final confrontation in the cave, it was getting pretty late in the day and the sun coming through the windows was fading out to evening.

John shook his head. "That took a lot of balls going into the cave. But there's something here I don't understand. You said the wendigos couldn't see you?"

"Damnedest thing. They were looking right at me. They could hear me, but their sight didn't work."

"Could it have been your coat?"

It was an idea I had floated with Harper, but she hadn't been able to confirm the hypothesis. Still, there wasn't any other explanation. "As far as I know. Nokemes put a lot of warding and protection into the brands. Part of that could have been to hide me from their sight. Or it could have been a call to Azeban to prank the wendigos."

John wrinkled his nose in distaste. "I was hoping we could add the patterns to the archive. Being able to hide from fae would be a powerful tool. But I'm not so desperate as to rely on a trickster god for safekeeping."

"Well, Nokemes is here, now. You could just ask her."

"Yeah. I might just do that. Would you mind leaving the coat with us?"

I shrugged uneasily. "I don't know, John."

"I would make sure it was returned to you. Besides, it's ripped up, isn't it?"

He wasn't wrong. Half the front panel was torn to shreds. As a piece of clothing, it was useless, and I had no idea if the protections burned into it still worked with the damage. "Bah."

"I'll even see if I can get the old lady to repair it for you. She might have enough free time on her hands."

"Well... I suppose it wouldn't hurt. But I want it back, whether she can mend it or not."

"I promise."

"Fine. But only if you put me on a flight to LA."

John grunted. "I was hoping to convince you to stay in Maine. Or at least in the north-east sector. We could use a man with your skills. Besides, there's Harper. She certainly looked happy to see you. A man could do worse."

"I'm not looking to settle down and have a family," I shook my head. "And Harper knows our arrangement is temporary. I didn't hide wanting to return to California."

"And she isn't interested in joining the Chapter?"

"I couldn't sell it to her. You're welcome to keep trying."

"Damn. I want her in the Chapter even more, now that I know how well she did in your investigation."

"Yeah. I'd love to have her as a partner. If she joins, I call dibs."

John laughed.

"But even so, I'm going to LA. My sister needs me."

"Well, you did your job and the wendigos are dead. I did promise. I'll get you on a plane by the end of the week."

I stood up and extended my hand. "Thanks, John. Maybe you're not a total asshole after all."

He snorted and shook. "Call your sister and see if she still wants you around. Maybe she'll give you a pass to stay in Maine."

"You're dreaming."

"Maybe. We're done here. Unless you have anything else, I want to listen in on the briefing."

I waved a hand. "No, I'm done. Have fun. I know I will tonight."

John chuckled and shook his head on the way out the door. I dug my phone out of my pocket and pulled up Alex's number. I felt an uncharacteristic nervousness as my thumb hovered over the dial button. I gave myself a mental shake. It was just Alex. Yeah, she was a lilin, but she was my sister.

I hit call and lifted the phone to my ear. It rang twice, then there was a scratchy sound and Alex's voice came through. She sounded exhausted.

"This is Alex."

"Alex! It's Ryan. I just got your messages."

I heard a soft thump. "Oh. That's good."

"Do you still need help?"

"You're a little late," she laughed, but there wasn't a lot of humor in it.

"Damn, sorry about that. I was off in the bush chasing this damn wendigo. They don't have many cell towers in the Maine backwoods. I could use some sun after this, though. If it's all right with you, I'll come back to Los Angeles and we can finally catch up."

"Yeah. I'd like that."

Through the door, I heard sudden shouting and worried calls of alarm. "Hold on, Alex. Something's happened."

I ran over to the other conference room and burst in through the door. Elijah was kneeling next to Nokemes, and the old woman clung to his arms, her tanned and seamed face pale. She was looking around wildly, her blind eyes rolling without anything to focus on.

I pushed through the crowd and knelt down next to her. "Nokemes," I said gently, "It's Ryan Halsin."

She reached out and grabbed my arm and her nails dug into my skin. "The lines are breaking," she said in a wavering voice. "I can feel them! Like ice cracking on a frozen river."

I looked a question at Elijah and he nodded. "I can feel it too, but not as strongly. Something happened to the west."

"Los Angeles?" I asked.

"You know something?" Elijah demanded.

"Maybe. I don't know. I'll get back to you." I patted Nokemes' spindly hand. "Nokemes, I have to go, but I'll be nearby, and I'll bring Harper."

The old lady nodded and released me. Her breathing was coming easier, though she still had a horrified look on her face.

I got out of the conference room and put my phone back to my ear. "You still there, Alex?"

"I'm here."

"One of the natives up here is having a panic attack. I'm not getting everything she's saying, but apparently all the ley lines just changed."

"Oh. Yeah, I suppose that makes sense."

"What makes sense? Alex, what happened?"

"Look," she said quickly. "I have to go, but call me back. You're still coming to LA?"

"If I can. Are you sure you're all right?"

"Things will work out. I hope. I'll talk to you soon!"

"Okay. Take care, Alex."

I hung up and frowned at my phone. Now I was absolutely certain that something was wrong in Los Angeles. Whatever trouble Alex had found herself in, it was affecting the ley lines clear across the country in Maine.

"Shit," I muttered. I looked up and saw Elijah staring at me from the door to the conference room.

"I do not like that look, Halsin."

"My sister is running into trouble."

His face took on an alarmed look. "The lilin?"

I winced and tilted my head toward the little conference room John and I had been using. "You mind?"

"Sorry. Sure."

I hadn't had much interaction with Elijah Moore. He was a contemporary of my father, and probably the only active hunter I looked up to. I was pretty sure he wasn't fully human, but asking about that wasn't really polite. Being in a small room with him felt like I was cozying up to a high-voltage wire. He had an energy about him that was volatile. If I didn't know him to be level-headed, I'd be itching to grab a gun.

"Speak, then," he grunted.

"You know the situation with Alex?" I asked.

"I know she is lilin, and is permitted to live because of her disposition."

"Yeah. I checked her out myself last year. Spent a week with her, helping her with a case she was working on. I can vouch for her mental state. She's one of the good guys."

Elijah nodded. "Your father said the same thing. You don't need to convince me, Halsin, I was one of the ones who put my vote in her favor."

I gave a sigh of relief. "I didn't know that. That's good to hear. But, well, I know she's a good person, but she's also vulnerable."

"All lilin are."

"Yeah. She needs someone that she can rely on, who's there for her when she needs moral guidance, and can stand with her in a fight."

"Is that why you've been badgering Baptiste to be transferred to the west coast?"

I nodded. "It is."

"Well, now I wish we had sent you earlier." He frowned toward the large conference room, as if he could see through the walls and was picking out a specific target for his irritation. For all I knew, maybe he could. "Consider it done. I'll put you on a flight tomorrow morning. Come by around nine and I'll have your tickets waiting for you at reception. I can't put you on a serve and protect detail, but you'll be in LA."

"Thank you."

He grunted. "You might wish you were back in Maine a few months from now. I'm not sure I'm doing you a favor."

"We're not exactly in this line of business for our health," I pointed out wryly.

"Isn't that the truth."

There was a knock on the door and it opened a few inches. Harper stuck her head in. "Ryan? There you are. I ended my walk early. I felt I had to return."

I shared a glance with Elijah. Maybe Harper had more of Nokemes' gift than she knew.

"You're not wrong," Elijah said. "You're Kawinse blood. I can see the facial similarities."

Harper swallowed and bobbed her head in a nod. "She's my grandma."

"Come in," Elijah beckoned to her.

She slipped inside the room and came to stand next to me, as if I could shield her from Elijah. "What is happening? Someone said something about my grandma having a panic attack?"

"Nothing so dramatic," Elijah answered with a small smile. "She sensed something in the ley lines and was disoriented for a short time. She is recovering in the scryer apartment now. I can bring you to see her, if you like?"

"I would," Harper said.

"Then if you would follow me?" Elijah opened the door for her and gestured for her to go first.

Harper's hand found mine and she pulled me with her. I followed her out the door, and saw Elijah's gaze flicker to our clasped hands. He didn't comment, though, and led us to the apartment suite at the other end of the building.

Walking into the scryer apartment was a bit of a shock. The rest of the floor was office-chic, with conference rooms, partitions, and swivel chairs. The apartment, in sharp contrast, was tastefully modern, with muted landscape paintings hung on the walls and deep shag carpeting. Nokemes was reclining in an arm chair in front of a huge TV, playing a muted nature documentary. The apartment was dimly-lit, and the shifting colors from the show cast mottled light across her face.

"Grandma, are you okay?" Harper called. She dropped my hand and went over to kneel down next to the armchair.

Nokemes reached out and touched her face with the withered tips of her fingers, and gave a small smile. "I'm fine, Harper. It was just a surprise. Ah... I hear you found your hunter."

Elijah glanced at me and crooked an eyebrow. I shrugged.

"I'm here, Nokemes. I have to thank you for your gift. It saved my life."

The old lady beckoned to me, and I went to squat down next to Harper. I got the same feather-light touches across my features, then she lay back in the armchair with a sigh. "I am glad. It took a lot of effort to make. What do you think of my new living space, Harper? My sister had good taste, didn't she?"

Harper frowned. "Your sister? I didn't know you had a sister."

"Twin sister, in fact. She stayed with the Chapter and I went to guide our people. It was the deal we made with each other. We knew the needs of both groups, and in this way, everyone got what they wanted."

"I had no idea," Elijah said softly. "I had always assumed the two of you had a falling out."

"Far from it, though it was a useful fiction. But now my people are settled in a home they can call their own, and are thriving. They do not need the guidance of one old, blind woman. The Chapter, however, does need me."

"You're staying, grandma?" Harper asked doubtfully. "I thought this was just a short visit."

"So did I. But the ley lines have gone wild. The fae will be coming through in numbers greater than anything we have witnessed in five hundred years. Without a scryer to guide them, the Chapter will not be able to manage. You witnessed first-hand what a single fae can do, child. It would be disaster."

"Is it going to be that bad?" Harper asked. She looked to me and Elijah, pleading with her eyes for one of us to refute Nokemes.

"I'm afraid so," Elijah said. "We were spread thin before. I can only imagine what the next months will bring. We need more hunters." He leveled his gaze upon Harper. I wasn't the target of his intent look, but I could feel Harper stiffen next to me. "You have experience in dealing with the fae, more than most. I understand you were considering joining the Chapter."

"I was," she said weakly.

Elijah nodded and dropped the stare pinning Harper in place. "Well. It is not a decision that can be made by anyone but you. Know that your addition to our cause would be more than welcome. I have pressing matters I must tend to. Halsin, I likely won't see you again before you leave. Good luck in California."

"Thank you, sir," I said.

Elijah nodded, bowed his head toward Nokemes, and strode out of the apartment.

"Jesus," Harper muttered once he was gone. "He's intense."

"He is," Nokemes agreed.

We stood in awkward silence for a moment, then Harper said. "Grandma, do you need anything? A drink? Food?"

Nokemes cackled to herself. "There's a kitchen right over there, if I need something. And a building full of people eager to help me if I want it. You can go. Spend the time you have left with your man."

Harper flushed, but bit her lip and shot me a look. "Thanks."

"Farewell, hunter," Nokemes said, and looked straight at me for the first time.

I swallowed. "Farewell, Nokemes. It's been my honor."

She nodded and turned her head to face toward the television, looking a few degrees off center.

Harper took my hand and led me out of the apartment. Back in the clinical boredom of the office, I shook off the feeling of unease the old lady had left me with. "You ready to get dinner?"

"I'm starving," she admitted.

"Then I know just the place."

Going out for a night on the town with Harper felt like the

most natural thing in the world. I was relaxed with her, comfortable, with the worries and concerns of the Chapter seemingly far away and belonging to someone else.

I brought her to a restaurant, a place I knew that had good food and a quiet atmosphere. We took our time eating, both of us more interested in each other than the food in front of us. We skipped dessert and went straight to my hotel.

Afterwards, we lay in each other's arms in comfortable silence, staring out the open window at the lights passing by in the harbor below.

"Ships passing in the night, you and I," she said softly. "I don't want this night to end."

"Neither do I," I said. I bent my head down to put a kiss on top of her head.

"I took some psychology classes in college," she said a minute later.

"Oh?" It wasn't the pillow talk I expected, but I was interested in what she had to share.

"It was an elective, something to fill out the units, but I remember reading something." She faded out, and for a minute I thought she had fallen asleep. Then she stirred and shifted around to face me. "It was about how people deal with their fear."

I nodded, but didn't say anything. Whatever thought process she was working through, she wasn't done voicing it yet.

"Nightmares, in particular. When I first read it, I expected some bogus nonsense about dream interpretation. Instead, it struck me as true. When someone experiences something traumatizing, the more they run from it, the less they are able to cope with their lives afterward."

'Suck it up' didn't strike me as a particularly educated approach to dealing with trauma, but I didn't say anything yet. She wasn't done talking.

"It was more than that, though. The only way to truly get over fear, is to find some way to regain control over whatever it was that brought about the trauma. Ever since the wendigo was destroyed, I haven't found a way to be the one in charge of my life again.

"I could go back to being a Ranger, but that would be me hiding from the truth. I think I would go crazy, knowing what I know, and pretending like nothing had changed. The nightmares wouldn't stop. Not ever. I could drug myself into forgetfulness with alcohol or prescription medication, but that would be worse than death."

I gave an understanding grunt. What she said made sense to me. It was why I hadn't abandoned the job. I didn't have the background to put the feeling into words, but now that she had voiced it out loud, it rang true. "You're a smart woman, Harper Hall."

"Maybe. But then, the only conclusion I can come to after that is a very stupid one."

"And that is?"

"To join the Chapter."

I laughed, and she gave me a swat on the chest, thankfully missing my still tender stitches. "I'm being serious, Ryan."

"Sorry. Why is joining the Chapter stupid?"

"Because it's a downward spiral. There's no win. To confront my fear, I have to put myself in a position where I will be exposed to more trauma. Once I join, there is no backing out."

"There is the five-year clause," I pointed out mildly.

"You know as well as I do that I could never take that escape," she said.

I pulled her into a hug and buried my nose in her hair. "Some people manage it. Your grandmother did."

"She left because she knew her sister had stayed behind. And look what it cost them."

"Maybe you're right," I said. "What will you do?"

"I've been asking myself that question for days," she sighed. "I'd be lying if I said part of me wasn't looking forward to joining. Helping people. The travel, the adventure, the challenge. You."

I lifted my head and frowned at her. "Don't get me wrong, Harper. I enjoy our relationship very much. But it would be a mistake to join the Chapter because of a man. No matter how good he is in the sack."

"And humble about it, too," she grinned. "But don't worry. I listed you last for a reason. I'm not expecting to get married or something."

It happens rarely, but every once in a while, I do the right thing with a girl. Instead of protesting the thought of marriage, I just nodded. "Well, the other reasons are good ones to join. And don't forget, facing your fears."

"That above all," she agreed.

"So... does that mean you will join the Chapter?"

"Haven't you been listening?"

"Sorry. Yes, I have been. I just don't want to put words in your mouth."

She sniffed. "What I'm trying to say, is yes. I've made up my mind. I'll tell John tomorrow."

"Really?" I gathered her up in a tight hug.

Harper lifted her head up to kiss me. "Really."

"Well, shit. Now I don't want to go to California right away."

She laughed. "No, you have to go, I understand that. I'll do my training here and meet you there when I'm done."

"Six months," I sighed, "if you're fast. That sounds like a long time, but it'll pass before I know it."

"Only six months?"

I grinned at her. "I told you before. You've got most of the skills already. I imagine all you'll need is an education in the fae. But don't discount it. It's going to be hard work."

"And then when it's done, to California."

"Yeah. Where your learning will truly begin. Don't let John push you around and try to keep you in Maine. Make him put your transfer to the west coast down in writing before you start your training, or he'll try and weasel his way out of it somehow."

"Oh, come on. He's not that bad."

"No, he just wants to do what's best for *his* neck of the woods. Which I suppose I can't really blame him for."

"All right." Harper stretched then rolled over on top of me. "But all that won't happen until tomorrow." She reached down between us and grabbed me. "In the meantime, I have you all to myself."

I grunted and felt myself start to respond. "I'm going to have to get some sleep at some point," I said.

"You can sleep on the plane. Besides, you're gaining three hours."

She wasn't wrong. I pulled her down for another kiss. Tomorrow I would be flying back to Los Angeles to find out what Alex had gotten herself into. With the ley lines destabilized, there would be fae coming through into the mortal all over the place. I'd have to find time for my sister in between putting out fires up and down the coast.

But for now, I had Harper in my arms and no obligations until morning.

Everything else could wait.

AUTHORS NOTE

Thank you for reading Haunt of the Wendigo! I hope you
enjoyed reading it as much as I enjoyed writing it.
If you did enjoy the book, please take a few minutes and write a
review. You would make this author a very happy man.
My website, http://devinhanson.com will have the latest news
and a blog about writing. Sign up for the newsletter there to
hear when new books are coming out, get free books, and
access extra content. I promise I won't spam you.
Ryan and Harper will return again soon!

Until next time,
Devin Hanson

ABOUT THE AUTHOR

Devin Hanson was born in Beaverton, Oregon. After a childhood spent programming computers and playing Dungeons and Dragons, Devin's career took a random turn to counseling. It was during his years as a counselor that he developed his insight into the human condition and renewed his interest in writing. Currently, Devin works as a web developer, spending his free time creating tales of fantasy and science fiction. For his sins, Devin resides in Los Angeles, California.

You can check out his website here:
https://www.devinhanson.com

Or follow him on Facebook;

 facebook.com/TheDevinHanson

ALSO BY DEVIN HANSON

The Dragon Speaker Series

Rune Scale

Rune Song

Rune Master

The Speaker's Son

The Cleric Scribe

The Last Incantor

The Immortal Archives

The December Protocol

The Matriarch Manifesto

Halfblood Legacy

The Halfblood's Hoard

Shadow of the Ghoul

Wylde Fire

Lilin's Wrath

Chapter Archives

Haunt of the Wendigo

Fate of the Magi

The Tome of the Magi

The Fractured Tower

OTHER AUTHORS AT HUDSON INDIE INK

Paranormal Romance/Urban Fantasy

Stephanie Hudson

Sloane Murphy

Xen Randell

C. L. Monaghan

Sci-fi/Fantasy

Brandon Ellis

Devin Hanson

Crime/Action

Blake Hudson

Mike Gomes

Contemporary Romance

Gemma Weir

Elodie Colt

Ann B. Harrison

Ingram Content Group UK Ltd.
Milton Keynes UK
UKHW011830140323
418553UK00001B/213

9 781913 904456